The Covenant of the Rin[g]

by Sidney Tomas

For Jessie and mums all over the world

In Loving memory of Irma

Prologue: Germany 1945

Sergeant Major Walker removed an untipped cigarette from a white and brown Players packet. He placed the much needed 'smoke" between his dry and dust-covered lips and lit the cigarette. The exhausted soldier inhaled the life-lifting aroma of the gold Virginia tobacco, rolled his eyes upwards then from side to side and surveyed the horror, confusion and destruction of humankind which lay before him.

He had endured a long hard grind from the initial landing on Sword Beach on that historic morning. D-Day 0631 hours on June 6th 1944. From the moment he set foot on that beach Bill Walker had witnessed horrors that could never have been imagined by a young man from a quiet North Yorkshire Dales village.

None of this venture into hell – and it was hell – would prepare him for what he was to experience on that day, April 15th 1945.

War was cruel, he thought; war was hell, war was savage. But in Bill's mind, war was executed by soldiers against soldiers, warrior on warrior. Be it right or wrong, wars had to be fought. What Bill saw that day as he was part of the British contingent liberating Belsen was not war, it was not the act of warriors. It was a crime which had never been committed before in the history of mankind. It was the systematic killing of men, women and children because of their religion, social standing, sexuality or lifestyle which did not fit the template of an Aryan race mapped out by a bunch of psychopathic criminals in Berlin.

Bill would comfort himself, by thinking despite all of this suffering, there would be hope. When the world discovered what had happened mankind would work to end atrocities and acts of human destruction and a repeat of the Holocaust would never be allowed to happen again.

Bill Walker closed his eyes and his mind drifted towards home and the memory of the lush green meadows, rolling hills and the sweet and well stocked rivers and streams of Wensleydale.

His trans meditational state ended abruptly when he heard the guttural and almost unhuman "CIGARETTAN BITTE"

A startled Bill cast his gaze right towards the source of the harsh command and to his dismay he was faced with a blonde haired man dressed in a black uniform and scuffed jack boots.

This was no ordinary uniform, it was no rank and file officer of the pay corps or infantry, this man was wearing the sinister attire of an Oberfuhrer of the Schutzstaffel, the feared SS.

The Nazi was heavily restrained on either side by two burly and un amused British Army Military Police Sergeants. The exercise was not an official detention, there had been no representation of defence as part of the decision process which had determined the next act. These two MPs under orders were accompanying the black clothed monster to a place of no return, he was in transit to the rear of one of the wooden billets which had provided rudimentary cover for the overworked and dying. This was the venue where the journey from Hitler Youth to a highly respected officer in the SS would come to a summary end.

Retribution and a cowardly death for a coward, commanded to kneel and feel the cold metal muzzle of the pistol pressing against the back of his shaved head.

A soldier's job is to protect civilians from danger not be the exemplars of their destruction Walker concluded.

The sergeant to the right of the Nazi retracted his hand and swiped his prisoner hard across the ear. "no ciggarettan for you pig, you soon will be smoke"

Bill had seen many Germans, but none had measured up to this blond-haired, chisel-jawed monster. His eyes were of blue cold steel, with no sign of emotion in the unlined face, no remorse, no conscience. His only goal was to serve the Fatherland and to deal with the sub-humans. There was not and would never be any willingness for this German to accept regret for his actions and those of his beloved SS.

"Cigarette, *bitte*," he barked in a precise, guttural and quite frightening tone. Although the prisoner was restrained he exuded menace and superiority and no acknowledgement of the fate that awaited him at the back of hut number nine.

Fumbling with the button, Bill flipped back the grubby pocket flap and withdrew the white and brown packet of untipped cigarettes.

He removed two cigarettes, placed them in his mouth and lit them both. He puffed on the Wills, inhaling calm, sweet-tasting smoke, approached the prisoner and with his right hand placed the lit smoke between the mouth of the SS prisoner, who gripped it in his teeth.

Fritz, Bill assumed the name was of his SS man, inhaled the cigarette, and as he exhaled, he closed his eyes. It seemed that for the first time he realised what was in store for him. Despite that, he gave no offer of thanks. The two guards adopted a less relaxed stance and started to guide the un-protesting prisoner to the corner of the block.

The guard on the left loosened his grip on Fritz's arm, which allowed him to remove the cigarette from his clenched teeth. It was clear that smoke was now irritating the German.

Pinching the cigarette between his first and second fingers of his left hand, Fritz removed the butt and threw it on the floor. As it passed the chiselled face, Bill noticed it for the first time. There it was, shining, contrasted against the dirt engrained third finger.

The German had noticed Bill's polarised gaze on the object, and in an almost programmed response Fritz held out his hand and nodded at the ring.

"vor ihre *kinder?*"

He then straightened his stance and stared almost through Bill with the piercing eyes of death.

In broken English he said again, calmly, "Please take the ring."

Bill turned to the guard on the right, who said.

"You might as well take it, mate. He won't be needing it. Tell this story to your grandkids. That's if you ever get out of this hell hole."

As Bill moved towards the German to remove the ring, Fritz nodded in approval.

"For you, take now."

Bill held Fritz's hand with his left hand and removed the twisted ring from his finger. Bill held it in the palm of his hand and looked at it. It was solid platinum, a snake ring of three coils. Almost immediately the two guards dragged the SS man away and he was gone.

Studying it further, he gazed at the ring wondering where it had come from and the horrors it had witnessed. He clenched his hand into a fist, closed his eyes and dreamed of home. He would soon be fishing for trout again with his little brother, Tommy.

He promised that he would wear the ring as a prompt, a verification of what horrors mankind could commit, and it would be a constant reminder of his need to be a good man for the rest of his life. He thought if things got difficult or unbearable, the ring on his finger would be a telling testament to evil, and that life had been much worse for others. He would be a good man for the rest of his life. He would never forget those days in Germany in 1945.

Chapter 1

Metropolitan Police Constable Aiden Simmons had not reasoned to challenge the driver of the dark blue van, in fact the 'Rookie" had only been with the force for seven months and did not feel that it was his place to question authority. After all the vehicle was representative of the model and age of the vans adopted by 'The Met's' armed response units. To under pin legitimacy the driver displayed the rank of Superintendent and the two passengers were both regaled in recognisable standard issue black police fatigues.

On that January evening the Wembley Arena was hosting a large public event and with the security alert at a high level it was perfectly in order to see the presence of numerous armed police units.

Safe passage approved the driver steered the van into the main car park situated to the East of the Wembley Arena and parked up next to a merchandising unit positioned approximately twenty metres in front of the main entrance.

Paul Wey inhaled the last breath of his cigarette and looked at the watch on his left hand, he glanced across the dark expanse of Car Park No 1 and briefly noticed the blue police van. He pulled his black hoody tight and mounted the step to the entrance at the back of the large unwashed white mobile retail unit.

When questioned by the Metropolitan Police later that evening Wey would report that he had no reason to be suspicious of the perfectly legitimate presented police firearms unit.

In the relative darkness of the car park the three occupants of the van sat in silence, the only background sound was the distance muffled drumming which emanated from the main concert hall.

The ambience of the van was eventually disturbed by the buzzing of a mobile communications device, the flashing of green electronic screen pierced the semi darkness and illuminated the cab.

The driver alerted to action by the communicator looked down and read the message displayed in green type. The two passengers remained silent, one of them was motionless however the man nearest the door appeared anxious and shuffled around on his seat in an uneasy manner.

'The heat will burn the summer of 66 R'

The driver stared at the communication, this was the message he had been programmed to act on, this was the clear un ambiguous call to action.

He turned and looked directly at the dark haired and boiler suited man sat by the passenger door and in a guttural accent barked.

"OK we go! get the holdalls and No 3 out of the back NOW!!!"

"Right M" the man hesitated then replied with a Middle Eastern enunciation.

M looked at the dark haired slim man sat on the middle seat.

"Get out now… grab your bag and join No 2 and 3"

The two men disembarked from van into the arousing cold night air and walked towards the rear of the vehicle.

M remained at the wheel and on the signal provided by the second slam of the rear door he wound down his window and gestured to the men who had appeared wearing the full uniform of Metropolitan Police Firearms officers. An informed eye would have spotted one anomaly, all three of the men were armed with semi-automatic rifles each loaded with a pair of magazines taped together. A nonstandard procedure for the police and a clear indicator that these individuals were fully prepared for a grave and deadly deed.

The blonde haired man who identified as M checked his black sports watch and with a cold un emotional gaze visually inspected his three accomplices and passed on his instructions.

"Go and take your positions and make sure that you all have got your ear pieces switched on?'

The three men nodded, one of them appeared nervous.

"Good now remember split up ….one through each door just as I showed you on the plan and don't forget to place your bags on the floor before leaving, just stick to the plan we rehearsed. I will give you the signal to commence and the signal to return. Understand?"

There was a momentary silence then one by one the three men acknowledged the instructions.

Ten seconds later the trio of ersatz police officers ventured off in the subdued light past Paul Wey's caravan and towards the glowing beacon of the venue foyer.

The middle and tallest of the three men had taken the lead towards the illuminated wall of blue aluminium framed glass which provided the final barrier to the assembled eight thousand plus excited daughters, sons, brothers, sisters and parents who had just listened to the final song of the evening.

Outside a stream of parents negotiated their way through the random gathering of police officers, merchandisers, and event security staff.

The firearms officer pushed his way past a frustrated man who was picking up dropped tee shirts, and positioned himself adjacent to the centre doorway, he placed the plain black imitation leather grip bag on the ground next to his right boot.

He looked right and left towards his two collaborators and raised his right black leather gloved hand to halt their movement.

The three men stood five metres apart, holding automatic weapons across their chests in readiness for action, no one doubted or questioned the authority of the men wearing black fatigues and chequered black and white baseball caps.

In an instant the deadened booming from inside ceased and was replaced by the banging of doors and the boisterous gaggle of teenagers as they decanted from the auditorium.

The leader of the trio observed the change in tempo and dry mouthed and heart pounding he awaited the order to move.

'it will all be over quickly' he thought,' *just remember the drill'* he reminded himself,

'six magazines and get out and back to the van, take full advantage of the confusion to make an escape' he felt assured.

His heart beat increased, his ears buzzed, he could feel the adrenaline warm his veins, to ward off the fear he thought about his escape and the financial gain waiting for carrying out this act. For a moment he dwelled on how easy it had been to walk into a large venue totally unchallenged whilst touting a deadly automatic weapon.

The brightly lit foyer filled up rapidly as the auditorium emptied, the atmosphere was one of excitement and joy as youngsters revelled at the experience of seeing their pop star heroes.

The door slid open onto the late cold night air and the babbling throng spilled out onto the large paved area between the venue and the car park. Thrilled teenagers, mainly girls were welcomed by a troupe of parents who were queued ready to meet their family members.

The leader felt a little agitated he wanted to execute the task and get out but there was still no instruction from his master back in the van.

M looked at his watch, and with the phone in his hand he opened the van door and stepped out on to the car park and proceeded towards the rear of the vehicle, He opened the rear double doors climbed in and closed the doors behind him. Under the dim illumination of the internal light he sat on a wooden crate and untied the laces on his ankle height black boots. He kicked of the boots stood up and unzipped the black fatigues to reveal a dark green pullover and blue denim jeans. M pulled on a pair of light brown leather slip on boots and grabbed a black waxed cotton jacket from a hook attached to the internal wood panelling of the van. He rose from the wooden crate and fumbled around in his right hand trouser pocket and recovered a single chrome key. The light from the mobile phone was just sufficient to allow him to unite the key and a lock on the box. He flipped the lid open to reveal the sinister contents, an electronic controller attached to a package of Semtex plastic explosive. With a gloved right hand M flicked a small toggle switch and the device powered up into life, the digital display flashed that the count down from 5 minutes had commenced.

M remained calm as he climbed out of the van, he locked the back door, put on the black jacket and joined the flow of fans who had left the concert early and headed across the car park in a direction opposite from the arena.

At 22.44 and 32 seconds M removed a smart phone from the side pocket of his coat and made a call which was relayed to the other side of the world then back to the device left in the locked van and a micro second later to the ear price of his accomplice.

Against the tide of departing fans, the three black suited officers unchallenged made their way into, and joined the manic activity in the foyer.

The leader raised his gloved hand and the heinous act was unleashed upon the innocent.

Hugo and his father had been waiting in the queue of cars and taxis which had furiously negotiated valuable territory outside the arena. They were both sat in the car, staring out at the dark evening illuminated by the river of headlights and the manic flow of people leaving the concert. Their daydreaming was suddenly disturbed when they heard the sound of gunfire rip into the night air and subsequent explosions which announced that a monstrous act was in progress

At precisely eleven minutes after the end of the concert a sinister, vile and rancorous sorcery of evil minds catalysed the exploding cordite which extinguished life, morality, and the immaculacy of human kindness.

The background of the excitement was ripped apart by the sound of automatic gunfire as it cracked above the noise of excited fans. Into this sacred space of childhood engagement and innocence had stormed three purveyors of destruction, representatives of evil itself. The black silhouettes provided a sinister backdrop against the muzzle fire of the Heckler and Koch semi-automatic assault rifles. Chaos ensued. Lights went out. The well-planned and programmed dramatization of suppression of purity had commenced. The entrance lights were extinguished. Glass was broken. The only illumination was the flames of death, yellow, white and orange, which exhaled from the muzzles of the black weapons.

For nearly two minutes the attackers discharged their weapons only ceasing the act of murder to change magazines, and refresh the weapons with another payload of death.

The central attacker ceased firing threw his weapon on the floor and in the confusion turned toward the door to make his escape and meet up with M as arranged.

The other two gunmen followed the lead, however, their plan for a safe passage was abruptly ended when M dialled a code into his phone which activated the detonators in the three black leather holdalls close to the three gunmen.

There was an almighty flash followed by an ear ripping blast and the odour of burning Semtex accompanied the smell of death in the foyer. The three gunmen were consumed by fire and torn apart by the catalysed plastic explosive.

Two seconds later the blue van exploded with a deafening boom accompanied by a large yellow and orange flash that burned like a large Roman Candle in the unlit car park.

The ensuing chaos provided a perfect opportunity for M to escape into the blackness of his surroundings.

There was no longer the orderly huddle of excited mums and children clutching souvenir programmes as they shuffled their way to the four main doors which exited onto the main street. The dark blue carpet was burnt and scattered with bodies moaning in agony, and in many cases taking their last breaths. It had been a place of excitement and good humour. The modern entrance, however, was not designed to cope with a huge gathering of mainly teenagers.

Outside the venue car alarms triggered by the exploding van rang out in unison with the screams of the dying and frightened on that fateful January night when a cruel and hideous act had transformed joy to unimaginable horror and tragedy.

Chapter 2

The morning silence was interrupted by the banging opening riff of a seventies rock standard, the muffled monotone from the mobile device heralded 05.30 a.m. and the end of Guy's sleep. Guy Walker was surprised he had slept so well, better than expected in consideration of the turmoil in his life and the many matters on his mind.

Fumbling around, his left hand silenced the screaming device, and his right hand carefully folded back the bed sheets in a manner that suggested the sleeper had spent some time in the British Forces. Guy rolled his legs out of the bed and sat erect on the edge of the white-covered mattress. His eyes surveyed the room.

It was the same scape every day: the impeccably polished handmade black English shoes placed carefully at the left edge of the wardrobe door. Hanging from the handle of the door was an immaculately laundered white shirt accompanied by an elegant 'off the Peg' dark blue Saville Row suit.

The same daily routine commenced, with 120 sit-ups and 50 press-ups. As Guy continued to the final exercise the tightness of his tanned skin revealed the scars on his shoulder, the result of a collar bone injury. Under his left arm there were three small but prominent scars, the brand left by contact with a hostile firearm.

47…48…48…50.

Guy exhaled through gritted teeth, jumped up and walked towards the en suite bathroom. He shaved and showered, dressed in a towelling robe and walked into the kitchen of his one-bedroom rented Mayfair flat. He stroked Tinkers, his faithful British Blue cat, and proffered his friend a bowl of food, which he placed down before her.

A breakfast of apple juice and cereal was consumed. No coffee or tea – as usual he would have this at the office. Guy was in his early 50s, average height and build, well-toned with a hint of a permanent tan, and he had a full head of undyed hair which he kept well-trimmed in a long, modern style. His friends and colleagues constantly questioned if his hair was dyed. Guy had many secrets, but this was not one of them.

Guy returned to the bedroom to remove his phone from its bedside charger. Standing erect with the phone in his right hand, he checked his email messages and as usual, there was little traffic. Guy was not a mailer, a point he relayed very strongly to all that knew him. He preferred to call, or meet- to 'press the flesh', as he termed it. Messages read or trashed he approached the dresser near the window, opened the top drawer and took out a pay-as-you-go phone. He switched it on, checked the emails. Nothing again to report. In the background the Radio 2 show streamed out the report on the horrific terror attack on British soil the previous evening, 62 dead and many serious injuries, then a report which updated the listeners on the challenge to the current leader of the Conservative Party and Prime Minister. The challenger was a young man called Phillip Medway, a respected investor, industrialist and ex hedge fund manager. *Well, successful*, Guy reflected. There was no hedge fund manager respected outside the fiefdom of the luxury car dealership network.

Well, Guy reflected, *if the man had the right to run the country, he knew about finance and he knew about lying, so he may well be a very strong candidate to be the next Prime Minister.*

This would be the subject of many a debate from now on, in the oak-clad clubs of Mayfair to the working men's' clubs of the County Durham pit villages.

Guy walked to his wardrobe and took a light blue Paisley tie from the rack fixed to the back of the door.

Despite a few dates and work life, he liked his own company, and his flat was his domain. It provided security for him, Guy was a loner, and lived not to rely on others. He trusted only a few.

Guy opened the bedside drawer and removed his golden stainless Rolex Daytona, and clipped it securely into place on his left wrist. This was the only jewellery he wore, except of course on the third finger of his right hand he wore with pride and affection and great sentimentality, his dad's - and before that Uncle Bill's – platinum snake ring.

He removed the immaculately pressed jacket from the hanger, admired the tailoring, and pulled it on and fastened the sole button. As he did this, the jacket rubbed the shirt and lightly pressured a scar on the lower part of his chest and abdomen and reminder of that day in 1991 in Gulf War 1.

He was now ready to deal with the issues that the day would throw at him. Maybe this was the day the deal would come.

One more look, the tie had to be corrected; a bit more hair fix. He had to look the part, elegant yet fierce, aggressive but polished. He after all was having lunch with Lukas Richter the billionaire fund manager. The appointment had come totally out of the blue, however a serious move on his part as Richter did not suffer fools. Folklore suggested that Richter had made fortunes from illicit arms deals in Africa. Rumour or no rumour, the Austrian financier was the maker of kings if he backed you.

Briefcase in hand he was ready to go and fight the battles to regain past glories.

It had been a little over three hours since the Prime Minister of the United Kingdom had arisen from a disturbed sleep of only two and half hours.

At the top of her agenda today would be a review on the murderous attacks in London the night before. She had been awoken from an early sleep with the news of the shootings and bombings at The Wembley Arena. Throughout the night and into the early morning Eileen Moss had fielded numerous calls from the Commissioner of the Metropolitan Police Force, The Home Secretary and the head of MI5. In only two hours' time she would head back to London for a meeting of COBRA to discuss the attack.

Eileen Moss was in residence at Chequers and had diligently and expeditiously consumed the contents of three red attaché boxes, which sat on the side of her work table.

This was the daily routine the hard work ethic which had been drilled into her by a coal miner father who was atypical of his comrades who dug for coal at Seaham Colliery, County Durham. He was a man who envisioned a better future for his family and powerless to improve his own prospects he would live out his own ambitions through Eileen his only daughter.

George White would work every hour and save every surplus penny for his daughter's future education.

Eileen left school with 4 A levels and headed for Cambridge University with a broad education in life and debate bestowed to her from her loving and dedicated father.

At an early age this young intellectual had gained an enquiring interest in politics, and unusually for a coal miner her father was a Conservative, he believed that hard work would bring reward.

As the recently elected Conservative Prime Minister these were challenging times for Eileen, and in many respects, she had inherited the poison chalice of a deeply divided minority Government.

Not only did she have to face up to a very popular, effective and well supported leader of the Labour opposition, Eileen Moss had a Judas in her midst in the form of the Home Secretary.

In a moment of reprieve from the world of politics she took a sip from the white china cup which had sat on the large dark mahogany desk, and revolving on the red leather chair she positioned her gaze to the world beyond the large white sash windows. The craved refreshing gratification of the beverage was abruptly eradicated as she drank the cold coffee, *' one day I will have time to enjoy my coffee hot'* she fantasised.

She moved to face her desk and her thoughts reverted to business and in particular to that slippery and treacherous Home Secretary, Philip Medway.

'This man was trouble 'she had decided '*he had come from nowhere, who was backing him? What were his motives? and what was his next move to disrupt matters?'* she hissed through clenched teeth.

One final sip from the white china cup and the tepid beverage was consumed. Eileen re united the cup and the saucer with a subtle clink.

Her thoughts returned to Medway. Damn, he was wrecking the party and could open the door to the opposition seizing power. He had come from nowhere, and aided with the financial power provided by very deep pockets had created a whirlwind in the party. Why now? she thought After graduating, he held a number of project engineers' appointments in East Africa and the Middle East where he amassed a substantial cash pile. The newly gained wealth had enabled him to buy a York based small air conditioning contractor. The rest was history. Today he sat on a substantial empire of UK businesses, mainly engineering, electrical contractors, and building services management.

The Prime Minister had secretly appointed party officials to investigate Medway's companies for foreign investments or any illegal and illicit dealings as funding sources. Nothing had come up except that the group had very little borrowings; in fact, zero. A company under the name Medway Contracting Holdings had defied gravity with what seemed endless cash piles and had made some ambitious acquisitions. Things were about to get more noteworthy as Medway was locked in a David and Goliath bid for Whitehead Industries, a $14 billion US based engineering business with interests in the UK, Israel and the United States. The company specialised in consultancy, process plant operation and the managing of large engineering infrastructure projects throughout the world.

Over recent months, Whitehead had suffered several misfortunes, which ended with the death of their Chairman and CEO in an executive jet aircraft crash. The Gulfstream 300 had just undergone its annual CAA check at a maintenance base at Biggin Hill. Interestingly, the maintenance company was run and had been recently purchased by one of Phillip Medway's old friends and former director of his company. The aircraft, fresh from its annual service, then collected Jim Massey and Bob Wilkes, CEO and Chairman respectively from Northolt air field, twenty minutes after take off and on the climb out the aircraft suffered an immediate and fatal catastrophic failure. The accident investigation board announced that one of the rear mounted turbofan engines had exploded and taken out the tail of the airframe, resulting in an out of control aircraft plunging into the Berkshire countryside and narrowly missing Newbury. There was one big mystery, the engine containment ring, which is designed to withstand an explosion and render the air frame safe, had not done its job.

Concurrently one of Whitehead's major suppliers had commenced legal action over a copyright infringement. The business was highly leveraged with senior debt syndicated with two major US and one major UK bank. The loss of leadership and pending legal action were putting new pressure on the shares. Social media was active with rumours of lack of performance on a number of large US and UK contracts for defence equipment. This amalgam of misfortune generated huge activity in the shorting of shares in particular, an Austrian hedge fund Tornado were taking out large positions on the stock.

To compound the problems, and like any thriller, the UK and EMA divisional Vice President was killed in freak skiing accident. Jason Turner was a rising star in the corporation and getting a grip on the contra issues. He died instantly after what appeared to be a minor and insidious fall. There was no witness apart from his partner and the doctor who had been on the scene with them. The doctor from Munich was the first to attend to Turner. Jason's partner Stephanie Davis, was shocked when the German Doctor announced that Turner had passed away. There was a short inquest, ruling death by misadventure, all backed by the Swiss authorities and the German's assessment of the incident that was so convincing. Turner's family were not so convinced and suspected foul play.

Chapter 3

Guy fumbled in his right pocket for the car key and gazed at the Range Rover, it was three years old. How he yearned to have a newer model or even something racier and Bentley perhaps.

A motorist pulled up alongside and disturbed the daydream.

"Are you leaving that space, mate?"

"Not yet, I'm afraid," Guy retorted.

Another voice bellowed out, "Are you going to move, now?"

For the second time, Guy announced he wasn't. He was just going into his car to retrieve some luggage.

Now was the time of atonement. The bill had to be paid for the excess of his past life. A cocktail of three failed marriages accompanied by a number of poor business decisions and investment failures built on highly toxic promises of unreliable funds. Guy had a huge financial hangover. There had been a rapid volley of successes in the late 90s and early 00s which made him a darling with the institutions and banks alike. The early success and associated trappings of cars, watches, beautiful houses, first class travel, had a profound effect on Guy.

This working-class boy was enjoying the fruits of his labour and was not willing to risk his hard-earned wealth on projects which did not interest him any longer.

He had rapidly gone through his cash balances and the final straw was two bad investments in businesses which went south in 2016 – 2017 as a result of the uncertainty of Brexit, and a number of customers going into liquidation.

Responding to the irate would be car parker, Guy said, "No, the car is there all day, my friend. I'm just getting something from the boot. Sorry."

Guy locked the hatchback of his car and with thoughts of the last of the dice spinning at max speed, he commenced his morning stroll to a rather congested Baker Street. Today was

Tuesday and he was still retained by the growing clothing retailer. One day a week was sufficient and his job was done, but the owners and the banks wanted Guy to sit it out and be in the office three days a week.

It was nine o'clock and the traffic was heavy – more heavy than usual.

Approaching the glass door which was the transit to the windowless basement office, Guy reflected upon the day in prospect and descended into the abyss of the overcrowded, soulless office.

Taking his seat, he fired up his laptop and prepared for three hours of number crunching on his twenty-first century abacus. The office was fully occupied with denim and tee-shirt clad twenty-year-olds going through their daily routine.

His smile was transmogrified into an arrogant but confident grimace as he concluded that his dress code would always win the day. He was a knight inspecting his armour prior to the battlefield. His low self-esteem would be masked and eclipsed by the robes of office which would protect him from the darkness and allow him to transact as an equal with the masters of finance.

He observed the lacklustre décor of the office and colleagues glued to their electronic masters, Guy reluctantly logged on, ready to establish any form of communication with those three meters away from him.

A string of emails erupted from the company's digital overlord, and as usual he ruthlessly deleted any communication which was not directly addressed to him. He had no time for gossip from the ether. All around him was the clash of keyboards, the servants to the Chinese manufactured flashing digital demigod in the sacred cupboard under the stairs as it blurted out the day's activities.

Guy removed an A4 view-per-day diary from his well-organised briefcase, a concession to the past. Surveying his notes – yes, one of those dying breed who still wrote things down. Neatly listed under the date were the actions for the day.

The highlight of the day was 12.15: an actual personal contact. A prehistoric act, a one on one Lunch. Contact with a human – well, at least Guy hoped it would be a human. He smiled to himself.

Lukas Richter was an investment banker who had made a fortune in Vienna and Frankfurt. A major player in Europe and New York he was relatively unknown in the London community. It was no secret that Richter was aggressive and a master of the 'short play', and to the discontent of his adversaries the Austrian was well-funded courtesy of mysterious backers with incredibly deep pockets full of cash. Guy had been monitoring and observing the performance of this aloof individual for some time. He had made some outrageous but highly profitable bets on the performance of a number of blue-chip companies. Did he have the Midas touch he wondered, or was it the work of a more Machiavellian dogma?

Richter's trusty assistant, Alistair Berry, had contacted Guy out of the blue. Learn from Richter? Guy thought. Was it the work of some prankster, or was it real?

The reality was Richter had invited Guy to lunch at Handell House, 12.15 that day, and he had to be punctual. Handell House club was not off limits to Guy – he had been a member for several years, until recent times. Familiar surroundings of elegant décor, wandering staircases and the welcoming maître d' would remove some of the anxieties of the meeting with the formidable Richter. Guy had never met or spoken to Richter on the phone and to receive an email from this titan would be as rare as sand in the Antarctic. On receiving the call from Berry, Guy was reminded of an introduction made to him with team sponsor of the 2015 Macau GP. That trip to Macau had been a dream come true, made only better by the holiday with full access passes to race week.

The first practice, the first morning out at Macau had been disrupted by heavy rain and eventually, due to the continuous downpour, activities ceased at 10.00 a.m.

Guy was not deterred by the robust downpour and decided to investigate machinery and activity in the pit garages. The Tornado Ventures backed AWS motorcycle racing team underpinned their superiority by holding court in two garages. The blue, white and black AWS team colours were eclipsed by the striking black and silver logos, bold statements that this was ownership of Tornado Ventures. They were the paymasters, fuelling the insatiable financial appetite of the multi-million machine which was road racing.

The racing community had to be prepared to persuade sponsors to part with up to 1.8 million US dollars to run a middle-ranking team. It was not a published fact that Lukas Richter's Tornado Ventures were the financial host of three million US dollars per annum for this team.

This was pin money for Richter, who although a semi recluse, did enjoy the trappings of a billionaire lifestyle.

This man was an enigma, appearing almost like a genie from a bottle from nowhere, but heavens, he'd made his mark. He had marked his territory in New York, Frankfurt, Singapore, and Swiss money markets. His investment vehicle, Tornado Ventures, was a financial missile. Richter had almost supernatural talent at picking blue chip companies about to announce bad news. The international financial community was totally perplexed as to where his substantial and never-ending initial seed funding came from. Two of the large US financial institutions had even gone to the extreme length to see if Richter was the facilitator of illicit funds. Despite numerous undercover investigations and highly covert examination of email traffic, no illegal dealings were discovered. It appeared that the money, or some of it, was from a secretive individual or organisation; however, it didn't appear to be involved in any international crime activity.

Spearheading this was top team director Dave Bright. An ex-racer with an MSc in Engineering,

Guy was miles away, transfixed by the technical genius of the team mechanics' ability to review data which allowed them to make minor adjustments to damping, ignition timing and a whole host of other parameters to improve performance. Suddenly he heard the broad Yorkshire accent of Dave Bright, not realising he was trying to engage in conversation with him.

"You're Guy, aren't you? We raced together back in the eighties. Do you remember me I was the young upstart who took you off at the tower bend at Croft Autodrome?"

Alarmed, Guy turned and realised that DB – as he was affectionately known – was addressing him.

"How could I forget?" Guy replied with a controlled smile. "It was at the end of my career, and you were a young upstart."

"What brings you to Macau?" replied DB, whose poker face did not give away that he was fully aware of the reason why.

The grimace evolved into a smile as Guy's ego was elevated in the company of a titan of motorcycle racing.

DB was just about to speak when he was interrupted by Paul Easton, the AWS Press Relations Director.

"Herr Schrader wants a word, and we can't ignore a command from our esteemed leader."

DB turned away from Guy momentarily and acknowledged the tall, dark-haired chisel-faced man in the corner of the garage, partially hidden from view by a large and expensive tool station.

Alerted, Guy's eyes moved towards the tool station and briefly surveyed the steely-looking upright individual staring at him. His cold blue eyes were locked firmly onto Guy, a look that made the recipient feel undeniably unsettled. Easton momentarily transacted his glance towards DB, ricocheting a subliminal message to him. *I want to see you now.*

DB turned to Guy. "Excuse me, one minute. The fuhrer wants to see me wait and I'll be back soon."

Impatiently, Easton disappeared through the door at the rear of the garage, and DB followed him into a very lavish blue and white motorhome.

Easton had unsettled Guy. There was something about this man which was sinister. He had never met him – again, he was not one for publicity.

Ten minutes later, DB arrived back into the garage and it was plainly evident that his mood had changed. Appearing far too friendly, DB said, "Let's go for a coffee, Guy."

As he rolled his lips and bit his tongue, Guy detected an unscrupulous opportunistic tone in his request, which inerrancy was a veiled demand.

"Let's get a cab to the team hotel. The coffee and the cake are first class. And anyway, I've finished for the day."

The verbal exchange in the taxi was a little more forced than the banter in the pit lane. Guy couldn't help but notice that DB was glaring incessantly at the ring on his left hand. The taxi pulled up outside the lobby.

"Go into the first-floor mezzanine, Guy, and I'll meet you in a minute. I need to go up to the toilet first, once I've settled the taxi."

In fact, Bright did not go to the rest room. He inched past a number of Chinese guests, in Macau for gambling, and made a call on his mobile. Call over, DB ascended the two stair cases made from polished marble with chrome balustrades, and walked over to Guy who was sitting on a white fake Italian table at the edge of the mezzanine.

"Coffee and cake on the way," Bright said and he sat down. One final glance at the ring on Guy's finger. He had seen a ring like this before, and only today.

Chapter 4

Jack Sharples awoke at 4.30 a.m. *This was too early*, he protested to the white radio clock on his bedside table

At precisely 5.10 he commenced his journey from his Cheltenham home located at the end of Montpellier Parade, and turned right at the roundabout on to the 'Golden Valley', which if uninterrupted would take him straight on to Junction 9 of the M5 and onwards to Manchester. His hopes of a burden-free transit to the motorway met a frustrating conclusion. As he approached the traffic lights adjacent to the filling station opposite the motorcycle shop, he noticed that two police cars had blocked the road which led past GCHQ. As he waited at the red traffic light, the silhouette of a police officer set against the background of blue flashing lights approached him. Signalling to the driver to lower his window, the policeman was temporarily disturbed by a crackled message which fired out of the communicator secured to the top left hand of his black stab vest.

Sharples lowered the driver's window.

"Good morning, sir. I'm afraid there's a potentially fatal road traffic accident resulting from a hit and run. This has resulted in the road being closed for many hours." The policeman announced

With a gasp of frustration, Jack enquired

"Is the road to next Junction North clear?"

"Yes, sir. If you turn right here, in two and a half miles the road turns left. The Tewkesbury road will take you to Junction 10 on the M5." Acknowledged the officer.

Jack nodded his head in acceptance but this was now making him late. He wanted to beat the Birmingham rush hour. And with no empathy whatsoever for this unknown victim, he replied,

"Thank you, officer."

Simmering with frustration at running late, eyes firmly fixed to the road he defied the speed limit past the railway station, he did not notice the light blue van which was parked opposite the entrance to the Cheltenham Spa station. The vehicle was a sixteen-plate light blue Transit, clearly adorned with vinyl transfers announcing that the van was the property of TET the global telecommunications provider. Jack and the sporadic flow of bi passers failed to know that TET did not operate vans in this colour, especially Transits of 2016 registration in this particular area, and the Company certainly would not have fixed decals in such an amateur fashion.

At that precise time, a thirty-three-year-old white male was being carefully positioned onto a drop-side gurney. Unconscious, he was attached to a heart rate monitor, an IV drip, and numerous other electronic paraphernalia which reported the ongoing flicker of life. The victim was loaded into the ambulance. As a paramedic worked to maintain a breath of life, police sergeant Ron Thomson talked into his mobile phone, and informed a tearful young lady that her husband would not be reporting for work that day. This thirty odd-year-old IT consultant would be heading to the crash department at Cheltenham A&E, and would possibly be transferred to Birmingham or Bristol by air ambulance later in the day.

As Thomson ended the call, he reflected on twenty years in the force as a traffic officer. Despite all of the tragic circumstances he had witnessed, he never hardened. It was still as upsetting as ever to tell a member of public that a loved one was fighting for their life.

While Thompson was on the call two telephone engineers were hard at it on their contrived stage show as they worked on, or at least appeared to work on, the large TET switching box placed outside the convenience store opposite the Cheltenham Spa railway station. At all times during the fanciful act of moving test probes inside the grey box, the whole stage show was being streamed live by videophone as the two erstwhile technicians went on with their work. During the simmering morning activity on the road, no passer-by thought to question what appeared to be legitimate repairs being carried out on the grey TET box. Only a trained eye would have noticed the small black device which had been connected by a series of wires to a cluster of terminals positioned at the bottom left hand internal corner of the equipment box. In a further twist is was not apparent to any on looker that this orchestrated operation was been coordinated by a man hunched over a keyboard many many miles away from this gateway to the digital high-speed internet freeway to GCHQ Cheltenham, the UK's spy centre. The GCHQ facility monitors all potential erroneous spurious electronic messages and provides vital intelligence to anti-terrorist organisations in and around the UK

Leaning over a computer in a bedroom in a large semi-detached house in St John's Wood was the slight figure of Hugo Parnell.

Hugo was the only son of a successful City lawyer. He had grown up in an uncontentious and slightly mundane suburb of north London. From an early age Hugo had shown an uncanny interest in all things electronic and had a vociferous appetite to research the latest technologies and state of the art computer systems, especially the wizardry that connected PCs and LANs, local area networks, to each other.

A genius at mathematics, Hugo was an accomplished amateur cryptologist and was an expert on the work of Turing, Knox and Flowers, the trio who had been the driving force behind the code breakers at Bletchley Park during World War II.

A loner, who did not socialise with the other boys he deliberately avoided partaking in football, cricket, or all things team sport, Hugo instead was content in the impersonal world of science and computing, and the faceless unemotional world of the World Wide Web

Hugo's physical reality was his home, his parents and his sister, Sarah, who he adored. And of course there was his forever-absent mother, Barbara, who was a senior partner at one of the magic circle law firms and was late home nearly every night

Little Sarah had been momentarily starved of oxygen at birth and had consequently suffered slight brain damage. The outcome of this troubled birth was a beautiful, blond-haired, happy and delightful little girl. This was a mask which covered a child who suffered severe learning difficulties. The son of two formidable legal titans never forgave the medical profession for Sarah's vulnerability to a cruel world.

Hugo achieved a First in Pure Mathematics at Imperial College London and was then accepted at MIT to study for a Masters in Mathematics and Computer Technology. His preparations were to fly to the USA were cruelly terminated on a fateful night in 2017.

Little did Hugo know that that sweet smile from his helpless nine-year-old sister would be her last. The image of his beautiful Sarah in Mum's hand was permanently etched on to his physical and mental memory.

Sarah loved pop music, and in particular the boy band Seven to One who was the love of Sarah's life. When the concert tickets had been announced, the general public only had minutes to stake their claim as demand outstripped supply by a huge margin.

When it came to hacking the ticket master site, Hugo held no morals. To him, it was only justice of quantum proportions for what the cruel world had inflicted on little Sarah. Satisfied their systems were impenetrable, the ticket agent pressed the button at 09.00 on that trading morning, and an explosion of electronic activity ensued. At 09.01 the server crashed – or it appeared to have gone down. What the thousands of highly intolerant, agitated, frustrated and, in most instances, furiously tapping keyboard warriors did not know, was that it was not quantity but quality of digital traffic that had was holding up proceedings.

Just like the Nazis believed the Enigma was unbreakable, eTicketUK believed that no one would ever crack their code.

Again, as with the Enigma, it was a human interface which provided the microscopic, almost sub atomic defect in the membrane, like a single cancer cell, which once established grew at lightning speed and corrupted the operation of the machine. At 09.00 plus 0.0005 seconds on that morning, two homemade servers designed and assembled by Hugo, a genius unknown to the wise men at eTicketUK, flickered into life. The box of wires provided the electronic switches which were fired up in a benign sequence of electronic patterns via invisible but hard connected highways in ninety percent of the PCs in the world. This unintelligible message had only two destinations; two connections to be made to create the covalent bond between one buyer and the main ticket server. In that nanosecond after 09.00 hours, Mr Steven Drake of 14 Walworth Crescent, Milton Keynes would become the only customer of that website. He did not know he was being used as a foil to block all the other traffic to the site. Actually, this was an immortal Trojan horse which allowed Hugo exclusive access to all tickets for the Wembley gig at that particular micro-second in time. Another micro-second later, the site was unblocked and free for the real Mr Drake to purchase his priority tickets.

The eighteen-inch screen flickered and revealed that Hugo was now the proud owner of two front-row VIP access tickets for the concert. For a moment his eyes glazed at the thought of the surprise he would give his little angel. The trip to Wembley Arena in the car would be the last time he would stroke her hair and experience the lovely innocence of her angelic gaze. As mum and daughter approached the VIP entrance, Sarah turned and with her blond hair covering one half of her face, she smiled at Hugo, a smile almost infant-like; a smile a two-year-old gives a mother when they receive the new life companion of a cuddly toy. Her blond hair radiated as she stood out amongst the backdrop of the thousands of excited children chaperoned by mothers and fathers hustling their way into the main entrance of the arena. She then blew a kiss from her left hand. That was the last act of affection he would see from her, and a final and eternal manifestation of childlike purity.

Hugo had reconciled that in a world of greed and capitalist dogma, innocence would always be sacrosanct. The dream was shattered by the malevolence of a separatist ideology, the result of which would kill, maim, and permanently scar the bodies of many innocent men, women and children and take away his lovely Sarah, perversely punish a little girl who had only brought joy and happiness to those hearts she warmly touched.

Fifteen days after the event, Sarah was laid to rest, and as he released a handful of moist earth that fell and landed with a gentle thud on the little white coffin, he stared at the sky and his blue eyes pierced the heavens and on a breath of rage he pledged revenge. He vowed on the soul of Sarah, and on the memory of Sarah, somehow, someday, he would avenge her killers. He did not know it but the wheels were already in motion to afford him that opportunity.

Chapter 5

Guy awoke from his trancelike state in the quasi parallel universe of his excel spreadsheet. He looked around, the bland office walls were still as plain as ever.

Lifting his head, in clear eyeshot was Abby, the Office Manager, whose piercing blue eyes were riveted to her PC screen. She was joined on the left by Davy, the cheeky Welshman, who was head of product, and on her right the ever ebullient and cocky Bobby Morley. Guy detested this over-confident, mouthy little shit. How had Guy, a formidable player, ended up in this dungeon? Lifeless, soulless, digital-powered light-yellow tomb.

An electric shock jolted Guy and he realised it was 12.05. God, only ten minutes before his meeting. He could not be late for Richter.

He switched off his laptop and closed the lid and looked at the black and gold dial of his watch which was deliberately set five minutes fast.

Rolling his chair back with an almost screeching motion, he stood up, and pushed the finger of his right hand through his incongruously medium-to-long dark brown hair and he thought,

"Well, lad. This is your big opportunity. Perhaps it will just be a lunch." Or it may prove to be a highly random event, a prosperous and decisive turning point which would provide the portal to transport Guy away from this office and back to the fortunes of the golden days.

A final utterance from the laptop signalled that would be corporate raider would be off the radar and released from the digital entrance to endless boring data of doubtful utility.

Placing his chair carefully into position at the workstation, Guy announced,

"I'm off, out for lunch. Ought to be back in an hour or so."

No acknowledgement from the incurious community to the cause of sales and margin increases.

"In fact, I hope never to return."

Still no response, as footfall, pennies, pounds and transaction sizes were being analysed. Only Davy lifted his head and gave a wry smile, then tutted in irreverence to his fellow team members.

Guy looked at the coat stand and removed his beautifully and skilfully tailored jacket from its dedicated wooden coat hanger. This was the final constituent of his uniform. Now the sum of the parts would provide the regalia of office which would energise Guy into the world of business.

Precisely seven minutes before the appointment, Guy was mildly nervous, and as he approached the steps to Handell House club situated on the north end of Portland Square, he placed his left hand on a well-worn brass handle to the immaculately painted black double-leaf door. Pausing momentarily, he felt the nerves ooze away slightly. This was familiar territory to him. Habitual ground it may be; however, it could not be concluded home ground, as it was Richter who had offered Guy the membership privileges of the day. He was still perplexed as to why Richter wanted to see him and, more puzzling, how the master of big money deals knew that Guy Walker even existed.

'Deep breath.' He said to himself.

Composed he opened the large doors to the familiar environment, elegant but tired, the well-worn marble tile floors, evidence of many decades of important traffic, a constant progression into the chamber of engagement. Deal making, both legal and illicit deals, reserved only for men of influence and wealth. Habit made him fumble in his jacket pocket, only to discover he no longer held the much-vaunted membership card. Today he was a mere civilian. No longer was he greeted with, "Good afternoon, Mr Walker," as the desk concierge indicated that he needed to sign in.

Guy observed that the layout of the reception had been changed in the progression of time. The formal counter had been replaced with a leather-topped mahogany desk behind which sat a thirty-something man of possibly Middle Eastern descent. The man dressed in a dark blue uniform raised his head and through his black-rimmed spectacles surveyed Guy's attire, which was a little obtuse as the only dress code at Handell House was that you indeed wear garments of some genre. Placing both hands flat, face down on the worn green leather topped desk, the receptionist terminated his visual inspection.

"Good afternoon, sir. My name is Omar. Is there anything you would like me to help you with?"

Guy's reply was suddenly and very deliberately guillotined, as a figure clad in a very expensive-looking two-piece business suit barked in an Austrian accent,

"Omar, it is ok. I will take this gentleman straight to Herr Richter."

Omar nodded in obedience and gestured for Guy to join the product of Aryan parentage who was framed by the ornate doorway leading to the main reception hall. As Guy walked on to meet Richter's man he did not notice the grey-haired man wearing a not-too-well tailored black suit. He was sitting on the low dark red leather Chesterfield two feet away from the large French Louis XVI fireplace. Resembling a 1950s newspaper hack, he was the living manifestation of many late nights looking at the bottom of a whisky glass and an empty packet of Marlborough red tops. As he turned to look at Guy, the three-inch scar on his cheek broadcast that he had a more sinister bloodline.

It would not have been fanciful to surmise the man's life had been punctuated from time to time by incarceration, probably in some godforsaken African hellhole.

Guy followed Richter's adjutant into the diminutive but nevertheless elegant high-ceilinged main hall of the establishment. It was just as he remembered, the two counter-coiling stone staircases ascending to the eclectic lounges overlooking Portland Square to the front, and the functional grounds at the rear. It was not grand, but elegant, and the buff yellow and gold crackle effect paint finish that covered the walls was testimony to the highly individual and mainly non-run of the mill membership of this highly selective London club.

This was not a venue to network with fellow members. It was a place of stylish solitude for the wealthy, successful and colourful individuals, some of whom had had a very unconventional and in some instance un reliable lineage.

Guy and his sentinel entered the first-floor lounge situated at the rear of the building overlooking the cigar bar and the garden, a regular haunt of Guy's in the past. He lamented the heady days, the last of the late-night drinking, smoking cigars in the company of beautiful women.

Acknowledging he had good health wasn't sufficient for Guy to his dissatisfaction he was now devoid of recognition in the high-rolling world of the financial arbitrage which he felt essential to his self-worth.

The lounge was approximately eighty feet by forty feet and the walls were decorated with the expensive fleur de lys print. An intelligently procured jumble of leather, green velvet, and blue patterned fabric sofas and chairs were positioned around the periphery of the room in a random fashion.

In the corner furthest away sitting on a white and red patterned sofa around which were formed a circle of chairs and a low-level mahogany coffee table, was a solitary figure. A man in his mid to late forties. He was sitting upright in the dark blue very well-tailored suit, complemented by a crisp white shirt and a red silk tie. He had a chiselled face and was subtlety tanned to round off his carefully coiffured medium-short blond hair.

What Guy was not visual with, were the steely blue eyes of this individual, the rose gold Rolex Oyster on his left wrist, and, placed on the second finger of his right hand, a platinum coiled snake ring.

As Guy was ushered to the quartet of sofas in the corner, his feeling of safety and confidence evaporated rapidly. He was about to meet one of the planet's most formidable financial warlords. This was after all Lukas Richter, a man with an oblique history and the autrach of the short deal, who attacked at lightning speed, vanquishing all in his path.

Guy arrived at Richter's temporary pitch, He felt drops of perspiration on his brow. All three were cognisant of their mutual presence: Richter seated, the other two standing in anticipation of the next move.

In a deliberate psychological move to unnerve his lesser, Richter refused to engage in any eye contact with Guy. The tactical silence eventually ended when Richter tapped the first finger of his on the right hand on the edge of the table. This was the clear mark for his subaltern, who announced.

"Guy, please meet Herr Lukas Richter."

Richter turned his head and gestured to Guy to sit down on the seat opposite. It was at this moment that Guy noticed the idiosyncratic scarce manifestation of a possible clandestine organisation. He felt uneasy at the sight of the snake ring, probably cast from the same die as the one he wore on his left hand. Guy was fully aware of the pedigree and background of this ring he was wearing, and thought, *'There cannot be any connection van there???.'*

Richter relaxed a little, and un fastened the top button of his suit jacket. In sharp contrast, his sharp blue eyes exuded control and a clear desire to win the day.

"So, Mr Walker, we meet at last. I have to apologise that I have not heard too much about you and your past successes. Herr Schreiber here brought me up to speed about your endeavours." Richter's top lip protracted to reveal a flawless array of white teeth. Through the grimace, he added,

"I may call you Guy?"

Guy nodded in agreement.

"As I hear, you were like your father and your uncle, a very accomplished motorcycle racer. Formidable opponent, I hear, reported to be aggressive both on and off the racetrack."

Guy, with a relaxed face, said,

"I'd like to think that I was passionate rather than aggressive, Herr Richter."

"Lukas, please. I insist. Well, I'm very pleased to meet you, Guy. My due diligence validates that you are hardworking, but more importantly a very intelligent operator. I hear that you have a strong ability at, as the Americans say, throwing a curve ball."

Richter laughed.

"And I am also told, that people think that you wear your heart on your sleeve, but no one really gets to know the real you. Excuse me, Guy,"

Richter said. He summoned the sommelier.

"A bottle of Montrachet, and one glass, for my pre-lunch drink. And my good friend here will have a lime and soda, please."

Guy, pulling back from his anxiety, rolled his eyes slightly and raised his greying eyebrows, thinking this man had done his homework.

Richter confirmed this by looking at his guest, saying,

"I believe Montrachet was your favoured wine before becoming tee total a few years ago, Guy? Mr Tee Total has done well, I see. You look in the pinnacle of health."

Richter spoke in a clear English with only a hint of educated Austrian accent.

The waiter, dressed in short dark green tunic and slacks, returned with an ice bucket in which he placed a bottle of wine and then carefully covered the open face of the container with a white napkin. He walked back to the bar and returned with a perfectly clean sparkling crystal wineglass. In a forced move the waiter gesticulated to Richter, who in return nodded and confirmed the approval of his wine.

The waiter placed a glass on the table, centre place in front of Richter, who tried the light golden nectar.

Savouring the final contents of the glass, Richter in a manifestation of authority handed the menu to Guy, the waiter, with precision, placed a beautiful glass tumbler on a wine coaster. Inside was a provocatively fizzing lime and soda. Richter nodded to Guy, raised his glass, and in a very clipped and forced voice, said,

"Good to meet you, Guy. Let us hope that it will bring good fortune to us both."

The response, Guy thought, should have ended with a click of heels and a toast to the Fatherland. "*The man is frightening*" he concluded.

Richter summoned the waiter over, at the same time tapping on the lunch menu. Guy seemed a little dreamy. he was anticipating a lovely lunch with an interesting and formidable player. This could be his chance. Just to be seen with Richter, in Handell House, having lunch, could be an endorsement to a path to future success.

Richter then displayed he was also master of the curve ball, by saying to the waiter.

"I will not be dining. Please look after my friend, and send the remaining wine to the lovely ladies sitting over there in the corner."

Richter nodded to the thirty-something classily dressed female on the blue sofa next to the bar. She was the younger of the two ladies, whose short black dress stood out against the powder blue background of the French designed velvet settee. Next to her and holding a glass of champagne, was a short, blond-haired, blue-eyed lady, immaculately presented, perfectly made up, complimenting her natural beauty. She was wearing a two-piece white Chanel suit, and a gold Rolex Oyster. Guy thought, good choice. Then he noticed it and felt a powerful shiver and a cold sweat. Around her neck was a fine white gold chain, at the bottom of which was joined a platinum snake ring embedded with diamonds.

Guy felt uneasy all of a sudden. This warm, quality environment was transmogrified into what felt like a place of Teutonic world order. What had he got into? Who was Richter, what was he? What was his agenda? And was Guy expendable?

In an almost laughable flash, Richter stood up and straightened and buttoned his blue suit jacket.

"Enjoy your lunch, Guy. My people will be in touch."

Turning on his heel, he was gone.

Confused and slightly dazed, a very unnerved Guy reflected on the last fifteen minutes. He concluded that he'd been subject to some kind of initiation process, which he hoped he passed. What he was unsure of was what he needed to do.

Tempted to find relief in as slurp of Montrachet, Guy elected for the security blanket of his mobile phone. He went onto Google and to the BBC news page. It would prove a distraction until lunch was ready. The financial pages bannered an announcement that Richter's Tornado Ventures had just placed a huge position on Whitehead Industries to buy shares. They had made a short purchase at least thirty percent below last night's market price; Guy thought this was a terrifically bold move considering the strength of this blue-chip company.

This was his stock in trade. He'd buy big blue chips hours before some adverse news that would have devastating effects on their stock price, allowing him to make big margins on the transaction shares. Richter always picked wisely, Guy thought. Then out of the blue: a ping. A text from an unknown phone. It read: '*Guy, great to meet you. You're my kind of man – passionate and with an eye for the finer things in life. I understand your fortunes have been low recently. I feel that we can do business which will rectify this situation. You are an honourable, trustworthy man, and we have a common bond, I believe. My people will be in touch. Please enjoy your lunch. By the way, Samantha – the elegant blond in the black dress – will join you for lunch. She is in the seat to my lovely wife. Ich enchen gut Lukas Richter*'

Guy smiled and politely said, "No, thank you. Have a great day." He resisted the temptation of the open wine and the prospect of drinking it accompanied by the beautiful blond, Guy decided to leave. He briskly exited the restaurant to avoid the gaze of Frau Richter and her very attractive companion. He descended the staircase and stepped on to the first landing which adorned the wonderful venue. How he missed coming here for a little liquid anaesthetic as he termed alcoholic beverage.

He passed through the small opening to the entrance, he was halted in his tracks. The Lebanese man behind the desk announced,

"Mr Guy Walker?"

"Yes."

"Herr Richter left this envelope for you."

Omar handed Guy a beautiful vellum cream A4 envelope on which Guy's name was written in elegant script, obviously the product of quality ink and a quality pen. As always, Guy was impressed. Even more impressive was the purple ink. Very unique, Guy thought. It was clearly the distinguished creation of an expensive fountain pen.

He thanked the concierge, and took the envelope in his right hand, which he folded and placed it in the inside pocket of his suit jacket. He decided he would go somewhere private to digest the contents of the letter.

Guy departed through the double doors, turned left from the club and proceeded down Baker Street and turned left and then north, 200 yards. Good, the coffee shop was empty. He could find a quiet corner.

He entered the large glazed front doors and walked to the counter and ordered a black coffee and a sandwich. He took the white cup and saucer and sat down in the far right-hand corner of the restaurant and waited for his order of a ham and cheese sandwich to be brought to him.

Five minutes later a young Spanish girl came over with a tray, on which was a white plate and the piping hot sandwich which would accompany Guy's super-heated coffee.

The young Spanish girl asked if he would like anything else, and she clumsily placed the white plate holding the sandwich onto the table, nearly knocking over the coffee cup.

With the barista out of sight, and his back to the till, Guy took out the envelope from his inside pocket. He held it in his hand, admiring the cream vellum paper. He carefully broke the seal of the envelope to reveal the contents: a neatly folded two sheets of vellum paper, with handwritten notes on it.

Guy thought that the composer of this letter was truly trying to make an impression and create the condescending role of the recipient. Greatly anticipating the contents, Guy unfolded the letter and began to read the handwritten message which had been carefully scripted in purple ink.

The beautiful purple writing on this wonderful cream substrate, was a work of art, not ink on paper but oil on canvas. Holding the letter in his left hand, Guy removed the glasses from his left-hand pocket. Glasses in position, and after one sip of coffee, he shuffled on the sofa, held up the paper, and began to read what Richter had penned.

Dear Guy,

What an interesting meeting we had. To get to the point, I like what I saw in you. I respect your abstinence from liquor and the ladies, the fine wine and even finer women. My research has highlighted two qualities you possess, which are non-negotiable when I consider a partner for a new business venture. To begin with, loyalty is paramount. If trust and loyalty is broken, we have to face the inevitable consequences. Passion to succeed and energy for the finer possessions and experiences of life are second on my list. You see, Guy, without this a man has no hunger and passion to succeed. It is not about money; it is about the trophy's money brings. My people tell me that you definitely like the finer things –I see your excellent choice in clothes and shoes, but you still remain grounded. I also hear that you are well-respected within the commercial banking sector and display a first-class working knowledge of structured debt deals in the mid-market.. A risk taker, I believe, but not reckless, evidenced by the fact you are still alive after an illustrious motorcycling career. You are a straight-talker, which is necessary if you have to work with a clear-talking Austrian. This conveniently brings me to the main point of the letter.

I am making you an offer, the best deal in town for you. It's clear you have the skills, drive and winning streak, and have demonstrated success in small deals. Well, the Americans say, it's time to stop fucking around with the small shit. Deal size is a skillset you do not need. You need the opportunity to exercise your skills and considerable talent. Like you, I'm a man of my word and there will be no lengthy contracts and other bullshit, if you'll accept what I'm proposing to you, and believe me you'd be foolish to reject it. I'm going to make you a star in the City of London. Well, here we go; here's my deal, my handshake to you:

1) Salary - £46,000 per month, up to 55% paid tax-free into a Swiss bank account. This I can arrange.

2) A man like you needs an expense account – let's say £5,000 per month.

3) If you return to Handell House you will find you will be able to collect your new membership – I have taken care of all the necessary formalities.

4) You have the free run of one of my numerous flats in Mayfair – let's say two-bed, two-bathroom first-floor flat, Mount Street, perhaps?.

5) A bonus package based on performance – up to £5,000,000 per annum.

6) First class air travel and rail travel, and use of my private jets when necessary.

I want you to head up a new crack team. I've set you up in a two-thousand square feet office in St James Street. The team are intelligent and hungry for success. They are loyal to me, and therefore you. This is the best offer in town, Guy. Ok, there will also be a stake in the fund for you. The main thing, Guy is I like you, I trust you, and I felt a bond between us, a belief in a higher cause, one which is fuelled by loyalty and trust. We can do many things together, and at the same time make a lot of money and bring success to Tornado Ventures London.

I can bring you the deals, you can work on the plan, the price, the margins, and lead it, execute it, drive it. I will fund it. You will be my right-hand man, my wing man.

I will give you the rest of the evening to ponder the offer and will speak to you at ten o'clock tomorrow. I'll phone you to get your yes. I am sure it will be a yes. Guy, I look forward to our call and working together to grow a business with meaning, one that will generate huge profits. We can invest and also contribute into special trusts and charities that are close to my heart and the future of humankind.

Staring at the final words on the page, over and over again, Guy was excited, but also looking for the catch. He would not need time to think about this, he was already on board and looked forward to saying yes in the morning.

Chapter 6

Hugo Parnell was a broken man, he was more than empty, one of life's loners felt undeniably lonely.

An irrevocable drive, a crusade for vengeance and a mission to right a wrong had maintained his sanity and a desire for life. If it were to be his very last act on the Earth, he would avenge the death of his little sister. He vowed to track down, flush out and bring justice to the animals behind the heinous act against good, murderers who followed a maligned and perverse dogma.

He had friends whose grandfathers had lived through the holocaust, and like the survivors of the camps, he wanted justice for the sinful and dark acts committed against humankind.

Track them down by any means possible and fork out justice to these criminals who had killed his little sister and stolen her from his heart.

His brain was fizzing with excitement at the prospect of finding the perpetrators of his sister's death and Hugo now needed solace in the only place he knew. He ran up the flowery wallpapered staircase and approached the white-painted door of his bedroom. He bounded onto his double bed, which was dressed in a dark grey duvet and a mixture of red and purple pillowcases. From the top of the light oak veneer side table he recovered his laptop and switched it on.

In cyberspace he would be happy. There was no need to deal with people on matters if they were just downright uninteresting. It was in the cloud of bits, bites, connections, codes, buzzes, clicks, whirrs and flashing lights that he wanted to find the killers.

He placed the laptop on the bed in front of him and repositioned three pillows against the headboard. Making himself comfortable, he prepared himself for the journey into the ether.

He remained online for at least an hour, and researched the Wembley attack, recent events in Paris and Brussels, ISIS, Al Qaeda, and MI5's ability to track down terrorists. The list was endless.

Hugo looked up at the wall, bit his bottom lip and scratched his head, deep in thought he considered the best gateway which would yield potential intelligence into these vicious acts. Special Branch, he thought. The good old British bobby. And after furious but well-guided taps onto the keyboard, he was on the Special Branch main landing page.

Using an illicit but undetectable programme he had written it didn't take him long to penetrate the system and get access to their network. The Special Branch computer verified his access and our intrepid cyber traveller gained full access to their files.

For five minutes he searched the server and then found what he was looking for: the medical and situation records written up from the night of the atrocities in London. His algorithm had allowed him to shadow one of the members of the organisation with the highest level of clearance. He obtained unfettered access to the full system which included reports to the Home Office and the Home Secretary. During the time on the site he left no trace of his activities, the cyber ghost would never exist.

Like a highly contagious and multiplying virus, Hugo's electronic pathogen penetrated the full extent of the Special Branch network and he was able to open all the files and glean all the information relating to the attack. He unlocked witness statements, photos from the coroner, and linked MI5 and MI6 intelligence briefings. At this juncture, he was not allowed access to the bits and bytes of the fortress and nerve centre at Vauxhall Bridge; however, the information he gleaned from the Special Branch network was be sufficient to start him on his journey.

Hugo was deep into digesting the words of a report by DCI Kath Smithson of Westminster CID. As he studied the timings of the carnage and analysed the CCTV, a freeze frame moment of the shot being taken, his eyes welled up in anger and sadness. He was fixated on the man in a black police boiler suit who did not have the valour or decency to show his face, which was shrouded by a black balaclava. What evil sat behind those eyes? Why did some intelligent humans sever the fine thread between good and evil and continue to perpetuate heinous and evil crimes? The assassin removed a Heckler and Koch MR556 A automatic assault rifle from a blue sports holdall, which now lay face down on the floor. Taped to the stock of this pressed steel and wooden apparatus of death were four curved magazines. This killer was not intent on taking one or two shots, he had mass murder programmed into his perverted mind, a mind polluted by a corrupt doctrine.

Hugo possessed an urge to delete this son of evil dogma from the screen, but what good would that achieve? He thought, don't get mad, get even.

He would continue in his quest to see if his logical brain, which underpinned a robust high bandwidth for complex analysis would discover a route to the killers. It would be this approach, he felt, which would champion the conventional police enquiry. Totally oblivious to the outside world, and the dimmed surroundings of his messy bedroom adorned with laptops, PC cables, and electronic paraphernalia was another stellar dimension. Hugo had crossed the boundary into a world not only that he knew well, but which provided him solace. Then it happened.

Ping.

Hugo jolted as if he'd stepped on a rattlesnake. He was in a state of shock.

A word appeared on the screen. Another being knew he was there. At the top right-hand corner of the screen there was a message:

'Hugo, would like to talk to you. We can help each other. You will get revenge.'

Aghast, Hugo bolted upright on the bed. At the same time, he pushed the laptop away from his waist. His eyes wide open, transfixed on the message. The shock faded. He attempted to reconcile two issues: who was it, and how did they find him?

He was perplexed. How could they have breached his electronic fortress? He was puzzled as to how he could help the organisation – whoever had the ingenuity to find him was clearly hacking into a government computer system. They – whoever they were – surely must have a similar or superior education in coding.

His mind raced, his eyes rolled, he looked around the room and dreamed. Who could it be? Mossad? MI6? CIA?

When he attempted to save what was left of the screen, all the digits and words melted away in self-destruction. He shouted in frustration at the screen.

"Who are you? You boys are clever."

Rolling his head back and clenching his teeth, the thought of a superior talent angered him, however, it would provide motivation to find out more on the entity, and possibly usurp them.

He carefully contemplated his next move and decided to respond. Hugo looked around the room one more time at the mess of computers, clothes scattered on the floor, he then stared at the ceiling and thought of his little Sarah.

Pulling the laptop back to his waist, he typed in the word, "How?"

Nothing was to prepare him for what happened next. The screen displaying the CCTV image from the police website vanished, and a message of black letters on a light grey background appeared. It was clear, bold type, and there it was:

'Hugo, we are sorry for the loss of your sister, Sarah. A tragedy. A wicked act. We possess information and reliable intelligence on who the masterminds are behind this debased act of violence. It is our righteous calling to route all the perpetrators and eradicate once and for all this network of death. We know you, Hugo – a bright young man, a solo flyer, highly enlightened and resourceful. That is 90% of the skillset we require, but you have the vital component: desire and motivation for revenge. We want you – in fact, need you – on our team. You are needed. Humanity needs you. Help us to restore good over evil.'

Emotions ran high in his head. His eyes glazed over with tears as he tried to make sense of the screen message.

Do not be directed by the anger of Sarah's death or the challenge of beating this hideous adversary.

Rolling his eyes towards the 8x4 photo frame on his messy beside table, he looked at the last photo of his beloved little sister. The tears swelled up. Swallowing hard, he returned his eyes to the computer screen, and typed in: *'How can I help?'*

A split second later, a tanned-faced man in his early thirties several thousand miles away typed in a reply:

'We will be in touch. Thank you, Hugo. Thank you very much.'

Hugo vigorously returned,

'who are you?'

On the screen appeared the final message:

'I cannot divulge this. Only that you will have to trust me and trust my organisation. We hold the same set of values and are looking to achieve the same goals. '

Whilst Hugo and his mysterious adversary or perhaps potential new friend conversed over the web, his father was negotiating his Mercedes CL600 off the drive and was totally oblivious to the blue BMW 530 parked one hundred yards away up the street. He was also unaware of the two suspicious thirty-something blond-haired, blue-eyed well-dressed men in sat the driver's and front passenger's seat. The passenger was wearing an earpiece in his left ear, and on his knee was a small electronic communication tablet connected to the web via highly encrypted protocol.

'We will protect you and your family, Hugo,' illuminated on Hugo's screen, the same message flashed up on the tablet in the BMW one hundred yards away from his front door.

Engrossed in the information on his tablet, the passenger and the driver had not noticed a red Honda Civic parked around the corner, approximately 400 yards away. This was not a resident's car, and the driver had never been in the area of London prior to today.

Hugo put down the laptop and walked to the bay window of his bedroom. He pulled back the dark blue curtain and peered out to see the rear brake lights of his father's car fading as he journeyed down the road. As he closed the curtains, Hugo looked right and noticed the two ominous silhouettes framed by BMW windscreen. The silence was broken abruptly by the ring of Hugo's mobile phone announcing an incoming call. He rushed over to his desk and recovered the phone. Number withheld.

He jumped onto the Star Wars patterned bedspread folded at the bottom of his bed and held the phone in his right hand, and stared at the incoming call alert with his finger hovering over the green 'receive' icon. Pausing for a split second, he assembled his thoughts. Do not reply? Or pick up and enter the world of espionage and danger?

They already knew where he was, so avoiding the call would not guarantee immunity from further contiguity. A gentle stream of warm and unnerving adrenaline moved through his body. This was fight or flight time. One million years of evolution had not quenched the human reaction to the unknown. Or was it just plain fear?

He felt his heart beat in his chest. This was foreign territory. Human emotion was vanquishing logic. This was a gut feel judgement call. Did he answer, or hide under the metaphoric bed covers?

Thinking of Sarah and clenching his teeth, the sweaty digits of his right hand touched the green circle, the symbol which would connect Hugo to a new dimension. This was a major turning point in his life. Things would never be the same again, as he placed the illuminated iPhone against his right ear.

A deep breath was followed shortly by a nervous swallow. "Hello? This is Hugo. But I guess you already know that," he said in a nervous voice.

The ensuing second of silence felt like an eternity. Long enough for Hugo to think, *what have I done?* Time to reflect on his decision.

Post-decision reflection was headed off at the pass as a voice at the other end sparked up.

"Good evening, Hugo. My name is George. Please go downstairs to the lobby. You'll find a small brown package on your doormat."

The message ended with a very deliberate click.

In a split second of reflection when excitement simmered and fear subsided Hugo concluded that these may well be the good guys. Why else would they want to engage with him?

Hugo had the phone in his hand, when he opened the bedroom door onto the illuminated landing. He rushed down the stairs, nearly falling as he skipped over the steps two at a time at breakneck speed. As he approached the base of the stairs, in clear view there it was, lying on the patterned carpet: An A4 unmarked brown envelope, bulging evidence of its contents. *A mobile phone*, Hugo thought.

He was indeed correct, as he was about to discover. Hugo picked up the envelope, felt the weight of it, looked around to make sure he was not being watched, and then swiftly returned upstairs and went back into his bedroom. He closed the white wood panel door and leapt onto his unmade bed. Ripping open the envelope, there it was: the GPS encrypted communication device, as used by the Western intelligence services.

Our would-be James Bond grinned. He was about to embark on a journey into a deep leftfield and covert cyber community, a world where he would feel great empathy. He thumbed the dark grey plastic phone which was encased in a peripheral aluminium strip. There was no on/off switch or similar facility to bring the devise to life. He noticed a shiny red pad approximately 12mm by 12mm, positioned at the bottom left hand corner of the device.

"Surely not"

He presupposed. How could they? But he was to take nothing for granted as he placed his right-hand thumbprint face down on the pad. After three seconds, the device flickered into life.

The top forty percent of the device lit up to present an LED screen display. In pure bewilderment, Hugo glared at the small screen which declared the device was the property of the Israeli intelligence service, Mossad. Why would one of the most covert, dangerous and ruthlessly impressive intelligence organisations want to engage with lowly Hugo?

He pressed the red pad one more time and the screen informed him of an incoming message in the ether. Hugo repeated the thumb action and placed the phone against his right ear.

"Good evening, Hugo. My name is Colonel Liv Abrahams of the UK desk of Mossad. I am sure that you have heard of us. Firstly, I wish to apologise for the approach and the rather unconventional method of establishing communication. Can you hear me, Hugo?"

"Yes, sir. Very clearly." He replied with a 'whiff 'of apprehension in his voice

"Liv, please. We don't go for such formalities in our organisation. We can help each other, and without question bring the killers of your sister and many others to justice. Well, it will be enigmatic justice. No newspapers ever reported the retribution after Munich."

"But how can I help you, Liv? What have I got to offer except my determination to bring these criminals to justice?"

"You, Hugo, have a distinct set of skills which will integrate well into our capabilities. More importantly, you will be operating outside the known intelligence community. We will never meet. At all times communication will be via this encrypted phone and the PC we will be sending you shortly. To obtain the modified laptop you will need to take your current machine to an address I will text you. To all intents and purposes, it will be under the guise of necessary hardware update to your existing laptop. What will happen is that it will be replaced with an identical unit, well, almost identical. The settings will be configured to connect you to us via the device you are holding now."

"When do I have to go to the repair shop?" he asked.

"Within the next twenty-four hours," Liv replied.

"The text will be with you within the hour, and the message will end now. And of course, please do not speak of this with anyone. If you receive any calls on any device other than this one, please do not engage."

"Yes, I understand, Liv. I will speak to no one and await your message."

"Thank you, Hugo. I'll leave you now. Goodbye until the next time."

There was a buzzing and a click and he was gone.

Hugo fell back onto the pile of pillows, and hand held tight on the device stared at the ceiling. What had he let himself in for? He wasn't fully back in the normal world when he heard.

"Hugo? Your supper is ready! Can you come down please?"

"Yes, Mum!" he replied.

His poor mother, he thought. She had inadvertently set a place at the table for the permanently absent Sarah.

Chapter 7

Guy left the coffee house and turned south on Baker Street and commenced the walk back to the dungeon of doom and gloom. If those soulless, dispassionate servants to the machine knew what Guy's next move was, they would see some money-raking asset-stripping dinosaur, the bad face of finance. The disgusting side of capitalism. This was his time. He had just been offered a seat at the top table with one of the recent greats of private equity.

He shed the daydream, he now needed to concentrate fully on negotiating the river of lunching office workers and tourists facing him as they blocked the sidewalk of one of London's busiest streets.

Guy descended into the bowels of the office, the windowless nerve centre of fashion retailing. Just as he entered the boundary to the office he was alerted by the small vibrations emanating from his phone lodged in the blue jacket pocket.

It was a text from Richter.

'leave your office now cross the road and wait at the left hand side of the entrance to the convenience store.'

Guy Walker needed no incentive to leave this 21st century mill, only that the noisy weaving looms had been replaced with the clattering of keyboards, and the new 'mill owner' did not live up the hill in a large house, the new master was a plastic box in an air-conditioned room.

On a mission Guy forced his way across the river of limos and blacked out 4x4s interlaced with reckless cyclists which was Baker Street. He pushed his way through the constant advance of pedestrians then eventually he reached his destination

As instructed, he positioned himself at the entrance of the busy store and awaited the next contact.

Parked opposite straddling the pavement and double yellow lines was a large blue Renault van.

At the store entrance he surveyed left and right and straight ahead. The absence of any contact and or any further instruction made him feel very anxious. Uncertainty, coupled with excitement, simmered the adrenaline in his veins as it pumped through his body, his throat was dry.

Guy's uneasiness was brought to a brief halt and replaced with abject terror. A potential adversary had approached him and was now straight in front of him: a well-built man dressed in a black suit, white shirt and no tie.

Guy's imagination, which was being fuelled by the bizarre events of recent days, now got the better of him. He deduced that this man was a hitman of European birth.

'Bloody hell,'

he thought. He knew this Richter business was too good to be true.

Guy's potential nemesis had a short, cropped blond hairstyle and a hardened face which screamed menace. The man had steely cold blue eyes, which no doubt had been the last living vision of many of his victims as he extinguished their mortality. This was no ordinary member of the public who was stood in front of our would-be hedge fund manager. The menace facing Guy was a man who revelled in making his opponent uneasy and scared. It was not the life changing event that Guy was expecting after the day's astonishing meeting with Lukas Richter.

Guy had attempted to move away from the door of the shop front on to the relative safety of the pedestrian flow, but Ivan, as he'd now been labelled, refused his contact any such move for cover. Then, as if a higher being had intervened, an old lady asked Ivan if he could pick up the white and green supermarket bag that had split, spreading the contents of all of her recent purchases on the pavement. It was the outcome of a cost-cutting regime at a supermarket, and the resulting thinning polythene bags clearly not fit for purpose, that had rescued Guy.

A very reluctant Ivan had to respond to the pensioner, this gave Guy the opportunity to make his move. This was his window of opportunity and he didn't exactly jump through, rather he squeezed past the man in front of him. As Ivan bent down to recover the contents of the ruptured bag, Guy pulled past and headed off through the pedestrian traffic, south on Baker Street.

Regretting his good Samaritan act, Ivan dropped a cabbage and a bag of carrots, and hotfooted it after his escapee. As he manoeuvred southwards through the torrent of blank faces, and the habitual smattering of those texting in preference to watching where they were going, Guy gathered what pace he could. He looked over his left shoulder as he dodged a texter and quickly noticed the advancing blond leviathan, who was clearly unsettled by the loss of his potential capture.

Guy sensed no other way out from his advancing foe and pushed past a Japanese couple then stepped onto the main road. His objective was the dungeon – his office – where he would be offered relative safety. His imagination had started to run wild. Could this be the adventure that he'd always craved? High finance, hijinks. He revelled in the chase, this was the stuff of spy thrillers.

Guy allowed himself a momentary wish for the lovely blond girl he had left back in the club he was now in an undercover world of espionage, he grinned. Despite his evasive moves, Ivan gained considerable ground on Guy. At a distance of ten feet, with both hands unencumbered and no bulge under his jacket, Guy concluded that this man was not armed. No Glock 13 to add spice to the day's event.

Guy moved put his hand against the door to sanctuary of his office, but it was too late Ivan had caught him. He felt the life drain from his veins at warp speed when Ivan placed a hand on his left shoulder.

'This is it he feared' as he turned to face his assassin.

Ivan pinned his quarry against the blockwork which surrounded the door, Guy could feel the total strength of this brute.

Guy overcame some resistance and rotated a folded right elbow towards Ivan' face.

Ivan blocked the move, and Guy planned his next pass.

"my friend stop I not hurt you" came out in a German accent.

"I have small package for you from Herr Richter"

Ivan added as he relaxed his grip.

Guy, his face red and heart racing turned to Ivan

"well let go of me"

Ivan let go and stood back and guy straightened his suit jacket.

With steely eyes fixed Guy stared hard at his advisory.

Ivan then produced a small but thick brown package from his inside jacket pocket and handed it over.

Guy looked down at the package and Ivan was gone, he had disappeared into the human jungle of Baker St.

Chapter 8

It seemed like days since Tom Leyton had left his beautifully appointed townhouse in Imperial Square, Cheltenham. In fact, it had only been four hours since he had slammed the dark grey double door on his not so perfect home life. Sustained by black coffee – how he hated drinking out of paper cups – and the lifesaving nicotine patches, he grieved the past days of strong black coffee and the untipped Gitane or Marlborough cigarettes.

In the world of modern coppering, Tom was perceived as a dinosaur, more the Sweeny's Jack Regan than Jack Ryan. He was an exemplar of the old ways.

He worked in a partitioned office at the end of a large open-plan space in Cheltenham Police section at GCHQ. The large open plan department was made of rows of light grey melamine desks on which were mounted standard-issue twenty-two-inch black LED screen computers, Tom's desk was distinguished by the piles of papers, open ring binder files and a bin overflowing with empty biscuit packets, coffee cups and sweet wrappings.

Leyton had loyally served the force for what seemed generations, his latest assignment was desk based operational role at GCHQ, a far departure from his days at the cut, shove and the thrust of the 1970s and 1980s. He now longed for retirement. The gold-plated pension he would receive in twelve months' time meant he would be able to spend a lot of time with the love of his life: golf, and attending matches at his beloved Gloucester rugby.

Eight years spent in the army intelligence corps had proved a good grounding for the life and the firm. Two years in Belfast had certainly influenced his unorthodox investigation style. Fluent in German, Tom spent three years in the British Army on the Rhine with intelligence gathering and had been involved in tracking down the culprits behind the Pan Am Lockerbie bombing.

This man had seen action and been at the dirty end of the business and the physical and metal scars were testimony to this.

Scanning the folks in the office, '*if only that lot know what he'd really been through, what he had seen, and the situations he'd had to resolve, sometimes with no questions asked.*'

Regrettably the young, innocent-faced, Twitter-following, bearded, tattooed generation of analytical copper viewed their governor with a little contempt. The new generation of 21st Century police officer deemed Tom's methods both dysfunctional and sometimes comical. In their mind's eye the figure head boss was a throwback to the seventies and eighties culture, a champion of the no longer compliant and once fashionable excessive drinking, and heavy smoking.

For what were to be the twilight days of his career, Tom had been assigned to GCHQ Cheltenham, heading up the listening station mainland counter-terrorism desk. He disliked the claustrophobic hellhole of the office, which was situated five floors below the ground in the 'doughnut' situated on the Golden Valley Road in Cheltenham.

The section was occupied by the police and was known as the Cheltenham Central. A 5 day 42-hour week shift pattern and the prospect of a good retirement benefits package provided compensation for this dreary life.

'Another coffee on the track to retirement helped sooth the prospect of a bland day,' he reflected

Then out of the blue on this cold, late January morning, an intercept was flagged up by Ron Willis, one of Tom's more loyal and broader thinking colleagues. Willis was a man in his early thirties, with short dark hair and black-rimmed glasses and a full time participant of 'dress down days', he sported dark blue pullover and black trousers. He had his back to Tom and was glued to one of the LED displays which occupied one of the workstations. He turned around to Tom and shouted:

"Tom! You've got to look at this."

Tom raised his eyebrows. "What, Ron?"

"Tom, come here. I need you. Please, it's in German."

Tom thought, *So it's in German?* He bit his lip and concluded that the excitement would be no more than a transmission of somebody trying to buy Champions League football tickets in Germany.

At Ron's insistence, he arose from his dark grey fabric chair with one arm rest, a witness to many tedious shifts in the post. Ron had been overseeing the routine daily checks of email traffic, Twitter, Facebook and phone calls which were analysed and interrogated at light speed by a large supercomputer. The electronic titan was entombed deep in the air-conditioned chambers well below their feet. Complex algorithms teased out and analysed specific words, strings of words, possible cribs, phrases which proved suspicious and partitioned to undergo another detailed level of scrutiny. During any interval in the process the documents could be sectioned for further assessment. The ultra-complicated software and the mega electronic processing speed sifted out any messages from the billions of daily digital exchanges. A hunt for a digital needle in a universe of a binary data haystack task to uncover communications which could suggest any activity which would threaten national security. The outputs were not just potential terrorist events, but anticipated cyber-attacks on government departments and financial institutions.

Leyton hurried over to Ron's desk and placing his hand on his right shoulder, he peered over Ron's head at the screen.

"What have we here, Herr Ron? What have the German's been up to? 'Don't they realise the war is over?" he retorted in a caustic note.

"Tom, the thing is, I don't get some of these words. As you know, my German is *sehr gut, ja?*"

Staring at the screen, Leyton quickly became excited by what he read.

"Ron, this is bloody High German. *Haute Deutsche.* It's the stuff of the nineteen-thirties and forties. Fuck me. This is the stuff of the Third Reich. It sounds like they're on the march again."

Ron replied,

"I guessed that, Tom. It's bloody unusual. Maybe just some dickhead pissing about."

"Not sure, Ron. I'll get Grace Wells over and see what she thinks about it. Can you print this out and keep it to yourself for the time being? Cheers."

"Wilco, Tom. Or should I say, *I vill obey your orders*?"

The working relationship between Ron and Tom was pretty good. Ron was the geek, the intellectual, the yin and yang of the hard-nosed field operative which was Tom Leyton. There was a lot of mutual respect between these two for their methods of working, knowing they would complement each other to obtain success.

Grace Wells was one of Tom's chosen few. Even though she was not from a field pedigree, Wells was a German History graduate with a First from York University. She was new to GCHQ, having previously worked in forensic computing with the Manchester police force. Although Wells was not a dirt-under-the-fingernails cop, Tom respected this very intelligent and pragmatic individual, a respect which was clearly mutual. They had worked very well together on a number of cases, Grace filling in the gaps in Tom's IT capabilities, and Tom bringing some hard-learned experiences to the table, to create a hugely effective fusion between these two individuals.

Tom was always consulting Grace on any matters which he felt required further validation and further investigation. Fluent in German, Grace was also a virtuoso in spoken French and Arabic. This was the obvious result of having a French mother and an English father who had spent the last thirty years in Bahrain in a senior role in a BAPCO national oil company. Her father had been chief engineer at the East Riffa oil refinery and a regular denizen of the English club in Manama. It was one Friday afternoon that he was introduced to the lovely Francine, a private tutor for the son of one of the Bahraini royal family.

Mr Wells quickly flew up the ranks at BAPCO to become one of the highest paid ex-pat members of the board. This was a marital status position, and when not at boarding school at Cheltenham Ladies College, Grace would spend her summer breaks around the swimming pool at the private villa on the Eastern Bahrain coast. Wells was recruited direct from university by the police in 2012 and spent two years in post before transferring to GCHQ.

Tom dressed in the usual un-ironed blue shirt, out of fashion tie and black slacks walked over to yet another light grey desk. This one was slightly messy with documents, USB sticks, and two mobile phones scattered across its top. Grace with dark brown hair hazel eyes was sitting in the black faux leather chair, deep in thought. She held an A4 sheet of paper between the thumbs and forefingers of both her hands; every so often she flicked her little finger against the white document, which made a cracking sound against the background of clattering keyboards and whirring printers.

"When our long-haired, bearded friend from over there finally figures out how to use the printer, I have something I want you to look at, Grace."

Wells placed the paper on the desk and ran the fingers of her left hand through her long brown, slightly scruffy hair which was resting on the black polo shirt she was wearing.

An impatient Leyton turned to Ron and shouted, "For f's sake Ronald McDonald, I retire in twelve months."

"I'm coming, boss!"

"I will launch that bloody printer off the Junction 10 bridge one day," retorted Tom.

The long, tall, skinny frame of the scruffily-dressed Ron appeared next to Wells and placed the two-page transcript on the desk in front of her. He then handed a copy to Leyton and returned to get one for his own reference.

"Sorry it took so long, Guv, but the actual copy is lengthy, and to be frank, it's a right pain in the arse."

Each of the copies was time-dated and confirmed the time of the original message across the top of each page in red. It was accompanied by the words 'Level 3 clearance only'. This suggested that the copying and circulation of the document was to be initiated by an officer on Tom Leyton's pay grade and above.

Tom extracted his reading spectacles from off the top of his head, which had the secondary purpose of holding his floppy, greying mop in place. Almost simultaneously, the three intelligence officers started trying to digest the contents of the paper, time-dated 09.33.17 January 31h 2017.

Periodically there was a cough which interrupted the otherwise stunned silence. Grace Wells was the first to finish reading the message, and she rested the paper face down on the desk and engaged full eye contact with Tom Leyton.

"What the hell? This language has not been seen in Cheltenham since we received the crypts from Bletchley Park back in the 1940s. I just don't get it. Why '*Haute Deutsche*" What is the thinking to use an almost extinct Language associated with one of mankind's darkest decades?"

Ron piped in,

“I don’t understand why they use such a controversial Language, bloody sinister if you ask me.”

Tom felt some mild excitement. Maybe this could be the big one to end his career

“Ron, get the coffee on and we’ll sit and discuss this and try and get to the bottom of it.”

He shouted,

Leyton shook his head from side to side, and chewing on his bottom lip, said,

“It’s almost as if they wanted to be found out. This content is pretty inert; or it appears to be. But the vocabulary is not. This vernacular is highly contentious in today’s politically correct world”.

He added

“And what is this obtuse reference to TET? What has our largest telecommunications company got to do with the Germans?”

Grace looked at Ron attentively and said, “You’re missing the real menacing core of this message.”

Grace read out the word for word translation in English.

A caffeine depleted, irritated Tom Leyton grabbed at a chair opposite Grace and sat back and listened.

“R, how was your trip to the home of 66 ? We are not disappointed with the outcome of the work, which was in your arena of expertise. I will be over to see you shortly, and don’t forget to stock up on TET credits.”

“So what do you reckon, Grace?”

Tom enquired.

“What do the Germans have to do with what was clearly an ISIS attack on the Wembley Arena concert and then a singular reference to one of the largest blue-chip communications companies?”

Wells looked at Ron then leaned forwards to Tom.

"Do we know the source of the message and the whereabouts of the receiver?"

"TET credit? What's all that about?"

Tom went on to explain,

"The scary bit, however, is that they knew the code for the attack, which is clearly only known in the police domain and MI5 and 6 and a few of us guys at Cheltenham. What we do know is that there was reference to the 'the home of 66 ' on some of the terrorist email and text traffic just prior to the incident. The security services are clearly linking this phrase with the order to attack the Wembley Arena."

A puzzled Wells gazed at Ron and then turned her brown eyes to Leyton, and went on to question their involvement with TET and what it was all about.

Leyton inhaled through clenched teeth, wishing he was negotiating the delights of a relaxing smoke, a Rothmans King Size perhaps. It relaxed him and allowed his brain to rotate like a mortal version of the colossus mechanical computer.

Tom exhaled and explained to the assembled party.

"we have to take this upstairs and the Fat Controller must be briefed."

The Fat Controller, or 'FC' as he was irreverently known by GCHQ, was Sidney Laing, who was head of home intelligence, counter-terrorism and mainland security at GCHQ. He was ex-public school, Oxford University, and a product of the English privileged classes. His father had come from some high up desk officer at Bletchley in World War Two. An abundance of high fat and high carbohydrate lunches accompanied by a nice claret had modelled Laing in to the typical style of a civil service mandarin. An image which was bolstered by the wearing of ill-fitting, grey, English tailored double-breasted suits and the obligatory red braces.

Leyton said.

"I will phone Pam now and arrange a meeting straight away"

Pam Staines was a very petite, pretty spinster, who was Laing's loyal PA of many years.

Tom gestured to Wells to hand him the receiver of the internal phone, in a mime reminiscent of a comic sketch he moved his lips, and relayed the silent message to Grace: dial 1281.

There was a click, and Pam answered.

"Mr Laing's office."

"Good morning, Pam. Is he free? Can we come and see him as soon as?"

"Yes, Tom. How is ten-thirty looking for you?"

"Perfect."

Tom placed the receiver down look towards his colleagues and said.

"10.30 at Laing's office OK"

They both nodded.

"Ron can you check previous email and electronic traffic to see if the name Dieter can be found elsewhere in connection with the Wembley shootings and bombing." Asked Leyton.

"Grace, my good lass, if there's any intel on any events relating to TET, please let me know as well. It's ten – ten now, let's reconvene at this desk at ten – twenty-five. Ok, Ron, get another control copy of the message. And somebody get me a bloody coffee."

Leyton depressed the brushed stainless-steel handle to the large door and entered the cavern which was Laing's office suite. They shuffled their way past Pam's desk and opened the second door into Laing's office. The office was in one of the grander working pods deep in the cavernous catacombs of GCHQ. The carpet was claret coloured; the walls were papered in a light floral pattern adorned with photographs of Laing in the Royal Navy and illustrations depicting several versions of recent frigates used by the navy. At the far end of the office was a large mahogany desk with a dark red leather top, sitting behind which was the large, rosy-cheeked, grey floppy-haired, portly figure of Laing.

He rose slightly from his chair and then sat down again. Laing then addressed his guests.

"Good morning and I trust that you are all well."

Before getting down to business, he made a further enquiry.

"Any news from the test match down under, do you know I cannot get my damn radio to work in the sub-terrain vaults of this spy centre "

"Good morning, sir."

replied Leyton.

"Our batting collapsed, I'm afraid."

Laing offered one of the four seats parked in front of his desk to his guests and beckoned them to come and sit closer. On his desk was a picture of him and his wife Shirley at the palace, which recorded the happy event when Sidney was presented with his MBE from Her Majesty. In the corner of the controller's office was a mahogany bookcase packed with the works of Shakespeare, great classics, Tom Sawyer, and a few biographies, and the usual supplements from Churchill, Obama, Thatcher, and of course Geoffrey Boycott. All show mused Leyton. He thought, what the hell has a biography and the odd literary work got to do with the security of our great country? This is clearly a display of pseudo-intelligence for this career civil servant. Laing was a man who had only ever been in the field with a Purdey side by side shotgun, warmed by port and a full English breakfast, firing at disorientated pheasants trying to avoid a shower of lead.

"Well, what gives me the honour of the company of this distinguished trio?"

opened Laing.

Leyton shuffled forward on his seat and began.

"Sir, we have a message which refers to the control command of the Arena shootings. What makes it chilling and engaging is that it was scripted in high German."

Laing looked up wide eyed then nodded in accord for Leyton continue.

"They also referred to Trans Euro Telecom. Very bizarre, sir."

"Yes yes very bizarre indeed Tom"

Tom Leyton handed a copy of the transcript to Laing.

Laing read the document and tapped the fingers of his right hand on the mahogany and paused in a moment of thought.

Tom Leyton intended to gauge Laing's interest?

"Do you really think that there is a connection Tom" enquired Laing.

Leyton nodded a gave a definitive.

"Yes"

"And what of the reference to TET have you any thoughts on what the connection could be" added Laing

"Sidney we cannot ignore this message further enquiry is needed"

Grace Wells jumped in.

"Sir they make reference to the code word for the attack, in an old language one very much associated with darker times, that is enough for me to be suspicious"

Laing stared at Wells and sat forward in his chair.

'What would be the next move be? Would further intelligence be required?' He contemplated.

Pointing at the transcript Laing summed up.

"Tom I would like you to go through recent telecoms and transcripts and find out if there have been any peculiar references to TET it is only a hunch but TET do control and provide the national communication infrastructure in a fashion" added Laing

"Ok I will get `Grace and Ron to dig deeper 'replied Leyton

In an unequivocal display of authority and a signal to wind up the meeting Laing slapped his hands face down on the table, the retracting sleeves of the grey suit jacket exposing white cuffs pinned together by gold cuff links and on his left wrist a vintage gold timepiece.

Keen to move onto other matters Laing announced.

"Ok Tom let's keep this Category 1 and within these four walls."

'Understood Sir, I just have a hunch that we may be on to something here, what I am not sure of, but something in these old and battered bones is sending me a strong signal that this is a biggie," replied Tom.

The three visitors bade their farewell, unseated themselves and left the comfortable surroundings of the' Fat Controller's 'office.

As Leyton moved swiftly past Pam's well ordered a clean beech veneered desk he noticed a red light flicker into life signalling Laing was requesting the attendance of his assistant.

No sooner had the office door closed the intercom on Pam's desk summoned her into Laing's opulent work space.

The petite blond haired Pam who was as always conservatively dressed in a navy blue suit, clutching a notepad and pen in her left hand entered the adjacent office.

She noticed that Laing's scruffy mop of greying hair looked more unkempt than usual and that he was displaying signs of being a little flustered. With Laing holding court so early on a Monday and in the company of three officers engaged in anti- terror, Pam had figured that something serious was be in play.

Peering over the top of his white china coffee cup and taking one last sip the milky sweet beverage Laing announced

"I need to speak with Sir Antony it is important can you exercise all of your charm and magic and track him down for me."

Acknowledging the request, the loyal PA turned on the well-appointed patent leather heel and headed back to her desk in the nest room.

As Pam negotiated her way through a number of human filters on the other end of the land line call she was not aware that that Tom Leyton was outside the door to her office and could clearly hear her asking for Sir Antony Jowett., the Permanent Under Secretary to the Home Secretary.

Tom Leyton was inspired and energised with this potentially exciting assignment, he felt that there was something deep and sinister behind the German scripted message.

A seasoned operator, he had interrogated a wide range of suspects using both conventional methods and, in some instances, employing techniques which tested the limits of legality.

Intuition was shouting out to this old school operative that all was not above board with Laing.

'Laing was acting too cool he hypothesised, yes it was all a little too breezy!'

"That overgrown schoolboy is far too relaxed for me Ron' Leyton declared.

"Do you really think so Tom, you know this is just one of the numerous issues on top of all that time wasting departmental politics that the fella has to deal with each day" Ron retorted.

"Yes Ron I get you, but this High German shit is spooky and as for the association with TET well something strongly suggests all is not what the eye is seeing"

Tom returned to his modest and disorganised desk and shouted for Grace to come over to see him. A little agitated he spluttered under his breath "where ae those bloody patches" as he rummaged through the badly arranged top left hand drawer of his desk.

There was a time past where the comfort of a cigarette would have satiated his need for calm and clear thinking.

He proffered a hand for Grace Wells to sit then arose from his desk to close his office door whilst at the same time he reassured himself that no one was with in ear shot of his office.

Seated, Leyton looked at Wells and assertively pronounced

"This meeting we are having now never took place do you understand"

A wide eyed and curious Grace Wells nodded agreement.

Leyton opened

"Grace accuse me of being hyper vigilant but I have a gut feeling that our red face over indulgent relic of the British Empire we refer to as Sir, is not playing a straight bat".

Grace who was clearly perplexed furrowed her brow and looked back at Leyton.

"Please let me in on this Tommy"

"Well I have undertaken a little bit of background research on our oafish leader. It appears that Daddy left very little in the way of inheritance to our man. It appears that Laing's Father liked fast women and slow horses and spent his mini fortune including the cash from re mortgaging the London family home. To put it bluntly notwithstanding the odd shotgun and a bit of second rate art our esteemed leader got nothing when his father died."

A slightly uneasy Grace Wells enquired.

"And where are you going with this Tom"

"Well my good friend Grace, I have discovered that Laing owns a large Holland Park house worth circa £2.9m so tell me how does the grade 6 or 7 with a potential salary 120k tops achieve this. Only 7 years ago he was in rented flat in Maida Vale."

"Most folk assumed it was inheritance well it was not!! Then there is the Range Rover and the 25 to 30 days shooting per year at one and half grand a pop, it does not add up"

Grace sat back and pondered what Leyton was suggesting, she hoped that he was off the mark as she did not want to even contemplate the thought of Laing being corrupt.

'Ok boss you may have a point and that gold Omega he wears would look better on me, he can keep that scary snake ring, horrible looking thing, but I cannot well do not want to consider that Laing is not on our side"

"The watch and ring two of the few pickings his father left him I believe"

"Another thought, and to keep you away from the pub tonight, find out what you can about his grandfather, paternal that is"

Queried Leyton.

"Evidentially he was from the landed gentry which evolved from the 19th Century 'noveaux riche', a small fortune made in the steel mills of South Yorkshire. His lucky break was the development of armour for warships"

"The business hit hard times in the 20s recession and the family lived off the reserves built up by feeding the WW1 killing machine".

"Then fortunes were reversed as WW2 provided a hot demand for the steel plate. What we do know is that our esteemed beloved leader's granddaddy was a known supporter of Sir Oswald Mosely's British Union of Fascists. During the 1930s he spent time in Germany trying broker a long term peace deal with Hitler. He became Conservative MP for Sheffield South and was on the government committee for assessing the industrial strength of Germany. The business specialised in high strength steels but it is rumoured that this capability evolved into the development of a low weight high strength aluminium based alloy used for aircraft armour."

Leyton handed an A4 sheet to Wells,

"Read on" he directed

Wells looked concerned and held the document in her right hand and occasionally looking at her boss she focussed on the words,

The document detailed that although the new alloy had been developed earlier it had not been offered to the allies until 1943 well into the war.

Wells read the document and then with a gasp exclaimed "but it declares here the Germans were utilising the British developed alloy 7 years before it was offered to the allies."

"That is the point before it was offered to the Allies, there are those who fear a conspiracy" added Leyton

"Ok Guv I will do bit of additional research and also see what else I can dig up on TET"

Grace Wells got up and turned towards the exit, as she laid her hand on the chrome door handle, Leyton spoke

"Thank you Grace please keep this to yourself and do not utter a word to Ronald MacDonald out there."

She engaged Leyton's stare and nodded approval of his request, she decided that her loyalties would lie with Tom Leyton well at least for the time being.

Chapter 9

Judiciously dressed for action in a dark grey flannel suit, crisp white shirt and paisley tie, Guy Walker, opened the un framed inner glass door, leading into to the air-conditioned marble chrome and brightly lit gateway to his future success. *This was really happening he smiled.*

The reception at number 40 St James Street although compact passed muster as a credible command post for his new financial venture, a very agreeable venue he reflected. Surveying the beautifully polished light coloured marble floor, his eyes then moved onto a cursory scan of the light blue painted walls, his vision locked onto the object behind the reception desk. With the razor like acuity of a laser weapon locked onto a target `Guy witnessed the endorsement to his new career. Behind the desk amongst the list of brushed stainless steel nameplates was Tornado Ventures LLP.

Clear as day displayed was the name of his Company at the high alter at the temple of financial arbitrage.

Guy was in the exclusive club albeit in the lower echelons of membership, but he was on board and with the full sponsorship of the high priest, Lukas Richter.

He romanced that Floor 7; 40 St James Street would be a wakeup call to the bigger members of the club the ones who occupied the large and expensively adorned offices which populated London's high cost city real estate.

The commissionaire, dressed in the trademark blue uniform and white trimmed peak cap, sat behind the reception desk and raised his head and nodded at Guy

"Good morning Mr Walker welcome to no 40."

Guy observed the, orange and white ribbons stitched over the top left hand pocket of the commissionaire's jacket, in a quiet voice he pronounced

"1991 I was there, God bless you my fellow and no more Mr Walker, I am Guy to a brother in arms 'you have my undying respect Dennis."

Dennis now dewy eyed and clearly moved saluted Guy.

Guy returned the salute turned and walked towards the stainless steel lift doors.

A firm press of the illuminated lift button and Guy entered the lift, he chose the no 7 directly above the black and chrome nameplate. After the almost silent passing of 25 seconds a ping announced his arrival at Floor 7.

This was it he reflected, the big one the pinnacle, he was on pole position at Monaco, on the centre court at Wimbledon he wondered what his team would be like. He swallowed hard to avoid tears, tears of high emotion rippled with pride. This was a long way to come for a working class lad from a large Northern town.

Opposite the lift doors were two large unframed slightly tinted glass doors furnished with highly polished chrome hinges and handles. On the left sash in quasi etching were the words Tornado Ventures LLP.

Guy felt the hairs on the back of neck stand to attention as he experienced the charge of a million electrons racing down the highways of his central nervous system.

He was alive and ready for combat in the sphere of International finance.

Guy pushed open the left hand door leaf and to his surprise Lukas Richter appeared from nowhere and presented himself in the entrance to the office

Richter held the door open with his left hand and grabbed Guy by the left arm and hauled him past Julia on the reception desk and straight through the open doors which lead into the main office and the trading floor.

They walked into a large open plan office adorned with private offices constructed from floor to ceiling glass partitioning which formed two sides of the space. On two walls were a bank of 60-inch TV screens displaying BBC Bloomberg and CNN updates.

Richter bellowed out

"Ladies and gentlemen, it is my great pleasure to be here today and would you please join me and extend my welcome to Guy Walker. Our new leader the figurehead of our wonderful new and exciting the London operation of the Tornado Financial Group"

The main office was set out in a very orderly fashion consisting of 4 rows of beech veneer desks and side tables each adorned with three LED PC monitors. The twenty-two occupants of this nerve centre were all standing and on Richter's mark they welcomed Guy with a rapturous round of applause. This was followed by banging of hands on the desks and robust cheering. Positioned in the far corner of the trading floor and enclosed on two sides by the glass partitioning was an individual office of approx. 6 metres by 4 metres. Centre stage on the high quality dark grey carpet sat a large rosewood desk accompanied with matching side table which was complemented with a full height unit positioned against the unglazed back wall

Guy knew immediately that it was his office as Richter had clearly done his homework. On one wall were large signed photos of Guy's sporting heroes the personalisation did not end there as behind his desk and on a floor, stand was a stunning Cherry Red Sunburst Gibson Les Paul guitar.

"Thank you for the welcoming touch Lukas this all too amazing for words" Guy said.

Guy was at home, in paradise he was in an environment fashioned to encourage and create success. A perfect setting where he and the first class team supported by financial resources courtesy of Lukas Richter, would build an execute deals like never before.

If there was a catch it was not visible and to be frank he did not care this is where he wanted to be. He was fully aware that he would have to deliver the goods but any fear was dampened by the fact he had a great team in this shrine to arbitrage and with the backing and pupillage of Richter he could not fail.

The master of Guy's destiny in an unusual display of affection wrapped his right arm across the shoulder of his protégé and announced

"Come into your office Guy and please make yourself comfortable sit down in your shiny new leather chair, it is important that we talk."

Establishing home position behind his new desk, and settled on the fine Italian black perforated leather, Guy adjusted his jacket and re set the lumber support.

Feeling like the new ruler of a hard won empire he swivelled right to take in the view of the trading floor, the engine room of wealth creation.

Richter sat opposite Guy and in a serious tone said

"Ok now let's get down to business.'

"Waiting outside and to whom I will introduce to you in a minute is Michael Stuch who has been heading up the operation in advance of your appointment., in effect he runs the show and will continue to under your guidance." He added

Richter leaned onto the new desk and in a clearly non- negotiable statement, he announced.

"Guy you will be the figurehead the Field Marshall, CIC, Michael will manage the operation under your guidance and instruction of course, and will have no direct report or line to me. You will be the face and culture of the venture."

"Clear lines of communication OK he reports to you and you to me understand ja?"

Guy nodded acceptance.

"I fully understand Lukas that is the only way I can work and you kind of know that"

"Stuch is very loyal to our cause and donates large proportions of his bonus to a number of the charitable bodies I head up."

"Where does he herald from" enquired Guy

Richter glared at his subordinate.

Reasoning that his question had been a little awkward Guy changed his tone.

"I will rephrase my question, what is his background?"

"Oh I see Guy, he is Austrian by birth and comes from a long line of bankers and interestingly he had an uncle who manufactured tractors until 1937.Well you can no doubt guess the replacement product", they still operate today in Voest Austria and Hanau in Germany."

Richter outlined the nature of the business assets held by Stuch's immediate and extended family. He enlightened Guy on the support the banking arm of the empire gave to help German companies to recover after WW2. The family undertook widespread cash investments in the "middlestaat" engineering companies during the late 1950s and beyond.

He enthused that these German homeland companies had become world leaders in many machine tool technologies.

Guys eyes were glazing over with Richter's account of family fame and fortune, what he heard next refocused his interest.

"And of course there was great uncle Fritz a Colonel in the Waffen SS, they say that he met justice at the hands of British Intelligence in 1945."

"that is all in the past let's move on "declared Richter

From his Lois Vution attaché case, Richter withdrew a pack of documents.

He pushed the files across the polished rich dark wood of Guy's desk and for the next 45 minutes Richter schooled Guy on current projects and key operation indicators.

Richter beckoned to Guy to pass him the A 4 pad resting on his side table.

Guy looked intensely as Richter sketched a number of diagrams illustrating how Tornado had taken advantage to short the stocks of Blue Chip Companies who were facing adverse problems. Guy's mind was polarised by the constant references to the huge cash pile he would have at his disposal.

"I can see that having such a resource will allow Tornado to move swiftly and give us the fire power to steal market advantage to maximise profit margins, but…"

Richter jarred by the word 'but' halted Guy in his tracks, and placed his flat hand out in front of Guy in a clear show of influence and power.

"but what Guy, but what I am not sure where you are heading" snapped the Austrian.

Guy was unnerved by Richter's move, '*was this an insight into the true man*' he reflected

"Apologies Lukas I did not quite get my words right only what I don't get is that you get the choice of target shares so right, you seem to have sixth sense yielding an ability to predict the misfortunes of otherwise robust and stable companies."

Challenged Guy

"Let's call it intuition and a strong hunch", Richter replied with a scarce grin.

"Yes I get that Lukas but knowing what, where and when to buy, well that is not my skillset"

"My dear Guy do not concern yourself with such matters we have means to predict the market shall we say' Richter replied with a cool and un fazed fixed stare,

"Outside this door, and under Michael's control, the traders with their algorithms and spreadsheets will take care of our positions, you just provide the leadership and become the face of our London operation"

Keen to move off the subject matter, Richter got up from the expertly upholstered leather chair, walked to the office door, pushed it open and waived to summon over Stuch.

On Richter's command he arose from the seat at communal table in the main office and approached Guy's office.

Stuch was six foot two inches tall had short blonde hair and 'his robes of office' was a dark blue Armani suit which clad a well-tanned and athletic physique.

The controlled figure of Stuch entered Guy's office and after closing the door, with a movement of radar scanner he scrutinised the environment, then fixed his chilling blue eyes directly at Guy.

Guy shuffled in an uneasy manner, Stuch responded with a tight lipped smile and with a sense of accomplishment he turned to Richter and with a more relaxed delivery.

"Good morning Sir "

Richter sensed Guy's apprehension at Stuch's presence and gauged that there would be no potential bon ami between these two driven bright but very different individuals.

Stuch drew back from the desk one of the brand new leather chairs, embracing the quality and aroma of the soft black covering. He sat down and positioned himself 45 degrees to the edge of the desk allowing him to have Guy and Richter on either side of his field of vision.

Richter began

"Guy, I have fully briefed Michael on your appointment and why it was vitally important that we need a respected English operator at the top of the London desk. Your appointment will give credibility and help to maintain compliance in this great city."

"I have made it clear to all and in particular Michael that you are in charge and you and only you report directly. After all we are Austrian it is in our DNA and therefore we are programmed to respect rank and levels of authority" Richter laughed.

A satisfied Richter looked at Stuch "Michael tell Guy of your recent success"

Stuch placed his hands on the top of his legs and swivelled his head between the visible engagement of Richter and Guy proudly announced.

"Well we have just made a clear profit of £1.13 BILLION, after costs, currency movements, and dealer fees."

After a brief pause to let the enormity of the win sink in he continued.

"How you may ask?", in his educated German accent and with clear precision he continued.

"We had intel that some large and damaging events were to occur at Whitehead Construction Grp, acts which would an adverse effect on stock price. With this knowledge and our cash reserves we put in play large short positions on the shares. We had a limited time slot to act before the Company had to make public huge overspend and underperformance on a number of government contracts. We had been watching these contracts for a while and with some feedback from two employees prepared how shall we say prepared to tell tales, we decided to make our move."

"They had a heavily geared balance sheet and the ensuing 60% southward movement of shares their debt and warrants were looking as worthless as bathroom paper."

"And guess what?" announced Richter

"We bought the debt at cents in the dollar and moved it on in packages at a good margin."

"The Home Secretary dropped the favourable bomb shell that there would be more funds for the loss making contracts so we had that double whammy of being able to trade what was no longer worthless paper" Rejoiced an ebullient Richter

"The timing of the Home Secretary's intervention was very advantageous to Tornado, almost scripted" pitched a dubious Guy.

"Yes Mr Medway helped the cause now let's move on." Richter replied.

"With that intel and the advantages of un encumbered cash you can strike quick"

"That is correct Guy and that is why we are called Tornado Ventures we had toyed with Lightning but the German translation to Blitz may have upset some of our friends in the City" yes we do move with lightning speed but this time we will stay away from Russia" laughed a grinning Richter.

Guy witnessed a deliberate and patently unsettling tone in Richter's voice. It was forced laughter to provide humour for his audience, but, Guy, sensed that that deep inside Richter's soul was residual hurt for Germany's loss to their former Soviet Enemies.

Richter, refocused on the here and now, removed a gold cigarette case from the left inside pocket of his jacket, and with a demonstration great proficiency flicked open the Dunhill Case, removed and place between his tightened lips a Sobrani tube of toasted Turkish tobacco.

Guy scrutinised the pre smoking ritual and reminisced of past days when smoking was cool and not vilified.

Fully aware of but in total denial of the UK smoking laws Richter lit the gold tipped black cigarette with a solid gold lighter.

The scene was a juxtaposition of style, and a purely manufactured rarity, an act of risky self-indulgence by crisp suited perfectly manicured modern day desperados.

These three men had all subscribed to the philosophy that gain without risk is not a gain which was worth living for and that a well fought and honourable defeat was more gracious than a silicic victory.

There was an almost affable mild crackling sound as Richter drew on the cigarette, the blue plume of smoke oozing the seductive sweet aroma of the fine tobacco.

Richter, placed the open gold case in front of Guy and proffered Guy to join him.

Clenching what felt like every bone in his body, and through gritted teeth and eyes straining Guy declined the cigarette.

Richter closed the case with a re assuring click, looked sideways at Stuch, a signal for to him enter stage left and commence his performance.

The show continued, Richter fixated on the half smoked cigarette he was in the process of rolling between his thumb and forefinger he licked his pursed lips and pointed the iconic smouldering baton at Stuch.

"Well Michael the master plan please it's time to talk about world domination."

There was a menacing tone to Richter's voice.

The board room could have been mistaken for a battlefield bunker from a darker era, occupied with officers in the black uniforms.

In Guy's mind this was not a man nor indeed an organisation to disappoint.

Chapter 10

"Hugo there is a letter to be signed for can you come down straight away."

"Ok mum on my way" he groaned in reply.

He was tired, a remnant of remaining awake for most of the night exploring the comfortable and familiar parallel universe of hyperspace.

He had been covertly browsing the servers of numerous organisations to garner as much information as he could on the Wembley Arena killings, and at all times remained invisible, his target hosts would remain unaware of his presence.

"Hugo for heaven's sake will get out of bed and come down here now"

It was a typical austere February morning cold damp and grey. Stood at the front door the be draggled postman who was on the edge of serious discomfort, and regretted his recent career move, made his impatience known to Mrs Parnell.

His mother hollered once more, Hugo threw back the bed covers and rolled out, feet on the floor, he scanned the blue carpet to sight his grey shorts and black plain t shirt.

He dressed quickly and clumsily and at one point he temporarily lost control of his arms hand and feet as they became tangled in the twisted garments.

"Come now or I will let this kind gentleman take your letter away." Protested the now impatient mother.

Hugo rubbed his eyes in an attempt for conveyance from a modality of semi oblivion to one of near reality, he ran down the staircase to be greeted by his mother holding the half open front door.

He yawned loudly as his mother gave a palpable look of pseudo denunciation.

Hugo held out his right hand to receive the letter from the despondent looking postie.

The postman in an almost damming act threw the brown A5 envelope at Hugo and in imperious gesture waived his freezing finger as a signal to sign the receipt.

The tight lipped postie held the pad and a grunting Hugo scrawled his name as evidence of his existence on God's Earth or at least for that moment in time.

The wet and cold delivery man turned around and headed down the drive towards the main road.'

"You could have been politer to that poor man he is only doing his job on this not so nice day"

Mrs Parnell continued.

"I just wish you would stop being so insolent and moody and spend more time in the real world instead of endless hours in your bedroom interacting with those sterile impersonal machines"

Hugo grunted disapproval turned on his heel and with letter in hand ran back up the staircase.

He slammed the bedroom door closed in a clear signal of defiance to his mother's semi scalding, and jumped on to the partially made bed.

He sat cross legged with his back against three stacked pillows propped against the headboard, and studied the envelope held in his right hand.

After a brief interlude Hugo chose the appropriate moment and tore back the perforated section which provided access to the contents of the envelope.

He was puzzled, the outer envelope bore an Indian postmark and an array of legal postage tender all displaying Ghandi. Removing the outside cover Hugo was left with a beautifully addressed hand written envelope.

A brief pause of anticipation and Hugo carefully opened and unsealed the wrapping that encased a letter typed on very high quality Conqueror paper.

It read 'dear *Hugo as you are well aware the Tamil Nadu Institute for Advanced Computer Studies has been for a number of years associated with your University.*

Hugo read on.

'Every year we hold a symposium on the future of algorithmic generated security protocols and this year we are hosting the event in Kochi, Kerala, India.

The event will be an informal affair, and will not only allow delegates to spend time deliberating the latest and near future concepts and technologies, but allow time for relaxing in loveliest surroundings. 'We read your final year dissertation with great interest and envisage the potential integration of your work with our current and future development programmes. 'Our programme is sponsored by Marino India who you may be aware are one of the largest players in the fast growing market for security protocols.';' recently ~Marino were purchased by the hedge fund manager Lukas Richter, and his financial backing has motivated a new programme of research projects. 'our committee values your good work to date and we feel that it would make huge sense for us to meet with you. apologies for the short notice, however we formally invite you to attend the seminar on 21 `February.

the programme is attached and you will see there will be time for relaxation.

The Richter Foundation has kindly arranged to fully fund all of your flights, accommodation and expenses. We would be honoured if you would accept and in anticipation we have booked Business Class travel departing Heathrow 19 February 'this will be a packed itinerary meaning that you will be away from home for 18 nights.'' We have prepared for your visa but you will need to call this number to make contact the Indian Visa Fast-track Service quoting reference 234749120.

A stunned Hugo recoiled on the bed. Why him? He wanted to go that was for sure. All of his adolescent life he had wanted to visit this mysterious spiritual country. He also recalled that his Indian friends from university were always good at maths.

Unfortunately, this wonderful trip would be at a time in conflict with his work for MOSSAD, and in an act of frustration threw the letter across the bed.

Fully prepared to enter one of deep solemn moods, his action was headed off at the pass.

Ping, rang the communicator

Hugo over to his pc desk and picked up the device.

The message read.

'Attend the Indian event at all costs and we need to talk tomorrow, G'

The message continued.

'In preparation we will send you an IP address, login in to a list of potential suspects which we need Intel on. 'the letter you have received contains a 'crib' a link or key you will need to use to decipher any messages on that IP address.

Hugo photocopied and scanned the letter, he then looked at the text and scribbled various permutations on the A4 copies.

The author of the 'crib' in, reverence to Hugo's prowess in mathematics, fashioned the digital keystone in a highly challenging format.

Hugo figured that the puzzle would be numbers based, after all he was a mathematician.

A highly imaginative logical somewhat obtuse thinker, this was proving a resilient trial for him.

Transfixed on the copied page, and in trancelike state all he could visualise were numbers, but nothing made sense, there was no pattern, no correlations, the message was not communicating with him.

He sat on the bed in the semi illuminated bedroom, the were curtains drawn and door closed to the physical world, his eyes scanned the script at light speed.

Gripping the paper tight he shook his hand and uttered "yes yes yes"

It occurred to him to scrutinise the letters surrounding IP ADDRESS'.

He picked up a yellow and pencil and furiously scribbled letters onto the paper copy, and processed letters for numerical sequences, the resultant numbers proved unsuccessful on numerous attempts to unlock the web address.

His frustration simmered and were unexpectedly subjugated by a ping, announcing the arrival of the numerical string *'876428£g?'*.

Hugo's mission centric un-emotional unconscious brain had identified the numbers as the key to cyber space and justice,

He made and assertive stroke of the return key and the monitor flickered into life and dragged Hugo into the dimension, the place, the cyber world where he always felt safe.

The screen rewarded Hugo's hard work with a garbled message.

The sender was not going to solely rely on Hugo's ability to solve the puzzle and gain access to the covert message.

Hugo had a strong hunch that the communicator had a secondary function as a number generator, similar those used to access bank accounts.

He gripped the communicator, and after two attempts guessed the login as 'SARAH DOB', he then input the corresponding numbers and letters and almost immediately a sequence of numbers lit up the LED.

Hugo juggled numbers and letters and fuelled the communicator with the results of his labour.

The decoded message appeared

'Liverpool CID have got Ali Amir Iqbad under surveillance in connection with the Arena killings. We are unable to gain full access to the police records and also, we require access to the TET secure server to investigate the transcripts of the suspect's communications. It is our desire that you find a way to break into the TET main server. We will bid you a goodnight and we will communicate with you at 09.30 tomorrow to discuss in more detail your trip to India. G'

Life expired from the communicator as rapidly as it had appeared only five minutes earlier.

Hugo closed his laptop, jumped off the bed and went over to three drawer set positioned in the bay window, he eased open the sticking top drawer and peeled back a pile of t shirts and placed the letter and copies on the base of the drawer then returned the shirts to their stored position.

He showered, pulled on a pair of recently purchased blue jeans and wriggled into a plain white t shirt, he completed the act with socks and baseball boots.

Hugo jumped up from his seated position at the edge of his bed he strutted over to his black desk and recovered a pile of coins screwed up notes and 3 credit cards.

These were rammed into his left pocket and I Phone pushed into his rear pocket of his jeans.

The final act to try and make him look half presentable was a mild dowsing of tap water to pat down his lengthening hair.

Hugo ran half way down the stairs then realised that he would need to return to his room to retrieve his house key.

Approaching the front door for the second time his mother shouted' Hugo where are you going now'

"out" was the stern reply, "I need to prepare for my trip" "trip?"

"Ah well the Richter Institute have invited me to and want me to attend a symposium on cyber security. "He replied.

"oh how interesting is it in London?"

"No Kochi"

Mum was no champion of geography; English language was her chosen following.

"no India" Hugo retaliated.

"India India"

"Yes mother India not the local assembly house on the Finchley Road'

"Well I don't expect me to pay for you no way"

"No need it is a taken care of flights, hotels booze, drugs and hookers" he replied caustically

"Now that is quite enough young man I will not have such contemptuous words spoken in this house".

"I need to go now mother, I am off o medical centre at Kings Cross for my injections, goodbye"

The door slammed and Hugo was on his way.

Chapter 11

“Sir Antony, I need to speak with the Home Secretary immediately, it is a matter of National importance.”

“Mr Laing please wait, I believe he is in office, and from what I understand he is extremely busy on governmental matters”.” Perhaps I can help you, direct you to a more appropriate source of assistance

“Sir Antony do please stop this procedural bullshit, stop messing me about and get me effing Medway this minute”

“Sir there is no need for you to adopt that tone, I find your manner most displeasing “

“Well as you are fully aware I and do not need to remind you I am GCHQ and not the local Police station.”

“And when you eventually make contact with your boss, please please emphasise urgency, and ask him, no tell him to phone me on the secure line thank you”

A premeditated click in Sir Antony’s left ear aurally pronounced Laing’s departure.

Back in GCHQ, Laing replaced the receiver, he rocked back on high backed charcoal upholstered chair, and stared at his large desk, the badge of office reflecting his status and pay grade.

His eyes refocused to the dark blue phone sitting in the open top right hand drawer of his mahogany and leather well-appointed work station. Two minutes wait and the flickering magenta LED signified an incoming secure message.

Laing nonchalantly claimed the receiver, and placed his left arm behind his head and heard the inimitable northern enunciation of Phillip Medlock, the Home Secretary.

“My dear Laing awfully nice to hear from you and what is the matter my good friend?”

Laing grimaced, and reflected that that bloody upstart Medway was no friend of his.

"Phillip I will get straight to point"

Laing continued in his upper-class accent

"hmm well we have a potentially sticky issue"

"I'm all ears 'interjected Medway

"Well Phillip that bloody menace Leyton and his lap dog Wells have intercepted a message, which in some way potentially link the Arena killings to TET, and this has set them on a path of deeper investigation."

"so what has this got to do with us?"

The laconic tone of Medway's reply, gave away an indicator that he was ready to curtail the conversation. He after all kept telling all that he had a country to run!

Laing's intuition detected Medway's slim interest, Laing paused and carefully chose his response.

"Well Mr Home Secretary, the intercept refers to the Wembley Arena and TET in one sentence and reports a job well done."

There was immediate silence, and after a ten second interlude, a clearly unnerved Medway tapped his right finger against the receiver and enquired.

"Well what is your take on this Laing"

"Clearly the crux is that Leyton is seeking to find the common thread to what logically and normally would be an uncommon connection between the two."

"At the time of the intercept the problems at TET had not surfaced, and born cynics like Leyton dig very deeply and he will leave no stone unturned, the man will be a nuisance."

"do you think that this will escalate?" Questioned a flustered Medway.

"well Phillip I have demanded all of his checked Intel on the matter, and instructed him not to spend too much time on the case"

"Furthermore I have designated it level 6 which means that he reports any future spurious activity to me and only me."

Medway jumped in with an ambience of underlying authority.

"Look Laing, conscious of who our paymasters are, you need to suppress this and discourage any further investigation"

Laing nodded.

"As I understand it our colleagues in India are preparing the ground to press the button on the TET Project,"

Medway continued.

"R and K are nearing completion of the financial positions."

"I understand fully Phillip; I understand"

Medlock sensed he was on a roll with mounting authority over the Civil Servant.

"This is the big one Laing; the gains are good for all" he asserted.

"Failure is not an option Laing …. not an option"

He articulated with chilling conviction.

"I suggest that we meet "and placing his hand over the mouth piece of his handset he turned towards his secretary, "Sir Antony what is my diary like today?

Sir Antony confirmed his only appointment, and at Medway's request Sir Antony rescheduled the meeting with James Stevens Chairman of Barclays Bank at Canary Wharf from1800 to 20.00 hrs. Medway then demanded that he give no excuses, claiming that the puffed up so and so could wait.

"Laing meet me at the Hilton Canary Wharf 18.00, no one needs to know where you are, so just go and book yourself a first class return from Cheltenham, now I must go" announced the Home Secretary.

Laing arrived at Paddington 1630 and hurried with the pack of passengers and negotiated the beeping 21st century stainless steel monoliths, the ticket barriers bordering Platform 4.

He lamented the buzz of London, and the great feeling of success which it inoculated into one's spirit, he walked taller as he entered the City of dreams, wealth and anonymity.

He gained track position in the race to the escalators and disappeared into the myriad of electrically powered arteries connecting the great city.

Bakerloo to Baker Street and pick up as lightly better presented Jubilee Line tube to Canary Wharf. Despite having not resided in London for many years, Laing had been able to retrieve the embedded iconic London "Underground Map' from his long term memory. With the adeptness of a seasoned commuter he arrived at Canary Wharf at 1752. He ascended the two flights of lofty escalators which transported commuters to the exit of the enormous vaulted terminal. With time of the essence he grappled his way through the onslaught of workers, and six minutes later he was sat in the lobby of the Hilton.

Art precisely 1800 the unmistakeable silhouette of a ministerial black Jaguar XJ6 pulled up outside the revolving glass doors that formed the entrance to the hotel. The driver's door of the Cabinet Carriage opened and a well-built black suited figure stepped out. He was equipped with an earpiece and the slight deformation of the left side of his buttoned jacket evidenced that this man was no ordinary driver.

The driver passingly surveyed the immediate area, and stepped around to the rear of the car, his head constantly scanning the close up environment. Satisfied that was no apparent threat he opened the rear door of the Jag signalling to Phillip Medway that the coast was clear and it was safe to step out into the busy hotel foyer.

Medway, sported a blue and white pinstriped suit, he turned nodded gratitude and muttered a message to the Special Branch guardian who led him into the hotel.

Medway strolled over towards Laing who was seated at a table for two adjacent to the large window in the far corner of the restaurant. Laing caught a visual glance of his associate and shuffled back his chair and stood up in readiness for the meeting.

The two men shook hands and exchanged welcome pleasantries. When asked if the journey had been comfortable, Laing bemoaned the new First Class coaches on the train.

"I suggest that we move to the opposite corner away from the window, we don't want the meeting to be obvious old chap "remarked Medway.

They both proceeded to as solitary area and sat down.

Cutting Laing short, Medway slapped his hand resolutely on the table and immediately stamped his authority on the conduct of the meeting.

"Now you sit there and listen to me Laing, I want a lid on this Leyton affair, and I do not care how you settle the matter. No more of your public schoolboy, civil servant old boy network protocol shit, just sort it, you have the power."

Medway's contempt for Laing beamed like a searchlight.

"Leyton and his crew have to cool and eventually kill this investigation by you surreptitiously denying them access to any intel which remotely has any bearing on this case."

Laing turned his gaze towards his antagonist and once more was rebutted by Medway when he attempted to control the conversation. The Home Secretary in a signal of defiance had placed his forefinger over his lips a clear and unambiguous pointer to silence Laing.

"Now get this my in-bred overpaid thick fat friend."

Medway verbally punched out in a clear display of his street fighting style, a man of humble beginnings.

"Both myself and my financial backers are the paymasters, and we pay out in both monetary and well I will impress on you non fiscal terms, so GET THE LID ON THIS NOW and keep me out of it." Medway commanded

"But Phillip…"

Laing was halted a second time by a very determined Home Secretary.'

"No buts do you get that you bloody pervert, not only are you on the payroll, we possess reams of news worthy material with you and your lovely young men in the Mayfair club."

Laing's arms slid down by his side and he retracted into the dark blue chair, his glazed eyes clearly reflected the soul of a deeply hurt man.

"TET will happen next week Laing, it has to, and to keep you focussed I have put half of million dollars' worth of options in your name registered in the Cayman Islands. And when it is all over you will have a packet of cash to spend on your rent boys." Remarked a Medway who was bordering on being vile.

"And one final thing Laing, good work finding Walker, he looks clean and semi corruptible, Lukas is impressed. That said and as a precaution I want 24 hr. surveillance on his phone and e-mails."

Laing acknowledged the request, and Medway rose from his seat and bade his farewell to the uncomfortable looking and the marginally raw Laing.

As a clear put-on to demean his guest, Medway removed a crumpled £20 note from his trouser pocket, dropped into onto Laing's lap, and said,

"buy yourself a coffee, sorry I cannot stay,"

As he approached the foyer and with the Special Branch man in clear view, Medway, signalled to his guardian that he was ready to leave.

He gave a firm wave, left hand fingers abutted tightly, a platinum snake ring curled around the third finger.

Chapter 12

Hugo rushed to St Johns Wood underground station, harbouring a whirlwind of emotions, predominately driven by excitement nevertheless tempered with reservation.

'What if this was a scam he pondered, or even connected with the making of a sinister act' he pondered

He concluded *'to hell with it'* and decided to give it is full attention.

He exited Kings Cross underground, and proceeded towards the new developments which had shot up out of the ground which was the old wasteland to the North East of the mainline railway station. As he walked past the new bars, restaurants and boutiques onwards to the large brick and glass towers, he was oblivious to the history of the area and how run down it had been until recent times.

The address he was given belonged to a twelve story fully glazed building graced with a huge high ceiling well illuminated reception hall.

Hugo entered the building via one of the three suites of chromed steel framed faintly green tinted glass revolving doors. The reception was cavernous its cathedral like proportions occupying at least three floors upwards. His dirty baseball boots looked incongruous on the immaculate 2m square marble floor tiles. There was an air of opulence in his surroundings.

Central to the reception was a row of glass wood and stainless steel counters shouldered either side by grand banks of shiny escalators leading to level 3.

Hugo approached one of the four receptionists, who were sat low level behind the counter.

A man of Eastern European origin, looked up

"Good afternoon sir can I help you"

"yes, I have an appointment with Dr Simpson of Premier One Two Healthcare, I think he is on the 5th floor"

"Let me see "replied the receptionist as he interrogated the flat screen in front of him."

The receptionist tapped on a silver keyboard and looked up at the screen hidden behind the counter top.

"Yes that is confirmed Dr Simpson is ready to see you, please take the lift to level 5, then turn right go through the double doors and report to his assistant Sister Brownlow"

At the request of the receptionist Hugo signed for the issue of a pass in to the building.

He avoided the advice to wear the identification around his neck and screwed up the lanyard and pass and rammed them into the rear pocket of his jeans.

The sinking feeling yielded and the bong announced the lift had arrived at the fifth floor and the doors glided open, Hugo departed and proceeded towards the doctor's reception.

"hello my name is Hugo Parnell I have an appointment to see Doctor Simpson.

A young nurse seated behind the light blue frosted glass reception counter looked up.

"yes Mister Parnell Doctor Simpson will not be too long please take a seat ".

Two minutes later, a grey haired middle aged man wearing light grey suit trousers, white shirt and a plain blue tie appeared from behind a large light oak door, situated at the right of the reception area.

"Hugo, please come this way "he proffered

Hugo entered the doctors consulting room and was immediately interested by the make and model of the PC on the practioner's desk.

The young IT whizz kid and mathematics genius had no motive to notice an item of mystery, one which represented a clandestine world, an exclusive covenant of terror and vileness. The respectable doctor a disciple of the Hippocratic Oath was the bearer of a platinum snake ring on the third finger of his left hand.

Hugo was ignorant to what the ring signified, a physical manifestation of and a key- a physical code to a highly secretive and encrypted world one which the numerous eco systems propagated from the laboratories of Silicon Valley could never replicate.

"Please be seated" requested the doctor.

"So I believe South West India is your destination, for two weeks" he muttered as he examined the file of notes on the desk in front of him.

Hugo nodded acknowledgement.

"Due to time constraints and as you are travelling less than three weeks from now we need to move fast so I have prepared an accelerated programme"

"OK as long as you are quick I am not too keen on needles" declared Hugo

"Not many are Hugo but it will be OK" replied the doctor.

"I have prepared the first stage of the inoculations, so you will have to come back in two weeks' time for the follow up."

"An appointment has been arranged just see my assistant on the way out"

The prospect of the four disposable syringes pushed Hugo into a cold sweat, as like most men he was averse to injections.

"Oh Mr Parnell please sign these forms and roll up both of your sleeves or better still remove your top"

Hugo removed his t shirt and Dr Simpson administered two injections into each of patient's upper arms.

A rather pale Hugo vigoursly rubbed his arms in turn in an attempt to remove the stinging sensation of the serum infiltrating his arm muscles.

Observing his patient's angst Dr Simpson commented.

"Are you ok?"

"I am alright I think but perhaps I could have a glass of water please" replied Hugo.

Rehydrated, and dressed Hugo said farewell to Dr Simpson acknowledging the next appointment.

Hugo departed the Doctors surgery and proceeded to the ground floor using the very rapid lift. As he exited the lift doors he was greeted by a blond haired man in his mid-thirties sporting a dark blue jacket over a grey polo shirt, chinos and brown suede shoes.

Already uneasy after the medical procedures, he was a little shaken when the blond man grabbed him by the shoulder.

"Hello my friend my name is Marcus Williams, and you must come with me, there is a car waiting outside"

About to speak Hugo was interrupted

"That is all you need to know at the moment" Williams asserted.

Williams ushered his captive through the glazed revolving doors, and opened the rear door of a black luxury 4x4 waiting on the bustling London street.

"Don't worry you are not in danger we are off to get your Visa arranged" spoke Williams as the 4x4 effortlessly accelerated down the road.

"I have not got my passport with me

"it is at home on under my bed"

With a cocky smile Williams produced the passport from the inside pocket of his jacket.

Hugo gave a look of amazement, and slightly shocked asked" where did …" Williams cut him short.

"don't ask don't ask, this is not the passport from under your bed but a perfectly legitimate copy"

'Who are these people Hugo? Wondered, they have influence that is for certain.

"And no need to go to the Indian Embassy" announced Williams, and laughing opened a page on the document which clearly evidenced the insertion of a 3-month visitor visa for the Republic of India.

In the back of the speeding vehicle Williams grabbed Hugo on the arm, and looking him full on in the eye, said

"Now listen to me clearly and remember what I am about to tell you"

A rather fazed and perspiring Hugo nodded.

“When you arrive at the conference in Kochi you will be shadowed by an Indian national called Ravi Sanjeera.

“He will ostensibly act as an interpreter, Hindu born in Trivandrum, educated in Bangalore, worked for the Indian Government then became an independent travel guide.”
“well the fact is, Ravi is one of us, Moshi Neumann born in Tel Aviv.”

“Ravi will be your aide for the duration of your visit acting as a rep for the travel company arranging the conference”

“But why do I need a travel Rep I am only attending the conference” protested Hugo

“There will be a weekend break during your trip and there are some tours arranged to the local lakes and the beaches at Kovalam,’ said Williams.

Williams explained that Hugo needed to feign illness and remain at the hotel that weekend, adding that he would travel to Madurai with Ravi. In Madurai he would meet with the team working on penetrating the communication network of the terrorists.

Hugo was getting flustered, this was all getting too bizarre to digest.

“Will I be a legitimate delegate “he gasped

“Of course you will, it provides the ideal opportunity to meet our people in India without raising suspicion.”

“So I will need to prepare a paper on my dissertation”

“Spot on my boy, and you will be receiving a full briefing pack on the event within the next three days’

“Ok my friend this is where we part company, you will be dropped off at Kings Cross station.” Declared Williams.

Ten minutes late, the large vehicle pulled up at the taxi rank between Kings Cross and St Pancras and Williams and Hugo said their goodbyes.

Hugo arrived at his home at 18.15 by which time his mother was well into her ration of afternoon gin and tonics. Since Sarah's death she had attended work less frequently and more time in the spirits section at the Waitrose on Finchley Road.

This was a legacy of Sarah's death, one which evoked conflicting emotions for Hugo.

He despised the vision of his mother destroyed by what had happened and the pain she suffered from her own physical injuries. There was also the mental scar. The flip side was anger, a deep resentment in his mother's inability to fight her personal torture. Why could she not just get on with life and do some good in her deceased daughter's name, instead of leaning on the illusionary affection of Gordons Gin.

"Where have you been Hugo" emanated a slurred tone from the kitchen.

"Just getting my stuff together for India"

"They want me to speak on my dissertation" "in front of some of the most distinguished and influential people in the field of cyber security."

Hugo paused and reflected for a moment, he felt a new pride in fact self-admiration, he had received validation and respect for his hard work. Recognition of his superior intellect he imagined with a suggestion of arrogance.

The self-congratulation was dealt a stinging blow by the caustic and alcohol infused twisted logic which erupted from his mother's tongue.

"Maybe you will get the offer of a proper job by one of the big banks or 'magic circle' law firms."

And with a slurring her words she added.

"You are wasting your intelligence on those silly electronic toys and spending irrecoverable time on that faceless internet." "Your father and I are tired of making excuses for you lack of career progress"

Hugo experienced tears of anger welling up, and clenched his fists to restrain his simmering rage. *Just ignore the woman.* he ruminated, do not react.

Holding back his contained rage Hugo made a rapid ascent up the stairs to his place of safety. Slamming his bedroom door, he jumped onto his bed and recovered the communicator from under his pillow. He had a message.

He logged onto the secure an IP address located safely and anonymously in the ether he decoded the message.

'We have strong intelligence which indicates that Trans Euro Telecom TET are withholding phone records and transcripts of e mail and mobile traffic in relation to the attackers. Both Manchester and the Metropolitan Police have confirmed their suspicions, TET systems are configured to maintain robust client confidentiality and we cannot get access to this information via the police networks. Furthermore, we understand that we are at risk of being identified as hacking the police records so we need to tread carefully. The authorities have approved access to the TET records but at this juncture they are not allowed to store any data on any non-TET sites. Even if we got full access to the police computers we still would have no visibility of the TET transcripts. Our organisation needs immediate access to the phone and e-mail records so we need you to gain undetected entry to the TET central secure server, the nerve centres the computers which generates and controls all passwords, encryption and protection protocols. Once we gain access we can rip into the data with our data trawl systems which are superior to those adopted by your Police. There are only 6 people who have the highest level clearance to enter the central operation server and all areas. Our attempts to break gain access have been futile, as their systems are sensitive to intrusion from overseas intelligence agencies. A solo flyer is required, a nobody who can sneak in under the radar. If that solo agent was to clone the login of one of the 6, well we could get in undetected. We have a proposed candidate David Leslie Thomas Moss. Moss is the Prime Minister of England's husband, the chairman of TET and heads up ethics and corporate responsibility, no one will ever suspect him. We have his e-mail and possible passwords which will give you a base to start from.it is imperative that this is all in place for the meeting in India. Finally, we must leave no trace of your ghosting on the server is than clear.'

Hugo read and re read the message and digested the quantum and the morality of the proposed task. He had been asked to find a way into the main sever of one of Europe's largest telecommunications groups. Moreover, he was using the PM's husband and Company chairman as a Trojan horse. In the wrong hands the breach of security would compromise the security of millions of individuals and hundreds of businesses. Such access could affect the financial stability of companies and potentially deep and irrevocable grief for a lot of people, he concluded.

He wrapped his hands around the back of his head and puckered his lips he then stared at the small screen deep in thought contemplating his next move. Comforted by the reality of helping Mossad in bringing the killers of his sister to justice he reasoned why he should go through with the request. After all he had vowed to bring retribution to the filth who had carried out the barbaric act in the cause of a disturbed dogma. '*my god he gasped what if these people are not legitimate but indeed terrorists, they could unleash hell.*' He contemplated why international terrorists would want call records and therefore access to this data and could it only serve good as a means to routing out the perpetrators of desperate acts of violence.

Hugo stared at the photograph of Sarah on his bedside table, his eyes filled with tears, he loved this innocent little girl and then she spoke to him in his head, a telepathy from beyond the grave, a manifestation to the undying and beautiful bond between them. A warmth seeped through his inner being as he heard the words in his head '*help catch these animals to prevent the deaths of other little brothers and sisters*' Hugo's brain was working overtime dissecting the scenarios.

The binary reckoning of his brain deferred to the trash bin of his mind any illogical scenarios and outcomes.

He concluded that hacking the TET server would only benefit good and dismissed that this intel would give any rogue organisation an upper hand.

His mind made up he grabbed the laptop from the edge of the bed and with a few well considered key strokes he initiated the mission to gain access to the TET server. Attaining entry would be one thing an ever bigger challenge would be to complete the task un noticed

Several hours, four tins of full fat Coke and three chocolate bars later Hugo was staring at his screen in full readiness to log on as David Moss, all he needed was his password.

The high level security of the system was configured to generate passwords on a random basis which could then be changed by the user.

Although the password may change, its fundamental background information would remain. This allows two things: firstly, that the password is given to the correct recipient and in the event of a login error, the system has a means to validate the user. He knew that he would be unable to guess the password to undertake his final task to generate the current list of validation criteria."

Moving to another computer, he opened up an algorithm he had developed many months ago. Into the programme he put date of birth, place of birth, mother's maiden name, and a whole host of typical personal security information. Probably could then be assigned to each entry field, both manually and from anecdotal and historical information. The algorithms made connections between the data, for example it would work using the mother's maiden name and favourite film etc.

On a third PC, Hugo trawled the usual websites for information on David Lesley Thomas Moss. The beauty of the information highway is the access to volumes of information, but the downside is the sheer wall of words and facts one had to sift through. What Hugo needed was the crib. This one phrase, the golden bullet which would start the process and allow him to look at options on validation data. There was nothing too sensational about this man: grammar school education, son of a mechanical engineer, a first in Engineering from Imperial College, London that provided the golden link to him gaining acceptance on a the much-revered management training scheme provided by an international manufacture of domestic consumables.

A succession of many job moves saw David Moss move up the ranks to eventually head up a division of a major oil company where he entered the field of corporate governance. Subsequent appointments involved corporate governance of TET and one of the "big five' accountancy firms, to name a few. He met Eileen White, at a Young Conservative event in London back in 1982. Two years later they were married, and over the years had two children, Victoria and James. One son, George a little angle, died at six days. A heart-breaking event which today evoked deep emotions and strengthened the loving bond between David and Eileen.

Hugo gasped. Little George: date of birth, date of death, days, hours… Yes, yes, yes, he stuttered with excitement. What he now had to do was run the algorithm of different permutations of inputs. But not TET yet, he exclaimed, banging the table.

He looked around.

'I'll try and find out the more sensitive login information from Moss', he thought. He was not a Facebook/Twitter person, but he would have store cards, airline card, loyalty cards. Hugo doubted he would use the information relative to George for less important accessible requirements, but he would be able to test other inputs.

Hugo needed to stop. He was hungry; he craved food. His belly was rumbling. He had to have time out to re boot up his own logical analytical process. Hugo left his machine switched on, locked his bedroom and ran downstairs to the kitchen.

"Hugo! What have I told you about running down those stairs? One day you'll fall and kill yourself."

Realising what she had said, she put her head in her hands and burst into tears.

"And where would Dad and I be without you both?" she stammered through a sentimental proclamation.

All of a sudden Hugo, the man on a mission, was arrested by his mother's emotional circumstance. She connected to his heart via the loss of Sarah. He felt a surge of empathy so unstoppable, he ran to his mother and hugged her tightly. He too was in tears by now, and though mildly sobbing, he expressed his love for his family and that he would do nothing to upset Mum or Dad.

She stood up from her chair and hugged Hugo hard, and for a moment in time they were united in their grief. It was only for a moment, as characteristically, task-orientated Hugo commenced his quest for food – and fast food it had to be. He was on a mission.

Releasing the hold on his mother, she almost fell to the floor before shuffling back into her chair. His mother almost abandoned, physically and emotionally, Hugo headed for the cream-enamelled breadbin on the granite worktop near the vast freestanding American-style refrigerator. Flipping up the top, he grabbed three slices of white bread, walked across to the toaster and commenced fabricating cheese on toast. The method was fool proof: bread in the toaster, grated cheese melted in the microwave. While this act of culinary master class was in progress, he walked over to the huge double-door fridge and grabbed a litre-bottle of orange juice. Placing the juice on the tray, toast on the plate, melted cheese on the toast: no heated words needed in the kitchen to produce a masterpiece in wonderful cuisine, he reflected.

Tray in hand, he kissed his mum and made his way back to his bedroom. He closed the door, placing the meal on the bed, and settled by his PC, concurrently grinding on the cheese on toast. Hugo started the task of seeking an easy-to-vanquish website used by the esteemed prime minister's husband.

Eureka! he uttered through teeth covered in half-eaten cheese. He had a store card, of an old middle-class reliable department store. It was almost obligatory to hold this esteemed loyalty card to be allowed into any notable dinner party within Hampstead or St John's Wood.

He set up a new account on the website in the name of David Moss, logged in on the setup another twenty-four accounts with different permutations of David Lesley Thomas Moss. He used a phantom IP addresses so the loyalty site would see several different applications from all over the world. Also, Hugo was able to apply for accounts at different times in the past and present to avoid alerting the store card to any levels of activity.

An hour had passed and he had 24 accounts, all containing at least two of the names and a whole host of memorable words. The exercise allowed Hugo to test for memorable questions and a strong inclination for what would be asked in a "forgotten password" scenario. He tested this on several of his fictional accounts and they all provided an outcome. The majority of accounts had elected for 'storecard'.com email, he assumed that David Moss would adopt the same email protocol. He was an important man surrounded by high levels of security, so he was subject to sensitive information. Surely, he would not offer his own email account, but elect to use the store client server for the purpose of the loyalty scheme. This would ring-fence his retail activity well away from his business and public office life.

Hugo sat back, crossed his arms over his head, glared at the 'storecard' login page, and pondered his next move. In fact, his next move was the third piece of crumbling toast and cheese on the plate.

Scoffing down the final remnants of his master feast, he was about to pass off as the husband of the UK Prime Minister.

“Fuck you,” he muttered on a cheesy breath.

“My little sister is dead because of your wife’s governmental inaction.”

The time had come to act. He logged in, password needed, and proceeded to go through the whole reset routine. He knew the probably of the questions and he prepared the answers, and within six and a half minutes he was logged in to David Lesley Thomas Moss’s loyalty account.

He clicked onto ‘my settings and preferences’ afforded the vengeful hacker a full inventory of old passwords, memorable names, important places and all transactions on his Moss’ account.

Hugo proceeded to log into David Moss’ TET account and interrogated preferences and personal information. In addition, he was now able to obtain clues to what validation data TET required.

In a large organisation such as TET the validation process was materially the same for a mere ‘mom and pop’ customer and the Chairman.

All of the data gathered from his intelligence exercise was ‘plugged’ into an algorithm and the results enabled Hugo to understand what verifications he needed to access the TET account of the husband of the UK Prime Minster

Hugo placed his hands onto his knees and wiped the sweat onto his denims. An emotional glance at the photo of Sarah validated his next move.

“This is for you little sis” he uttered in an almost tearful proclamation

Within 4 minutes and 28 seconds he was logged into David Moss’ high level encrypted account. TET were unaware of this intervention and it would remain off the radar in perpetuity.

He remained on the site for 63.82 seconds and in this period performed a brief but targeted ‘reccy’ gaining visibility to all aspects of the organisation. Thoroughly satisfied that he could now meet and offer Mosad the Trojan horse they so highly sought; in fact, more like a microorganism than a Trojan horse, he thought, clapping his hands. Job done. TET would never know.

He did not know that 86 miles away in GCHQ Cheltenham his activities had been flagged up on Grace Wells' screen.

Chapter 13

Sat in his high-back hand-finished leather office throne, Guy swivelled twenty degrees left and twenty degrees right and surveyed his team on the trading floor through the glass-panel wall. Contemplating the next move, little did he know what was about to happen.

Richter had issued Guy a new Nokia fully encrypted GPS phone as used by the security services and military. The device had a distinct ring just a boring monotone alert. It was Richter.

"Guy."

He placed the phone against his ear and swivelled back in his chair.

"Lukas. Nice to hear from you."

"Likewise, Guy. But to business. Can you and Michael meet me at Private PrimeJets's hanger, Biggin Hill, at 13.50 this afternoon? If you head for London heliport now, we'll have you both picked up. My Dauphin is en route as we speak."

Nice, thought Guy, Eurocopter Dauphin three and a half million Euros, twin pilot full IFR.

"Ok, I'm on my way. Do I need anything?"

"No, only you and Michael."

The phone clicked to end the conversation.

The captain of the Dauphin gave a thumbs up to proceed for the rotors-running embarkation of his passengers. Guy always found this thrilling, helicopters so visceral. The noise, the air movement, and the fact they defied the laws of physics and finance.

The two orange-vested loaders ushered Stuch and Guy towards the pulsating machine and the aroma of burning Jet A1 evoked wonderful memories for Guy.

Belted in, headsets positioned, door secured, the captain wound up the throttles, pulling on the collective and the four-tonne machine gracefully hovered taxi towards the departure point. Pointing to the River Thames, the helicopter lifted to approximately eight feet from the ground, the nose tipped forward and they transitioned away to the north east. The twin turbo power plants pushed the luxury aircraft effortlessly to seven hundred and fifty feet. Under strict instruction of West Drayton, the helicopter made a climbing turn to a heading of 150, a direct route into Biggin Hill.

During the twenty-five-minute flight Stuch and Guy passed pleasantries but were very much aware of the need to maintain silence in all matters relating to business. Guy felt the helicopter slow and commence the final approach to the commercial airfield and, as a pilot himself, he had an understanding of what was going through the captain's thought process. The dark grey machine made a perfect helipad approach to the north H at Biggin Hill, then hovered taxi over to the Prime Jets terminal.

Guy noticed Richter's Gulfstream at station on the apron. A perfect touchdown and the two passengers were ushered away from the helicopter by three ground staff. Guy and Michael were taken through the two sets of glass doors into a reception area furnished with an array of black, grey and claret leather chairs and sofas cushioned on a granite-coloured commercial Wilton carpet. To complement the seating facilities were an array of coffee tables, newspaper racks, and a free, unmanned cocktail bar in the far corner.

On the two sides of the reception were four meeting rooms, two kitted out with sofas, two with formal boardroom-style tables, each framed by twelve black leather and chrome chairs. In one of the informal rooms, sitting on the sofa, was Lukas Richter.

Today he was casually dressed in a plain black tee-shirt and light blue expensive-looking jeans.

Richter gestured for his visitors to join him and ascended from his seat to open the door.

"Good afternoon, gentlemen. Please be seated."

Guy sat opposite, and Stuch to the left of Richter.

"Well, let's get to business,"

Richter said as he sat down in a comfortable leather chair.

"My intelligence reliably informs me there has been an almighty screw-up at TET and the lid is about to blow."

Guy looked at Stuch, who was staring intently at Richter.

"We're talking major shit, my friends. Someone at a very senior level had his account hacked and very soon there will be an enormous data leak. We are talking personal data, which may be readily available to all and sundry, but there's also information related to key corporate governance matters. Now, it gets me juicy."

"Please tell me more, Lukas," Guy was enthused.

"Well, it appears that one senior executive – I'm talking top, top – has been a little carefree with his password recovery validation data. It's transpired that some minor hack got into this big-hitter's account via his online shopping account. It gets better. Then man in question is David Moss, husband of your Prime Minister."

Guy exhaled, rocked back.

"Bloody hell. This is going to hit the TET share price."

Richter put his elbows on his knees and looked intently at Guy.

"Precisely, Guy. We're going to short TET large."

Guy looked at Stuch, and behind his dark blue eyes he concluded that the brain was already working on strategies.

"Now, all the City is expecting are robust numbers for TET, a prediction that their German mobile interest has outperformed expectations. Furthermore, there have been renegotiated debt costs and the use of cash reserves for future investment in high fibre rollout."

Stuch, leant forward and piped up.

"Coupled with solid customer retention figures and general important business sector, the boys in red braces have been very bullish," he declared.

"Well, we know different. My assessment is that the anticipation of a favourable performance is yet to be priced into the stock, I say plus ten percent, on the basis we'll have no issue in writing contracts with a low margin to buy shares from a strong short position. What do you think?" Richter asked his aids.

Guy thought, looked at Stuch, and replied,

"Well, let's say there's a ten percent potential uplift, so one's predicting, say a hundred and ten value, we offer eighty-five to ninety. Then we get the short in at, say, sixty to sixty-five."

"I agree, but let's say eighty, and we sell then at a hundred and replace at sixty-five, making double bubble."

Stuch added,

"Ok," said Richter.

"This is the plan. Through our Frankfurt, London, New York, Singapore offices we need to transact four billion dollars. This has to be spread out thinly so as to reduce our visibility. We buy short sell contracts to place, based on the expected good fortune."

"And funding this, Lukas?" enquired Guy.

"That's not your concern, Guy. You will have a billion dollars in your account in the morning. Get to work, gentlemen. The key to this is to spread the work around. Guy, this is where I need your input. Get to work on your contacts. Two million here, three million there. And gentlemen, this is between us. Finally, the profits are being earmarked for a big one. A really big one. But we'll say no more that this stage. It goes without saying, leverage the cash back at least four-to-one. Time is critical. We need to get contracts to sell and place now as anticipation in the market builds. It's about a time horizon of ten days. I expect the big bad news in ten days. So start thinking about those short contracts. Any questions?"

"No," said Guy.

"Not at all," muttered Stuch.

"I believe your chopper is ready to take you back to London."

There was silence all the way back to Battersea, there was only the whooshing of the perfectly balanced articulated helicopter blades.

Back in the office, Guy and Michael made a beeline straight to the boardroom.

"How many contracts are you good for, Michael?"

questioned Guy.

"I reckon I've contracts both ways for, say, seventy to eighty million."

"I can get a bit more if I call a few old mates," said Guy. "Each of the trades are good for, say, twenty million each, so we're a bit short," he said, with a modicum of panic in his voice.

"Ok," said Stuch, "we may need some help from your friends from the North London community."

"I don't get you."

"The Jewish community."

"Ok, I see. Do you have any contacts with those boys?"

"Yes, I do."

"Good thinking. We can do a little syndication with them. I also have some friends who move stock."

"It's still not enough," asserted Stuch. "We need a friendly investment banker. One that brings in the big boys."

"I may have the man," Guy said, looking for affirmation from Stuch. The cold German just nodded.

Guy bit his bottom lip and shook his head and looked into the blue eyes of his adjutant.

"I know just the man, just the very man," he rejoiced with authority.

He needed to score with the German, and gain credibility to more than justifying his involvement. After all, Stuch was Richter's man.

Stuch's granite appearance warmed a little as he smiled in approval at Guy's momentary superiority.

"I always knew you would have the answer, Guy," the German said with a mildly sarcastic approval, and for that moment Guy felt he had won over the cool German.

Leaning forward and tapping his mobile, he continued on his quest to triumph over the German,

"I'll make my call now." he said,

His tongue brushing over his very expensive upper dental work, Guy raised his gaze towards Michael Stuch, stood up, grabbed his phone and reaffirmed his governance. He announced in the style of a true leader,

"I will have this in the bag before tomorrow this time. Now, Michael, my friend, get on your phone and whip up your contracts. We need another quarter billions of contracts by close of play tomorrow."

"Yes, sir, consider it done," Stuch replied in an almost obedient tone reminiscent of a subordinate military officer in a black and white war movie.

Guy closed his office door behind him and with his back to the trading floor, tapped out a sequence of numbers into his phone. Placing the device to his right ear, he was welcomed with the soft New York tones of,

"Guy, how the hell are you? I thought you had disappeared."

"Not me, my friend," he replied. "I'm out in the big bad world reinventing myself. How are you Steve?"

"Life's good at Red Dawn Capital."

"Still playing with those big bully Russian investors?"

"Well, Guy, I have to say, they still have a pile of money, and there is a wall of Dollars in the east awaiting the right deal. My issue is London's property market is flat and Dubai is giving pretty useless yields at the moment. You know me, Guy, old school trader. I like full on high arbitrage deals. So what's with you, man? Are you still playing around with mid to low end UK leverage shit?"

"No, Steve. I've opened a desk in London for Richter. I was knocked over when he approached me; as you New York Italians say, he made me an offer I couldn't refuse."

"Fuck me, man. You're soaring with the eagles. I don't know how he does it – sixth sense doesn't even attempt to describe it. My investors have made most of their money from doubtful activities and they now want good returns on their clean cash. The current landscape is offering nothing like the returns they seek. As you know, our mafia friends from Russia have pushed most of the cash into Israeli-based instruments. Being Jewish, they avoid any investment in properties in Dubai and the rest of the Middle East."

"I need something juicy for them," Steve expressed with a huff of desperation, "or I'll just be running property and blue-chip yield stuff for the good old city boys."

"Steve, I've got a big one for you: a short on a very big English blue chip, and option to go long too, as the market expecting a good result. But somehow Richter has a different view."

"Tell me more, Guy, you old fox. Let's meet at Handell House, say four o'clock this afternoon?"

"You're on, my friend. Consider it a date."

"Good afternoon, Mr Walker. Nice to see you back as a member."

These were the words that raised Guy six inches in height. He was back. He had returned to the stage where he would act out the final world-beating performance. Adjusting his cuffs, he replied, "Nice to be back, Mohammed," and patted the maître d' on the left shoulder.

"I have your favourite window table reserved, sir."

"Perfect," replied Guy.

As he walked through the dining room, he passed the green leather circular banquets which curved around the tables in the centre of the room. The tables were beautifully dressed in white linen, playing centre stage to the best food and exquisite wine which would lubricate high finance and deals. Mohammed retracted a bottle green leather-backed chair and Guy sat down at the table set for two positioned by the floor-to-ceiling period sash windows overlooking Portland Square.

The position allowed him a view of the entrance. Guy remarked, "this place has not changed a bit, but I have. This will surprise you, my friend: sparkling water, please."

"Sir, when I heard you were coming, I prepared to cool a nice bottle of 2000 Montrachet for you," Mohammed expressed with surprise.

"No more, my good friend. No more, I'm afraid. But your beautiful food is well truly in my sights."

Mohammed nodded, and reclaimed the wine list and turned to procure the non-alcoholic beverage. He took two steps and Guy intervened.

"Ah, but Mohammed, my guest, who you'll recognise, will no doubt need something stronger when he comes in. Please leave the list."

Guy, swivelling his iPhone between the fingers of his right hand, surveyed the eighteenth-century room, which had been tastefully decorated and furnished with a blend of period and contemporary design. This was an environment in which he thrived; a venue where he played out his best performances. He was a natural storyteller, and the sacred eighteen hundred square feet was where he would make his greatest curtain call. He smiled, looked out the window, and in his mind's eye, imagined the day he would collect the keys from one of the two-bedroom apartments which graced the Square.

Was he dreaming? No, he was playing out to the end what would be a red-carpet performance. Guy Walker was set to become one of the private equity community's big stars. His hand prints were about to be cemented into the industry 'Walk of Fame' for eternity. He was elated by what was in prospect and was about to metaphorically put pen to paper on his own story.

"Guy! How the hell are you?" shouted Steve Gibson in his American drawl.

Guy was extracted from the quantum existence in his parallel universe.

"Don't get up – I'm sitting right down. I've already checked in and your man is bringing me a scotch and soda. It's on its way."

Steve Gibson looked the archetypical 1980s Wall Street trader who had outlived the numerous boom-bust cycles of the last thirty years. He had survived, unlike some of the young bucks who had started with him on the trading floor back in Lehman Brothers, New York 1982. He was a good-looking man in his late fifties and the blue eyes and boyish smile were crowned with a full head of greyish hair, slightly longer than regulation, deliberately slicked back in the style of Gordon Gecko in the movie *Wall Street*. Steve had moved to London in 2004 to head up the oil desk at a major investment bank. He was known to be a risk-taker, a solo flyer who pushed the limits, and dabbled at the edge of the regulations. Twice investigated for potential insider trading, his employer could no longer be seen to have an operator in their new cleaner-than-clean format. They paid for one of their best white-collar crime lawyers to get him out of the crossfire of the FSA and the CPS. This was, however, his Waterloo, and he was let him go with an undisclosed payoff.

In his inimitable Wild West style, Steve saddled up and ran out towards frontiers new. He did not head into the gold rush of the West, but the East, and the emerging markets in Latvia, Estonia, Lithuania and the Ukraine. This was a land of opportunity, awash with freshly laundered money from underhand Mafia operations. Also, there was money for large property and infrastructure projects, which proved irresistible to Steve. Huge returns were made, but countered with immeasurable risk, not only to one's balance sheet, but possibly to one's life.

Steve's aggressive approach and fearless and insatiable desire to make money delivered him great success. In addition, his charming character and ruthless attitude attributed to drink, drugs and fast women, gained him a reputation of a man to have a good time with. He made many friends; friends who, without doubt, would have become dangerous enemies once the rich seam of lucrative deals and wild living became barren. Steve returned to the UK six years later to a seed change in market. Hot money was flooding into the UK to find large property projects, leveraged by low interest rates and asset prices which had been depressed by the financial shock two years prior.

For those who had the backing of a large cash pile it was a land of milk and honey, and through complex financial structures and vehicles, his prior misdemeanours would have been forgotten. With his complex money paths and contacts in the East, he sanitised the products of dubious activities and turned them into gilt-edged legitimate returns. At the same time, he opened up the growing London property market, a safe haven for his client's ill gains and genuinely earned profits.

The tightening of money laundering and increased due diligence introduced by FCA on foreign investment, and the softening London market, did not bode well with the community of investors who had enjoyed very exciting returns and critically an opportunity to convert blood money into bricks and mortar. He had looked at opportunities in Africa, in particular Zimbabwe; however, the fearless and highly imaginative Gibson was not prepared to trust his fortune and life with a bunch of ruthless crooks who had an insatiable appetite for money and the spilling of human blood.

"Guy. It's so good to see you back where you belong. We all know this place is your grazing ground."

"Well, Steve,"

Guy paused and took a sip of water and he placed the glass back onto the table continued.

"I've a big 'play' for you. It's too good to be true. It's a big blue-chip British institution. The market is expecting robust earnings from the last quarter, the Company has a good strategy, and stable products in growing markets. Our initial intel, however, is that there is not a headwind but a cyclone approaching, and we see a huge opportunity to play a big short."

Guy had grabbed Gibson's attention and the American leaned forward, he was keen to hear more of

"You want cash from me, Guy? I thought Richter had bottomless resources."

"No, Steve, I need you to create liquidity in the stock. I want you to set up long and short positions on this particular asset."

"What asset Guy I cannot figure out a plan until you tell me the target" Gibson replied with a tone of excitement in his voice.

Guy pushed his right hand out in a move to stall Gibson.

"We can be bullish at the moment, as the market expects a good return with a ten percent arbitrage opportunity on the upside. But here comes the rub. We will short by thirty percent. Work out the maths. Steve, use your cash and your contacts. Wine, dine, blackmail – do what the fuck you need to do, but I need one 'Bill' access to stock, but without any vis."

Gibson thrust his arms out across the table and looked Guy straight in the eye.

"Ok Guy who are we stalking"

Guy leaned forward and with a deliberate look, whispered

"TET"

Gibson recoiled in his chair and threw his arms behind his head,

"What? You're crazy. T E Fucking T?" he ranted in his New York accent. "T Bloody T? Are you mad? You short TET, it would be suicide. Well, for me, I would not need to take my own life, it would be taken out of my hands."

"Trust me, Steve. When this is over, there's another big one in the pipeline."

"But Guy –"

"No 'but Guy…' Are you in, my old buddy? Say yes, and let's order some risotto."

Smoothing back his greying hair with both his hands, he rolled his eyes from left to right, then fixed his soft blue boyish eyes at Guy, grinned, and said,

"Risotto it is. And a bottle of cold white."

Chapter 14

Captain Russell Oliver scanned the horizon and surveyed the instrument cluster, then he visually locked on to the primary display system of the Gulfstream G550. It had been a long flight, assisted by his trusty first officer he commenced the pre-landing checks and routines.

Unlike the days on the large airlines, they would be making a VFR approach to a landing site on a remote private airstrip. Visual Flying Regulations were fully necessary for two reasons, the primary one being that the receiving airstrip had no instrument landing capabilities, and the second consideration was the GS550 N55628 needed to remain off radar as much as possible.

He had mentally pushed through the alarms and warnings which aurally and physically announced the transition from automatic pilot to manual controls.

"I have control, Russ," First Officer Tom Stevens gave the assertive signal that the Gulfstream was now in his competent hands, a twenty-two-thousand-hour pilot.

Captain Oliver pressed the intercom switch on the control column.

"Cabin, prepare for landing in ten minutes. Clear conditions. There are no issues to anticipate."

In the rear cream leather seat, Lukas Richter fastened his seatbelt and pressed his head back into the soft napa upholstered headrest. Ten minutes later, the twenty-five-million-euro jet was tracking down a private tarmac airstrip, seventy-five kilometres south of Parzana in the Argentinian province of Entire Rios. The aircraft rolled out on the perfectly manicured runway, which was set in a clearing framed with some of the last remaining Yatay palms in the area. As the aircraft turned to taxi, Captain Oliver became visual with two other executive jets: A Swiss registered bombardier S Global and an Estonian registered Gulfstream S550, both very capable long-range luxury aircraft.

Oliver applied the parking brake and shut down the two rear mounted turbo fans, which both flamed out to an unpowered slow rotation. With the first officer performing the shutdown checks, Oliver turned to Juliet the cabin assistant and announced.

"J I am unlatching the door and lowering the steps so we will be out within a minute"

Juliet patted Oliver on the shoulder turned and walked through the low headroom cabin towards her passengers.

"Herr Richter Captain Oliver has unlatched the door we are just about ready to depart"

"Thank you, Juliet, and pass my thanks to the pilots for a trouble free flight" replied Richter

This was the for Richter, he unbuckled his lap strap, stood up, stretched, and collected his cream linen suit jacket and light brown leather briefcase. It had been a long flight through the night; however, this version of the aircraft was equipped with a rear stateroom and bed. Luckily, he had managed seven hours sleep but he needed a shower.

The door opened, and with a definitive clunk and the powered steps were disengaged from the flight position. It was February, and therefore summer south of the Equator. As the door opened, the cold conditioned cabin air was greeted with the warm and humid ambiance from the outside.

Richter stepped out of the door and stood on the top step, stylishly positioning a pair of chrome-framed Ray Ban Aviators to shade his blue eyes from the local sun. He held his case with his right arm, jacket over his shoulder, and with his eyes adjusted through the mirrored non-polarised glass, he descended down the dark red carpet-covered treads of the access steps.

"Lukas, welcome *meine fruenden bist du glucklich*," roared an elderly man dressed in a white linen suit, powder blue shirt, and a Panama hat which sheltered his thinning grey hair from the midday sun.

Richter waved in acknowledgement and the man in the linen suit approached the bottom of the stairs to greet Richter.

The conversation which ensued was transacted in perfect Haute Deutsche

"Gunter, it is good to see you, my friend," Richter announced with a degree of joy.

As Richter stepped onto the smooth concrete apron, Gunter Schmidt wrapped his arm around Richter in a strong embrace. Gunter's golden tanned hand contrasted against his guest's crumpled white linen shirt. On the third finger of that golden hand was a silver snake ring.

"Lukas. It's good to see you. It has been too long. Our friends are looking forward to spending time together over the next few days."

"Gunter. Yes, it has been too long. But as you know, I've been very busy, ja?"

"Well, my friend, the car is waiting to take us to the farmhouse, you'll be able to freshen up and rest for a while."

As Richter climbed into the back of the Mercedes M-Class, cold air in the vehicle brushed his face, a feeling he welcomed. He was never at ease in hot climates.

His luggage was firmly placed in the back of the vehicle, the driver pressed the power tailgate button and proceeded to take up his position as captain of the testimony to German engineering.

"Well, Lukas, please give me an update on our next move in the great plan to complete the task started many decades ago."

"Gunter, we'll soon be taking controlling positions in the required assets, and then we need to agree a plan of action from there onwards."

"Well, my friend, let's discuss this with our associates once you've had time to recover from your journey."

The black Mercedes limo decelerated and approached a large pair of steel gates, shouldered by white concrete pillars establishing the entrance to the hacienda *Los Chinos*. The black vehicle halted at the gate and a swarthy man holding a well worn black machine gun signalled to his accomplice who controlled the gates. The black steel barriers opened inwards and the car turned into a long driveway bordered by well-maintained poplar trees. Either side of the road was a combination of Pampas, green fields and areas of palms. Eight hundred metres from the end of the drive was a large, sprawling, and single-storey cream painted Argentinian style farmhouse. The transport arrested its motion with precision, next to the entrance to the building and two men appeared.

The first was an Argentinian man in black trousers and a short white tunic, Richter presumed that he was obviously a servant of some description. The second figure was a more menacing, six-foot, fit-looking man in his mid-thirties. He was dressed in cream chinos, a tight-fitting white short-sleeved shirt which accentuated his tanned, well-toned biceps. Neatly tucked in his belt in the rear of his trousers was a Glock 13 automatic pistol. On the third finger of his left hand was a silver coiled snake ring!

Gunter disembarked from the car, and followed by Richter, walked into the building, acknowledging the muscle, not the man in the tunic. The entrance hall was large, with a solid dark hardwood floor. The odour of wax revealed that the surface had recently been polished by one of the ten staff employed at the farmhouse. In the centre of the hall was a four-metre round wooden table on which an array of porcelain vases filled with water which offered the last remaining essence of life to a beautiful arrangement of white lilies.

On the periphery of the hall were a number of doors, and in the absence of windows, six ceiling fans offered the only opportunity of air recirculation. A hundred and eighty degrees from the entrance door were two wooden-framed, glass panelled doors leading on to a large room. Scattered around the walls were paintings and sketches of polo games, pampas grasslands, sympathetically complemented with black and white photographs of Buenos Aires.

"Come here, Lukas," barked Gunter, as he led him to the double doors, which were in the act of being opened by a rather large and overweight man in his seventies. The proxy doorman was wearing a pair of dark blue trousers and a long-sleeved white shirt. His facial expression clearly illuminated, vindication that he knew Richter.

He proffered a rather chubby hand, the root of four rather fat, stubby fingers. Richter responded and the hands met, resulting in a firm and vigorous handshake.

"Lukas, it is so good to see you. Your excellent work for the cause is beyond the call of duty," he said in High German.

"Friedrich, my friend, it's so good to see you and of course these achievements would be impossible without your support and dedication to the cause," Richter responded in the same outdated and often avoided dialect.

Friedrich ushered his guest into the large open-plan living room, where in the centre lived four large brown leather sofas positioned at 12, 3, 6 and 9 o'clock around a very large glass coffee table. Assembled on one of the two sofas were two middle aged men, and seated on another were two men of more advanced years. They were engaged in a lively conversation in the now-familiar *Haute Deutsch*, which was abruptly terminated when Friedrich shouted in a guttural tone, "Gentlemen! Comrades! Our final guest has arrived."

All four men stood up abruptly and simultaneously, two of them clicked their heels in concert. The oldest of the four men, a balding, grey-haired, slightly overweight individual, greeted Richter with open arms.

"Lukas. It's so good to see you. I suppose that you want to freshen up. We have much to talk about." He clasped his hands together. His left wrist flaunting a solid yellow gold Rolex Oyster Day Date; on the index finger of his left hand a coiled snake ring.

Richter acknowledged the greeting and responded,

"Hermann, Michael, Andreas, Johann it is so good to see you all. I have much to report. Things are moving forward at a pace and we need to agree the next step. Please excuse me for an hour, I will need to refresh."

Led by Hermann, the balding grey man who welcomed Richter, all four men sat down on their respective sofas. On the glass table, there were six identical cream dossiers, each with an eagle on the top right-hand corner and in bold black type on the left side of the front page were the words, 'Operational Stinging Serpent' overprinted in red letters, 'strictly confidential'.

On the other side of the World, in the sleepy town of Cheltenham, Grace Wells was studying a series of abnormal communications transacted on the TET central server. One relay in particular puzzled her: why had David Moss logged in to the high-level server and needed to validate his password? Since the spurious reference to TET in connection with the Arena killings, on the instruction of Leyton, Grace had configured watching software to find and track odd traffic from the main TET server.

She looked at the screen and tapped her fingers on the desk. '*Why? she said to herself. What the F?*'

She had been alerted to the activity of a main board member indeed the PM's husband' and the need for him to validate his password. Goliath, the supercomputer at Cheltenham, flagged up this activity not only because it was TET but because it was configured to flag up any activity relating to the PM's family or close associates. This was normal security protocol with senior government members and their immediate families. She was puzzled more by the fact that the login had, on the face of it, not come from a computer not in the UK network, and was fully aware David Moss was at Chequers with the Prime Minister.

This was not normal behaviour, she thought, and decided to dig deeper into the activities connected to Moss and TET.

She called Freddie at the IT department.

"Fred, my lad. This is a level four from above. I need a drill down on unusual and abnormal traffic from the PM's old fella and any big news from TET."

"Give me five, Grace, and I'll have it up to you."

"Cheers, Fred. And keep this to yourself, my fella."

"Wilco, my dear girl. And do you fancy a beer at 131s later?"

"Maybe tomorrow?"

"Sounds like a plan, my old friend."

Grace Wells logged in to a different subdivision of the server and typed in 'David Lesley Thomas Moss'. She then added new accounts, passwords, validations, Trans Euro Telecom password change, date of birth, validation phrases. Wells impatiently tapped her digits again on her desk as she awaited the data to illuminate the two flat screens.

On the seventh appeasing tap she was presented with a wall of information on one screen, and the rolling listing of emails on the left-hand monitor.

"My goodness," she muttered. "Where do I start?"

She furiously grabbed and unfolded the pages of an A4 pad, and removing the pencil from between her teeth, she started scribbling diagrams. The output was a series of boxes and arrows: TET, David Moss, Lesley Moss, password validation, login request.

'Why did Moss forget his password for one of the most secure servers in the private sector?' she ruminated.

Parking that line of thought for a moment, she received a list of new account openings from the past seven days, they included the four names of the PM's spouse. She scrolled down David Thomas Lesley Moss. There was a welter of applications for new credits cards, email account openings, car registration, and driving licence applications, and even a declaration of personal bankruptcy. The activity was unrelated except applied name permutation only.

Then, as she scrolled down pages of random electronic traffic, a trend was exposed. In the last twelve hours there had been multiple accounts opened in what appeared to be an abundant combination of the four names. There was no visibility of where the applications were posted; however, a major high street store appeared several times.

"Yes!" she screamed, "There's something here!" and slammed the pencil down on the desk. She turned around and caught the attention of Tommy Leyton, who was sitting behind the desk in his office.

She interrupted Leyton on one of the many occasions when he had placed his feet on his desk, wrapped his arms behind his head, and stared blankly into space.

"I'm thinking," he would always retort.

"I get paid to think. And how I go about it is my business."

Grace waved at Tom, who awoke from his semi dream and signalled for her to come into his office.

"Tom, we need access to a high street store main server. Can you pull some strings and get us clearance?" she asked.

"It'll be difficult without pulling the Fat Controller's braces."

Grace explained what she had observed and the strange trend in credit card applications.

"I buy it, Grace. Give me some time, and I'll get you in at Bracknell. Can you source the point of application?"

"No, Gov, they're all ghosts, including the first lady's request for password validation."

Leyton smirked at the reference to the first lady; the whole country was aware who wore the trousers in the Moss household. *It was only a pity she didn't adopt the same level of control with her rabble of treacherous cabinet.*

Grace returned to her desk and awaited clearance.

Call it a hunch Grace Wells elected to spend a bit more time and carry out due diligence on the TET activity.

She reclined in her chair and swilled the final drops of the sweet white coffee from the Bath Rugby mug.

About to take one last sip, she noticed a message appear on the screen.

The tired policewoman leaned forward, placed the mug on the desk, all of a sudden, she became transfixed with the illuminated words in front of him.

"Red Dawn Investments were trading high volumes of contracts in Trans Euro Telecoms shares"

'Ok these are popular shares, she held a number herself, however good trading was expected' she thought

'So why are Red Dawn taking large short positions which is counter intuitive to the market sentiment' she muttered.

What perplexed and alerted Wells was the involvement of Steve Gibson, the larger than life trader who employed underhand tactics and who remained as slippery as a snake and as dangerous as a shark.

The GCHQ chiefs were well aware of Gibson's alleged connections with a number of Russian underworld figures.

The report detailed an extensive list of e-mails and electronic communication, it appeared that Gibson was adopting a wide spread approach to the financial transactions, ordinarily this would keep such activity under the radar of the FCA.

Grace Wells was hungry for more information, and desperate to unearth more on she decided to access Gibson's telephone records.

The hold point to her enquiry was her lack of clearance to the required level, but she elected to bust the rules and use Laing's login code.

'*to hell with Laing'* she muttered *'that overgrown overweight in bred will never notice such an intrusion, he is blinded by claret skewed vision'* she added.

Wells tapped in the password' CHUKKA123', Laing's love of the polo set made it easy to guess, *well he liked hanging around the polo scene and getting drunk with his wealthy friends.* She smiled at the thought.

A few carefully chosen key strokes and the illicit and substitute Laing was presented with a list of calls to and from Gibson's mobile phone.

Amongst the wall of information, she was looking for the free radical a one off call, and there it was, 12.32 and 15 seconds and 13.51 and 56 seconds yesterday, to an UK mobile which belonged to Guy Walker.

Biting her bottom lip, she studied the finding, *'was this the electronic key she was looking for, the one to unlock the mystery'* she pondered.

She walked over to a neighbouring vacant desk and logged onto the pc, searched on google for Tornado Ventures LLP.

In a flash a very expensive looking website erupted onto the screen. Two taps of the 'our people' button and she was presented with the much hackneyed black and white 'power photo' of the senior team. Top centre was Lukas Richter, the Austrian with the Midas touch and one who had very secret deep pockets. This made sense to Grace as it was common knowledge that Richter was the architect of the short play.

'*but why TET it defies logic they are a safe bet, a highly profitable company'* she gasped

She scrolled down the page further and was presented with a very familiar face, Guy Walker, it was the same cool player who appeared in the photo on display in Tom Leyton's office.

Guy Walker was indeed an old friend of Tom Leyton, and old mate, ex drinking buddy and past best man.

'Surely Walker is not involved in any covert financial transactions. It was well known that Richter was a king maker.....an enigma, with insane levels of well-guarded funds.'

She closed down the computer, jumped up and headed towards Tom Leyton's office and muttered *'I need more on this man'*

Somewhere in her psyche she knew Walker and Richter were accomplices in some deceitful activities.

"Grace come over here please I have some very interesting info for you" barked Tom Leyton across the office.

Grace Wells was prickled with Leyton's highly audible demand and as an act of retaliation elected to take her Bath Rugby mug with her. This would hack off the Gloucester loving Leyton.

Armed with the mug she entered Leyton's office which enlisted a response.

"Now you can take that bloody thing out of my office" joked the 'Guvnor'

Leaning against the wall, Wells announced "I'm all ears Guv "

Rocking back in his chair Leyton commenced.

"Well I have chopped old baggy breeches out of the loop and gone straight to my old mate Johnnie in London"

He continued.

"I have a comprehensive list of all applications made for store cards within the last 48 hours."

"Here it is for you to get stuck into, passwords, date of birth, validation data, memorable names, places, and pets names the bloody lot"

Leyton smiled, he felt that he had demonstrated his value asserting his seniority in the organisation.

A not so celebratory Wells replied.

"thanks Guv, I will go and continue my detective work"

She nodded at Leyton as she left his office and headed over to her desk in the main office and sat down at the vacant workstation.

The GCHQ standard issue flat screen powered into life and requested the predictable login data and password inputs.

An orchestrated rattle of the dark grey keyboard and Wells was reunited with subversive world of cyber surveillance, 'the snoopers charter' for the benefit of the liberal press.

She opened a number of applications and a specialist programme which identified trends in data.

"BINGO"

She had to mute her voice in all of the excitement, in the moment of triumph.

The electronic routines had flagged up the numerous applications in various combinations of David Leslie Thomas Moss for store cards. Furthermore, the it was evident that the applications were made with validation data intrinsically the same as that used by Moss for access to the high level TET server.

She jumped up from the chair, and ran to Leyton's office, who noting the enthusiastic crusade signalled for his assistant to enter without delay.

A clearly enlivened Grace Wells close the door behind her and catching breath she spluttered.

"Tom, I have it, I bloody well have it, I believe I know what is happening"

Leyton rocked back in his chair, and manipulated the pencil, his surrogate Rothmans, between his dry lips. At moments like these he missed the relaxing and mind polarising effects of nicotine.

"I am all ears Grace fire away "

"This is my assessment Tom:

Leyton listened intensely.

"David Moss did not log into the TET server that is obvious, he has an alibi, and he would never forget his password. We have a ghost a hacker who attempted to login on two occasions and was eventually successful after presenting correct validation information."

Leyton leaned forward "and?"

Wells continued.

"Tom it is my opinion that some individual with the intention to go unnoticed has been through a routine which has allowed access to the highest echelons of the TET server, and this is the best bit they cloned David Leslie Thomas Moss.

"Ok I hear you but what is the motivation of our ghost"

"what are they trying to achieve" Leyton interjected.

"Well guv I have some other intel which is worthy of further scrutiny"

"Go on."

Grace Wells updated her boss with the knowledge she had on the connection between Steve Gibson and Lukas Richter.

Tom Leyton appeared mildly interested, however his mood was about suddenly change to one of concern.

"Tom, I have some other intel which I am not sure you will like" said Grace.

"Try me Grace, I am too old and ugly to be shocked by much these days" replied an indifferent Leyton.

"Well Tom it appears that your old friend Guy Walker is tied up in this"

A clearly surprised Leyton became silent.

He reflected on what Grace had told him, and decided that he needed to know more

"go on" he said with a disturbed tone.

"Well Tom he is associated with Tornado Ventures; you know that Richter fella"

"So what Grace the man has to earn a living what is the issue?" replied Tom Leyton.

"Ah but Tornado and in particular Walker are linked to Steve Gibson and this merry bunch seem to know something about TET we don't know, in fact what even TET do not know"

Tom Leyton was suddenly uncomfortable, he knew Walker well and hoped that this would not compromise his position at GCHQ.

"Tell me all you know Grace"

"What puzzles me is that Richter is predicting misfortune at TET, this flies in the face of current thinking, it is a solid company with an undervalued share price if anything." Said Grace Wells.

Tom Leyton was clearly unsettled at the potential involvement of one of his friends and the uneasiness was evident in his voice.

"Whaaat what do you think Guy's" he hesitated "I mean do you think he is in deep?" What are the angles here Grace?"

"Well Gov my guess is that Walker is being used as a conduit for Richter to the UK financial sector"

Wells paused and noted the concern on the face of the normally ebullient leader.

"My hunch is that is far as it goes he is the fall guy on the periphery only of something bigger and potentially more dangerous."

Leyton lingered deep in thought for a minute and responded.

"Perhaps we can bring Guy on board, I know him well he has his threshold to risk and if he senses that he is wrapped up in some covert act he will bottle it, I can almost guarantee that"

"And what perplexes me Gov is the veiled connection with the London terror acts, what are the motives ?.the links? I need to get my head round the whole thing Guv"

"Good work Grace, I need time to digest all this, attempt to understand the potential connection between arbitrage on TET and international terror, and crucially figure out how I can recruit Guy into our ranks"

"Ok Guv I will get back on the case and allocate effort to finding the source of the bogus Moss login"

As Grace Wells was leaving the office, her superior sighed.

"Get me more on Walker please, I want to know where he goes what he does who he does it with and what he is up to, and leave no stones unturned, understand?"

"Wilco" responded Wells, and she closed the office door, leaving her boss deep in thought.

Chapter 15

The immaculately presented Qatar Airways stewardess, offered a beige covered arm and gently tapped the shoulder of the sleeping Hugo.

Over the soothing ambient whirr of the Rolls Royce Trent engines, occasionally interspersed by the inimitable 'bongs' courtesy of the passenger call button, she whispered.

"40 minutes to landing sir, can I get you a coffee and a small snack?"

The weary traveller who had gained very little value from the faux sleep in the low pressure aluminium tube, powered his business class seat back to the landing mode.

He rubbed his eyes and shed the mediocre quality airline blanket in which he had been cocooned for 6 hours.

As a frequent flyer with parents who never 'turned right' this was not an alien habitat for Hugo.

Coffee and croissant consumed he grasped the seat arm rests as the Boeing 777 touched down on one of the warm asphalt runways which served Trivandrum Airport South West India.

It was 04.30 local time Saturday, the tired Hugo was warmed by the prospect of an undisturbed sleep when he arrived at the hotel, there was no lectures planned for the weekend.

The transit through immigration was seamless and at 05.20, he appeared though the gateway into the noisy, hot and bustling arrival hall.

Through the mass of bodies, he sought out and located the white board which displayed his name, Hugo signalled his presence and he was quickly united with his driver.

"Good morning sir my name is Seshi I will be taking you to your hotel"

Seshi relieved Hugo of the large grey case and ushered him out of the terminal into the warm early morning air and towards a black Audi saloon.

The trunk opened automatically and the perspiring Seshi deposited the case into the luggage space and closed the lid.

The driver dressed in black pants and a sweat soaked white short sleeved shirt, gestured to and opened the rear car door. Through the illuminated aperture which lead into the beautifully appointed, chilled interior, Hugo was surprised to see a passenger sat on the black leather seat.

The man was in his mid-thirties and welcomed Hugo in the unmistakeable accent of a citizen of Germany.

"Good morning Hugo my name is Hans; I will be accompanying you on your trip to India."

"Trip?" quizzed a very confused Hugo

"What about the Hotel?"

"Ah well we are not going to the hotel, we will now be driving to Madurai"

"Our plan has been moved forward we need to have our special meeting later today, so please get comfortable it is a tedious journey" requested the German.

Seshi now behind the wheel turned to Hugo

"There is fresh coffee and pastries in the central console please help yourself"

A startled Hugo sank into the soft seats and buckled his seatbelt in preparation of what would be at least a seven-hour drive.

Hugo was correct in his prediction, it was not to be an easy journey, the Indian freeways were notorious for rather atrocious road works. Fast flowing dual carriageways were without warning transformed into a scene reminiscent of the cratered fields of WW1 Flanders.

To add to the motorist's abject peril were tank like lorries, cows, camels and mopeds travelling the opposite way down the carriageway.

From and initial conversation Hugo had gathered that Hans was not fully briefed on the meeting, and was purely there in the capacity of protection of a valuable cargo. That cargo was Hugo Parnell.

The tiresome, seven and half hour journey eventually came to an end, and the Audi pulled up in a rammed back street which ran parallel to Station Road in the centre of Madurai the capital of Tamil Nadu state.

Seshi alighted from the driver's compartment, swiftly moved to the rear of the car and opened the passenger door exposing Hugo to the moist and putrid air from the market district of one of Southern India's largest cities.

Hans disembarked and joined Hugo at the rear of the car where Seshi was extracting the cases from the trunk.

"Come with me Hugo" barked Hans

The bewildered Hugo, obeyed and followed his presumed guardian. In the receding daylight which shone down the hectic alleyway, he had observed that his luggage was nestled between two black and aluminium hard cases similar to those used by the military to protect sensitive electronic equipment.

Hans closely followed by Hugo, pushed his way through the torrent of pedestrians and small motorcycles, only to encounter the trials of the shattered and cratered sidewalk.

They eventually arrived at a door adjacent to SPS Electricals, an open fronted garage like property packed full of boxes of electrical fittings together with reels of cable.

There was nothing unique about this store it fit the template of the numerous shabby and poorly presented retail units which populated the full length of the chaotic street.

Hugo was overwhelmed at the sheer volume and variety of rubbish which inhabited both the unmade road and the pavement. He was then shocked to see untethered cows as they wandered aimlessly around the streets.

The doorway opened onto a steep staircase lined with light blue walls desperate in need of maintenance, the dirty marks above the bannister line evidence of many years of service.

The three men ascended two flights of the poorly lit stairwell and on reaching the second floor Seshi stopped at a badly chipped brown painted door, which was encased behind a welded steel fence.

The door was embellished with a white notice informing the world that this was the entrance to the offices of AB Singh Engineering Consultants.

Hugo was hot and sweating profusely, and desperate for a drink of water.

Hans produced a key from his right hand pocket and unlocked the door which led into a lobby approximately three metres long with a single white door at the far end.

Hugo shuffled into the space and welcomed the breeze of cold conditioned air which kissed his sweat coated skin.

'It begged the question why such a scruffy hallway was clinically air conditioned' Hugo pondered.

Seshi closed the outer door from the staircase and Hans fiddled with a bunch of keys finally making the correct choice to open the white steel door.

As Hans manipulated the key the coiled snake ring on his left hand went unnoticed.

The German finally negotiated the high security lock and opened the white door to reveal a wall of white light that masked the contents of the room.

The trio were greeted with another waft of cold air as the entered the large open space.

Hugo was surprised by what he saw, the room and its contents were incongruent with its location in the back streets of an Indian city.

Pristine white walls bordered a space approximately eighty square meters enclosed with a high quality suspended ceiling furnished with neatly laid out high power lighting cells and ventilation grilles.

Securely planted on the dark grey carpet were an array of chrome and leather office chairs and six black melamine work stations each equipped with two flat screens and a black keyboard? In the far corner of the room was a locked glass partitioned room in which lived two black flashing servers connected to a myriad of cables.

At one of the work stations, sat two men of possibly European origin, one was dressed in a white button down collared short-sleeved shirt and Chinos, the second man wore a lightly chequered t shirt and black denim trousers.

Both men had blue eyes and short cropped blonde hair, Hugo observed that they were talking in fluent German.

Sat opposite the two Europeans was an Indian man whose complexion suggested he was a descendant of a higher caste, his frame and demeanour a testimony to a life shy of hard manual work.

The Indian man was engrossed with his work and fixated to a peculiar looking lap top, so much so he appeared to be oblivious to the recent entrants to the room. Hugo was not familiar with the computer, in fact, he had never seen the like of the chunky black machine encased in the fabricated aluminium protective container. He surmised that it could of military origin probably similar to the machines used to launch nuclear weapons.

Hans closed the door with a secure clunk which alerted one of the blonde haired men who arose from his seat.

"Hans it is good to see you, and you must be Hugo" he announced.

Hugo was a little bowled over to hear a supposed Israeli agent speak English with such an obvious German accent.

"Hugo I am Jacob Riemann of Mossad, yes and before you ask I am based in Germany in station at the Embassy."

"Intelligence gathered to date would have us believe that the terror cell we seek are embedded in Germany, in fact we believe that they are an evolution of the team who were involved with the bombing of the Pan Am 747."

"I apologise for any confusion but it is necessary that our agents maintain the ability to speak fluent German. My grandparents who were fortunate to escape Nazi Germany, passed on their native tongue to all of the children." Declared Jacob.

Hans took the perplexed Hugo by the arm and walked over to the desk where the industrious Indian was still engaged with the laptop.

"Hugo this is Sanji,"

The young Indian man stopped typing raised his head and offered out his hand.

Hugo and Sanji shook hands and all three men sat down around the space age lap top.

On the mark from Hans the other German joined the trio.

"Hello Hugo my name is Liv I too work on the German desk in Berlin."

"Ok let's get down to business" announced Jacob.

"We have a strong reason to believe that the British Government is withholding vital information and mobile phone transactions, linking one of our known terror groups to the Wembley Arena killings"

He continued.

"Our covert access to GCHQ has been limited and we run the constant risk of being discovered"

"access to GCHQ wow that is impressive "piped up Hugo

"We have re thought our approach and have decided to focus on breaking into the Trans Euro Telecoms server to access the call transactions on the network.

"This is where you come to our aid Hugo"

"Well ok, well yes I can well I emm.... Well I already have got into the em.... Server" A pensive Hugo stammered.

"But how am I relevant? I don't get it," challenged a now concerned Hugo.

Jacob removed a packet of cigarettes from his top pocket, removed one and polluted the room with a whiff of toasted tobacco as he lit up.

There was a light crackling sound as Jacob inhaled hard on the tipped cigarette, he continued.

"The difficulty is that we are known to the British Intelligence Services and Special Branch, so we need a foil a Trojan horse to obtain the records."

Exhaling the blue smoke, Jacob attempted to console and to an extent encourage Hugo.

"The thing is my friend with your help Hugo we will be able to bring the killers of your sister to a swift and final justice"

He rocked on his seat, gesticulated with his right arm and flicked ash on the desk, Jacob continued.

"Ok let's get let us get on with the task in hand, Sanji here has penetrated two firewalls and gained access to the main TET sever, what he now needs are the necessary password and validations to login in as David Moss to ensure that we get in at the highest level."

"The work you have done for us will allow access fully undetected by M15, M16 and Special Branch."

"I see, but why do we need to be in India, I don't get it" questioned Hugo

An assertive Hans charged in, raised his hands in the air.

"Look, we're not here to ask questions. We have a job to do. So I suggest we continue or we go home."

An uncomfortable Hugo attempted to return Hans's glare, but the blue eyes proved too much of a challenge for him to look at.

"Ok, for Sarah," muttered Hugo.

"The connection is made, Jacob, we are ready to go," Sanji reported.

"They will never locate us."

"I have relayed the IP through twenty different world locations," he added.

What they did not know was that six thousand miles away, Grace Wells at GCHQ was tuned into any activity involving David Moss, TET and the JBL Contracting industrial conglomerate. Wells was able to examine this login, but the source of the message at this stage was impossible to locate.

"Over to you, Hugo."

He slid the military-looking laptop towards the Englishman. Hugo was at the end of Sanji's desk and received the machine. He spent a couple of minutes surveying the keyboard layout to familiarise himself with this chosen weapon against terrorism.

Hugo floated the fingertips of both hands over the rather chunky keyboard, he looked at Hans and Jacob, then returned his gaze to the monitor. In the illumination of this windowless, white-painted room Hugo buried his head into some very sophisticated high-tech equipment, the young Englishman felt comfortable and ready to undertake the task in hand. There was silence, the only disturbance to the ambiance was the clatter of keyboards as Hugo opened up one screen after another on the laptop.

After three or four minutes of manipulating the keyboard, Hugo was engrossed in the world of the web a quasi-extension of his own brain. This was a place where he was comfortable. It was normality to him. He penetrated different levels of security, found back doors into areas where hackers had failed in the past. He was a natural. Even Sanji, a competent computer expert, sat there in amazement at Hugo's skill and ability to break the codes one after the other.

After another minute of Hugo and the Web working in concert, he announced with great satisfaction that he had achieved his goal. He had found his quarry. He had vanquished his adversary.

He turned to the three men and simply said, "I'm in. It's all yours."

Hans looked at him. "Yes? What do you mean, you are in?"

Hugo gave a short reply. "You have access to TET. All of their accounts via David Moss. I have also set up a routine embedded into the software, which will not register this activity ever happening."

Back at GCHQ, as a result of previous suspicious activity, Grace Wells had instructed the IT department to monitor any traffic between David Moss and TET. This check was outside the normal TET loop, and although TET would not see a record of activity, GCHQ would have full visibility on all email and electronic communications traffic.

"Ok, over to you, Sanji, please. Ensure that you have all of Hugo's login details saved so as not to allow ongoing access to the server. We have a lot of work to do," said Hans.

Hans again positioned himself as leader. He said, "Ok, Sanji, you have your list of tasks. Jacob, please report to the boss and let's get back to Kerala with you and Hugo."

"Is that it?" Hugo sparked up in surprise. "I've come all this way for ten minutes on a pc? I want to catch the killers."

"Leave that to us now Hugo. Your job is done. Also, you have a conference to attend and that is the reason you're here. It would blow your cover if you're absent from Kerala for too long."

Hans rose to his feet and put on his black jacket and signalled for Hugo to get up.

"Goodbye, gentlemen, and thank you for your help," said Jacob.

Hans unlocked the white internal door leading out to the lobby and beckoned his fellow travellers to follow him. Four minutes later the three were securely seat-belted into the Audi as the driver negotiated the insane and busy backstreets of Madurai.

Chapter16

Lukas Richter towelled himself down after a much-needed shower and, taking care not to slip on the highly polished wooden floor, he walked through to his well-presented bedroom. Shuffling across the luscious thick beige rug, he approached the king-sized bed beautifully attired in freshly-pressed white cotton linen. Laid on top of the bed were his clothes for the evening: a white shirt, cream linen slacks, and white cotton socks to be worn under light brown suede slip-on shoes.

Five minutes later, fully dressed and giving off a waft of expensive French cologne, he entered the reception room.

"Good evening, my friends. It's good to see you all together again," Richter said with sincerity and joy.

A steward in black trousers and a short white tunic offered a tray of drinks, and Richter took a glass.

"I can't believe it – J W Black Label. My favourite! The rock star's drink. Thank you, my friends. It is good to see you again," voiced Richter with joy.

"Lukas, you're a longstanding servant to the cause and to the Fatherland."

Richter replied in perfect German. He raised a glass. Jorge stood erect and clicking his heels in an act of obedience, barked, "Danke meine Oberfuhrer.

Richter, standing head-on to his five colleagues, raised a glass.

"I propose a toast: to the cause, the Fatherland, the covenant and our dear Fuhrer."

All five replied: "The covenant!"

"Gentlemen, before dinner we have business to attend to."

As they took their respective seats, Friedrich handed out the five cream dossiers. As they were seated one by one they opened up the documents.

The reception room was cavernous and in the centre was a large, low level mahogany coffee table with a glass top. Four rather large leather chesterfields formed a perimeter around the coffee table. and it was to these seats they took their positions.

Friedrich assumed the Chair of the informal meeting. He looked at Richter.

"Lukas, can you please give us an update on matters?"

Placing his dossier face down on the glass-topped coffee table, he said,

"Gentlemen, the situation is as follows: the central funds by a series of, shall I say, staged and lucrative transactions have allowed us to amass a very large reserve of US dollars, Euros and Stirling."

He continued.

"To date, as you know, we have taken large positions in Western Labs, Western Labs Bioscience and aided Philip Medway in the acquisition of Whitehead Holdings and the JBL Contracting Industrial and Construction Group. Thirty-five percent of the current funds have now been allocated to support both long and short sell positions in the English telecommunications giant Trans Euro Telecom. The anticipatory return at greater than 200%percent will provide us with liquidity and opportunity to take full control of Western Labs, Western Labs Bioscience and of JBL Contracting Industrial Group, in particular JBL Contracting Infrastructure Services Ltd. This is a company which is part of Medway's empire he gained through the acquisition of Whitehead Industries. He will give us control of his Companies as he pursues his political career. This is the former Whitehead division which is working on contracts to manage and merge the water supplies to Tel Aviv, Jerusalem and a number of major towns. The assets under management include the de salination plants at Sorek, Ashkelon, Palchaman and Hadera that account for 75% of the fresh water provision to our Israeli friends."

Friedrich shuffled the document and looked at Richter

"And what is the current status on these contracts Lukas? Are we in control of our destiny? Enquired Friedrich.

"The contract will be awarded very soon and our new PM elect will ensure that our friends in Israel push the folder in our direction" "very good let's not take the pressure off those connections are vital I the achievement of our objective" said Hermann

"I agree; you must not let anything slip Lukas do you fully understand Lukas" stated Friedrich

Richter nodded continued.

"Moving on"

"The TET arbitrage will happen within the next forty-eight hours. Parallel to this, the whole world will view that David Moss, the husband of the English Prime Minister, was culpable in the release of private records. Mrs Moss is already hanging by a thread and this event will no doubt topple her"

Friedrich paused and sipped his whisky.

"Our friend Laing will ensure that there will be no serious challenge to Medway's leadership. Over the past twelve months he has been amassing information and evidence on the activities of the main contenders. The Tories always have a weakness with sex and there would be enough information to hold off any challenge to Medway's position. In my estimation, England will have a new PM in two to three weeks and we will have full control of JBL Contracting Industrial Groups.

"The final timings are all dependant on the process of Western Labs' Laboratories, or should I say the parallel work being carried out in Argentina by your people, Friedrich."

"With that, I will update you all," offered Friedrich.

"As you and the world are aware, bio-scientists are working on a cure for malaria, in fact a preventative cure for malaria. It involves an antidote developed from a natural organism which has been genetically modified. It can be introduced directly into the drinking water of any potentially infected area. The trials have been underway for the last three years and the World Health Organisation is going to recommend that the product is phased into the water supply across the world. The programme is being funded by our friend in America, the Internet billionaire with deep pockets, who wants to meet his creator with goodness in his soul. We also know that our outgoing PM is hot on this subject and will commit overseas aid to rollout the project."

Hermann jumped in.

"It's all progressing well, my friends. But where is the relevance to our project to finalise that we started in 1942?"

"Stay with me, Hermann," barked Friedrich.

"Our laboratory in Argentina as you know has been working on a parallel project under the control of the esteemed doctor, Johan Monkall, or should I say, Mengele Yes, his one and only grandson."

Johan sat erect and moved his hands in front of him. He took a crystal glass, poured water into it, and took a sip. He commenced his report.

"Please turn to page two of the dossier."

There was a ruffling of paper.

He continued,

"If you read the summary you will see that our laboratories have developed a bioweapon that is colourless, tasteless, highly toxic and very highly concentrated. With knowledge gained from my grandfather's experience and experiments I have been able to genetically develop a bio agent which will attach itself only onto particular DNA groupings and principally those from a non-Aryan origin. Yes, my friends, we have developed a bio agent which will attack those predominantly of Jewish parentage. As protection to our friends, there are particular constituents in the malaria prevention additive which normalises the effect of the anti-Jewish agent. I've named the killer bio agent Viper, as it will strike with a deadly effect."

The room fell silent for a short while and the German continued.

"When we administer the malarial protection to states surrounding Israel just as a precaution, say, three weeks before, within four weeks we will be in a position to upload Agent Viper into the water supply of our Israeli enemies. The beauty is that the victim does not have to directly digest Viper, it can be absorbed through the skin. Death will take place within three days. Once infected with this virus it can be passed on through bodily contact to others. Our prediction is that that state of Israel will cease to exist in under five months."

Looking up, Friedrich enquired,

"How did you develop Viper?"

Richter closed his dossier, and looked Johan straight in the eye.

"How convinced are you that Viper will be effective against the Israeli population? After all, research on race has determined that there is no direct correlation between DNA and race."

Johan placed his hands on his knees and sat up straight, in preparation to address his audience.

"Gentlemen," he said, as he placed his palms in the air. There was a pause before the other four members of the meeting looked at him intently.

"My grandfather carried out extensive research into genetics. He had the advantage of a large population of human specimens. Due to circumstances and the huge anti-Nazi sentiment, his work was never published. In fact, a lot of it was smuggled out by our brotherhood prior to Auschwitz and the other camps being liberated. It appears that Josef Mengele had concluded research which was far in advance of any work undertaken by Crick and Watson. His highly secretive and unorthodox approach examined the DNA blood type and genetic markers from Jews and non-Jews all over Europe. He noticed some DNA markers varied in Jews from different countries and various levels of orthodoxy. Even today, some Rabbis in Israel are requesting DNA background checks before they agree to marry Jewish couples. Modern research in genetics has found that more than seventy percent of Israeli Jewish men have inherited a Y-chromosome from some paternal ancestor. There is also a raft of written work on the DNA trends of the Ashkenazi Jews. Add to that the activities of the last forty years where the members of our brotherhood have been working in hospitals all over the USA, Europe and Israel. The have successfully collected blood samples of patients with mainly Jewish parentage, which have been forwarded to Argentinian scientists. The scientists in the Argentinian jungle laboratories have continued what some would describe as the in humane work started by Mengele. We have, however, found out that there are trends between DNA and race."

"Utterly amazing, in fact mind blowing" said Friedrich

Johan continued.

"The laboratory has developed a virus which we believe will attach itself to the DNA of eighty percent of the Israeli population. This will guarantee an early, effective and high mortality rate. Tests on humans that do not possess the target DNA markers have shown that the Viper dies within an hour of entering the bloodstream. Furthermore, the waterborne malaria prevention agent provides secondary protection during the incubation period of the virus. What we have, gentlemen, is a once and final solution to the Jewish – well, Israeli – question."

There was silence in the room. Only the ticking of the large grandfather clock three feet to the right of the fire contributed to severing the ambiance.

"Goodness," gasped Richter, "you really believe this can work?"

All eyes moved to Johan. Another pause.

Johan surveyed his fellow comrades, looked at the buff folder, looked directly at Richter, and tapped his left finger on the folder, and in a chilling monotone said.

"Yes. Totally."

"And the delivery system?" asked Friedrich.

"Ah. One of the JBL Contracting companies within our total control holds the IP for technology and maintenance operations for the large desalinations and water treatment plants situated at Sorek, Ashkelon, Palchaman and Hadera. They are pitching for the contract to update these plants with the latest technology developed by JBL Contracting, and also to manage the ongoing operation of these facilities to improve environmental efficiency and provide higher quality water. They are under the skin of the company, shall we say. With our contacts in place and total control of the companies, our operatives will be able to get into the plants and dose the water supply." Replied Richter

"How do you intend to get the large volumes of the virus into the country?" Richter enquired.

"Well, Herr Richter, we're not talking large volumes. It will take the form of eight containers each holding six litres each of the virus. The only issue is that that Viper has to be supported in controlled conditions whilst it's being shipped. The plan is to send the containers to the UK in refrigerated beef cargo container, move it by land to Western Labs where it will be stored ready for distribution to Saudi Arabia, Libya and Egypt, as malaria prevention water additive. The shipment designated for Egypt will then be taken across the border with a container of construction components for the two planned modifications of the desalination plants being built by the company. Our people working in the organisation will then take the small containers to each of the four plants in Israel."

There was still silence.

Richter continued,

"Our maintenance operatives will then inject the Viper virus into the outgoing water supplies. This will take a period of two hours. I have to admit that this is the riskiest part of the operation as we have to ensure there is no interruption, so it is imperative that we have our best men on the ground. They have been handpicked and are undergoing training in Austria as we speak."

Richter stood up. The Austrian financier reflected as he looked around at the wood-panelled walls, the polished wood floor, the huge fireplace, and the fans in the ceiling in this quiet ambient pleasurable environment on the edge of the Argentinian jungle. He concluded that *the future of Israel was being determined. In fact, it was being determined that Israel would have no future.*

He reminisced on the stories his father and grandfather had told him about the glory days of the Reich. He was proud to be Austrian, and like many others, felt that the master race still had a position in history. He rolled his tongue around his mouth, adjusted his shirt, bent down to pick up his glass of blended whisky. Standing straight, he raised his glass to the ceiling.

"A toast. A toast to the success of the brotherhood and the Viper. And to the covenant of the ring."

All six men stood up, raised their glasses high, most of them looking to the ceiling. Everyone was wearing a platinum snake ring on one finger of their left hand.

They all barked,

"The Reich!"

"The Reich!" barked Friedrich.

In concert they shouted,

"To the covenant of the ring!"

They sat and replaced their glasses on the table. They all shuffled back into their leather seats.

The doors opened and Jorge entered the room. "Dinner is served, gentlemen."

"An appropriate place to cease our discussions," Friedrich stated, and closed the velum folder in front of him. He stood up and pointed towards the double wooden doors, which were now opened, leading on to a beautifully dressed twelve-seated dining table.

Grace Wells was so deep in thought that she almost did not notice the message as it appeared on the screen. If it had not been for the forewarning of a synthetic ping, her attention would not have been refocused to the important work in hand.

'Re booted' back in to hear and now, Grace Wells clattered away at her keyboard and was presented with a synopsis of David Moss' activity on the TET server.

She studied the list of activity over the previous 12 hours, a log in event at 12.15 GMT of today, a Saturday, grabbed her attention.

'Heavens it was Saturday, and she should be at the Rec watching her beloved Bath Rugby destroy Northampton Saints.'

In act of pure frustration, she lifted the receiver off and using the lead dragged the internal telephone set across her messy desk towards her.

SIX TWO FOUR FIVE was hammered into the key pad.

"Frankland can I help:" emanated from the dark blue receiver.

'What an officious twat Peter Frankland was, he was a character from a past era, a servant of the Empire.'

In no disposition for chit chat she spoke.

“Peter, Grace Wells here, ‘code orange 426’. This was the code level for the day as relayed by Tom Leyton.

“OK fire away” replied Peter Frankland.

“Straight to the point: where was the PM, and, more particularly, the PM’s husband, today between 12.00 and 13.00 GMT?”

“Leave it with me, Grace, I’ll get straight back to you.”

Wells went back to figuring out how Guy Walker could be involved in all of this. Was it just a coincidence?

The phone buzzed. Wells collected the message.

“Peter Frankland here Grace. Just to report that both the PM and Mr Moss were at lunch at the US Embassy today all day, they were joined by two high-ranking generals and a prominent businessman. Special Branch confirm that they never left the building and all of their phones were switched off.”

“Thanks, John. Enjoy the rest of your day.”

Grace Wells tapped into the system to review the phone and email transactions of Guy Walker during the past three hours. Nothing of interest except of course for Steve Gibson.

“To hell with it,” she thought, and place in her earphones on her head and tuned into the live commentary from the Rec.

Chapter 17

Guy arose earlier than usual for a Monday morning, the reason being that he had a six-thirty breakfast meeting with Steven Gibson at Salvadoris in Virgo Street. He went through the usual rigmarole of dress check, final check, and just one last glance in a full-length mirror, he was tooled up and ready.

The cab pulled up outside Salvadoris and Guy paid the driver.

At the entrance he announced to the manager he had a table booked. This was one of Guy's favourite haunts. He loved the informal ambiance, good food, low levels of chat, and beautiful wine list which he could no longer partake in of course. There were always the nice-looking ladies to observe.

The maître d' confirmed that his table was ready and that his guest had already arrived and was sitting in the corner table near the window. Guy walked through the busy restaurant, bumping past two waiters and several people hustling around. This certainly was the place to breakfast, he thought.

"Good morning, I'm a bit late."

"No, Guy, I'm early," said Steve.

"Have you ordered?"

"No." Guy summoned the waiter.

Clasping a pen and paper, he arrived and awaited instruction. Guy pointed an open hand to the grey-haired his guest who was well presented as usual, dressed to kill in a black suit, crisp white shirt and dark blue tie.

"I'll have two poached eggs, brown toast, smoked salmon, topped with spinach, black coffee and apple juice," Steve said in a Soft New York accent.

"Do you know what? Make that two," Guy said. "Don't forget the coffee now, please."

The waited nodded. "Yes, sir."

Guy was about to open the conversation when his mobile phone delivered a ping, announcing the arrival of a text. Ordinarily he wouldn't have answered this; however, this was the designated signal for messages from Richter.

In a reference to the past TV advert for TET, the text read *'Busby will be freed at 10.05'*. Guy knew this was the signal that bad news would be on its way for TET. Another ping: '*Ensure all pieces are in play. No call backs.*'

Guy silenced the phone.

"apologies for that Steve but it is a message highly relevant to our meeting"

Gibson waived his hand in approval.

Guy was only too aware what this meant: he had worked frantically with Stuch and colleagues in Singapore, New York and Frankfurt, all he needed was for Gibson to confirm contracts were all drawn up.

Guy placed the phone back onto the table face down and was just about to speak, when Gibson halted the conversation by holding his hand out flat towards Guy.

Gibson with a huge grin announced

"No need to ask what that was about, Guy. And the answer is yes, we are ready to go. And fuck's sake, please do not let me down. I have some nasty bastards who are expecting their money back and change."

"10.05, Steve, that's the trigger time. 10.05."

"Well, let's enjoy breakfast."

The waiter poured coffee and two minutes later, a brace of immaculate white plates was positioned on to the crisp ironed tablecloth adorned with polished silver knives and forks and clear-cut crystal glassware.

Six thousand miles away, four and half hours ahead in time, in a second-floor office in the backstreets of Madurai, India, a certain Sanji Patel was busy toiling over a laptop.

...

Guy Walker arrived at his Mayfair office at 9.56 GMT and as he entered the main floor, all appeared to be calm with a little less of the usual shouting and frantic activity from the traders. Three large TV screens reported the daytime news; nothing exciting, no boats had been rocked. A few minor blue-chips were posting results. With TET numbers not expected for seven days there was little to vibe the office.

Just after ten, Guy walked over to and sat behind his desk. His door closed he wanted to cherish the quiet moment and catch up on a few personal emails and a few calls, then coordinate with Samantha, his PA.

Just as he was taking a sip of his toasted Columbian blend, Stuch burst into his office.

"Guy, Guy, Guy! Look at the TV! Look at the TV monitors!"

Guy stood up slammed down his mug and bounded out of his office and onto the main floor. There was silence. All staff were standing, glued to the screens. The news they were digesting was unbelievable but not totally unsurprising considering the deals they had been putting in play over the last few weeks.

On the BBC news screen, the newsreader was talking about some scandal at TET. The red banner whizzing along the bottom of the screen shouted out the news: "Prime Minister's husband implicated in scandal; release of one and a half million customer bank details, dates of calls and login details."

Also TET's website had been jammed, allowing any member of the public to login and examine any customer call records.

"My God, this will end a few marriages," Guy reflected.

David Moss was being mentioned time after time, accusations of a national security breach were being used extensively. There was total outrage in the Houses of Parliament, two minutes after the news had broken. It also appeared that the PM had her personal email account under the control of David Moss and now this was public knowledge.

Guy looked at one of the trading screens and there was a small wall of red on the telecommunications and banking shares. TET's share had fallen 62% in 34 seconds.

Guy shouted,

"Now, get to work! We have contracts to satisfy. Get on those phones get on those phones, pronto!"

Andy Davis, one of the senior traders, pulled Guy by the arm.

"Boss my book has just made two hundred and seventy million. That's fantastic. How did we see this coming?"

Guy shrugged, looked at the ceiling, and said.

"Let's not ask too many questions. Let's just reap the benefits."

Guy went back to his desk, sat down, and put his head in his hands and gasped. Outside his office there was craziness, mayhem driven by the greed, motivated by the unforeseen event, wringing every last drop of misfortune from one of the world's most powerful telecommunications companies.

Little did Guy know that Richter and his merry band from New York to Frankfurt had also bet against the pound sterling. Richter was already aware of the source of the leak and the impact it would have on the already faltering PM. Richter's fortunes were real on all fronts and the cash was amassing at the rate of the water from a breached damn.

Guy muttered,

"My God. I'm fucking rich. Well and truly back on the map."

Raising his head, he surveyed the ongoing frenzied activity outside his glass partition. The advance to an even greater profit-making territory had started. How could this have happened? How could Richter have predicted this event?

But now was not the time to question. He sat there dreaming of his trip to the Jack Barclays Bentley dealership where he would be king again for one more day. Then a loud ping announced a message from Steve Gibson.

Glancing at the iPhone, Guy read the only words:

'Fucking hell, Guy. Incredible. The Russians want me to run for president'.

Then a smiling emoji.

By eleven o'clock TET had corrected the breach and secured all the server connections. However, the damage was done. Shares were down fifty-two percent below the morning opening price. The sterling was 4.2% down on the dollar and 6% against the Euro.

Guy put his head in his hands in an extraordinary play out of relief. My goodness, he thought, this is beyond my wildest expectations.

The distant ping of his mobile signalled a message from Richter.

The message was brief and to the point: *Stage one complete. All on plan. We have to meet on Wednesday at 13.00 at HH.*

The message puzzled and elated Guy. "Stage one?" he hissed through his teeth, puckering his lips.

"All in place? What plan?" He recoiled into his chair. The brightness of the ceiling light made him squint temporarily.

Closing his eyes, he pondered the text for a few seconds. Glancing at his mobile, he muttered,

"Well, in for a penny, in for a pound."

He bounced up from his chair, walked over to the chrome and black coat stand in the corner of the office retrieved his jacket and left the office.

As he walked through the main floor, he was welcomed by a standing ovation from all his office staff, which was led by Michael Stuch. He gave a monarch like wave in acknowledgement, said nothing and headed for the exit.

Walking down the stairs, he saluted the commissionaire and burst through the main doors into St James Street. He needed air. Although it was a London polluted vintage, it was a relief from the manufactured environment of his office.

His head was in a spin. He needed a distraction so proceeded to the corner of St James Street, Piccadilly, and hailed a black cab. The cabbie wound down the window and over the familiar knock of the diesel engine, he heard the ever-familiar phrase,

"Where to, guv?"

"Thirteen Saville Row, please."

The cabbie nodded his head and Guy got into the black vehicle and slammed the door, and embarked on some retail therapy.

Wells burst into Tom Leyton's office.

"Sorry, boss, but you have to hear this."

Leyton was midway into devouring his midday snack, the delight on this occasion a custard-filled doughnut. He feverishly swallowed the treat and wiped remnants of custard and sugar from his lips and his fingers, and for the finale he folded the paper napkin and threw it into the bin.

"What the hell are you on about, Grace? Are we at war?"

"No, boss. TET have had a massive security leak. David Moss is implicated and the Prime Minister is on thin ice. Shares are through the floor and here's the stinger: get this: Steve Gibson's fund and Guy Walker's Tornado Ventures made huge gains on shorting the shares."

"Are you sure this is for real?"

"Yes, boss. I knew those two buggers were up to something," she said.

"Ok, Grace. This is one for the FCA boys, insider trading is not our bag."

responded Tom Leyton who was trying to appear unconcerned.

"Tom, are you forgetting TET was in the transcripts of the killings? There is a connection, I'm sure. I feel it in my water."

"Well, go get a coffee Grace, and let this city police deal with it."

"Tom, I know you and Guy Walker have a connection, but you cannot let the friendship compromise an investigation with potential ramifications for national security. After all, who broke into the TET server? There is a dark force on the side-lines."

Wells brought Leyton up to speed on the false login on Saturday night.

"Ok, Grace. I need to get to Walker. I need the bastard to get us in on what's happening."

"There's one other thing you need to know, boss."

She handed him the transcripts of the two texts Walker had received from Gibson and Richter.

"Bloody hell, Grace, what do they mean, 'stage one'? Is there something deeper going on here?"

"You're correct, boss. I'm going to find out if we can get a source for the TET login."

"Ok, Grace, dig deep. Leave no stone unturned. You've got my authorisation to phone tap. I feel there's more to this Herr Richter than meets the eye.

Seven thousand miles away in a facility nestled amongst the palm trees of the Argentinean jungle a group of men in light yellow suits and respiratory equipment were busy at work. This was not the work of honest men, but the travails of an evil regime that had remained dormant for four generations.

In an underground bunker a team of technicians were filling six-litre containers with a clear liquid. They were working in a predominantly white decorated clean room in sealed negative pressure conditions. This was the climax of a heinous and perverted research programme which had its origins back in 1943 in the not-so-clinical environment of Block B in a camp in Upper Silesia, Poland. A perverted, twisted and inhumane doctrine of the ways preached by the ambitious Dr Mengele. A mission to manipulate the genetic code to proliferate the master race and at the same time aid the destruction of those who did not fit the Aryan template. This research was only known to a few SS officials and even Adolf Hitler himself was not aware of the full extent of the potential precipitate of these vile experiments. This was the brainchild of Heinrich Himmler himself and the programme had been directed by Reinhard Heidrich until his untimely death in 1943 at the hands of the Czech resistance.

The men working on filling these canisters of death were no ordinary research scientists or technicians; they were descendants of members of the SS and in particular members of the highly secretive sub-section of the bearers of the 'Totenkopf 'deaths head. All of them had been brainwashed into the doctrine of the master race, and to find a final solution to the Jewish Question – in the present tense, the destruction of Israel.

It had taken many years to develop the Viper virus through an intensive programme of research and testing on animals and even human beings. This new generation of the sect exhibited even stronger beliefs in the need for the world to be led by a master being.

Within two days they would be finished. All of the canisters would be filled and enclosed in temperature and pressure-controlled transport containers. They would have worked tirelessly for the covenant and they would continue to give themselves and their lives to the cause, as a number already had. Several had volunteered to act as human Guinea pigs in experiments to validate the antidotes. The favoured outcome had not always been achieved, and the warriors to the cause of racial cleansing were early victims. Up and until they were released from their agony by death itself, these followers of the vile and chilling cause exhibited loyalty to the end.

Sixteen kilometres away from the bunker of Satan, Lukas Richter boarded his Gulfstream. He buckled up his lap strap and digested a perfectly chilled glass of Krug champagne. The pilot punched in the ten-point coordinates that would navigate the aircraft all the way back to Biggin Hill in South East England.

Chapter 18

With the first of the day's lectures over, Hugo's brain was feeling a little punished by the tidal wave of new knowledge he had been exposed to. The young genius inserted the key card into the hotel door, located it into the power slot, and threw himself on to the king-size bed.

The perfectly adjusted air conditioning refreshed him a little, but he needed a drink. He rolled off the bed and on to his feet and headed for the mini bar and pulled open the black plastic door and retrieved an ice-cold Coke Cola – full sugar, of course. *They never seemed to have any diet products in India,* he reflected.

Eventually he found the bottle opener, popped off the cap, and downed the refreshing, high-sugar drink in three gulps.

He only had thirty minutes to shower and change before dinner in the restaurant downstairs at the hotel. He decided to leave the necessary cleansing and dressing to the last minute. Repositioning himself on the bed, he pulled up two pillows and picked up the TV control.

Within ten seconds he'd championed what mere mortals need five minutes to figure out: how to find an English-speaking channel. Sorting through the usual rubbish, she stopped abruptly at the BBC World News Channel. When he saw the banner at the bottom of the screen, he sat up erect, looking at the TV in amazement.

He turned up the volume and was brought fully up to date with the news from back home:

"TET in new security leak; PM's husband, David Moss, implicated."

"Jesus Christ," he belted out.

"What the hell? My God, what have I done? What is the relevance of this to my work? What has this got to do with Mossad and fighting terrorists?"

He lay back on the bed, head in his hands, feeling panic pulse through his veins. He placed his hands over his eyes. The panic brought him out in a cold sweat and he started panting for breath. The thought of what he'd done ripped through his very heart and soul.

"I've destroyed lives," he gasped. Emotions fuelled by the realised consequences of his actions. The natural loner was now feeling too alone. He needed to talk to somebody, confess his sins, seek redemption for the pain he had dealt the innocent. Alone in India. Yes, he was alone, and would not discuss with his host and his fellow techies. They may well be part of the conspiracy, he concluded.

Hugo jumped off the bed, he paced around the room and felt perspiration of fear rolling down his brow. His logical mind had never had to deal with such emotion. Yes, he'd been devastated by Sarah's death, but that was not by his hand.

"God," he muttered, "I need to speak to somebody."

Naturally he had no close friends, his only confidants in life were the black and grey electronic gateways to the cyber world and such a faceless connectivity wasn't any highway to redemption. To make matters worse, whilst in the secret haven in Madurai, Hugo had aided his accomplices in hacking into two more companies. The Mossad man, Jacob, had convinced Hugo that Western Labs were funding the ISIS organisation and JBL Contracting Construction with their Middle East connections were involved with it too. Middle Eastern offices and construction were a recruiting hotbed for terrorists. Jacob had also convinced Hugo that the international communications network of the contracting company had been using an illicit pipeline to pass coded messages between terrorist cells.

Jacob claimed that Mossad had hacked into the TET network but were soon found out, and their access denied. He explained that Hugo's skills and methods gave them visibility without the target ever seeing any breach of the electronic security.

Hugo sat on the bed, knees up to his face, hands around the back of his neck, tears in his eyes as he contemplated the further consequences of what he had done. The raid on TET was shocking, but what could happen Western Labs and JBL Contracting he did not want to even consider. This would affect thousands of lives; pensions would lose value; jobs would be lost; careers would be folded. Overlaying all this destruction' *what was the real motive for Jacob and his crew. Why would Mossad want to bring down these companies? Not for financial gain, surely? For foreign intelligence reasons, definitely not.'*

His mind was now racing. His usual latent imagination was unleashed and a vista of sinister scenarios ran through his mind.

"My God," he thought. He was in the welfare of these people. They had his return tickets and controlled his life for the rest of the next two weeks. He had to escape their physical and mental clutches. But how?

Unfolding his body, he walked over to the desk, and surveyed the two phones in front of him: his personal mobile and the one supplied by Jacob's organisation, whoever they were.

He'd have to play a gamble. The Mossad device no doubt was tracked at a minimum. His own phone was a pay-as-you-go, and in preparation for the journey he had elected to buy a new sim card before he left the UK. As far as he was aware, Jacob's men didn't have the number, so to use it would be the safer of the two bets.

Checking the hotel room door was locked, he turned up the volume on the TV to provide a sound foil to his proposed conversation. He wandered into the bathroom, locked the door, put down the toilet seat, sat down on the white WC and dialled the landline number.

"0207 7511238," was the reply.

With relief, he was greeted by the homely voice of his father.

"Dad, it's your son," he bleated out in a tone of desperation.

"Hugo, are you ok? You sound troubled," his father replied.

"No, Dad. You need to come and get me. I'm in big trouble. I'm in danger." The words were leaving his mouth in increased velocity and the time and speed of his delivery alerted his father that all was not well and something erroneous had happened.

"Now, slow down, Hugo. Just slow down and tell me what the situation is and what we need to do to get you home."

Hugo sensed real love in the voice of this man who was normally too consumed with his work to show real empathy for his son.

Taking a deep breath,

"Dad, I've been brought to India under false pretences. You're never going to believe this, but I was recruited by Mossad to help investigate the recent London terror attacks."

"What?" his father interjected. "That's preposterous. This is unreal. How on earth…?"

"Dad, stop the cross examination. Just get me out. They – the Mossad – or whoever they are – they say they're Mossad – well they wanted me to find out under the radar how to get into the TET server in order they could obtain telephone messages from the London terrorists. They told me that British Intelligence would not allow them access. Well, I did it, and I did it for Sarah. At least, I thought I did. I bloody well hacked into the TET main server using David Moss's account, and nobody knows it."

"Well, they bloody well do now, Hugo. Have you seen the news? We may even have a new PM soon."

With a strong note of desperation in his voice, Hugo said,

"Get me out of here, Dad, please. I'm so afraid for my life."

"Ok, son," his father interjected some authority into the conversation.

"I'll get things moving at my end and I'll speak to one of my loyal clients. He has a private jet and he owes me one. I saved him a hundred and eight million in a deal last year. Keep your phone by your side and keep the door locked. I'll get back to you as soon as I can. Also, give me the login details to the pay-as-you-go account and I'll top up your credits."

"Ok, Dad. Please be quick."

"Stay calm, son. Act as though nothing has happened."

Hugo ended the call,

"I love you, Dad."

"I love you, my lovely boy."

A click ended the quasi-security of hearing his father's voice and Hugo was instantly plunged back into the darkness of the reality of where he was.

Hugo did not notice the flush plate mounted in centre of the white emulsion paint of the ceiling. He did not realise that the room also had a wall-mounted sprinkler unit and no need for an additional unit in the ceiling. The ceiling plate was a dummy, and encased in this was a listening device. His not so friendly hosts had recorded the full conversation.

They were not alone in this act of covert surveillance.

In the depths of GCHQ supercomputers which managed thousands of messages per second were searching for digital strings which represented particular sets of words including phone emails and electronic communications. The parameters had been set up by Grace Wells, London Wembley Arena terrorism, and the TET share price

At 04.35 in the that Monday morning Grace received notification of a mobile telephone call, a pay-as-you-go Vodafone SIM The GCHQ surveillance instrument of cyber interrogation had picked up the random use of words from Trivandrum in India to a landline in Hampstead, North London. When Grace read the transcript from the full conversation, the pre-programmed words were plain to see. What Grace was not prepared for was the references that had been made to Mossad.

Perplexed and surprised, Wells read the message one more time.

"Mossad?" she uttered under her breath. "Mossad?"

Leaning back in her chair, hands behind her head, she pondered her next move.

'*Stop grinding your teeth*,' she warned herself. But this was a lot to take on and she knew she needed to tell Tom. She wanted to check something out first.

Closing down the computer, she got up and went to one of the empty desks in the meeting room which bordered the main office. On a secure landline, she typed out a number retrieved from her memory, of a mobile phone.

"Hello, it's Yitzhak," a man's voice in a clipped, Middle Eastern accent replied.

"Yitzhak, it's Grace Wells. I hope it's not an inconvenient time?"

"Grace, good to hear from you. In fact, wonderful. How are you? It's been too long."

Yitzhak Avraham worked as an oil analysist at an investment bank based in Canary Wharf. He was in charge of reviewing oil movement and production levels in the Middle East and Russia with the prime objective of predicting supply and demand patterns and spikes, keeping the daily traders up to date with the fluctuating price influencing data.

To the outside world, that was his day job. Yitzhak, like all young Israelis, had been called up for national service, and the bright university graduate ended up in the intelligence services. From there on, he was recruited by Mossad and worked on many assignments on counter-terrorism activities. It was in 2013, on secondment to GCHQ Cheltenham when he met Grace Wells. He fell for her long brown hair and beautiful big brown eyes, wit and intelligence. She was smitten by the tall, handsome, dark-eyed, tanned, well-toned man.

For a year and a bit and not to the knowledge of their superiors they shared alternative beds in their respective rented houses. Grace resided in a second floor flat in Montpellier, and Yitzhak in a three-bedroom house in the Suffolks, the bohemian residential area of Cheltenham.

To avoid being noticed together by the five thousand alleged school teachers who lived and worked in Cheltenham, they spent much of their weekends in London. Grace had been devastated when Yitzhak was relocated and the relationship eventually fizzled out.

Yitzhak's good looks and charm meant he had no shortage of admirers in the London financial community. It was a driving factor that finally guillotined their 'golden' relationship.

Yitzhak was no ordinary Mossad field officer. His uncle Piero Levy was a high-ranking officer in charge of all Western European counter-intelligence, a fact known to Grace.

"Grace, it's nice of you to call, but I know you too well – there's a reason. Other than your good looks and charm."

My goodness, he's not changed, she reflected.

"I'll get straight to the point. I've come across some very interesting intel connecting Mossad to two large recent events in the UK."

"Tell me more, my lovely girl, I'm all ears."

"Can we meet? I don't want to discuss this over the phone. Time will be of the essence."

"Well, Grace, I have the essence. Do you want to meet tonight? You're only two and a half hours away."

"Ok, I'll get the 17.02 from Cheltenham Spa. We'll meet at 20.00 at the Hilton in Paddington. My last train home will be 22.04. That gives us two hours."

"Perfect. I look forward to seeing you, my dear."

"Thank you, Yitzhak. It will be good to see you again."

Unusually, the GWR train pulled into Paddington dead on time, an effortless journey allowing Grace to catch up on some sleep. She encountered the everyday carnage of passengers jostling for position in the aisle to leave the train, and decided to remain seated and wait to allow her to be a little calmer the meeting with Yitzhak. Once the carriage had cleared, she disembarked and headed down the platform towards the exit barriers which were open, as all tickets had been checked en route.

She proceeded to the large air-conditioned shopping gallery at the end of the platform and leapt on to the escalator then walked through the double door entrance to the Hilton Paddington. She progressed through the second set of double doors was confronted with a floor colonised with busy travellers pulling trolleys and businessmen on mobiles, all rushing to catch the last train home. To the left of the open plan coffee area, sitting solitary at a low veneer table, there he was, looking at his mobile phone. How she still fancied him. He had not changed. Rugged, handsome looks, the floppy light brown hair and those deep hazel eyes.

As she approached, he turned his head. It was a typical look of affection, an intense animal attraction. They made each other dissolve. He lamented those nights of closeness, pure intimacy, when he held her close and looked into those deep brown eyes. He would stroke her long brown hair while she was asleep.

Yitzhak tilted forward and upwards from the dark red upholstered seat and cast aside his mobile. He looked at her longingly.

"Grace, my love. It's so nice to see you. It's been a while, but I've never stopped thinking of you, ever."

"Still a smooth talker," she smiled.

Walking over to her he hugged her and kissed her on each cheek, then nature took its only course and they kissed on the lips, a deep, affectionate kiss. In fact, more than just affectionate. The energy, love and chemistry of attraction. A virtual molecular bond still existed between these two good-looking, intelligent high achievers.

They sat at the small round coffee table and there was a moment of touching. More to the point, an electric-inducing contact of legs under the table. They became totally oblivious to the hectic surroundings of the busy coffee shop.

Yitzhak hailed the waiter.

"What will it be, Grace?" he asked, fully looking into her sensual eyes.

She looked at him.

"I think I need something stronger than coffee. A large glass of chardonnay, please."

She craved the hit and the first caress of alcohol in her mouth, a necessary anaesthetic to take the edge off her hectic day and also relax her in the presence of the man she still wanted deeply.

"Let's make it two," he said, and winked at Grace, displaying one of his renowned boyish grins.

There was a silence for twenty or thirty seconds as they sat back and admired each other. How he longed to be with her again, and the feeling was evidently mutual. The pause button was reset when the waiter brought two perfectly chilled 250ml glasses of the honey-coloured liquid.

Grace grinned as she placed the glass against her lips and took a sip of the much-needed relaxing properties of the fine specimen of French wine. Placing the glass back on the table with a soft clink, she said, "Well, let's get down to business."

He finished his drink, looked at her and nodded.

"What, we need to get a room?" he responded in a jocular tone.

God, how she wanted to take him up on this offer. It would be a perfect way to spend the evening – and the morning – with this man, curled up in white cotton sheets.

Temptation was chained up firmly and with a hesitant and nervous laugh in her voice, she replied.

"Not this time. Not this time at all. I have serious business to discuss, Yitzhak. We have a problem."

Out of character, he sat motionless and silent as Grace brought him up to speed with all information on Richter and Mossad. She covered all angles: terror cells, mobile calls from India, Wembley bombing and David Moss, and of course the TET affair. She talked for thirty-five minutes, briefly stopping to catch breath, and of course to take the relaxant of the Chardonnay wine.

She rounded off the informalities by looking him in the eye, this time not with lust, but in need of serious discussion, and help.

"What the hell are Mossad doing, being involved in TET, Richter and Wembley Arena?"

He dwelled on the question and digested what he had just been told. Yitzhak rolled his head back and flipped his brown hair from his brow. With clarity and brevity, he declared,

"Nothing to do with us. Nothing."

"How can you know that? How can you be sure?" Grace questioned.

"I am sure. I work directly with my uncle, and let's say he affords me a bit of privileged information on our activities in the UK. I can categorically guarantee this is not one of our operations. These are not our people. What I can tell you, however, is that Herr Richter is on our radar. This man has a very secretive past. A dark past. He's believed to be connected with a very dangerous, sinister and heinous organisation, who by the way are not involved with any of the terror on the UK mainland. What he and his vast society stand for is much deeper and wide-reaching than a few terrorist incidents. We know for a fact their ultimate goal is the destruction of Israel and the homeland of the Jewish people."

Grace looked puzzled. "Please tell me more."

Yitzhak continued

"Over the years we have placed several undercover operatives into the companies and the organisations controlled by Lukas Richter. Every one of these men and women ended up dead: a car crash, a heart attack. Sepsis, a rogue shot in a hunting accident, and can you believe even a bite from a venomous snake in India. We managed to retrieve a landscape of random information but we have concluded so far that this Richter is high up in an organisation – or, as they term it, a covenant – of fanatics who are descendants of some of the most ruthless and feared members of Himmler's SS."

Grace looked perplexed.

"Surely not. This sounds like fantasy."

Yitzhak's posture stiffened he was confident that this was no fantasy.

"Now hear me out Grace"

"OK I'm all ears" Grace replied

"From our trusted sources and personal testimony, we know the SS had an underlying loyalty to their Fuhrer in Germany and made an undertaking to eradicate the Jewish people from the face of the planet. Four years ago and just before the snake incident, we did manage to – let's say - interview one of Richter's foot soldiers. To avoid suspicion, we staged his death in a hotel in Rouen in France, and our friendly coroner replaced the body as Richter's man. In fact, we had him and an already-dead body perished in the hotel fire that night. We managed to bring him back to Tel Aviv for some intensive questioning, and before he suddenly expired, he gave us some useful, though not conclusive, information."

"Expired?" Gasped Grace.

"Yes, it was just a shame that such a strong, fit member of the Aryan race, had a low threshold to sodium pentothal."

"You used a truth drug on him?" Grace screamed in an assertive and disappointed voice. "That is banned by international convention."

Yitzhak huffed in disapproval.

"So is the mass murder of innocent people, Grace. You must know that."

"Well, who was he?"

"He was working for one of Richter's companies as a managing consultant and located in Rouen attending a regional board meeting. Off site, of course. We know he was one of the loyal disciples, as he like Richter and a number of Swiss bankers was the bearer of a silver snake ring on his left hand."

"A silver snake ring? What is the significance of that?" enquired Grace.

"Well, what we've gleaned is that the wearers of this ring belong to a secret covenant, an underground organisation that has disciples placed in prominent positions in Swiss banks, international finance houses, large corporations, governments. If we can believe it from our friend in Rouen, the British Intelligence."

An exasperated Grace said, "My goodness. And who are these people? What is the covenant? What is their mission?"

"Well, they are all descendants of high-ranking SS officials. In 1943, predicting the end of the war, two separate undercover factions evolved. One was a group of generals headed by field marshal Rommel, which culminated in the attempt to kill Hitler in the Wolf's Lair. Their objective was to remove Hitler, and this group who were not fanatical Nazis wanted to cease the killing of innocent civilians and broker peace with the allies. The other, and a more covert and perverse group, were made up from fanatics from the SS. In the main, they were recruited from the senior positions in the death camps and ranks of the SS involved in the organised killing and transportation of Jews. They had an unshakable belief in the master race and a vocation to rid the Western World of what they termed the sub-human species. What we term innocent men, women and children. They were inciting the hideous doctrine of racial purity and a master race that could evolve by the mass extermination of any undesirable which did not fit the genetic template of the Aryan breed. It was rumoured that even Hitler, Bormann and Goering were not aware of this cult, and that it was under the direct and underhand control of Reichsfuhrer Heinrich Himmler.

"my god is this for real" expressed Grace as she cupped her face in her hands.

"A key figure also in the organisation was Dr Josef Mengele the' angel of death', responsible for carrying out vile and evil experiments on the abundant stock of human guinea pigs who were extracted from the ramps at Birkenau 2. Mengele was one of the founders of genetic engineering research and as a consequence of these hateful methods he made some new and ground breaking discoveries in the field of human genome theory. The work of course was quickly squandered by the allies. The results were laundered over a number of years into new and widely adopted theory and practice by other renowned scientists. To the dismay of research institutions working in the field of genetics, they are totally unaware of where their legacy research comes from. From what we understand, in 1944 Mengele was involved in the seeding of Aryan women with cloned cells. The result allegedly was the birth of racially pure babies. The children would grow up in the protection of three main groups of surrogate parents. They were smuggled to Argentina to be brought up by families of escaped SS officers and sympathisers, which comprised members of the covenant. Several children were repatriated to wealthy families in neutral Switzerland. In many cases, the families were bankers who for generations now have been the custodians of the vast amounts of stolen gold and money plundered by the Nazis from the transportations to the East."

Yitzhak paused and took a sip of water. He scanned the room full of business types and tourists and returned his gaze to Grace. He felt compelled to tell the world his story but it would compromise bringing these evil people to justice.

Yitzhak cleared his throat and continued.

"Finally, a number of prominent German families were chosen, although not fanatical Nazis they would receive huge financial rewards from the illicit funds in Geneva and Berne to bring up and indoctrinate their adopted 'kinde '. A number of these German families also managed to emigrate to the United States, the UK and France after the war. The host countries were never aware that they had provided homes for former Nazis and would allow these anti-Semites to grow up and flourish. The objective was that these children would grow and evolve to believe in racial purity, an irrevocable belief of the master race. Through a network based in Bern and Buenos Aires, they would receive ongoing training and education in the precedent of a master race taking over the world."

A shocked Grace shook her head and continued to listen.

"In years preceding the war, many of the children grew up, and via personal attainments and/or a combination of corrupt dealings, they reached prominent positions in large financial institutions, industry and even government. As adults, they met at several undercover locations to further confirm their learning of the dark ways. Their ultimate goal remained that one day they would by whatever means eradicate the state of Israel. We are talking dangerous people here. These people are embedded in our banks, large organisations, and offices of influence. And they're all fanatics and followers of the evil from 1944."

Yitzhak rested. Grace, transfixed by the conversation, was in disbelief.

"Phew!" she said.

"Who are these people? Where are they now? Have they got anything to do with what I've discovered?"

"I figure so, Grace. What you've told me fits the pattern. They crave legitimate wealth in the money markets of the world, buying and selling securities and currency. They also buy up and control companies which one day may assist them in their goal of world domination. You've got to understand; this is a different war. They will have control of our economic instruments and destroy Israel by any means at their disposal. I said they make profits on legitimate markets, but what we perceive is they have insider knowledge allowing them to make pre-emptive bets on stocks."

"I see. So they were implicit in the TET fiasco by creating bad news to the share price?"

"Exactly," said Yitzhak.

Again there was a pause. Grace took a slip of her wine. Yitzhak stared at her beautiful brown eyes and the luscious red lips as they touched the glass.

"So what you are suggesting is that they operate under a guise of Mossad to gain access to sensitive information on TET, only to release confidential data into the public domain to create financial gain."

Yitzhak replied,

"Yes, that may be the reality of the situation."

Grace thought carefully for a moment, aware of time. She asked.

"Is Richter the top man?"

Yitzhak shook his head and closed his eyes momentarily.

"No. I believe there's another one above him who pulls all the strings. A very senior banker in Berne, Switzerland. Get him, we get them all," he said with passion. "Well, Grace, you know all I know about the 'covenant of the ring."

Grace Wells had not noticed that when she had been checking the timetable her old flame had caught the waiter's attention, tipped the rim of his empty wineglass and mimicked the order of two more glasses to be brought to the table.

The waiter, fully understood the command, returned and placed the two chilled glasses down on the table.

“Well, Grace, how about supper for old time’s sake?”

Looking down at the wine, she raised the glass and licked her lips, her eyes narrowed. She leaned forward and whispered in his ear,

“I would prefer breakfast.”

She leaned back, threw her return ticket on the table. It was not for the evening, but for 07.30 the next day.

Yitzhak experienced a churning sensation in his stomach. He raised his glass and blew a kiss at Grace. “To old time’s sake.”

Grace tipped her glass.

“To you and I. Just give me a minute.”

He nodded approval. Grace got up, walked in a rightward direction to the hotel lobby, putting her mobile phone to her ear. “Boss, can you meet me at 08.30 in the morning? I’m on to something big. Keep it to yourself, I’ll explain in the morning.”

“Sure, Grace. Do I need any assistance?”

“Tell no one. Especially that bastard, Laing.”

She did not trust Laing. He had too many of the wrong friends in high places to give her comfort in his authority.

Chapter 19

"Sanjeev. Sorry to bother you," said Hugo's father.

"Hell, that's not a bother, my friend. How can I help you?" was the reply.

"Sanjeev, my old friend, I have a very serious problem involving my only son, Hugo. I haven't got the time to go to the authorities and I need help urgently. In fact, I don't think the authorities can help me."

Sanjeev paused.

"Of course, I'll do what I can, my friend. After all, I owe you one many times over."

"Well, I need to get my son Hugo out of India rapidly. He's in a Travancore Heritage Beach Resort in Trivandrum, India, and I fear for his life."

For a top lawyer, used to playing the poker position, uncharacteristically Martin Parnell was exhibiting signs of distress.

"Ok, calm down my friend. I'm on the case. Vijay Saran, my old friend, owns that hotel. I have stayed there many times myself. I'm going to be on to him now. Meanwhile, pack a bag. Travel light, don't tell anybody, and get down to my house within thirty minutes. You need nothing but yourself and your passport. I will accompany you to Northolt where I'll get the jet prepared. We can sort details on the way. Just get moving now."

"Sanjeev, that's fabulous. Thank you very much."

Hugo's father ran upstairs, pulled out a small case from under his bed. His wife was alerted by the noise and shouted,

"What's the matter?"

"Nothing, darling. I've had an urgent call from Sanjeev. He needs me in New York for a couple of days. Taking me over in the Gulfstream."

"Oh no, I don't want to be on my own."

"Look, my love, why don't you go to your sister in Grange Park? I'm sure she will be good company for you for a couple of nights. Danny's away in Dubai for the rest of the week, I believe, larking about in the A380 again."

"Ok, that's a good plan. I'll call her and lock up once you leave."

He hurried down the stairs, placed his brown leather case on the hall floor he put his arm around his wife, and kissed her goodbye. Martin retrieved his case and made his move the door slammed closed, and he was gone.

En route, Sanjeev phoned Hugo's father and asked for his son's mobile phone number. He also reassured Martin Parnell that the police and other measures were in play to protect his son.

"Vijay, hi. Sanjeev here from England. How are you my friend"

He was surprised to hear from his old friend so late in the evening.

"It's wonderful to hear from you. Have you got news for me??

"Please listen. A good friend of mine and I are on our way to Trivandrum as we speak, we have a crisis and need help to try and avert. In the meantime, you can give me some valuable assistance. Please listen carefully. You have a guest staying in your Heritage Hotel, Mr Hugo Parnell. He's in grave danger and I need you to get him from the hotel in safety. Pull all the strings, my friend."

"I'm all ears. Just tell me what to do."

"This is my plan." Said Sanjeev.

Three minutes later, Hugo's father pulled up at the elaborate black wrought iron gates which punctuated the high white walls surrounding the palatial property of Sanjeev Pakhim, property developer, investor, and owner of several engineering companies in the UK and the United States. Hugo's father's Mercedes pulled up at the gates and the night guard approached the car, recognised the occupant, returned to the hut, activated the gates, and waved him through.

The distinctive sound of rubber on gravel ceased as Hugo's father pulled up his SL Class Mercedes next to a dark grey Bentley Mulsanne. The lights of the Bentley were on and the engine running, and the driver was in 'office' ready for departure.

Just as Hugo's father was terminating the life of the purring ten-cylinder AMG engine, one of the mirrored-finish gloss black doors of the house opened. Through the doorway and down the stairs proceeded a fifty-year-old Indian man, slight build, greying hair, gold-rimmed spectacles, wearing a pair of jeans, a polo shirt and a tweed jacket. He was carrying a Louis Vuitton bag and a light brown leather laptop bag.

As Sanjeev approached the rear door of the Bentley he looked at Martin and shouted.

"Martin we must go now!   please get in my car"

He beckoned his friend to get into the rear of the grey luxury saloon. Hugo's dad felt the soft-close doors take over and he settled into the black and white stitched quilted leather seats.

Sanjeev, with his bag on his knee, was already buckled in.

"My friend, it is good to see you. I admit, the circumstances could be happier."

"Good to see you again, Sanjeev. I'll never forget this."

Sanjeev put his right hand on Hugo's father's knee in an unspoken gesture of comfort. The Bentley silently crept forward and the rear lights illuminated red the white stonework of the mansion as it left by the exit gate.

"The jet is in readiness, Captain Lewis advises that the flight time is 8 hours 45 minutes, so perhaps we can get some sleep. I have a double crew on board which will allow us to return once we have your boy"

'yes my dear boy' Martin Parnell reflected

A boy who had been neglected – not vindictively but deliberately – by overworked career parents. Added to this he had suffered the horrific trauma of losing his little sister and witnessing his mother's life changing injuries. Hugo's father made a pact with himself there and then: when this was all over, he would spend more quality time with his only son and his wife, and less time in the office.

As the Bentley gracefully sped up the A40 towards RAF Northolt, Sanjeev updated Hugo's father on what actions he had put in place in India.

Ten minutes earlier, Hugo, still locked in his room and frightened for his life, had received a text from Sanjeev. It set out exactly what was going to happen, and instructed him on what to do. To validate the message, Sanjeev had added some information personal to his father, that none of his captors would ever know, guess or find out easily. It was the name of his father's first pet dog, Mackie, a black highland terrier.

Still frightened and very anxious, Hugo awaited the next move. He was tense. His stomach was churning. He was sweating.

A long, painful and tense ten minutes passed and a white and orange Mercedes ambulance followed by a black BMW 5 series pulled up at the entrance to the Heritage Hotel.

Two Indian men, one who carried a medical bag, and both casually dressed disembarked from the BMW. The rear doors of the white ambulance opened and two male nurses dressed in light blue tunics removed a trolley, allowing the wheels to collapse and make contact with the tarmac surface. They were met by the hotel manager, who directed the party to Room 407 on the fourth floor.

At the same time the medical contingent entered the lift in the lobby, two men approached the door of Room 407. The taller of the two banged on the dark green painted door.

"Hugo, it's Jacob, can you come out? We need your help with an urgent matter."

The other man was the menacing figure of Hans, the passenger of the Audi in Madurai.

As Jacob raised his arm again to remind Hugo of their presence his jacket opened momentarily, revealing a leather strap across the white shirt, positive identification of a shoulder holster. Hans was not so discreet. In the dim light of the hotel hallway, tucked in behind Jacob, you could see the Glock 9mm sticking out of the belt of his trousers.

Hugo froze when he heard the familiar and sinister voice, all of a sudden, a cold chill flowed through his body, he felt a fear he had never experienced before.

Jacob who was getting impatient up the tempo and hammered on the door one more time

"Hugo, please come out. We need to talk." he shouted in a menacing tone.

"Please make them go away please God help me. Forgive me" Hugo uttered under his breath and cupped his now sweat covered hand and gripped his fingers hard.

Hans shook his head and Jacob removed a duplicate electronic key from the pocket of his black jacket.

"Let's see if this works," he grunted under his breath.

Hugo's eyes filled with tears, he was helpless and paralysed with fear, he knew that he could not defend himself against the mountain of a man. He surmised that his assailant would be armed and just hoped for a swift end.

'*what am I thinking, they will torture me first for information it will not be swift, my life will end in pain alone in a foreign country'* concluded a now semi delirious Hugo.

He looked at the plain surroundings of the bathroom, and then then all of a sudden, the radiant glow of the two down lights was terminated, he was in darkness,

"No no please do not let this happen to me" he whispered. This was it, he was resigned to his fate, unable to move, he had lost all hope. Only a forty mm thick wooden door and a low-tech electronic lock provided the barrier from the living world to that of infinity and eternal blackness.

Jacob inserted the key into the aluminium lock assembly, the two microchips facing upwards the green light illuminated. Hugo's heart was in the pit of his stomach as he heard the whirring noise that all tired travellers are relieved to hear when they arrive at their hotel room, that *the door is finally unlocked*!

Jacob pressed down on the door handle, and in a swift move grabbed his pistol and held it above his head ready for action.

Pools of perspiration were assembled on Hugo's brow. He could hear his heavy breathing in his ears and his now confused mind. The pearls of sweat resembled water droplets sitting on a freshly polished car's paintwork. His mouth was desert dry. He was in a state of panic. He clasped his hands to stop the shaking but it would not abate. The fear was overcoming all of his physical strength.

In the darkness he saw the green signal on the lock and the door handle slowly move downwards. He was frozen to the spot.

'Why me, he thought. Why do I have to die? Why me'

He was a millisecond away from a brutal death. These men would want information from him first, before they powered him down to eternity.

Taking a breath and closing his eyes, he thought about his little sister, Sarah, then nothing.

He heard the door handle return to its rest position. A setting he never believed it would ever revisit. It signified remission. Something had happened to save him, to yield him more minutes of valuable life.

Locked inside the room Hugo had not witnessed what had happened a microsecond before Jacob was about to burst into the room. The lift doors had opened four metres from room 407, and out which had appeared two men in civilian clothes, and two officers in local police force uniform. Hans had swung around to take aim, but the officers in the police force had already cut him down with a 9mm machine pistol.

After he had witnessed the swift death of Hans, Jacob thought better than retaliate so he dropped the pistol turned and ran for the emergency stairs at the end of the corridor

The police officers were slowed down as they stumbled over the lifeless body of Hans, the loss of inertia allowed Jacob to make a swift escape.

Hugo had been so scared and transfixed on the sound of the door handle, he had blocked out all other aural signs from his petrified brain. His trance of pure raw fear was punctuated, however, by the shout from outside:

"Hugo, are you ok? I am with Sanjeev. Mackie dog. Let me in. Mackie dog," announcing that he was not a foe, but indeed a friend.

"Hugo, we are coming in now. Do not be concerned."

The door opened, and in bounced the doctor, his assistant, followed by the medics and the trolley. Still dazed, Hugo was still not convinced who was friend or enemy, but after a few seconds figured out that these guys might be on his side.

"Hugo, I'm Dr Singh. I want to get you out of here. To do that, we want you to lie on the trolley and fake that you are ill. We will cover you with a blanket and place an oxygen mask on your face and insert an IV drip into your hand. I want to make this look authentic to any onlooker. Hugo, do you understand me?"

The doctor looked him straight in the eye and waved a hand across his face. "We need to get away. You are in extreme danger."

Not able to speak, the still scared and tearful Hugo nodded his head to accept the terms of rescue. The two medics helped their perilous patient to his feet and shifted him onto the trolley. The mere fact the oxygen mask was not dispensing any gas and the cannula was only taped to his hand helped Hugo to believe that these men were trying to help and rescue him.

As they wheeled him through the hotel room door, one of the medics deliberately turned Hugo's head to one side so he would not be visual with the corpse lying in a pool of blood on the green and dark yellow patterned carpet.

Seven minutes later, Hugo was sat up in the back of an ambulance, speeding towards the airport.

Chapter 20

Grace Wells was woken by the buzzing of her work secure mobile phone. It took her a few seconds to become acclimatised and connected with unfamiliar environment she had found herself in These were not her bed sheets, and the evocative aroma of the Christian Dior aftershave prompted a rewind the events of the evening.

Next to her wrapped in the beautiful white cotton sheets was Yitzhak.

'Oh no,' she thought then replaced the it with '*a good time!*'

She fumbled for her phone, and knocked over an empty wineglass on the bedside table, however the potential sleep halting noise was attenuated by the deep pile dark red Axminster There was a buzzing and Grace looked at the flashing phone which signalled two things: it was 03.52 and it was Tom Leyton.

She picked up the phone.

"Ms Wells, I hope I have not disturbed your beauty sleep, or should I say your act of détente with our Israeli brothers in arms."

"Hey Gov it just after three what is going on we are not due to meet until later today" she replied

"Well, Grace, I am at this moment thirty minutes away from Northolt. I want you to get in a cab and hotfoot it to the main gate. Show your pass – they're expecting you."

"What yes well ok, boss. On my way."

She rubbed the sleep from her eyes, got her brain into some form of semblance and stepped out the of bed and got moving.

Showered and dressed she leaned over towards the tanned skin of the one that she would always love. She opened the mini bar and grabbed a bottle of still water and crept out of the hotel and headed towards the lift. She departed from the front door of the Hilton on to the main road.

A hard tap on the window of a black cab awakened the driver from his semi-sleeping state. As the cabbie rubbed his eyes, Grace was already in the back of the vehicle and had closed door.

"RAF Northolt, please," she said, "fast as possible."

The black cab's diesel engine erupted into life with the familiar signature knocking sound

"OK, miss. On our way."

Settling in for the journey she decided to call Tom.

"What's going on?"

"Where are you, Grace?"

"In a cab."

"No place to talk. When you get to the main gate, they are expecting you. They will direct you up to the private flight lounge."

"Ok, gov. See you soon."

"Where do you need to be, miss?"

Grace awoke from her semi-sleep and checked a news website on her phone, no *major events had transpired overnight, what is so important that Leyton wants me now? She thought.*

The cab tuned off the A40 and negotiated the quiet side roads and approached Northolt airbase.

Grace recognised the destination and leaned forward towards the Perspex shield which defined the driver's space.

"By the main gate, please."

The cab pulled in and a solider carrying a machine gun addressed the open driver's window. Grace jumped out and thrust her GCHQ pass towards the man.

"Oh, good morning, miss. Please follow my colleague over there to a car waiting to take you to Mr Leyton."

She settled the cabbie. "Keep the change, but can I have a receipt, please?"

The white Vauxhall pulled up at the private jet lounge, which was in partial darkness.

"The door on the left through the main reception Miss."

"Thank you, Sergeant."

Wells thanked the Sergeant who had delivered her to the private aviation terminal. She entered the partially lit reception and opened the front door on the left as instructed. Sat in two easy chairs, enjoying fresh coffee, was Tom Leyton and another man she didn't recognise.

The man stood up from his seat. He was in his mid-forties and hard-faced, with granite eyes which had no doubt witnessed the expiration of many a poor man's life, probably on more than one occasion. He had the stance and gait of a military man, and even though he was dressed in jeans and a white shirt he was impeccably turned out.

Tom Leyton looked his usual self: hair uncombed, unshaved. The 'I've-just-got-out-of-bed' fashion statement.

The stranger spoke in a clipped accent which provided evidence of his time in the military,

"Robert Smith. Pleased to meet you, ma'am."

"Call me Grace, please. Or Wells, but don't annoy me like that man there and call me Gracie."

Smith managed a small grin, which offered some hope of humanity in this highly trained killer.

Grace thought to herself, '*I've just met the real James Bond.*'

Leyton piped up,

"Robert is one of our cousins from across Vauxhall Bridge."

“That’s correct, Grace, I’m MI6. Your findings have been escalated and there have been further developments.”

Once seated, Leyton produced three pieces of A4 paper from his briefcase, which he pushed on to the light wood veneer coffee table which formed the hub of three beautifully dark red upholstered designer low chairs.

Leyton commenced.

“To save time I will now tell you what it says: the number dialled from the location India received the following message from a number that belongs to Sanjeev Pahkim, the renowned businessman. Further investigation and West Drayton Air Traffic Control informed us that a Captain Lewis filed a flight plan to Trivandrum Airport South West India for a Gulfstream jet belonging to Sanjeev. It departed six hours ago from this very airfield with Sanjeev and a lawyer called Martin Parnell as his guest who is the father of young man in distress in India. They have three hours to run to their destination, and have filed a reciprocal flight plan back to the UK leaving one hour after arrival. The manifest indicates that Hugo Parnell, the son of Sanjeev’s guest, will be on the return flight. We want to intercept and question them when they eventually arrive back at Northolt. In the meantime, I am sure that you would like to bring us up to speed with the results of your information-gathering exercise with Colonel Yitzhak Avraham.” Tom Leyton grinned.

Grace gave Leyton a wry grimace, Smith remained poker faced and looked un interested

“Ok Tom I fully understand but what I am about to tell you defies belief but the reality is it presents a disturbing and credible threat to world security” said Grace.

For the next hour, Grace divulged to an alarmed Tom Leyton and poker faced Robert Smith all she had learned about the covenant of the ring, nearly word for word she recited the report which Avraham had given to her.

“My goodness” exclaimed a clearly concerned Leyton. “this is unreal”

“So, what you’re telling me is that these little Nazis are working in our banking and government offices and large industrial concerns.” He added

"Yes, Tom. Except they are not all little and they wield a lot of power. It seems they are coordinating vexatious and evil acts. Recall the word 'plan' in the message"

"Yes, I do."

Robert Smith stood up stared at Wells and broke his silence.

"What has our little nerdy friend in India got to do with all this?"

"Well, the little nerd was the anonymous little nobody who slid under the radar and into the TET server as the PM's husband without leaving a trace."

"I'll take great pleasure in dealing with this young man when he arrives," said Smith.

"That won't be necessary." exclaimed Tom Leyton

"More coffee, I think," said Grace.

The Mercedes ambulance sped through the streets of Trivandrum, the sirens drowned out by the background noise of cars, motorcycles blasting their horns in a move to establish territory on the busy highway. Hugo had moved and was now lying on his back looking on the rust peppered white painted ceiling of the vehicle, he was still in a state of semi-shock and had no idea that one of his would-be captors had lost his life.

The ambulance and the black BMW trail arrived at the airfield and were directed to the private executive terminal by an officious moustached gentleman who was wearing a dark brown uniform which displayed ribbons of medals he had most probably been awarded for years of service and not military bravery. On the poorly-finished and ill-lit road the vehicles proceeded to the terminal.

The ambulance jolted and arrested to an abrupt halt at the entrance to the terminal and Hugo grabbed the rails on the trolley to halt a fall.

Vijay and Dr Singh jumped out the rear of the BMW as it was still running to a standstill. They both ran around to the rear of the ambulance and surveyed the vicinity, to ensure that it was safe to open the door of the ambulance. The yellow glow on the inside of the ambulance could be seen for quite a distance in the moody ambiance of the airfield. The light provided a perfect backdrop for Hugo as he stumbled down steps aided by one of the medics who then helped him out and into the terminal building. This indeed provided a perfect lightshow for the onlookers who sat in the Toyota four-by-four vehicle parked one hundred metres North of the terminal. The blond-haired passenger in the Toyota turned to the two men in the back and said.

"That's him."

The front seat passenger tuned to each of the other occupants in turn and said.

"The flight is due to arrive in sixty-five minutes. It will be cleared to go direct to the terminal. It will need to refuel, and I expect the return flight to be underway in an hour from landing, so it gives us a little time to make the grab."

The menacing figures remained silent and nodded their understanding of the situation.

Hugo was escorted through the double aluminium-framed glazed doors into an unlit reception area, off which four white doors led to offices, one of them which was the main departure lounge. One of the blue-uniformed medics who had gone ahead into the lounge flicked the switch which illuminated a very plush and well-appointed accommodation. The walls were painted a pale blue and were overlaid by a tapestry of photographs of an array of small jets and old Indian Air Force fighter planes.

At the end of the space was a pair of light oak double doors which gave way to the departure area. Scattered around were high-quality leather and material quilted sofas and armchairs fenced around beautifully adorned coffee tables. All of which were cushioned on a beautiful dark blue patterned Indian-themed carpet.

The second medic sat his patient down on a black leather sofa, and Dr Singh brought Hugo a bottle of water mixed with electrolyte.

"Drink this up, please. You've had a shock and you need to remain fully hydrated."

Hugo unscrewed the top of the water and gulped down several mouthfuls of the strange-tasting liquid. The Indian doctor knelt down in front of Hugo and looked him in the eye. With his hand on Hugo's hand, he said.

"Hugo, listen to me. Your father and his very good friend Sanjeev are en route from England and will be here within the hour to take you home. I have to leave now, as does Dr

Patel, but my two colleagues will remain with you until your father arrives. Nobody else knows you're here. You're safe now. God blesses."

"Ok, doctor. Thank you. I owe my life to you, I could not thank you enough. Thank you and please accept my best wishes."

Still semi-shocked, Hugo was rambling on. In fact, he still had not fully acclimatised himself to what had happened over the past hour.

"I just want to go home, Doctor. Please let me go home."

Dr Singh placed both of his hands on Hugo's shoulders.

"Listen, my friend. It's all ok now. You're safe. You're with two of my most reliable colleagues here." "and please drink the fluid you need replenishment after the shock you have suffered."

Hugo nodded unscrewed the top from the bottle and gulped down several mouthfuls of the salty tasting clear water.

One of the medics followed Dr Singh and Dr Patel to the exit the building, when they were gone he ensured that the door was locked safely behind them. The last of the medics announced himself.

"Hello, Hugo, I'm Ravi and I'll be here until your father and his friend arrive."

The BMW departed and the driver concentrated on negotiating potholes in the dim light. None of occupants of the departing car noticed the four-by-four and its sinister occupants parked near the terminal. As the BMW drew up all four occupants of the Toyota ducked down to avoid any visual contact. It worked. Jacob returned to the seated position in the vehicle and the others followed.

"Right, they have locked the door on the terminal from the inside, so we cannot gain access without making a noise.

"This is the plan."

Pointing to the two in the rear.

"You're coming with me. We will need to cut a hole in the chain-link fence which will allow us access to the apron on the air side of the terminal." Nodding at the driver, "You remain here until the operation is complete and we have the prisoner."

Jacob then announced in a chilling and steely tone.

"And he will be the only prisoner. I want the father and the air crew and the Indian dead. Silence at all times. Our air crew will be arriving in ten minutes and will park behind us until we complete the take. It is imperative that we do not make a jump until just before they are ready to go. We need the aircraft to be refuelled and a departure flight plan to be filed. Do you understand?"

"Yes," they all nodded.

It was a perfectly coordinated and unemotional response.

"Ok, sit tight until the Gulfstream arrives."

Approximately forty minutes later, three white lights illuminated the taxiway as the Gulfstream repositioned to the executive terminal.

"Will you require fuel G-SANJ?" the message crackled into the headset of Captain Lewis.

Affirm 4000 US gallons Jet A1," Captain Lewis announced to the tower,

"I will arrange the credit card" he added

"Proceed to stand and shut down and refueller will be waiting. Do you need any other ground supplies?"

"Negative," replied Captain Lewis. "We will be taking one POB with us for the return flight."

The jet turned on its illuminated nose wheel and came to a halt and Captain Lewis spooled down the General Electric turbofan engines. The First Officer disabled the switch lock and powered up the cabin door latch and the retractable passenger stairs which touched the warm concrete. This was Hugo's stairway to freedom. Captain Lewis popped his head from the cockpit door and shuffled down the passenger stairway and shouted.

"45 minutes' maximum before we depart so do not waste any time"

He gave the all clear and his two passengers descended the aircraft stairs. As Sanjeev stepped onto the concrete apron he was greeted by the roar of the diesel engine powered yellow Ashok Leyland refuelling truck.

The airside door of the terminal was in darkness as Ravi opened it to welcome the new arrivals. Hugo felt the warm night air and the unmistakable odour of jet fuel rush into the air conditioned terminal building. His spirits erupted when heard he heard the welcoming voice of his father.

"Hugo, are you there? We're here to take you home. It's Dad. Where are you, my son?"

For the first time in many years, Hugo felt a true empathy, even a vague essence of love in his voice. Hugo was in tears. Tears of joy; tears of fear, tears of confusion. But tears all the same.

His father caught sight of Hugo through his own tear-filled eyes. He was relieved to see his boy. Hugo ran to his father and they embraced in a tight lock for what seemed minutes.

"I need a drink. Where's the bar?" joked Sanjeev. "Ok, water will do. The champagne can remain on ice until we climb out on our return journey.

Captain Lewis entered through the access door, Ravi made sure that it was re secured behind him. Hugo sat next to his father and Sanjeev remained standing as Lewis briefed his passengers.

"Ok, let's get it done," he said in clipped RAF speak. "We are taking fuel on as we speak and our planned departure is in thirty-eight minutes. I suggest that you all remain here until I call you."

"Yes, sir, Captain," bellowed Sanjeev.

"Dad, I'm so pleased to see you. It's all such a mess. I really thought they were going to kill me. Please forgive me for bringing disgrace to the family, but I only thought I was doing my best to avenge Sarah. I was in my world, one I felt safe in, one where I never expected to encounter real villains and murderers."

"Oh, please do not fret. It's me that needs to apologise to you. My work has always taken precedence over my family. You just get sucked into a parallel world of winning, greed, power and esteem. Well, my only boy, that will change when we're back home. I'm going to take substantial time off with you and Mum and rethink my life."

His father told him the whole story, the sequence of events that led to them being in that terminal building on that warm morning at this airport in southern West India.

Unknown to the occupants of the terminal, thirty metres away from the aircraft three men dressed totally in black fatigues and balaclavas were approaching the chain-link fence, which constituted the boundary between air side and the general public. Crouching down, Jacob turned to his accomplice.

"Cutters, please."

He nibbled a hole approximately one metre by one metre from the base of the fence. A quick look around and they crawled through.

"Ok. Go slowly to the edge of the building and wait until I tell you to move." Pointing to one at the rear: "You will go up the stairs and hold the crew. No shooting in the cockpit. Get them down the stairs and we'll dispatch them outside the terminal."

Pointing to the other man whose dark silhouette melted into the shadows.

"You follow me to the door. As soon as they appear, take them all out except the boy. And I mean that. That's my instruction."

His blue eyes irradiated against the backdrop of the dark night, he said.

"I repeat, kill them all except the boy."

"Clear," was the cold reply.

As Captain Lewis stood on the apron and signed for the fuel, the three attackers moved to their assigned positions at the edge of the terminal. Lewis ascended to the cockpit and five minutes later returned to the door of the dimly lit departure building. The door opened and Lewis shouted,

"We're ready to go. Get your things and await my call."

Hugo and his father arose from their seats to join Sanjeev, who was already stood up and eager to leave. Nothing was said all of a sudden, the atmosphere had become tense, they were on their way but not home yet.

Overhearing the Captains instructions, Jacob turned to his two henchmen and his finger against his lips he moved his hand and pointed at his rear man then signalled towards the aircraft steps. Jacob held his 9mm machine pistol and with his gloved left hand screwed in place a 250mm long silencer. They remained in waiting, a big cat in the long grass ready to pounce on it's prey when the moment was right.

Inside the terminal lips were tense, heads were low there was only the faint sound of breathing and the whirring air conditioning unit.

The passengers were only a matter of yards and minutes from the ride to freedom, but Hugo had experienced the guile of these men, the cold blooded killers who had duped him He was scared and was unable to let it be known to his saviours. One medic stood by the door whilst the other was in line behind the three passengers, the silent trio stared at the floor then the walls. To focus on the gleaming white jet awaiting them was too much as to them it was still very very far away.

The driver looked in the rear-view mirror and observed a vehicle not using any form of light pulling up behind him.

"Ah, the pilots," he thought, and relaxed a little. Under his breath, he muttered, "All on schedule."

Back on the apron, Captain Lewis walked from the Gulfstream towards the terminal, and provided the cue to Jacob that it was nearly time to move. Jacob pointed at the rear gun and followed up with hand movements signalling that he wanted them to move towards the aircraft.

The unlit apron provided perfect cover for the killers to move towards the aircraft. The lit open door provided a beacon for him to home into.

Lewis knocked on the door and the medic unlocked and opened it.

Lewis shouted,

"Ok, move it, now. Get across the apron as quick as you can and get into the aircraft."

Thanking the medic, he turned towards the aircraft.

This was the moment to move, knew Jacob. His woollen-gloved hand held the machine pistol and he cocked the instrument of extinction with his left hand.

"Ok," he said.

He turned to give number two his orders to move. As he focussed on the man behind him, he was confused. It was not Schmitt.

He did not have time to panic, react, or reconcile the situation as Sergeant Dave 'Jim'Reeves emptied two rounds of muffled 9mm pistol munition right between Jacob's eyes. He was killed instantly. Behind Reeves was a limp body, throat cut from ear to ear courtesy of Corporal Ravi Ravhindran of the Indian Special Forces, who was currently being trained by Reeves and some of his mates from the mob.

Unaware of what had happened to his accomplices, the third attacker had made his move. As he emerged from the shadow towards the bottom of the aircraft steps, he fell to the floor at the receipt of two bullets from a silenced machine pistol, this time placed in the highly trained hands of Steve "Tom" Jones of the Regiment Special Air Services.

The driver checked the rear-view mirror and for a millisecond saw the black-clad figure in the back of the car. Then there was blackness. His head flopped forward over the steering wheel, blood gushed from the huge wound which exposed the severed jugular vein.

The regiment had done its job as instructed by HQ. Jim and the four servicemen had been stationed in Augarabad helping the Indian Special Services in counter-terrorism training. In fact, they were delighted to be able to provide them with a real-life 'reccy'.

Back in England, once Leyton knew the severity of the situation, he had made calls to the right desk in the HQ of intelligence. This triggered the whole chain of calls to Augarabad and ministers on both continents were awoken. India over the years had had its own dose of terrorism, resulting in huge loss of life. Today they took homeland security very seriously, understanding threats from within as well as foreign terrorist organisations and in some instances, actual countries. You only had to visit New Delhi airport and witness the heightened security checks and the intense deployment of troops to guard the terminals.

When the appropriate ministers were aware of the situation, they were more than happy to cooperate with the UK and provide their own Special Services with some real action

Chapter 21

It had been a gruelling twenty-four hours for Lukas Richter. A big event with his colleagues and then a long flight back to the UK. Though he managed to get some sleep he remained wide awake when he arrived back at his Holland Park house late that evening. Freshly showered, he lay on his bed in an attempt to get some shuteye.

The ringing of his mobile phone and the coupled message provided the perfect antidote to tiredness.

An educated European accent: "Lukas, we have a problem." In perfect German the caller reported,

"Your little computer whizz kid has gone rogue on us."

"I'm sure Hans and Jacob with help from their associates will deal with it."

"Sorry to interrupt, Lukas, but you need to be told the full picture. Hans, Jacob and their colleagues are all dead. It seems India's Special Forces were tipped off. That to one side, our little computer boffin has spoken about his activities and Sanjeev Pahkim turned up in India in his jet to bring him home. So now the intelligence services have got wind of it all and have dealt with the problem to protect Hugo."

Richter was just about to reply when the caller continued in a voice that was becoming slightly and deliberately raised, his tone hinted that matters had escalated:

"Def Com one to five, as the Americans say."

"Well, they're not bringing him home for mother's cooking. My money is, there's a reception committee waiting for him."

Not even Captain Lewis heard the two discharged SAS weapons. In the shadows the bodies of the attackers had been removed. Lewis stood at the bottom of the aircraft steps welcoming his passengers, as all times with his back to the blood stains that lay on the fringe of the dark shadows and the soft illumination of the concrete airfield.

Ten minutes later the Gulfstream was climbing from 27 right hand.

Sanjeev bawled,

"Time for a glass of champagne."

Hugo was already asleep, lying in his father's lap. Unbeknown to him, the water bottle had contained a sleeping draught as well as electrolytes.

The caller was unquestionably angry, a normally calm operator who communicated in an educated European accent, barked his displeasure through the handset. The situation in India was of huge concern to him.

"Lukas what the hell has happened it is a catastrophe, one which compromised our plan, now get the lid on it now.do you get it" berated the irate caller.

Richter' attempt to interject was cut short.

"You and your team have been shoddy Herr Richter, and now we must bring the end date forward and compress the timescale"

"I hear what you say......"

"Herr Richter let me finish please, I have neither the time nor the appetite to hear the feeble excuses"

Richter listened with growing unease.

"you need to speak to Friedrich without delay, work your men hard, no rest bite, we need to achieve in 4 weeks that was planned for 3 months"

The caller shouted.

"no more mistakes, no delays no excuses"

There was a familiar click in Richter's left ear and the call was ended.

Angered at the shambles in India and left a little ragged after his tense call, Lukas Richter adjusted his towelling bathroom and sped down two flights of stairs and into his office.

The large white regency door opened onto a sympathetically designed contemporary study space.

Centre stage was a large smoked glass and polished stainless steel desk undoubtedly crafted by the hands of skilled Italian artisans. The walls were finish painted in a whimsical array of grey, black, magenta and primrose yellow panels. Two tall piano black and mirrored glass cabinets garnished the wall opposite the pair of floor to ceiling sash windows. Tradition was retained in the form of a white regency fire place. Richter opened the glass doors on the left hand unit, to uncover the mirrored internals of a cocktail cabinet. A large cut crystal tumbler afforded the perfect vessel for a single malt.

Whisky in his left hand, Richter walked over to the window and retracted the original 19th Century vertical shutter. He swilled the whisky inside the fine Irish crystal, pondered his next move, stared at the outside word, raised the tumbler to his lips and downed the drink in one.

Downing Schnapps in one was programmed into his DNA.

The fine unblended scotch hit the spot, and revitalised he placed the tumbler on the table, with a heavy thud. Lukas Richter sat in the high backed dark red leather chair, and with his mobile phone grasped in his left hand he dialled a number.

Twenty-three seconds later a familiar noise proclaimed the connection.

"Lukas" a drowsy Guy Walker whispered.

"Yes Guy correct it is I, we need to meet today in fact, let us say 0700 at my house "

"why the call at 03.30 please?" Leyton protested.

"well Tom, if I cannot sleep why should you" he laughed.

"now get some sleep and instead of counting sheep, figure out how we get immediate control of two companies within 10 days. I will see you 0700 sharp"

Click and the call was over

A dreamy Walker still startled at being ripped from the 'arms of Morpheus' to listen to Richter's ridiculous demands, threw the mobile across the bedroom.

He reset the alarm clock to 0545 and elected to go back to sleep.

'*that arrogant man Richter can wait until tomorrow morning'* he muttered.

Four kilometres away in an apartment overlooking the Thames close to Vauxhall bridge, a mobile phone rang out loudly.

The alerted occupant of the super king sized bed rolled over and reached out for his phone ringing out on the bedside table.

Phillip Medway grabbed the phone and noted the flashing display, it was Lukas Richter.

"Lukas what the hell its three bloody thirty, what is the matter" remonstrated Medway.

"never what the hell me ever again, never forget who you work for" barked a clearly displeased Richter.

"Without me you would still be digging fucking holes in the ground, now you listen to me and listen good"

"Ok Lukas, but it is just gone 3.30 what is the panic?"

A slightly acquiesced Richter jumped in.

"OK Phillip I am aware of the time but we need to talk, there have been some developments."

"Just give me a moment Lukas I need coffee"

Medway shuffled out of bed and phone lodged against his left ear, he carried out a well-choreographed routine and managed to pull on a dark grey towelling bathrobe.

As Medway, headed downstairs and into the kitchen the caller brought him up to speed on the events in India.

"Bloody hell Lukas this is not good" replied Medway as he tried to engage with an over complex coffee machine.

Ten minutes and one Americano coffee later, a slightly relaxed Medway was exchanging ideas with Richter.

"OK Lukas I will 'rattle' a few door handles in the corridors where the 'Mandarins' reside and get those contracts approved, from a regulatory perspective, and then nothing will stop us.

"I understand that JBL are still in Israel, in a consultancy role, and also there are Engineers working on pre commissioning activities at four water plants"

Medway continued.

"The work is all pro bono in an attempt to warm the hearts and cheque books of the Israelis"

"Look Lukas we are well embedded and therefore with the contracts in place we will be able to get our men close enough to the action for us to complete our task.,"

"and' said Richter

"I will push the 'powers to be' to get heads of terms in place and kick some ass to get the trade clearances." Replied

"Top of your list Lukas will be to be to take full control of JBL CONTRACTING CONTRACTS and get your men in place."

"Yes Phillip I have already got the wheels in motion" declared Richter.

"I will get on Lukas" said Medway. The conversation ended with a more lucid and conciliatory ambiance."

Guy arrived at the Holland Park Road address at 06.55, paid the taxi driver and bounded up the half dozen stone stairs which fronted the opulent cream 4 story town house.

He stood in front of the beautiful gloss black painted door, turned his head and scanned the exquisite neighbourhood. *He was in the 'valley of the kings'*, the *residential homes of business billionaires, and a host of music, stage and screen stars.*

He was just about to press the gleaming chrome door bell, when the door opened and the face of Lukas Richter appeared.

"Please come in Guy, we need to get started, and I apologise but we have no time for breakfast."

Richter led Guy into a large first floor kitchen which overlooked the tree lined road.

The kitchen was a juxtaposition of classical high ceilings ornamented with 19th century plaster coving, and the modern high gloss white Italian kitchen units.

An array of high quality German stainless steel appliances complemented the beautiful cabinets.

Richter pointed to high legged quilted leather topped stool, and they both took their places around the stainless steel trimmed island unit.

"Guy I will get straight to it, there has been a serious breach of security"

Richter continued for 35 minutes and acquainted the caffeine starved Guy, with the recent events which had led to the meeting.

"So what can we do to override this mess?" questioned a weary Guy.

Richter leaned over the immaculate stainless steel worktop and replied

"Nothing other than accelerate our plans, so you need to coordinate with Stuch and swiftly acquire the requisite volume of shares in JBL CONTRACTING" "it is imperative that we gain full control of the board and company" stressed the Austrian.

"Thankfully there will be regulatory resistance from the authorities, that has been taken care of"

"Furthermore over the last 6 months we have gently squeezed our influence by appointing our people in key operational roles within that organisation

Richter continued.

"This has allowed our people placed in JBL the opportunity to carry out advanced due diligence on the workings of the water treatment plants in Israel. To date they have been able to show off the operational efficiencies and cost saving benefits of the JBL patented technologies" "in some instances clean water output improvements of up to 11% with cost benefits approaching 15% have been enjoyed."

"What about competition for the contract" enquired Guy

Richter opened a buff folder which revealed a summary on the project and passed it to his understudy.

He pointed at the third light green highlighted paragraph of the document.

"See here, the un copied and highly protected technology and supporting process software is a clear winner with the Israelis and they have a real appetite to work with us to improve upon the country's fresh water supply."

Richter found time for a smile.

"They want us, in fact they need us, not only for retrofit technology to existing water treatment and de salination plants but for all new builds"

Richter grinned and placed his hands in the air, his palms facing Walker.

"They have no time to go elsewhere or develop their own solutions"

The Austrian continued with a hint of excitement in his voice.

"The backing of the UK government who will place future restrictions on JBL ownership will give the Israeli government full comfort in regard to any matters of national security"

A grinning Richter was on a roll and Guy listened intently.

"I have spoken with both Phillip Medway and the CEO of JBL and insisted that Heads of Terms are in place within 5 days"" concurrent with that we must take full control of the Company"

"It is imperative that we have full access to those plants within weeks."

"My goodness weeks, why the sudden rush" Guy questioned.

"That you do not need to bother yourself with Guy all I ask of you is get me control of JBL, do what you need to, pay the market rate the funds are there, and try and keep a low profile so not to spook the markets"

A slightly battered and weary Guy, who by now was craving nourishment and coffee replied.

"Fine Lukas I fully understand and I will get things moving today."

He paused for a moment to figure out an approach.

"We will go for a spread approach and as I understand it Medway's shares are well hidden in the Cayman Islands?"

"Correct" affirmed Richter.

"Guy we have no more business I will let you go and start work"

"OK Lukas I will get started" replied Guy with an inflection of moderate foreboding in his voice.

This did not fall into Guy's plans for the day, he had hoped to go and spend the recent spoils of victory. He had planned a day on Saville Row, and a spot of 'tyre kicking' in Purdey's gun shop. He had after all made £2.3m a day before, so work was not top of his agenda.

The peerless black door quietly closed behind Guy and he made his way down the stone steps and onto the pavement. Shaking his head re rolled back the cuff on his dark blue suit jacket to expose his beloved Rolex. It read displayed five past eight, *'sod it he had time for a much desired breakfast'*, and he headed off in the cold morning air towards the nearest tube station. As Guy wrangled with the flowing mass of morning rush hour, his mind was so focussed on coffee, eggs and toast, that he did not notice the two men who were following him.

The men did not move together but indeed were allied, however, they did not look out of the ordinary in the morning hustle and bustle. The carriage of the Jubilee Line train was packed to capacity and Guy had managed to grab a seat next to a rather large man wearing a black chalk stripe suit, who's attempts for total occupation of the arm rest were rebutted by Guy on numerous occasions. Sat to his left was a short haired man probably in his mid - thirties, who was casually clothed in a denim jacket, white t shirt blue jeans and canvas boots. He held a mobile phone which was connected to ear plugs via a white lead, oddly the irritating hiss of music coming from the ear pieces was absent.

Unbeknown to the commuters, one of the innocuous looking ear sets was actually connected to a communication device, the model used by the British Secret Service and Special Branch.

Further down the packed carriage, stood in the aisle was a tall man in chinos, trainers and a dark blue wax cotton jacket. Nobody noticed that he was also wearing and ear piece identical to the one used by the man sat next to Guy.

The train slowed on the approach to the Baker Street stop, and Guy got up from his seat ready to disembark. His eventual destination would be a well renowned breakfast restaurant situated at the corner of Baker Street and Bickenhall Street.

It was now eight thirty and any pedestrian progress was impeded by the mass of peak period passengers, this allowed the two men furnishing ear pieces to overtake Guy as they fought their way across platform 6.

Guy departed the final escalator and tapped an Oyster card onto the turnstile which allowed him free transit to the Baker Street North exit. He proceeded to the outside world onto the most polluted road in London, to Guy this was still a welcome relief from the hot dirty claustrophobic underground.

All of a sudden and to Guy's alarm his progress was obstructed by the man wearing the denim jacket, in response Guy pushed back in an attempt to prevent the block.

The counter measure met with resistance and the denim clad man delivered a robust intervention and grabbed Guy firmly by the right arm.

"Hey what is you game man "Guy protested

Within a second the other man with ear piece came along side and grabbed Guy by the left arm. In a reflex Guy turned his head left and shouted."

Hey asshole what is your problem"

Guy was now in fight or flight mode, with the former taking over, the adrenaline flowed fast, his pupils narrowed and he was set and ready to engage with these two would be assailants.

His mind working at lightning speed to figure out what to do next, however, his actions were abruptly halted.

"Mr Walker. can you please relax we would like you to come with us" announced the denim clad man, who flipped open a brown leather wallet to reveal a Police warrant card.

"I am Chief Inspector David Bishop of Special Branch, and on your left is Sergeant Paul Brown"

"WHAT" A very fazed Guy exclaimed.

"Just come with us sir we need to talk to about some recent activity carried out at your brokerage"

"We are acting on behalf of the FSA"

Guy was not convinced with the reason, "*it was far too soon, it had only been yesterday, no way would the authorities act so quickly'* he reckoned.

Then for a fleeting moment he thought that he may have been framed, a 'patsy' for Richter's illicit dealings.

"Well if you let go of my arm I will come along; it looks as though my options are limited.

"Am I under arrest ?" quizzed Guy.

"No sir not at the moment, but we do need to talk to you in connection with some very serious matters of National security"

Outside the entrance to the tube station a Black Range Rover Sport SVR straddled the pavement and road, the driver had placed his warrant card in the window to ward off any overzealous traffic wardens. Bishop opened the rear door of the SVR and ushered Guy into the vehicle. Guy got into the 4 x4 and was accompanied by the surly Sergeant Brown. Sat behind the steering wheel was an officer with short hair and stubble beard, the menacing figure was wearing a tight blue polo shirt which projected the well-toned bi ceps of the karate black belt

'Not a man to cross' Guy summed up.

Bishop hopped into the front passenger seat, slammed the door and belted out in a north London accent.

"Let's move it Rockie"

DC Richard 'Rockie" Allen, rolled his glance towards Bishop.

"Northolt Gov?"

"Northolt Rockie" Bishop affirmed." And give us the display of blue lights, the A40 traffic will be heavy so we need all the help possible"

A spooked Guy shouted out.

"What the f is going on, Northolt, that is military not the Old Bill"

Bishop turned and through the gap between the black leather seat headrests he stared at Guy.

'it was a stare that had, 'we mean business and do not try anything with us' written all over it'

Guy did not respond the, *'message was loud and clear.'*

The covertly positioned blue lights were powered up, the supercharged petrol V8 roared into life and the passengers were pushed back into their seats as the 550 BHP engine accelerated the vehicle the wrong way down Baker St.

At speed they turned into Melcombe Street, the high authority of the blue lights paving the clear track through the minefield of commuter traffic.

Ten minutes passed and as they arrived at Hanger Lane and Guy grabbed Bishop's attention.

"What is all of this about Inspector, this has nothing to do with the FSA has it?"

"We will be asking all of the questions Mr Walker, all in good time"

Bishop replied indignantly.

The Range Rover, slowed from the law breaking speed and turned towards the main entrance of RAF Northolt. The vehicle stopped at the gate and the Special Branch men were received by two Military Police Sergeants. One of the MPs examined the drivers pass, then peered into the vehicle.

The driver uttered a coded sentence, the policeman signalled to his compatriot who raised the red and white striped barrier.

Rockie had been to Northolt many times, and being familiar with the layout he squeezed the shift stick into drive mode and steered the vehicle left towards the Executive Jet Terminal.

It had been several hours since Leyton and his visitors had arrived at the Terminal, and in the intervening period the facility had become fully operational and was now occupied by the day time staff. To maintain privacy and confidentiality Leyton et al had been relocated to one of the secure meeting rooms situated at the rear of the building, a section of the facility reserved under lock and key for the Intelligence Services.

The windowless room provided a reasonable level of comfort thanks in the main to well-chosen lighting and a near silent air conditioning system. The furnishings were austere in comparison to the main terminal, an oval beech veneer table provided centre stage to twelve dark grey cloth upholstered chairs. Tom Leyton sat furthest from the door at the far end of the table with Grace Wells at his right and Captain 'call me Robert please' Smith opposite Wells. It had been a long night and the three tired occupants had exhausted the small talk, Leyton had resorted to rocking on his chair whilst the other two just stared into space.

The peace was interrupted as the door opened and DCI Bishop led Guy into the brightly lit room. Guy Walker stopped in his tracks when he saw Tom Leyton sat at the far end of the room.

"Tommy what the hell is going on, is this a pisstake?" blurted out the clearly ruffled Guy.

A very controlled and trite Grace Wells responded with a hard stare and replied.

"No Mr Walker this is not a pisstake that I can guarantee, you are here as part of an investigation which concerns National security, I suggest you sit down and listen"

Leyton look at Guy and nodded his approval of Wells' instruction.

Guy sat down and pronounced."

I am all ears Tommy and if you do not convince me soon of what is going on here I will demand my lawyer"

On this mark Captain Smith lunged towards Guy, slapped the palms of his hands firmly on the table, and with unyielding eyes locked onto his victim, he screamed.

"Walker now listen to me and listen good, there is no place for lawyers in this room, we just do not recognise them, so stay seated shut up and listen to the man"

Guy had seen this type of man before, he knew what they did for a living. He elected to acknowledge Smith's orders.

Smith addressed the two Special Branch men.

"Gentlemen can you please leave us now and remain outside, thank you."

Bishop and Brown nodded left the room and closed the door.

The definitive click of the door lock being activated sent a cold shiver through Guys soul. Tom Leyton placed his elbows on the table and looked at each occupant of the room in turn.

"Well Guy let me begin and I shall in this instance start at the end, I hope this will make sense in good time. I have a lot to tell you but we are under time pressure so I will present the outcomes."

A confused Guy nodded.

On the floor next to Tom Leyton was a 1980s style hard shell black briefcase, he bent down opened it and removed a dark pink A4 folder which he placed on the desk.

Tapping his finger tips on the folder Leyton stared directly into Guy's eyes,

He then made his pitch.

"Well my friend I have three outcomes to present to you and for the sake of yourself and the Nation I sincerely hope that you chose the final option."

Leyton rubbed his teeth with his tongue, nervously bit his bottom lip, inhaled deeply and presented the alternatives to a very attentive Guy.

"Option 1 is as follows. I have sufficient evidence in this folder."

He paused for a minute after which he tapped the document then the GCHQ man leaned across the table towards Guy and in an act of unequivocal authority dealt by a man who was confident of being able to execute any threat, he continued.

"To put you behind bars for at least 20 years, charges from insider trading to treason, the evidence real or not will stick I warrant that and you will serve a lot of time."

A very unnerved and restless Guy, Leyton's words resonating in his head, did not doubt that the people in that room could deliver on their threats,

'He thought that the TET deal had been too good to be true, he had been dragged into some large scale fraud and act of international espionage.'

Guy Walker remained silent and returned a look of disbelief at Leyton *'how could his old mate Tommy do this to him the Judas.'* He shook his head in disproval at his so called friend.

Nothing in his wildest dreams and his large imagination could have prepared him for what came next, option 2!

In fact, Grace Wells was stunned by what Leyton said next.

"Option 2, well option 2 involves me or us handing you over to my colleague Captain Smith, and he will deal with you."

There was silence. Guy froze to his seat, Wells wide eyed looked at Leyton and Captain Smith gave a sinister smile.

Leyton continued

"And before you ask I have full authority and I have orders from the highest office in the land, so to avoid any doubt ...... repeat I will hand you over to Smith, do you understand."

Guy walker was motionless.

"Captain Smith here is highly trained in creating quiet out of noise if you get my meaning!" continued Leyton.

Guy felt the blood leave his body, he had encountered many sticky situations in his life, he had survived suspected gas attacks in the Gulf War, and missed colliding with the trees at over 100 mph at Oliver's Mount race circuit.

'This was major league shit, like he had never known before and with no probability of survival.'

For the first occasion in his 50 odd years he was frightened, desperate, terrorised beyond his wildest imagination.

"Fuck" he uttered under his breath and in a slightly broken and noticeably nervous voice he squeaked.

"And……and option 3?"

Leyton sat back in his seat and shuffled the document on the table with his right hand, looked at his two colleagues and gave his answer.

"Well Guy my old drinking buddy Option 3" he acted out another well designed pause and then continued.

"You fully cooperate with us it is that simple"

"Cooperate on what" responded Guy.

"You help us get Richter and help us penetrate and close down his evil empire, and assist us in stopping an attack he is organisation is planning"

Guy relaxed a little, *this was a temporary reprieve from the executioner*

"Ok Tommy I am all ears", "Confused but all ears." he replied.

Leyton gave a sigh of satisfaction, Wells gasped relief and Smith exuded disappointment.

For the next two hours Leyton and Wells told Guy all they knew about Richter, the Covenant, developments in India and the prediction that the Covenant were working on some terrorist plot of unimaginable proportion.

Just after 11.18 GMT the Gulfstream owned by Sanjeev Pakhim touched down on runway Two Seven at Northolt Airfield England. It had been a very intense, emotional and confusing four hours for Guy, starting with Richter exerting pressure only to be followed up by quasi arrest by Special Branch and then to be put under the threat of his own mortal existence. All of this surreal, intimidating and terrifying activity on an empty stomach. Low blood sugar levels had set Guy's head in a spin resulting in a thumping migraine and impaired reasoning.*my goodness what had he got involved with* he reflected as mild panic began to creep into his psyche.

Then to eclipse all of the insane events, he had to listen to an account of a worldwide conspiracy, funded by a legacy of Hitler's Third Reich, and a covenant of 21st Century Nazis hell-bent on killing 'undesirables', and the creation and rise of an Aryan master race.

Acts of terror and murder veined with echoes of the past, inhumane acts on a large scale carried out by monsters. All bank rolled by funds from mysterious backers in Europe who through pseudo legitimate financial arbitrage continued to multiply their ill-gotten gains of the early 1940s. Then grand finale, the revelation of the provenance of the silver ring Guy wore on his finger. Leyton has explained that this was the physical symbol which identified members of the evil, secretive and unassailable club.

Guy blocked out his mind from his immediate surroundings and reflected on his only recent reincarnation into the world of finance, '*it had been too good to be true he concluded, to opportune, and again he wondered why had Richter courted him?'*

Then out of the blue he was hit with the reality of why he was involved, it was a moment of gut wrenching blind panic he broke out in a cold sweat, he experienced deep nausea and a chilling sensation which speared the marrow of his honest bones.

"My God my God" he spluttered "they think that I am one of them, a ring bearing descendant, a member of the evil clan, I wear the ring that is it "that is the reason I was chosen"

An astonished Grace Wells chirped in.

"Yes got it one, you have it right on the nose, they or at least Richter believes that you are one of the covenant, you're a bearer of the ring"

"One born from the ashes of the evil empire of Nazi Germany, more a Firebird of Satan than a Phoenix" added Robert Smith.

Leyton clapped his hands.

"Now listen they clearly believe in you and have no reason to think otherwise, so let us use this or more precisely use you to our full advantage."

A clearly uncomfortable Guy protested.

"What you want me to risk my life, be as stooge, and try and get to the top of this organisation, and help you foil plans for some hypothetical act of terror."

"If they find out what I am up to they will kill me Tom" he halted as he realised what he had said.

“At least option 3 allows you some conduct over your fate Guy, please do not underestimate our willingness to exercise the other two options.” said Leyton

“My God “remarked Grace Wells. “you would really go through with option 2”

Tom Leyton gave her an acute sideways look; he was not bluffing.

Leyton leaned down to his case and retrieved a mobile phone. And in the style reminiscent of a salon bar owner serving up bottle of whisky in a determined act he flung the mobile down the table top to Guy. Just like in the movies Guy caught the object as it skated across the polished surface.

“Guy this is a secure encrypted phone with access to Grace and I only and one other number of vital importance to you”

“And what is the other number a direct line to the Pope, the PM, God?” replied a churlish Guy.

“No Guy that speed dial will go straight to Captain Smith here, and to be used if you are in danger of losing your life” affirmed Leyton.

“One call and Robert and his friends from Hereford will be at your disposal, also use this contact to let us know if you become aware of any immediate threat to the public”

“My goodness Tom I feel important. Said Walker in a laconic tone

“Do you fully acknowledge Walker.” a scowling Captain Smith asked.

“Yes, it is clear and what do I do now “

"Go back to work and carry on as usual, keep close to Richter, and keep us informed on any salient developments., I suggest you call us on a daily basis as matter of routine, at all times use the phone I have given to you." Instructed Leyton.

"We will also be giving you direction on what we need to know" added Wells.

Tom Leyton arose from his seat.

"It is time to leave us for now Guy, one of Bishop's men will take you back into town, and yes he will stop for some breakfast en route."

In an act of mock surrender Guy stood up and held his hands in the air.

"I have no option but to follow your instructions"

He pushed the chair back and exhibited a clear desire to leave.

"Now I must go and I need breakfast" Guy announced.

"Goodbye and good luck "said Leyton.

"Yes good luck Guy" said Grace Wells who was still trying to make sense of the events of the last four hours and in particular the possible destiny of Guy at the hands of Captain Smith.' *I suppose this is one of the realities of working with the intelligence services nothing must compromise national security and the protection of the innocent public.'* She concluded.

Captain Smith remained silent.

Grace got up and moved past Guy and knocked on the closed door, which alerted Bishop to enter the room.

“Chief Inspector please take Mr Walker back to a place of his choice oh and get him a good fry up on the way he will need his strength for the day ahead” instructed Tom Leyton.

Guy turned and left the room to a chance freedom, the only exit route which would offer him any hope of survival.

“Guy don’t forget your phone “shouted out Leyton.

“It is safely in my inside pocket” Guy shouted in reply.

Without moving his head more than 10 degrees Smith focussed his emotionless eyes at the door and bawled out.

“Good luck again Walker you will need it”

‘What a cold bastard he is, I hope I never need to see him again.’ Guy resolved in his thoughts

Chapter 22

There was a reassuring bounce of the front tyre as the handbrake was applied to Gulfstream G-SANJ and demarcated the end of a long flight direct from the Indian subcontinent.

Captain George Silvers rolled back the throttles and First Officer Monty James powered up the passenger door which retracted open activating the staircase. First to descend the steps into the clear daylight was Sanjeev, who in his normal outlandish fashion punched the cold morning air in a sign of victory. Mission accomplished.

He was followed by a very pale Hugo, who was being steadied by his loving father as they gingerly climbed down the steep aircraft steps. Sanjeev saw his driver and personal protection guard, Geoff, and gave them a big welcome wave. He noticed the troubled look on his aid's face and this was validated when Geoff shook his head.

Sanjeev mimed,

"What?"

The large-framed Geoff in his trademark black jacket and jeans nodded his head towards the terminal, bit his bottom lip and rolled his eyes. As Sanjeev's cream Gucci slip-on shoe touched the sacred tarmac of his home, Tom Leyton appeared in the aperture of the terminal door, accompanied by Grace Wells and another man, who was not Robert Smith. Over the top of Hugo's head, his father's trained eye observed something was amiss and he had a sinking feeling that they would not be home for some time.

Leyton approached Sanjeev, produced his identification card, and announced in a very officious tone,

"Mr Sanjeev Pahkim, I am Tom Leyton, and this is Grace Wells, from British Intelligence. The gentleman at my rear is Colonel Yitzhak Avraham of Mossad, the Israeli Secret Service. ....Before you ask, he really is."

Not long after Grace had left the warm bed in Paddington Hilton, Yitzhak had received a call from the UK desk in Tel Aviv, updating him on the crisis in Trivandrum. In the car, on the way to Northolt, he received a briefing from General Avi Schein of the Mossad in Tel Aviv. '*Oh hell'*, gasped Sanjeev as he turned to Hugo and his father.

Five minutes later, the three new arrivals were positioned at the meeting room table with Leyton, Avraham and Wells. Robert Smith had left twenty minutes earlier in a black helicopter. Leyton opened up the meeting, again behind doors securely locked by Inspector Bishop.

"We are fully up to speed on what happened at Trivandrum airport, the hospital and the reasons why you, Hugo, were in India. What you will not know, however, is that just as you left, Indian Special Forces, aided by men from our Special Air Service were involved in an operation to secure your safe departure."

"What do you mean?" asked Sanjeev.

Leyton updated the three bewildered civilians on the operation and how there had been an attempt to capture Hugo, and the need to save the lives of his father, Sanjeev and the four air crew. Totally out of character, Sanjeev was completely speechless. Eyes wide open, he folded his arms behind his head in disbelief.

It was all too much for Hugo to take in. His logical brain had been fried by all the obtuse and surreal activity.

Hugo's father asked, "What happened to the assailants?"

Tom's silence and shaking of his head said it all.

An almost half-drugged Hugo said, "Who – who was trying to capture me?"

"A gang of individuals who work for a sinister undercover sect who are plotting some unspeakable act of terror. What, when and where, we do not know."

"But there is no "if, "it *will* happen," asserted Wells.

Hugo rubbed his eyes in an attempt to refocus his thoughts, and asked.

"So that Jacob was a member of the gang of the bad people? He duped me, he conned me to help the bad guys?"

Yitzhak Avraham leaned forward, looked at them all sat around the table, and announced.

"Jacob was one of ours. He was Mossad. He had penetrated the lower echelons of the organisation and yes, he was instructed to recover you."

There was a stunned silence in the room. Tom Leyton and Grace Wells had never been part this highly secretive information.

"But - but – he tried to kill me," Hugo blubbered. He burst into tears, the whole emotional torment had got the better of him.

"He was going to kill me and my father," he screamed.

"Hugo, he could not blow his cover. You would have perished at the hands of the others in any attempt. He also created a delay at the hotel to give your rescuers time to get into the corridor. Furthermore, he knew Special Forces were going to be at the airfield and cynically planned the operation in such a manner to allow the good guys the full advantage. When he went to the airfield he knew he was going to die at the hands of his allies. He was a brave man, Hugo. He gave his life for the bigger cause."

Hugo blubbered,

"I don't give a fuck. We nearly died! And I aided terrorists."

Leyton intervened. "Look Hugo –"

"Don't give me 'Look, Hugo,'," his father said.

"I've had enough of this bloody murderous circus."

Wells turned to Hugo's father, elbows planted on the table.

"This is not going to happen, sir."

"Don't you bloody 'sir' me, my dear. I know the law, it's my field. My colleagues will rip you to shreds."

"Well, let me make it patently clear to you to avoid any doubt: this law you wish to tout does not apply in this room."

"What?" Hugo's father screamed. "I know my rights."

"Yes, sir. But I repeat myself: this room is immune to any form of the law that you refer to."

"I demand that we leave now!"

Sanjeev, in an attempt to calm the situation, placed his hand on Hugo's father's left arm.

"I understand, you're right. But these people were involved in saving our lives. I sincerely believe we should listen to them. Martin"

A very riled Martin Parnell brushed Sanjeev's arm away and threw his hands in the air, then banged the table in utter frustration.

"Ok, Sanjeev. I'll do this for you. I owe you that much."

Tom Leyton sat forward, his eyes red from a late and weary night. He knew that there was still work to be done. No time to rest now, he began.

"We are on a time critical mission to find out the key members and the foot soldiers of the covenant, and critically what their next move is. The sabotage of TET and the act of embarrassing the Prime Minister, whose career was already on thin ice was a clear sign they are amassing for something big and memorable."

Tom Leyton revealed his full hand.

"I'll come clean with you. When I heard about Richter's involvement in the TET shares situation and the goings on with or without Mossad in India, I decided I would not trust my immediate boss. It is common knowledge that he is a close friend of Phillip Medway and my hunch is that Medway's very rapid rise to fame and fortune is at the dirty hands of Lukas Richter. So I went way above my pay grade, put everything on the line and contacted an old friend of mine, David Greenway. We were in the Secret Service together many years ago. His seniority and loyalty were rewarded and he became one of the personal bodyguards of David Moss. Yes, the PM's husband. I phoned him and put him in the picture and he put his job and pension – even life – on the line to tell David Moss."

He then went on to explain that at two o'clock in the morning he had a phone call from the PM's office, from Mrs Moss in person, and a conference call with her husband. To begin with, it was not friendly. She said she did not approve of public servants, especially in the security services, breaking rank and confidentiality. In usual and predictable, single-minded fashion, she verbally reprimanded him. She threatened that both Greenway and Leyton might face disciplinary action, with a guarantee of at least five years behind bars.

After a long pause, which was tantamount to that of a senior member of the judiciary holding back before announcing a sentence, she said, in these circumstances, and in the interests of national security, she would accept what Leyton had to say. She then added that they would be allowed maximum priority and would speak to Sir Richard Levine, head of MI5 and MI6, who was to contact them shortly. He was told in no uncertain terms that he and his department would give Leyton and Wells their full support.

Leyton said.

"There we have it. One hour later I'm on the phone to Sir Richard Levine, operation Montpellier is approved, and I am to report to him directly. Two hours later, I come here and I'm greeted with one of Richard's men, Captain Robert Smith. The plan is now as follows: to begin with, we need to get Hugo and his father and mother to a safe house. I then need to get you, Hugo, to GCHQ as we need your knowledge and the full electronic power of the donut to break the covenant's communication network. We have to figure out what they are up to."

A car was waiting for Hugo and his father, which was to take them to a large house in the Cotswold countryside just outside Cheltenham. The door opened and Inspector Bishop entered.

"Mr Leyton, our boys went to the house and there was no one there. It's all locked up and dark. We went to collect the mother and Hugo's belongings to take to the safe house."

Hugo's father turned to Bishop.

"That's ok. I told her to go to her sister's house in Grange Park. She thinks I'm out of town on business."

"Ok, Sir. Phone her and tell her we're on our way. And the address?"

"It's 48 The Chine, Grange Park."

"Thank you, sir. We'll meet you at the safe house, Mr Leyton."

Leyton nodded.

Sanjeev stood up with a semi-grin.

"Am I not needed in this real cloak and dagger stuff?"

Leyton said, in a stern, one-hundred percent, no-nonsense delivery.

"Sir, this is no game. People have already died and the lives of many more are potentially in jeopardy. This is real life. Serious." Then he paused and punctured the silence with a killer phrase

"This is a matter of life and death to you all. Get it?........... Good. Let's move."

As they got up from their chairs as instructed by Leyton, Hugo's father was on a mobile phone trying to reassure his panicking wife, who was starting to worry.

"Look, calm down. We're safe. You are too, just take a big breath and listen to my instructions. Stay by the phone, lock all the doors. In about thirty minutes Special Branch will come and collect you. You'll be reunited with Hugo by early afternoon. I love you, Barbara."

A tearful Barbara said, "I love you and Hugo, too."

Chapter 23

The black Ford Mondeo estate car pulled into The Chine Grange Park London.

"Number forty-eight is at the top of the bank on the left-hand side, according to my recollection."

"Thanks, Sergeant," replied Inspector Wright.

The vehicle slowly proceeded up the road towards the entrance of number 48, a large detached house. Wright had an uncanny feeling. He had noticed a black saloon car parked fifty meters up from the road end, with a middle-aged man sat behind the wheel appearing to make a call on a mobile, but Wright was not convinced of the man's true intent.

He glanced at his sergeant as they continued to drive up to the top of the bank to turn left into the entrance of their destination. As he approached the gates, Wright noticed that the front door of the house was ajar and the hall light was on. The absence of any light behind the curtains suggested that the front downstairs room was not in use. The Inspector put his hand on the sergeant's shoulder and said.

"I think there are intruders in the house. Probably armed. She must be a target for the boy's silence."

He increased his grip on his colleague's shoulder and Inspector Simon Wright looked with reassurance into the eyes of his sergeant and said.

"Ok, this is what's going to happen. I'm going to make my way back down the road, to probably number thirty-eight, where I will leave the street,"

Sergeant Anson nodded his comprehension of the proposed move.

"My plan is to enter the back of forty-eight via the garden. Let us agree now that I radio call you when I'm in position in the garden at the rear. In the meantime, Sergeant, call for armed back up and a helicopter."

Wright continued

"When they're in place, send me two texts in succession. Please also make sure that one of the lads from Firearms tackles the guy in the black car. I think he's got something to do with a potential getaway. I suggest also firearms block both entrances to this narrow road."

"Ok, Gov, I'm on the case." Replied Sergeant Anson

"And don't forget if necessary you have the authority to shoot to kill. That is the protocol."

"Plain as daylight, Sir." acknowledged a pensive Sergeant Anson.

Wright carefully closed the car door behind him and made his way down The Chine and kept close to the edge of the pavement to avoid being seen in the streetlight of the cold winter night When he arrived at number 36, and with the black car out of sight, he entered the driveway of the double bay window fronted property.

The house was positioned on a slope, so Wright had to ascend four steps only visually aided by the dim porch light to the front door. He faked putting a key into the door and then rang the bell, and as the occupant opened the door, Wright pushed his way in, holding out his warrant card in full view. He was greeted by a very shocked man in his mid-fifties dressed in white tee shirt and jeans who firmly closed the door behind him.

The very dazed occupant of the house was then thrust against the wall. Out of the kitchen appeared a young man, probably in his twenties, dressed in a tee shirt, shorts and flip-flops. He too looked dazed. Obviously, the man's son.

Wright clenched his warrant card between his teeth and threw both hands forward and waved them in an effort to keep the men quiet. In a swift action he retracted the flapping warrant card using his left hand, and announced,

"I'm Inspector Simon Wright of Special Branch. I believe there are potential terrorist activities in progress at number forty-eight. I will need you to remain in the house and firmly secure all the doors. Armed police units on their way to secure the road, and hopefully this operation will be concluded very quickly. There should be no casualties and no need for any concern."

The frightened man was holding on to his son.

"Will the terrorists come to this house?"

"No, Sir. We believe that they are attempting a kidnapping at number forty-eight. Her son is helping us with our enquiries and some intelligence activities. My colleague and I are tasked to come and take Mrs Parnell to join her husband and son at a safe location."

The man did not look totally convinced however he felt some comfort that he was in safe hands

"If you do as I instruct; you will be safe."

Wright reiterated what they needed to do and reassured then again that they would all be safe once the armed police arrived.

Looking at the older of the two men, Wright said.

"Look, Sir, I now need to leave the house. I will exit via by the back door and I will return when the operation is completed. Please ensure that any motion-activated lights are disabled and lock the door behind you."

The frightened man nodded.

The gardens at the rear of the houses were large, which allowed Wright to move around well out of view of the adjacent properties. It was a cloudy night in the middle of winter, and illumination levels were non-existent one hundred feet away from the rear of this very English property. Numbed by the cold of night Wright climbed fences, shinned up trees, crawled through hedges, tumbled on grass, hacked through rose bushes and fought his way through a whole host of vegetation one would expect in a middle-class, Middle-England commuter belt garden.

Under the cover of darkness, ten minutes later, he finally arrived at the boundary fence of number forty-eight. He stopped to survey the landscape and warmed his freezing cold fingers under his armpits. Wright then proceeded to move closer to the rear of the brick built house. The policeman shuffled along the ground, repositioned himself and hid behind the summerhouse at the end of the partition in the garden. This move presented him with a full view of the large sliding doors to the patio and the single door to the kitchen. He felt the phone buzz in his pocket and removed it. The two texts acknowledged that the firearms officers were now in position. The cold, scraped and scratched Special Branch man was just about the make his move when heard a scream. Through the bare patio window there was a clear visual evidence of two tall men, both dressed in black, throwing with force a middle-aged woman to the floor.

The woman tried to get up, however, one of the men slapped her across the face with the back of his hand so hard that the sound of her cry could be heard through the sound attenuating double-glazing. The other man caught the woman just as she was about to fall to the ground.

"Where is she?" the man shouted. "Where is your fucking sister?"

The weeping woman, now on her knees, through tears stuttered,

"I – I – I've told you, she's not here. She's not here at all."

One of the men slapped her again and she screamed. A granite hard and guttural voice said, "Stay there and do not move."

Looking at his fellow kidnapper, he said

"Ricardo, you concentrate on searching down here. I'll go upstairs. If she tries to escape, shoot to maim not kill. Remember: maim, not kill."

Words that sent a chill through the confused and very frightened and in pain woman.

The man in black flicked three switches at the base of the staircase, which illuminated the hall, the staircase and landing. At the top of the stairs was a very large landing, which double-backed to a window that overlooked the front door. There were five doors leading on to four bedrooms and one family bathroom. He opened each one in turn, slamming wardrobe doors open and closed, looking under beds, kicking doors down to the two en- suites. Meanwhile, Ricardo was looking under the stairs, which was a storage cupboard for the vacuum cleaner, wellingtons and a whole host of old curtains and an array of pictures.

As Ricardo dragged out the vacuum cleaner from under the stairs, he unintentionally repositioned a loose piece of carpet, revealing the outline of a frame in the floor. He screamed upstairs to his friend,

"There's a door to the cellar! She must be down there."

"Good work, Ricardo," shouted his accomplice from upstairs.

Ricardo, in a controlled rage, aggressively and rapidly decanted the full contents from the under-stairs cupboard and uncovered the whole frame to the cellar door.

Ricardo's accomplice rushed down the stairs and into the back room where the frightened woman was, and shouted.

"Stay there, you bitch. Remain on the floor. If you move, I'll come in and kill you."

He then went to join his accomplice and attempted to open the cellar door.

"You'll have to force it open, Ricardo. It appears she's got it bolted from the inside."

Ricardo produced an eight-inch commando blade knife from his black bag, and using the blunt side of the weapon tried repeatedly to lever open the cellar door.

Only one metre below, fully aware of this frantic attempt to capture her, was a very scared Mrs Barbara Parnell.

When the two assailants had originally come to the house, Mrs Parnell's sister had held them at bay long enough to allow Hugo's mother to access the relative safety of the cellar. Cowering for her life in the corner of the dark, cold cellar, Hugo's mother was hiding behind an old desk. She noticed the glow on her mobile phone, which announced the arrival of a text. With shaking hands, she picked the phone up to recover the content of the text.

It said: '*My name is Inspector Simon Wright of the Special Branch. I'm here to save you. The building is surrounded with armed police. I just need to know how many men entered the house.*'

Fixated on the screen, shaking, this was a lifeline she had been looking for. She took deep and calculated breaths to calm her thoughts. She held the phone in one hand, she re-read the message on the glowing screen and was warmed with the prospect of being saved from this hell.

She typed "2" and sent the message back.

She then texted, '*Under the stairs. I'm in the cellar.*'

The response from Wright said, '*Ok. Stay calm and cool. Be quiet. We are coming to rescue you and your sister. Trust in us.*'

She placed the phone face down and put her head between her knees and pushed herself against the wall in the pitch black, waiting for her saviours to arrive.

Barbara Parnell cowered quietly in the corner, her eyes fixed on the white halo of light which defined the doorway from the cellar to the under-stair's cupboard. To her it was the door from hell; the gateway to death. The light was a reminder of what lay at the other side, five-eighths thickness of plywood held in place by one bolt was her only saviour from a certain death and or torture. The door was pulsating with the constant onslaught of Ricardo's hacking away to try and release the bolt in the aggressive attempt to get to his target.

'What will be the next step, she thought? *What happens now? I may never know.'*

She could not stare at the door any longer. She closed her tearful eyes. Every blow, every bang, every clawing sound every contact of that knife sent a wave of terror through her whole body. Bang, bang, hack.

Screaming Ricardo saying,

"I'm going to get you! We're coming for you!" All in an attempt to break her morale.

She closed her eyes and put her hands over her ears and just hoped that Wright and his men would arrive in time to save her and her sister.

All of a sudden, the halo from hell disappeared as the lights in the house all were extinguished. There was the sound of scuffles. There was the of shouting, some muffled bangs and cracks, and then a thud over the top of the door. And then silence. She heard what sounded like something being dragged across the access door and out of the downstairs cupboard. The lights were then switched on and a man banged on the cellar door and announced,

"Mrs Parnell, we are the police. You're safe. My name is Sergeant Chris Miller of the Metropolitan Police Armed Response Unit. I repeat, you are safe. Please open the bolt and we will take you to safety."

Thirty -five minutes later, a very shaken Mrs Parnell and her even more bewildered sister arrived at Northolt air base and were being examined by a female doctor and medical officer from the Royal Air Force.

In the morgue of The North Middlesex Hospital, on three separate gurneys, lay the bodies of Ricardo, his assistant, and the man who had been sat behind the steering wheel of the black BMW. They were being guarded by two dark-haired, black-suited individuals from MI6. Two of the bodies were stripped to the waist and exhibited evidence of entry wounds to the front chest under the heart and below the throat. The third victim, the driver of the BMW, had a six-inch cut from one side of his throat to the other. He too bore a bullet wound to the head, as delivered by a British military standard Heckler and Koch machine pistol.

The door opened. A Royal Air Force medical officer addressed Mrs Parnell to say that she was now ready to go back to join her husband in Tewkesbury. She'd been through hell, and the trauma of the day was there to witness in the look on her ashen face and her wide-open eyes. It had all been too much for her, being on the edge of death and witnessing the British Intelligence and the Secret Services at their best when it came to killing terrorist opposition. She had showered and was given clean clothing by the military at Northolt.

As she walked out of the room, she approached the double-glazed doors at which her sister was standing, looking outside at a black Range Rover Sport, illuminated, engine running, ready to take them to their destination.

Four hours later, the Range Rover Sport pulled up outside a large detached house on a modern estate just outside Tewkesbury on the edge of the Cotswolds. Before the lights were extinguished on the black vehicle, Grace Wells jumped out of the front seat and opened the rear passenger door, allowing Mrs Parnell to disembark. An MI5 man who had been in the pursuing black Jaguar, opened the rear door, allowing her sister to get out of the vehicle.

Three minutes later, and after many tears and hugs, Hugo was reunited with his mother once again.

Grace and Inspector Bishop remained in the kitchen and made tea whilst the three family members and the mother's sister had the chance to update each other on the events of the day and make up for lost time. Outside the house, three armed uniformed officers were positioned: two outside the front door and one at the rear.

Grace opened the plain white door from the kitchen to the drawing room. Bishop, who was carrying a tray of six mugs of tea entered the room, he carefully spun around and closed the door with his right foot and joined the Parnell family.

Bishop said,

"I'll get some breakfast brought in soon. I'm sure that you would welcome something hot. You must both be very hungry."

Mrs Parnell replied, whilst keeping her hand on Hugo's shoulder,

"I'm afraid I've no appetite after what's happened. I'm just glad to be alive."

Bishop held out the tray and each occupant of the room reached out and grabbed a mug of the perfectly shaded, warm, reviving tea.

Chapter 24

In the large drawing room of the house in Tewkesbury the silence was only interrupted by the occupants taking large slurps of the hot tea. The room was twenty feet by fourteen, with double patio doors to the rear. It had a grey carpet, lightly coloured walls, chrome handles to the white doors, and venetian blinds. It was typical of many houses on this new development. Untypical were the people sitting around the coffee table, they warmed themselves on the much-needed amber revitalising beverage. Their day had been far from typical, and the last forty-eight hours of their lives had changed through the sequence of events, and the inert and innocent surroundings of the room would never bear witness to what had happened to the four members of Hugo's family

Leaning forward, with her elbows on her knees, and holding the cup with both hands, Grace looked up at Hugo.

"Hugo, we need you to help us. This will be your chance to do good. What you can do to assist us will only help and bring peace to the world."

"Who exactly are you?" Hugo's mother asked Grace.

"Ma'am, I'm Grace Wells from GCHQ and now on special assignment with MI6, Vauxhall Cross. I have full authority from the chief herself. The trauma of the last forty-eight hours has been dealt to you by the blood-stained hands of an evil organisation with roots back to the darkest times of European history. Hugo has been briefed, but for your benefit, Mrs Parnell, this is who we are dealing with."

For the next forty-five minutes, a wide-eyed Mrs Smith, grabbing on to her husband's left arm, listened to Grace Wells and the summary account of the ring bearing covenant of terror.

The distressed Mrs Parnell sobbed and had to be comforted by her son her husband. With tears in her eyes, and with her inner being still chilled to the bone, she held her husband even tighter. She then looked at Wells, and with quivering lips said.

"No. We will not help you. Get us out of this place – we need to get home. This family has been through enough. You people have no compassion."

Her husband turned to face her.

"Barbara, we need to help the British Intelligence. They will protect us and for all of our long-term security and the countless innocents at risk, Hugo needs to do all he possibly can."

"No! No," she screamed, crying, sobbing, throwing her cup down on the table in protest.

"Yes. Yes," Hugo said. "Let's help these people. They've already saved our lives. We owe that to them."

"Ok, ok. I just want this nightmare to com e to a conclusion and for us all to go home."

Mr Parnell hugged his trembling wife, kissed her on the forehead, and whispered in her ear. Grace placed her mug on the grey carpet and seized the moment.

"Right. Let's get down to business."

Looking at Hugo, she put her hands on the table, and said,

"Hugo, this will take thirty minutes. We need to get into the car and go down to GCHQ in Cheltenham. Mrs Parnell, you will remain here, under armed protection. We cannot risk moving you all at the same time. Once at GCHQ, they will want Hugo to gain access to the high-level communications of Tornado Ventures and in particular, the traffic to and from Lukas Richter."

She also explained that the organisation had one of their little helpers close to Richter, and later today, employing a clever box of tricks, would enable them to get access to Richter's private and scrambled mobile phone.

"Scrambled?" questioned Hugo.

"Yes. It is under encryption. Any normal intercept to the message would only witness noise."

Wells stood up and clapped her hands with authority.

"Now that you know what we're dealing with, we're up against the clock and we must master the advantage. Furthermore, they're on the march, clearly, and sinister events are certainly on the horizon."

Grace stressed the imperative was to seek out what the evil organisation were planning. No doubt it would be some act of unimaginable terror and mass murder, and how they needed to be rooted out and closed down. The real determination in Wells' voice added urgency to the matter and motivated the family in a call to action. With the convincing delivery, Grace moved to the door.

"I don't know about you lot, but I need some breakfast." She opened up the double doors to the dining room. On the table was cereal, toast, jam, bacon rolls and hot coffee. She said, "Breakfast is served."

As they all jockeyed for position, at the end of the table was a middle-aged lady in a white apron, carrying a tray of tea and hot water and fresh orange juice.

"This is Mavis. She'll be looking after you for the next two or three days, whilst you're living here for the duration."

"Duration?" scowled Mrs Parnell.

"We have no intention for it to last any longer than it needs to, as we are up against the clock and must get a resolution to this matter soon."

After breakfast, a black Range Rover driven by an armed officer, with an equally effective latent killer sitting in the passenger seat, pulled up beside the house. Noting the transport was there, Wells and Hugo headed down the drive and jumped in the back of the vehicle. Just over thirty minutes later, the car pulled up to the Gloucester Road closed gates at GCHQ in Cheltenham. An armed police officer examined their passes and allowed them over to the part of the car park closest to the door, which was used by the director or members of the Government. The vehicle pulled up adjacent to a dark grey steel security door. The officer in the passenger seat jumped out, looked around, and helped Hugo out from the vehicle. He ushered him to the door, which had been opened by Wells.

The door led to a small sterile corridor, illuminated only by industrial lights in cages fixed to the mid red painted wall. Wells approached a panel adjacent to the metal door at the far end of the hall, which had no hinges or handles attached. She then placed her right eye over a retina scanner and the door opened immediately.

Only Wells and Hugo entered the room behind the grey door, which led the way to a stainless steel lift access and another retinal scanner. They were allowed access to level four below ground. Stainless steel doors opened onto to a light grey corridor, laid with black industrial grade UPVC flooring and the by now familiar caged industrial lighting was fixed to the painted block walls. Hugo was ushered to a door at the end of the corridor. One more scan of the dark brown eye, and they were inside a room containing eight desks and chairs, each with three large flat screen monitors, all ready for action.

It had the look of a sterile City dealing room, walls lined with TV screens displaying not results from financial markets around the world, but ongoing World events fed from live news streams. This is where the similarity ended. The silence and the caustic atmosphere were not congruent with any of the gambling establishments in the City of London.

The office appeared empty, but all of a sudden, a twenty-five-year-old woman popped up from behind one of the grey laminate desks.

"Oh, hello, Grace. Just trying to sort out this cabling. When will they effing get these things to work properly?"

Jumping to her feet, the tall, slim woman who had long blond hair, and wore jeans and a dark red sweatshirt, said, "Hello, there. You must be Hugo? Very nice to meet you. I'm Holly Jackson, Senior Systems Analysist attached to the anti-terror desk at the doughnut."

"Hi, Holly. Will you be assisting me?"

"Sure will. I'm here to give you all the help you need."

Wells looked at Holly and inquired what the current situation was.

Holly was a girl in her mid to late twenties, obviously of graduate stock. She had long blonde hair, blue eyes and wore spectacles for reading. She looked the studious type, and Hugo immediately felt a great empathy towards her. He felt a comfort that only people involved in the world of cyber space could share. Like Hugo, Holly was an advocate of the world beyond the email, the world beyond the back of the screen, the black hole of cyberspace, the digital chain of information, information that could yield the clues to finding the sinister people that were a threat to World security.

In fact, Hugo was correct in his assumption: Holly had graduated in Mathematics from Manchester University and gone on to have a career with GCHQ from their graduate intake programme seven years ago.

Wells looked agitated and she tapped her fingers quite impatiently on the top of the desk. She needed answers now. Time was of the essence, and the world was getting short of essence.

She touched Holly on her right arm and said.

"Where are we, currently, Holly? I need to know what our status is."

Holly pulled her gaze away from the computer screen, pushed her glasses back on her head and looked at Wells. She said convincingly.

"All we know is the information we're getting from the non-scrambled phones and emails and texts. All of the traffic comes in and out of Tornado Ventures. I have the locates on Richter's and Guy Walker's scrambled phones, but we need to crack the code, as at the moment all I get – as predicted – is a lot of noise."

Holly said.

"Hugo," and beckoned him to come and sit next to her at the desk to allow the three of them to look at the bank of screens in front of them.

The conversation in the room was accompanied by the brief clatter of the keyboards and with the typing completed Holly pointed to a bar chart on the left monitor.

"See these are calls Richter has made from his scrambled phone but we cannot decipher" Holly reported and added.

"You can see these six main contacts but until the code is cracked, these telephone numbers really do not yield any information of any use."

Taking a sip of coffee, she looked at Wells and said.

"Once we break into the conversations and obtain the key to the code, we can then define the location of all the calls throughout the world and that will give you sufficient information to act. Until such time as we get the codes, we cannot get anything for you."

Wells closed her A4 book and said.

"It is all over to Walker now, he has got to deliver this now. I'm afraid, Hugo, until we get this information, we're just going to have to sit tight."

Five thousand miles away, two large sea going containers were secured in the bowels of the MV Lawson on course for Rotterdam, with an ETA of 10.20 UST, February 28th 2017. Eight miles to the south of the Lawson, another large container ship, the MV Colorado, was steaming in a direction that would take it to the port of Southampton. Deep inside the cavernous depth of the large steel hull of the MV Colorado, positioned amongst the array of blue, white, green, and red containers, was a brown rust peppered twenty-foot refrigerated container.

On the face of it, the container appeared to be nothing out of the ordinary. It was just the same as the numerous anonymous dormant steel storage units inside the great structure of the container ship. The container had originally been destined to be shipped to Rotterdam on the MV Lawson; however, its eventual destination had been re determined three hours before embarkation. The container was being transported on a trailer which was hauled by a white Ford tractor unit. With only twenty miles to go, the large Ford truck had been flagged down to a halt, by who the driver thought were police.

The driver was tired and had experience a long and tedious journey. He had just wanted to get to the port to turn around and then get back to his family. Who was he to question the legitimacy of four immaculately dressed officers of the local gendarmerie? He pulled the juggernaut up to a halt, took it out of gear, and over the background clatter of the diesel engine ticking over, there were three shots from a 9mm Browning pistol. The driver would not have known what had happened to him and he would never see his home again.

One of the policemen stepped up to the cab and opened the door. He pushed the driver to one side and positioned himself behind the driving wheel.

The policeman in front of the truck waved a torch and the vehicle was repositioned to a small, unlit side road off the main highway. The police driver parked the vehicle next to another GMC articulated tractor unit, and the trailer was removed from the Ford tractor. After ten minutes, the tractor units had been swapped over and the white GMC truck was on its to the port with the container firmly positioned with one of the assailants at the wheel.

Whilst the load was being swapped over, the police driver had removed his ersatz uniform and had put on the overalls of one of the trucking company employees. He was also handed a modified manifest, which diverted the contents of this container not onto the MV Lawson, but on to the MV Colorado, bound for Southampton.

All the paperwork appeared to be in order at first glance: all originals. What the paperwork and insurance documents did not declare was the deadly payload inside the container. The manifest informed the reader that the containers were packed with best chilled Argentinian beef destined for the restaurants of Europe.

The next morning at 6.30 an Argentinean police patrol car discovered a burnt-out Ford truck in a forest clearing. When he inspected the inside of the cab of the truck, he discovered the charcoaled remains of the driver huddled on the floor of the passenger side foot well.

Several days later the coroner would rule accidental death. His report would make no mention of the three bullet holes – one through the temple, one through the neck, and one through the chest. His only conclusion was that the driver had pulled over for a sleep, and whilst in the arms of Morpheus, he was transported to the arms of his maker, courtesy of a faulty electrical connection.

Chapter 25

Despite the trauma of the last thirty-six hours Guy had to forgo a long sleep-in and once again a familiar sound rang out at the same ungodly time in the morning. He rolled over to the bedside table in protest at the arrival of 5.30 in the morning, picked up his iPhone 8 and flung it at the floor.

Knowing it would not cease, he remedied the error of his ways, picked up the phone and disarmed the alarm. His head was heavy, not from alcohol, but from the pure and simple brain punishment he had experienced in the previous one and half days. The tiredness and stress had bludgeoned his brain and aberrated his vision, it was like he was seeing the room with the acuity of a 1980s grainy pop video.

Guy quit the comfort of the large bed and stumbled to the bathroom, turned the shower on, and jumped under the refreshing deluge of warm water, which helped in some way to prepare him for the day ahead. He dried off, and returning from the shower room, looked at his mobile phone and noticed a missed call from Tom Leyton 0602.

"Does that bastard never sleep?" he muttered under his breath.

Guy sat on the edge of the bed and returned Leyton's call

"Tommy do you know what time it is" protested Guy

"Yes Mr Walker I do, I have only managed two hours sleep, so be good fellow and let be in" responded Tom Leyton

" whatttt!!!"

"Never mind shrieking, I am outside your apartment, so be a good fellow and do as I say and let me in"

Enjoying only the security of his towel, Guy shuffled through to into the main living room, pressed a button to release the front door and allowed Leyton access into the main apartment block. He then unlatched the door to the apartment and left it ajar to allow Leyton in.

Leyton walked in as if it were his own apartment. He was holding a square cardboard carrier into which three paper coffee cups inserted. In the other hand he had a large bag of breakfast pastries.

"Not let's sit down and have coffee and breakfast," smiled Leyton.

"Three cups?"

Before Tom Leyton could explain, a young man in a cheap grey suit entered the room, he was carrying a light brown leather briefcase, exactly the same as Guy's.

Leyton sat down and retrieved a croissant from the bag, annoyingly casting flakes of pastry over Guy's clean carpet. He then offered the bag to Guy, who shook his head. He only wanted coffee at this time in the morning.

Leyton munched on a bun and spluttered, "Please meet Jeremy Parr of our electronic surveillance department. 'Q' to you and I, and the public."

The caffeine hit had woken Guy slightly and his mood started to improve with every mouthful of the hot dark liquid. He decided to take one of the pastries, and with a hand proffered for Parr to take a seat on the large cream sofa next to Leyton.

For a moment the three of them sat gulping coffee and devouring the fluffy sweet patisserie. It was almost as if nothing had happened and the three people had never met, and were just sitting in a place of communal eating watching the world go by.

But it was soon back to business in the confines of Guy's luxury one-bedroom Mayfair apartment. Leyton brushed the flakes of pastry off his trousers and his jacket and opened up the dialogue.

"Jeremy has a new briefcase for you, Guy. To all intents and purposes, it's exactly the same as the one you carry every day as your companion. There is one new feature, however."

"Don't tell me. Hidden dagger. Pistol. Bomb. Helicopter blades." Mocked Guy.

"No, Guy. Be serious. Inside the spine and part of the framework of the case is a device which will allow us to hack a mobile phone within a range of four metres. For it to work, however, the phone to be investigated needs to be used for at least five seconds. An RF receiver or let's say Bluetooth system, will link the device to your case. We'll be able to upload all calls, all addresses, all contacts, everything from that device directly into the storage facility into your leather bag."

"And why do I need this?" questioned Guy.

"Well, Guy, I want to access all the traffic and contacts on Richter's scrambled phone. We need to know who he speaks to. Obviously, yourself, and no doubt the paymaster, and it is most important that we get these details."

"There is one problem, Tom. The phone is scrambled."

"Yes, Guy, I know that. If you call him whilst you are in the vicinity of the briefcase and say at least five words, we can break the encryption sequence."

"But that would look a bit stupid," said Guy. "I'm four metres away from him and I make a phone call to him and speak to him? Surely that would arouse suspicion."

"No, that's how the system will work. If you follow our instructions, we'll get the data we need. Just attend the meeting and do as we instruct and we'll get full access to all the information we seek. Now, get yourself ready and go to the office as if nothing has happened. We'll leave you."

"Roger over and out, Tommy. Tell matey boy with you go pick up all the coffee cups and food wrappings and take them with you."

As Leyton was just about to leave, he turned.

"Just act normally at the meeting. Do make it work. Call him, make it look like a genuine error."

"Yes, Tommy. Now, let me prepare for the next round of this crazy mad existence."

The décor and furniture of the boardroom was textbook 1990s office development: a dark grey carpet, on which was positioned a very long, elliptical ash-veneer table, which was truncated at both ends to accommodate two leather armchairs. Around the table were positioned ten leather-backed and chrome chairs on each side, and in the centre was a speakerphone. Either side of the speaker were placed a nest of glasses, bottles of water and decanters of lime and orange juice to complete the table setting. At the far end of the table sat the Chairman, Paul Woodcliff. He was a man in his mid-fifties, with greying, thinning hair, who now needed the assistance of his gold-rimmed glasses for reading. Next to him, either side, were a cornucopia of blue, grey, and pinstriped suits representing the remainder of the board. They were strategically positioned at Woodcliff's end of the table to give the appearance of solidarity towards the failing chairman. This resulted in the board table nearest the entrance door being totally empty, and gave out the physical statement of a definite 'home end' and 'away end'. These ground rules would predict the conduct and outcome of the meeting that was about to take place.

During the next hour there would be a huge shift in the power base of this company. The away end would become the definitive home end under a new leader.

Richter, Wallace and Guy were led into the boardroom by Julia, Woodcliff's PA. The steely eyes of Richter surveyed the room, and gazed in turn at each of the men positioned at the home end of the table. He judged that they appeared defeated, and certainly if they hadn't been defeated prior to him entering the room, his cold steely stare would embed defeat in their minds.

Looking up to the back wall, eyes firmly fixed on Paul Woodcliff, Richter announced.

"Good morning, Gentlemen. For those who do not know me, I'm Lukas Richter. This is Steven Wallace, to my left: my lawyer. On my right is my right-hand man, my wing man, Guy Walker, head of Tornado Ventures, UK. We will shortly be joined by John Mawgan, who is on his way."

Standing, Richter placed his briefcase on the table and studied the room again, ensuring that he had asserted his authority on the quasi-defeated board. He deliberately sat opposite Paul Woodcliff, adjusted his immaculate black suit, fiddled with his red tie, and decided that he would keep his prey in direct sight throughout the whole meeting.

Richter flicked open the chrome latches of his leather briefcase and took out twelve documents. He put them into two piles and pushed them down the table towards Woodcliff. Guy and Wallace positioned themselves either side of Richter, they both engaged with their briefcases, removing notebooks which they placed in front of them on the table.

"Well, gentlemen, let's get straight to business," Richter said. "In this pack of information I have given you the following documents: an agenda for today's meeting and completed minutes of the meeting for your signature, Mr Woodcliff."

He explained the minutes were there to legalise and validate the outcomes of the meeting and all the points that were discussed. In fact, there was to be no discussion; it was a case of validating the will of steel of Lukas Richter. Momentarily removing his stare from Woodcliff, Richter eyed each of the directors individually, placed his hands in front of him, and said

"To put it bluntly, the meeting is over, and all the points have been actioned."

"What no meeting" protested Woodcliff."

Richter jumped in.

"Yes that is correct no meeting, we now have full control of the Company in terms of shares, and the shareholders have just elected myself and my two colleagues to the board.

Woodcliff slammed his hands on the table and protested.

"You cannot do this! It's preposterous. It's illegal."

Richter looked at his agenda, turned towards Wallace, and then nodded his head upwards into the gaze of Paul Woodcliff. He gritted his teeth and picked his moment.

"I suggest you shut up, my friend, and go back to the safe work of audits, from where you came. I want to introduce an entrepreneurial spirit to this business, one that will make the rapid-growing Company one to be cherished, and give profitable returns to its shareholders. Re engage the spirit this company grew on, and was growing on, Mr Woodcliff, until you arrived and put the brakes on it with your over-cautious strategy, caring more for the outside world and the environment than the shareholders."

Richter explained further points on the agenda.

"The fact is Woodcliff that due to the revised size of the company and the evolved structure of the shareholders, we no longer need specific committees for remuneration and corporate governance. The Company is now going to be private.

Woodcliff retorted.

"But I was brought in with specific experience in this field."

"Well, my learned friend, your contributions are no longer needed."

concluded Richter and announced

"I refer to the agenda, item three."

David Wood, the group financial officer intervened.

"You can't be for real. This is not allowed."

Richter turned to him pointing a finger straight at him, and said.

"Mr Wood, listen to me. This is for real. This is really happening."

"You mean that you can take the Company back to private ownership?" questioned Woodcliff.

Wallace stepped in to the discussion and said.

"As from 16.00 on Friday this week, this will become a private company. Your services are no longer needed. It will be headed up by our brand new team. All the board will be redundant."

He then passed out a pile of well-stuffed envelopes from his case to the men in front.

"Here, gentlemen, are your terms of surrender."

Richter added, "We have made you an offer you cannot refuse. You will all leave with dignity and a fat pile of cash."

Woodcliff stared through the silence at Richter and attempted to display some strength of character. He was on a losing wicket. He would soon succumb to the fierce blue eyes of his adversary and bow his head in concert with colleagues; or ex-colleagues, to be precise.

Richter closed his briefcase.

"Well, gentlemen. Business concluded. Let's have a glass of water. My friend Mr Wallace here will talk you through your severance packages."

Guy looked at his phone. There was a message.

"Excuse me, Lukas, I need to contact Michael. He wants some information urgently."

Richter waved his hand in approval and Guy left the boardroom via the single glazed door.

As Guy left, he pulled his phone from his pocket and dialled '1'. Two seconds later, Richter's phone rattled out a familiar tone. Richter held up the phone and answered. "Guy, a stupid man, you've phoned me instead of Stuch."

He turned and acknowledged his anger by shaking his head at Guy, who was standing on the other side of the glass door

Guy played out the game and phoned Michael Stuch, and appeared to be in a heated exchange for two or three minutes before the calm was restored. Inside Guy's replacement briefcase, in hidden depths, the electronic circuitry covertly connected with Richter's phone.

Richter returned to the officers and reiterated the offer and the attractive package that was being proposed by Wallace. Rolling his eyes again, he stared at Woodcliff in an attempt to garner some approval. Woodcliff just shook his head, his gaze fixed at the London skyline.

Twenty minutes passed and there was much shuffling and movement of paper on the table as Wallace explained each line of the severance packages to the outgoing board. The door opened and all heads at the away end looked up, eyes became fixed on the six-foot blond-haired well-dressed man who appeared in the opening.

The man was immaculately turned out in a black Italian cloth suit, white shirt, red tie. He was holding a black attaché case. He raised his hand in a presidential wave, and in a strong Texan accent announced

"Good morning. I'm John Mawgan, the new Chief Operating Officer"

His eyes scanned the room and he placed his case on the table and sat down next to Guy, close to the halfway line. He leaned forward and poured a glass of water from the decanter. The ring on his left hand was seen clearly by Guy.

"Only water?" he protested. "Where's the coffee? Get me some coffee, please!" he bellowed.

Richter banged on the table and the gaggle of voices ceased. He held silence for a moment and gave a scrutinising look to each man sitting around the table. Again, Woodcliff attempted revenge, but folded under the dangerous stare and cruel eyes of Lukas Richter.

Lukas Richter placed his hands on the table in front of him.

"Well, I will leave Steven to finalise the packages and recover the statutory paperwork. John needs to speak with you and your project team working on the Israeli water treatment project as a priority. I suggest you meet here at 08.00 tomorrow."

John Mawgan piped in with an introductory speech."

"Gentlemen I have reviewed this business and the current market and see a significant growth opportunity in the water treatment market with good long-term prospects for project work and recurring maintenance contracts. On this it is imperative that the deal with Israelis needs to conclude soon and it is vital that we see immediate progress on these contracts currently under review by the British Government"

Woodcliff piped up.

"But the deal with the Israelis will possibly be blocked, there's nothing you can do about that. It puts us in a difficult position with this project."

Richter jumped in.

"Mr Woodcliff, I'll just remind you, you're no longer 'us."

The gutted Woodcliff gritted his teeth, flushing red, and fervently tried to swallow his anger. He would no longer hold back once his passion got the better of him.

"I'll get you back, you bastard," shouted Woodcliff as he banged his fist on the table.

Richter looked at the celling, smiled, and dismissed Woodcliff with one of his damning gazes. He then caustically said.

"You are correct on one thing, Mr Woodcliff, and one thing only. Yes, I am a bastard. Now get out of my bloody boardroom, you pen-pushing, puffed up, overpaid clerk. I never want to see you again. And by the way, if you break the conditions of silence on the contracts and severance deals we have given you, the courts will not protect you. Now go."

Richter got up out of his seat

"Guy and I will be leaving you all now, Wallace will finish up all of the business and Mawgan will keep you all under control."

Guy and Richter exited the room and closed the door on a stunned silence.

Out on the busy London Street Richter said farewell to Guy and flagged down a cab.

Guy elected to walk for a while, so as to clear his head, and figure out the next move. He was thirsty and needed coffee, he chose to avoid the chains and found an independent Italian Coffee shop. Just as he sat down to enjoy the Americano, the GCHQ phone buzzed, the text requested that he meet Leyton at 20.30 at Guy's flat the purpose to swap briefcases.

Guy acknowledged receipt of the message using the agreed code 'Senior TT', he also confirmed the meeting with Richter had gone to plan.

Guy paid for his coffee and headed off outside to face the cold London day.

As arranged Leyton arrived at 20.30 and Guy paused the movie he was watching got up and opened his flat door.

Ten minutes later the switch had been made and Guy returned to the film and his now cold pizza

A police motor cycle illuminated the tarmac and stationary traffic blue as it threaded its way along the congested A40.

A dark silver Eurocopter EC135 helicopter, was positioned on the ground at Northolt with rotors running. The police BMW pulled alongside the humming helicopter, and a RAF

Police man removed a brown briefcase from one of the white rear storage panniers. Keeping his head down the blue uniformed figure ran across to the red flashing beating visceral flying machine. He handed the case to the co-pilot, then he ran back to the safety of the white line which defined the boundary of the heli pad. A thumbs up from the pilot and with a smooth delivery of gas turbine power the ground appeared to shake as the 3000Kg machine lifted from the tarmac and ascended into the night sky.

Forty minutes later the relative peace and tranquillity of the car park at GCHQ was interrupted by the thundering roar of the EC135 as it powered down to the hover and eventually settle on to the car park. The pilot rolled the throttles back sufficient to enable the rotors to keep running. He gave the thumbs up to the security guard waiting at the green door adjacent to the car park. The guard ran over. The rear door of the aircraft slid open and he was handed a brown leather briefcase.

The guard carrying the briefcase returned to the illuminated doorway leading down to the huge techno vaults of GCHQ. The pilot gave the all clear signal and returned into the night sky. Two minutes later nobody would ever know he'd been there.

The security guard handed the briefcase to Grace Wells, who was waiting inside the door leading to the car park. She hurried away down through the various lift systems, each time having to give retinal scans to validate her authority. The case was handed to Holly, who would start work with her team, and it would take another six uninterrupted hours before she was able to crack the code and interrogate all the information on Richter's scrambled phone. It was going to be a long night at GCHQ.

Chapter 26

Back in his Mayfair flat at 23.15, Richter picked up his scrambled phone and phoned Friedrich in Argentina. Updating Friedrich on the events of the board meeting, and announcing that the company was securely under their control, he added that Mawgan would be working hard with the team to ensure that the company won the Israeli contract not only for the supply of the two new desalination plants, but more importantly the ongoing repair and maintenance and upgrade for the existing systems. He also reported that Mawgan had already decided to employ three more consultants at the desalination units on a pro bono basis as a sweetener to win the ongoing contract.

Richter was then updated on the progress of the shipment of the Viper canisters from Argentina.

"The container ship will arrive in Rotterdam thirty days from now," announced Friedrich.

"We must ensure that our people on the other end are ready to receive the goods."

Friedrich explained the new plan. Due to the breach in security, the brotherhood had agreed to bring forward the timed release of the Viper virus. Friedrich asked whether Richter was at his desk.

He replied, "No."

Richter got up from his leather sofa, turned on his heel and went towards the wood panel door that led into his rather contemporary office. The room was decorated with white painted walls, an ash laminate floor, and in place by the window was a chrome and smoked glass desk and a leather-backed chair. As he entered the room and switched the lights on, he noticed the yellow package placed in the centre of his glass desktop.

Friedrich told Richter to open the TNT document that had been placed on his desk earlier. Richter took a place in his seat, swivelled in his chair, and picked up the yellow cardboard envelope. He twiddled it around in his thumbs and tore open the serrated strip, allowing him access to the documents and contents.

Some of the documents were related to share transactions at the New York office which required Richter's signature. To the onlooker, this was just another instance of top-level documents, thousands of which travelled the Atlantic daily. Even in the modern electronic world, paper still had to travel across the Atlantic for validation and it was by such means that the whole financial system between New York and the United Kingdom maintained life. He looked inside the cardboard envelope and found another A4-sized TNT sealed envelope. He removed it, placed it on the desk in front of him. With the steady hand of a surgeon, he gently pared away the layers of paper and came across a very small microchip. He discarded the envelope into a black mesh wastepaper basket, and placed the chip on a white piece of paper on the desk.

He got up from his chair and went across to his cupboard, unlocking it with a key he took from his left-hand pocket. With the door open, he removed an electronic reader. Returning to his desk, he powered up the laptop and attached the reader. From his inside pocket, Richter produced a small USB stick, which he placed into one of the ports of the laptop. After several refreshes of the screen, a matrix of information appeared, which would give him the code to access the information on the chip. After a few key strokes, and the input of passwords and memorable events, he was able to upload the message. In the subdued light of the office in the evening, Lukas Richter put his elbows on the table and concentrated on the message which appeared in front of him on his Apple laptop. It read:

'Lukas. The shipments are on their way. Due to time constraints and the breach of security, we have to deliver Viper by alternative means. The containers destined to be shipped on the vessels out of the Argentinian port were intercepted by our operatives in Argentina. The canisters have been removed and we have arranged to ship them to the UK by alternative means. When the Chairman and you fly over to Argentina next week for the event, we will make modifications to your aircraft, which will allow you to house the tanks secretly in the airplane. We have arranged for the aircraft to undergo timed checks at Biggin Hill in the UK in the following days and our operatives will then remove the containers. More details of our plans will be discussed on Saturday after the polo match in Argentina'.

To legitimise the constant travel back and forth to Argentina, Richter, a huge polo fan, had ensured that all of the companies in the Tornado Group sponsored a Berkshire based polo team. In the winter months this team trained and played in Argentina at a competitive level at one of the numerous haciendas they owned. On the coming Saturday they were sponsoring a huge match on the outskirts of Buenos Aires and it would be an opportunity for the team to get some well-needed practice in prior to the tough season in the UK. He would also be accompanied by the UK team manager, who would be looking for new talent, both human and equine.

It was 8.15 in the morning at GCHQ and Holly and her team had worked right through the night. They had cracked the encryption code on Richter's phone.

Hugo was lying on the settee in the corner of the office, clasping a bottle of water, half asleep, half awake, trying to listen to the conversations around him.

Grace Wells cleared the numerous empty coffee cups and plates on which the piles of crumbs bore witness to the biscuits that had been consumed with vigour throughout the night. She shouted to Hugo to join her at the end table, where Holly and one of her assistants were sitting, looking intensely at the three large LED screens.

"Ok," Holly said. "We've cracked the code.".

Gasping, she added.

"We just had enough traffic between Richter and Guy to crack the code, but due to the short message, we had to run the algorithms for a long time before we actually managed to find the key."

"And there was another problem, in that the crib the key to lock that is which was programmed to change itself. We eventually figured out the future reiterations by using complex algorithms we developed during the night."

She continued.

"The team and I managed to decode several of Richter's scrambled calls, GCHQ will now be able to unscramble any calls that Richter make to and from his secure mobile phone."

"This is a major step forward thank you so much Guys" said a clearly pleased Grace.

Although Hugo had not had the benefit of a full night's sleep, he had managed to get some shuteye on the settee and was feeling the best he had for days, a feeling probably motivated by the fact he was now back in the world he loved: the cyber world. He not only felt rested but also felt secure in the capable hands of the GCHQ team. In the previous thirty-six hours, Hugo had been appraised of what he had spawned by his actions in that small room above the dingy shop in India.

He was not a rounded individual, and found big swings in emotion difficult to cope with, so he rationalised the situation into a logical supposition. Hugo figured out that had he not got involved, he still would not have stopped the juggernaut of these animals and they would have discovered another way out to crack the information he had given them. To achieve further comfort in his mind, he also convinced himself that his involvement would accelerate the process of capture and potentially save many lives.

With beaming eyes, he said.

"Well done, Holly. You seem to have it cracked. Self-generating encryption code sequence. All from three calls. That is so impressive. They'll never guess that we've got this far."

Holly gave a wry smile and held her breath, thinking, '*I shouldn't need to impress you, arrogant little shit. We are, after all, GCHQ*'

At that very moment the door swung open, which allowed the high-level illumination from the hall to flood into the room. In walked a blue-suited Tom Leyton. He was there to find out two things: had they cracked the code of Richter's phone, and to understand who he communicated with on a regular basis.

An ebullient Holly bounded up and rejoiced in confirming that the code had been cracked, and also a ghost connection to Richter's phone had been created.

"Good work, Holly," Tom announced with an infrequent smile.

"Here is a list that detail the main numbers Richter has phoned in the last forty-eight hours, with volumes alongside in the proportion shown in a bar chart studied earlier in the week.

Leyton reviewed the document.

"Ok, we need to locate the source of these mobiles and record all voice transmissions." He said

"Already done, Sir," replied Holly, who was now trying to look accomplished in front of Hugo, Grace and Tom Leyton.

Leyton read and re-read the script of the messages between Richter and Friedrich.

"You say this Friedrich has a German accent?"

"Yes, boss," Holly replied. "Educated, too."

Leyton looked down at the document and bit his lip. What he read deeply concerned him. They were describing a shipment of a Viper product on a ship bound for Rotterdam. The constant reference to the plan accelerated disturbed the seasoned intelligence man. Experience and gritty intuition made him conclude there was about to be a large terrorist event on the immediate horizon. What were they planning? Where? How? Who were these people?

He stared at Holly. "Are you sure you cannot locate the source of Friedrich?"

"No, sadly," said Holly. "He's using a relay burner phone."

Leyton looked towards Hugo with a sense of disappointment blended with a touch of despair. There was silence for a minute as all four of them sat at the grey desk to compose their thoughts.

Hugo slapped the table.

"Yes, we can do this! We can do this; we can do this! My guess is that the server in Madurai India is the key. It will all be channelled through there."

Leyton and Holly listened to Hugo as he detailed how he would access and interrogate the server in India.

Anxious to know the outcome, Holly emerged from her seat and shifted over to and sat on the desk in front of Hugo. She crossed her legs and leant forward, stared insistently at who she thought was a nerd, and demanded to know more about his plan to break into the communications of this divisive covenant.

A slightly unnerved Hugo looked at Grace and glanced sideways at Holly for acknowledgement, and explained.

"If we work on the premise that the secret communications – in fact, all the communications of this organisation – go through the servers in that Indian office above the shop, I can gain access to that server and with some trickery hopefully find out where the dummy remote burner phone is located."

Wells looked at Holly sternly and resisted asking why GCHQ had not come up with such a logical solution to the matter. '*It had needed the intervention of a twenty-three-year-old civilian computer geek*'. She reflected

A slightly ruffled Holly put her hands on the desk, closed her file, looked at Hugo, and said, "Well, Hugo, you had better get on with it. If you do need any help, I'm here – as are the rest of my team. I'd be very interested to see if you can locate the dummy burner phone."

Holly, who had just seen her crown knocked off by a student, picked up a comforting glass of water and sipped on it, this helped steady her mind temporarily. She placed the glass down on the table, looked at Hugo and in an attempt to regain authority, stated.

"Please let me know as soon as you have any breakthrough."

Leyton closed his notebook, looked at Hugo, Holly and Wells and said

"Yes, and make sure I'm the next to know. We've got to move quickly on this, we don't know what their next act is going to be, but they are planning something big and something sinister, and it's all about accessing their communication network."

Leyton bade farewell and left the room. Hugo took up the keyboard. Holly went to her desk, and still fighting with her emotions, logged on to her workstation to carry out further analysis on calls made to and from Richter's phone.

Six hundred and fifty miles away, in the wood-panelled study of a French style chateau in the hills overlooking Lake Geneva, a mobile phone rang. The man relaxed on the larger chair was savouring the delights of a Romeo Y Julieta Wide Churchill when he received the call. He rested his beloved hand-rolled cigar on the dark red ashtray, leaned forward on to the expansive mahogany desk, and picked up the phone.

"Yes, Lukas? What news have you got for me?"

Richter explained in detail the change in plans and how the Viper delivery would be rerouted when they met up this weekend coming for the polo tournament in Buenos Aires. He also explained that after he'd been dropped back to Geneva private airfield, his business jet would be repositioned to Biggin Hill for its hundred-hour service, at which point the cargo would be removed for further dispatch.

Richter also explained the outcome of the meeting with Woodcliff and his cronies and explained that Mawgan was on the case now, with a view to getting at least the maintenance contract for the four desalination plants and water distribution system in place within the next seventy-two hours. He also added that Mawgan would be now preparing to assemble his team, equipment and people to go out to Tel Aviv as soon as possible.

"And Medway?" questioned the man in Geneva.

"Well, Sir, Medway knows what to do. He will ensure that the competition authorities and the Foreign Office stamp all documents as a matter of procedure. All licences to export the products and the services will be in place to correspond with the signing of the contracts."

Gazing around the room and admiring a treasured Klimt original hanging on the wall of his study, he turned his head and gazed through the leaded glass window which overlooked the flickering lights on Lake Geneva. He picked up his cigar, rolled it around in his fingers, gently placed it between his lips, and sucked on the decadent tube. With the phone on hands-off, he asked a few more questions about the timings for the weekend, exhaled smoke and said.

"Well done, my friend. This is good work. We will soon be able to achieve what our forefathers could not achieve. A covenant that will last for a thousand years. I must go now; I'll see you on Friday at Buenos Aires at the hotel. God speed, and have a safe trip, Lukas"

The man is Geneva pressed his left hand on the mobile phone to eradicate the call. The works of Klimt and Klee were able pass witness on the platinum ring on his second finger, a coiled snake.

Three hours later the details of the telephone conversation would be sent to Tom Leyton, Grace Wells and Sir Richard Levine head of MI6.

Chapter 27

John Mawgan placed his matching black leather briefcase and hand luggage down on the maroon upholstered chair in the British airways business class lounge at Heathrow T5. He was accompanied by four colleagues, Dan Hunt Projects director, Steve Hopkins Project Manager Retrofit Applications, Johnny Dunn Project Manager Project Mermaid (New Build) and Kevin Harrison Operations Manager Retrofit. All five of the men were travelling to Tel Aviv for a pre-contract meeting with The Israeli Water Provision Authority.

Checked in for BA 153 departing 2110 they would arrive in Tel Aviv in the early hours of Thursday morning, which would allow then only four to five hours rest at the Carlton Hotel, before they had to attend the meeting.

It had been a very hectic and stressful 24 hours for John Mawgan, starting with appointment at JBL Contracting Projects resulting from the shakeup of the board. It had only been twelve hours since the UK and Israel had signed a letter of understanding allowing JBL to formally tender for the refurbishment of four existing and construction of two new de salination and water purification plants. These facilities were of high importance for the security of Israel's clean water supply for decades to come, and the proposed work would require guarantees from the UK government as to the financial and political stability of JBL Contracting.

Unusually the process had been led through the UK Government Trade Department, by Phillip Medway the Home Secretary. With all the red tape replaced with red stamps Medway and his team had promoted confidence in JBL and the Israel Authorities were also given comfort by UK Government guarantees. It was indeed the Home Secretary that would be overseeing the vetting of all key UK citizens working on the project. Medway had personally led the due diligence on Mawgan and the senior team. It was this intervention by the Home Secretary had carried a lot of weight in the agreement between the two governments.

The stewardess on reception announced the boarding of BA153 to Tel Aviv and on this prompt Mawgan and his team left their unfinished drinks and snacks, collected hand baggage and headed off to the gate.

The white and blue courtesy mini bus pulled up at the reception at The Carlton Beach Hotel Tel Aviv, first to disembark was a bleary eyed Steve Hopkins followed by his four travelling companions.

In turn they each collected their luggage from the driver, which with the exception of personal briefcases was loaded onto a baggage cart by a bell boy dressed in a blue uniform.

All five men checked in and agreed to meet in reception five hours later at 10.30 allowing them sufficient time to get to the meeting. The venue was only half a mile away at the Authority's office on Ben Gurion.

The ping announced that the lift was at the 2nd floor, the stainless steel doors opened and John Mawgan turned left and made his way to Room 221.

The weary traveller inserted the key card in the lock and with a whirr the door was unlocked, he entered the room switched on the lights and flung his two bags on dark blue bed spread.

He opened the wardrobe door, and hung up his light grey suit jacket, in the illuminated closet.

As he approached the bed his phone rang, it was Richter.

"John are you alone"

"I am Lukas go ahead"

"Good, well your meeting will be soon, and with all clearances in place there should be no reason that contracts or at least Letter of Intent, should not be signed off"

"I totally agree Lukas; hell we have had operatives at those four plants for over a year now"

"It is vital that you get dates for Hopkins and Harrison's men to gain full access to the sites I have twelve technicians ready to fly and they are fully security cleared."

"They are all UK citizens on the face of it, however, unbeknown to Israeli's they are all fully trained members of the covenant" "as are Hopkins and Harrison"

Richter continued.

"You need to stress the importance of the requirement to fully install all final retrofit valves, controllers, burners and the up to date process control software, push the cost saving angle hard. Another key consideration for the Water Authority is the increased output of fresh water which will be I demand as the dry season approaches."

"Lukas I fully understand, and the recent discussions I have had with Yoshi Edri, who as you know is the man heading up the project from their side, he has confirmed that they are as keen to move forward as much as us"

"In our last correspondence he informed me that all work permits are in place for our retrofit teams who will working on all four plants"

"furthermore he already has import licences for the first consignment of equipment to be delivered to the existing four working plants"

"The tight timescale will dictate that the initial supplies will have to be air freighted, and believe this or not I had a call from the MOD, a Group Captain Mike Hudson, informing me that the powers from above have placed 4 C130 Hercules freighters at our disposal for two return flights."

A knowing Richter replied.

"Yes, our Home Secretary friend has pulled a few strings, we are looking all set to go"

"Lukas I need to catch some sleep, now my meeting is in four hours" Mawgan calmly protested.

"OK John I will leave you now"

Four hours later the bedside phone rang tearing John Mawgan away from a brief albeit deep sleep, he fumbled for the receiver and the automated message, which for some odd reason had a Californian accent, announced the arrival of 10.00 in the morning.

The receiver re united with the phone, John got out of bed, showered and dressed in a light pair of grey suit trousers which had been carefully folded and retrieved from his hand baggage. He buttoned a white short sleeve shirt and a dark blue tie was hurriedly signed off with a schoolboy knot, he grabbed the suit jacket from the wardrobe hanger and he was ready to go. A loud ping proclaimed that the lift had landed at lobby level, the doors opened and John exited right and toward the coffee shop. As he entered the large open plan eatery which was bordered on two sides of floor to ceiling glazing overlooking the ocean, he notices his four colleagues sat at the far end. Mawgan walked past mainly empty tables and chairs and arrived at a six seater table next to the window.

He took a seat next to Steve Hopkins, who was also wearing a light grey suit and white shirt

"Good morning fellas "

A volley of 'good morning John' ensued.

"Grab a cup John the coffee is nice and fresh. I also recommend the eggs and salmon; the bagels are lovely" Said Steve Hopkins.

The conversation around the table was muted, a consequence of tiredness and nervous anticipation about the meeting, they all knew that so much was hanging on winning the contracts. All except John Mawgan, he knew that the meeting was just a formality, he knew that wheels had been turning in the background, courtesy of Phillip Medlock the UK Home Secretary.

At 10 30 the five executives, left the restaurant and assembled near the rotating doors which formed the exit from the hotel.

"I have arranged the hotel shuttle to take us to the offices" announced Dan Hunt

"Sir your transport is ready" heralded the bell boy

John Mawgan looked at his colleagues

"Thank you, ok team, let us go and do it"

Ten minutes later the hotel mini bus pulled up outside a modern eight story office building situated on the corner of Ben Gurion Prospekt and Wiesel.

Steve thanked the driver and the five men passed through mirrored glass doorway and into a large minimalist reception. The visiting contingent all approached the dark grey stone effect reception counter, and John spoke to the middle aged brown haired lady sat behind the desk.

“Good morning Ma’am, I am John Mawgan form JBL Contracting Industries, myself and my four colleagues have meeting with Yoshi Edri of the Water Authority.”

She clattered the keys on the black keyboard, and after studying the screen she looked up.

“Messrs Mawgan, Hopkins, Hunt, Harrison and Dunn I see”

“That is correct” replied John.

“Could each one of you in turn say your name and look at the camera to have your photographs taken”, she said, and pointed at the small black encased digital lens sat on the counter top.

“I would also like to see your passports please”

Johnny Dunn was the last to have his photo taken and with the task completed the receptionist handed five photo IDs attached to blue lanyards, and the stack of passports to Mawgan.

“John it is so good to see you” resonated behind John’s back and he turned to see Yoshi Edri. They had never met before but with the wizardry of teleconference technology, they instantly recognised each other.

John replied

“Yoshi so good to meet you at last” he then introduced in turn each of his in turn each of his lanyard toting associates.

“Thank you Racheal I will escort my visitors to the third floor, the meeting room is ready”

The lift delivered the contingent to the third floor and Yoshi lead them straight ahead to a door at the end of the short corridor. The unlocked door led into a large conference room set out with a large oak veneered table and fourteen dark red upholstered boardroom style chairs. Centre to the table were two stainless steel trays hosting two large water decanters and a compliment of glasses. At the far end of the table adjacent to the window were seated three man in short sleeved shirts and ties and one woman wearing a light cream blouse. Directly in front of the female were two identical suites of six documents, comprising the formal contracts for the two new build and the four retrofit projects.

The four hosts got up from their seats and Yoshi made the formal introductions

"Hello to all, these good people are the key members of the projects team for both the new built and installed upgrade from left to right are Abir Cohen Vice President Projects Division, Nadiv Levy Construction Director New Projects, Abigael Darhan Project Director Existing Plant Upgrades, and Aaron Mizrah Operations Manager Existing Plant Upgrades."

Yoshi's team stood up to receive their visitors and John Mawgan responded by introducing his colleagues.

The nine men and one woman all shook hand and exchanged business cards.

Yoshi sat down at the end of the long table followed by the rest of the group, and when they were all comfortably seated he addressed the meeting.

"Good morning everyone I am pleased to greet our friends from the UK, who will be spending most of the day with us, to discuss the proposed works to the four existing water treatment and desalination plants at Sorek, Ashkelon, Palchaman and Hadera and the two new plants to be based at two of six potential locations. The priority to day is to concentrate on the upgrades to the existing facilities, to allow us to be fully on line for peak usage. With the majority of pre tender work completed on the two new installations and all points agreed I suggest that we officially sign the documents and enter into the contract for the mechanical, electrical and system design, equipment provision, installation test and commissioning of two new desalination plants. This will allow you to proceed with time critical system design and the placement of orders for long lead time items. That should not take too long after which we will discuss the roll out programmes for the upgrades to the existing units."

Yoshi was greeted with a unified nodding of heads and "agreed" confirming acceptance of the schedule for the day.

Two hour twenty minutes of discussion and page turning of documents concluded with Yoshi and John signing one suite of documents.

A light lunch was served in the board room which provided a forum for the parties to engage in convivial chat for an hour.

An hour later and after last remnants of lunch had been cleared away Yoshi opened up a detailed discussion on the upgrades for Sorek, Ashkelon, Palchaman and Hadera.

Yoshi re opened the proceedings

"In summary we are delighted by the work carried out to date by JBL and in particular the onsite teams based at the four locations. It is so pleasing that our respective Governments have agreed terms and that the extensive due diligence has not flagged up any past current or future issues for National Security. The supporting guarantees offered by the British Authorities regarding the performance on these contracts gives us added comfort."

He continued

"Our respective teams have thrashed out the scope of supply and ongoing support and all 'I's' and have been dotted and "t's' crossed." So from our standpoint we are all good to go the scope and schedule of costs are all I order, lets us sign the documents and get moving."

The ten minutes it took for both sides to sign the contract documents, did not reflect the amount of work, hours upon hour of redrafting, that it had taken to get to that juncture. I wish to thank all of you for your hard work thanked all and nominate Steve Hopkins as JBL Contracting's senior representative supported by Kevin Harrison who be in charge of all operational matters." Replied Mawgan.

"Yes there has been a great deal of work carried out by both teams and I want to confirm that Abigeal Dahran will be the project leader for the Water Authority, with Aaron Mizram as her appointed deputy." Responded Yoshi Edri

Abigael announced.

"It will be necessary to hold detailed programme meetings at each individual site, and we need to start these activities forthwith."

"The detail aside as Yoshi pointed out time is of the essence so we must ensure that work on site commences as soon as possible"

Steve Hopkins responded.

“The benefit of having our operatives on your sites for the past months has given many advantages, mainly we have been able to understand the individual characteristics of each plant allowing us to model specific systems control routines. The upshot is that our engineers know what control equipment is required and the optimum software updates.”

Abigael jumped in.

“Very good so we now must put words into action and on the basis each site will have a nominated project manager for each facility I will now table a provisional high level programme as follow”

“with today being Feb 26th here are my suggested milestone dates”

There was a lively round table discussion an eventually a list of key activity milestone dates was agreed.

John Mawgan reviewed the redlined programmes and jotted down in leather bound note book the main event start dates. *These were the dates which Richter would need to know, timings which would determine when the special supplies, and covenant operatives would need to arrive at site, and finally the date when the plants would be re commissioned back into service.*

With all key parameters agreed the discussion around the table continued in a friendly and semi social and less business like fashion.

John stood up and over the chatter announced that he needed to make some private calls.

“Please John use the vacant office across the corridor, whilst you are gone I will arrange some fresh tea and coffee” responded Yoshi.

Yoshi displayed clear affection for John and his team and had said on many occasions that ‘*both he and Abigael were looking forward to working with John and his colleagues’*

Mawgan got up from his chair and left the room virtually unnoticed, such was the flourishing ‘bon ami’ between the two parties.

He entered the empty office, closed the door, and made himself comfortable in one of the grey chairs placed midway down the large oval conference table. With his note book in front of him with clear sight of the door, and using his encrypted phone he sent the following text message to Lukas Richter

'Contracts for new build and Upgrades all signed. On site date for all equipment and personnel to start refit 7 March all 4 locations. Commission to be complete for full operation 21 March.'

A ping heralded a reply.

'Noted John, I will work with F to ensure V is ready to send with install teams, 21 March will be an historical day for our cause L'

Deep in thought Tom Leyton scrutinised the words on at the A 4 sheet clutched in his left hand. He was puzzled by what he read and after the third read he became agitated and he refocused his gaze to Grace Wells.

"Grace I just cannot get my head around all of this, what is this cause? Has it anything to do with this bloody covenant of Nazi scum I wonder?"

"And what is the relevance of 21st March, what happens on that date? You say this is from a text from John Mawgan at JBL Contracting"

"What is this cause and what is special about 21 March?" Leyton quizzed Grace Wells.

"And these 4 plants, are they in Israel ?, we need more intel, Walker needs to get us into JBL Contracting "

"Yes and we need some our own people in JBL, to find out what is being planned in Israel" replied Grace Wells."

"Richter and his henchmen are clearly up to something, they blow up four water treatment plants and there is no fresh water to some time, but that can all be fixed in time, and it will be disruptive that is for sure but not yield the deaths of many"

“No there is something more sinister in play this could just all be a diversion” responded Leyton

A clearly unsettled Tom Leyton lunged forward and grabbed the black mobile off the top of the desk and punched in 10 numbers, the audible tone validated the hands off mode.

“Hello Tom” the muffled tone Guy Walker announced.

“Guy your good work has helped us to monitor and fully decipher all communications to Lukas Richter’s encrypted phone” “an hour ago we received the following transmission from John Mawgan at JBL”

A slightly hyper Tom Leyton brought Guy fully up to speed with recent communications and in particular the one referring to 21 March.

“Guy, I need to know what John Mawgan is doing in Tel Aviv and what legitimate activities JBL have got planned in Israel”

“We need a man on the inside one who is close to these projects furthermore we require full detail on what works are planned at the four water treatment plants”

“OK Tom I will do what I can”

“Do what you can is not enough Walker” snapped Leyton

“I need to know everything and I insist we recruit a key player in JBL”

“And by the way Guy”

“What’

“Make sure they don’t wear a bloody snake ring” affirmed Guy

“OK Tom, but what I do know is that several days ago Richter instructed myself and Stuch to buy up shares in JBL’s parent. Sufficient to gain control,”

“Go on” asked Leyton

“Well we did and I was at the meeting where Richter fired the whole dammed board and put this American John Mawgan in to run the show.”

"And yes before you ask the six-foot odd ex quarterback was wearing one of those bloody rings!"

"OK Guy I will leave this with you and with March 4th only around the corner you need to act swiftly"

"Guv I think we need to let Mossad in on what we know" said Grace Wells

"Ok you go and speak with Jitzac meanwhile I am going to bring the PM's office up to date, lets meet back here in say 2 hours and compare notes,"

The click confirmed the connection, and Yitzhak welcomed the caller.

"Grace my darling it is so nice to hear from you, have you called to arrange a beautiful meeting or is it mundane business?"

"Boring old business I'm afraid but who knows what will happen" she laughed.

During the two-minute call she appraised Yitzhak with details of traffic between Richter and his lieutenants, and the further actions Tom had requested Guy to undertake.

Yitzhak told Grace that he was aware of the work on up grading the four water treatment plants and the need to build additional units to safeguard clean water supply for the nation. He had obtained this knowledge from his cousin Abigael who was Project Director for the National water supply company. He added that it was common knowledge that work was needed to upgrade existing facilities and that for some time work had been undertaken by an English company under the watchful eye of both governments.

Grace digested what Yitzhak had to say but she had one key unanswered question in her mind.

"Thank you, Yitzhak, but the one thing I do not understand is why have the Israeli government put the fate of the nation's water supply into the hands of an English domiciled company.?"

"Yes I thought the same Grace however there have been some extensive due diligence undertaken and robust guarantees given by the UK Government as to intellectual property and security. In fact, your new PM elect Phillip Medway has had his hands all over this project since its conception."

"Grace you have to understand that JBL technology is world leading in terms of efficiency, output, performance and environmental credentials, or at least that is what I have gleaned from my cousin. Also many political commentators see the project as precursor to new trade relations between Israel and the UK about to be freed from the shackles of the European Union."

"Well Tom believes Medway has too much influence but always comes out whiter than white. What concerns us is that Richter is too closely involved for comfort"

"The problem we have Grace is that there will be huge resistance from our government to hold up progress on the projects, we need the water supply, and other options well this late in the game are not an option"

"But Yitzhak we have a potential national security issue, it is within our remit to act, there is far too much background chatter for this to be ignored."

"Give me and hour Grace I will make some calls"

Yitzhak ended the call and got up from his chair, left the main office and headed towards one of the four empty meeting rooms which populated the Canary Wharf building where he worked in the clandestine role as an oil analyst.

He entered Room 1542 closed the door and stood by the window and made the call on his mobile phone.

"Hello Uncle Piero it is Yitzhak; I need some help…."

Chapter 28

The Swiss Registered Executive jet touched down on Runway 170 at Ezeiza International Airport Buenos Aires at 1732 local time on the warm Friday evening. Captain Stefan Pascale taxied the aircraft to the InterJet ground handling facility and executive jet terminal located on the north side of the airfield. As pre arranged Captain Pascale repositioned the jet directly inside InterJet's western hanger.

Lukas Richter hurried down the power fold steps, and closely followed by a luggage carrying aide, he walked with vigour across the light grey painted concrete to the reception office. He entered the plush reception and he was greeted by Friedrich and a slightly overweight yet dignified well dressed German speaking man. The light grey suited unnamed figure was the owner of the white and blue Bombardier S Global long range corporate jet parked next to Richter's luxury liner. The three men shook hands embraced and then headed outside to and got into an awaiting black S500 Mercedes. Richter's aide and two other men dressed in black pants and polo neck pullovers loaded a mixture of luggage into, and then joined the driver in a Mercedes people carrier,

The limousine closely followed by the black mini bus sped off towards downtown Buenos Aries.

Forty-five minutes later the two vehicles drove through a gap in the black railings and "sentried" entrance to the Palacio Duhau- Park Hyatt on the Ave Alvear Buenos Aries.

The door to the S class was opened by a bell hop wearing a dark green suit trimmed with gold braid, who was joined by two porters who then decanted the luggage from the pursuit vehicle onto two mobile carts. Richter and his two associates marched through the open entrance and into the late early 20th century colonial influenced grand entrance. He was greeted by a petite man sporting short black hair complemented with a thin moustache and who was attired in a plain dark grey suit.

"Herr Richter welcome, it is our pleasure to have you at The Palacio Duhau once again" he delivered in impeccable German.

Richter returned the greeting with a warm handshake,

"Thank you Signor Garcia, it is so good to see you once again my friend"

"My colleague Suarez will take you to your usual suite on the second floor, I received your advanced instructions and I will arrange for dinner to be served in your room, with two additional places set for your colleagues."

"Perfect Juan, did my people check the room out in advance of my arrival"

"Yes Herr Richter, and no one has entered your suite since they left"

In fact, is was Friedrich's men who had carried out a sweep of his and the two associate suites on the second floor. Doors and window locks had been checked all drinks bottles in the bar replaced with new sealed units and a full electronics sweep had been undertaken to check for bugs and hidden cameras.

"Very good my friend, now I will make my way up to the room and freshen up after my flight",

Richter looked at his gold Rolex, it was 1910 local time.

"let's meet in my room at 2000hrs" he instructed Friedrich and the other German.

They both nodded and proceeded toward the grand oak staircase.

"Juan can you have Suarez available to prepare cocktails a 1950 and perhaps we can commence dinner are 2015"

"Of course sir and if there is anything you want call me night and day" replied the manager.

"Thank you as always Juan and please accept my invitation for you and your lovely wife to join us at the polo tomorrow, I would be delighted if you could come along and spend the day with me at my private enclosure" "as you know my Company sponsors the challenging team"

"Herr Richter, you are so kind. Marjorie and I would be honoured to join you"

In an act of true affection Richter patted Juan on the shoulder and proceeded to the lifts.

The doorbell to suite 221 reverberated and Suarez opened the door to the awaiting Friedrich and the man who had arrived from the airport with Richter.

Richter arose from the claret shaded velvet upholstered settee and walked over to greet his guests. He had showered and was casually dressed in a pair of white linen pants, powder blue shirt and light tan suede shoes.

"It is so good to see you looking so well Lukas, I trust that you have had a little time to relax"

"Not too much time I am afraid, there has been little time since I landed, but any occasion to see my good friends is always welcome"

"Suarez has just given me the signal that dinner is almost ready to be served so I suggest that we take our seats around the dining table' added Richter

The suite boasted a spacious reception area with three floor to ceiling windows dressed with long grey and silver patterned drapes overlooking the well presented gardens and terraces at the rear of the hotel. To the left was a satin white painted large wooden door which led to the main bedroom dressing room and twin bathrooms. The reception space was host to a seating area comprising two dark red settees, a light oak coffee table, a white linen adorned six seat setting dining table and in the far right hand corner stood a well stocked bar unit.

Friedrich and his guests took their places at the table, and remained silent as Suarez partially filled three plain crystal glasses with a perfectly chilled 2012 Grand Cru Chablis.

With a charged glass in his right hand Alfred toasted his fellow diners in high German.

"My friends it is good to see you again and I toast success in our undertakings to create a better and a pure world and to conclude the work started by our forefathers" the guttural delivery rang with an air of superiority and sinister determination.

"Thank you, my friend," replied Friedrich "I suggest that we wait until after dinner and not in the presence of Suarez and his staff to discuss our final plans.

For the next two hours the three comrades enjoyed an exquisitely prepared and presented dinner of scallops, fillet of beef concluded with vanilla soufflé, and complemented by an array of fine French and Argentinean wines. The conversation was restricted to views and prediction on the following days polo match, and the benefits of private aviation.

"Gentlemen let us sit on the comfortable seats" announced Friedrich and gestured to his guests to move to the sofas.

“Just leave the brandy and three goblets please Suarez and you and your man can go now I will see you in the morning”

“Thank you and goodnight gentleman” replied the assistant hotel manager as he left the room.

A light but reassuring slam heralded that the door was closed and provided the prompt for the business of the evening to commence.

Alfred and Friedrich sat silently, occasionally sipping on the brandy as Richter brought them up to date on events in Tel Aviv.

“Is the Viper agent fully developed and ready for use” enquired Alfred

Friedrich nodded “yes, it is”

“And you have assurances from the laboratory team that it will remain stable during transportation”

“Yes Alfred we have carried out numerous tests as and provided the virus remains in sealed air tight containers which are not exposed to temperatures over 45 degrees Celsius there will be no degradation, of that I am assured”

Richter shuffled awkwardly from his reclined pose, and leaned forward in the direction of Friedrich sat opposite.

“So what you are saying is that we need all resources in place by March 21 so that we can release the Viper agent” questioned Friedrich

“That is correct, however, we need the supplies on site well in advance, they can be hidden in our on-site stores which will be controlled by our people at all times.” Replied Lukas Richter.

Alfred who had been listening intently to the conversation leaned forward and placed his brandy goblet on to the coffee table and broke his silence.

“All good but what I am concerned about is the not insignificant matter of getting Viper out of the country and all the way to Israel”

For the next thirty minutes Richter described in detail how the Viper canisters would be shipped out of Argentina to England and forwarded onto Israel. He also explained on how a handpicked team of followers of the cause acting as employees of JBL would be in post at every step of the process, to ensure that total control was maintained.

"I can assure you that Mawgan and his team have everything in hand and that security will not be compromised" added a weary Richter.

Alfred shuffled uneasily on his seat and a gave a cursory glance towards Friedrich which progressed to a locked stare engaged onto Richter's sharp blue eyes.

"OK I will leave all matters in yours and the very capable hands of my friend Friedrich" Alfred replied in an unemotional tone.

"Let us drink up and retire for the evening we have a long but enjoyable day at the Polo tomorrow" announced Friedrich.

Alfred stood up, his rather large frame had left a noticeable indentation in the seat cushion of the dark red velvet settee, he walked over to the dining table. Friedrich and Richter remained seated as Alfred made his chilling closing proclamation. He took the final swig from his brandy, and with the vapour of the sweet liquor suspended on his breath he looked at his two companions and announced.

"We will now succeed where our fathers failed, we will complete the task and once and for all eradicate the world of our eternal enemy," and as he slammed down the empty goblet, the glass hitting wood of the unclothed dining table he barked.

"Failure is not an option"

The door closed and he was gone.

Friedrich stood up headed towards the door, halted mid step and turned towards Richter.

"Well Lukas this is now in your hands, you and your team must secure a place in history, you have the resources and have had our full backing all of the way, the time has now come to make the vision a reality"

Richter nodded to his friend and raised the fine crystal glass to his lips he relished the final sip of the Louis XIV brandy and reflected on the task in hand.

The yellowish headlights of the white GM van barely illuminated the dimly lit internal perimeter roads to North Airside of Ezeiza International Airport Buenos Aires. The driver was hunched over the steering wheel to aide visual acuity and through strained eyes he spotted the entrance gate to the InterJet's complex.

As the vehicle approached the red and white sentry barrier to the chain link fenced compound a dark blue uniformed security guard appeared from a white portable building.

The van pulled up at the boundary and the overall clad driver wound down his window in response to a nonverbal signal from the security man.

"Good evening can I help you"

"I have a delivery of airframe items for the mechanics working overnight repairing one of the executive jets."

The guard stirred the beam from his machined aluminium torch around the internals to the cab of the van, he than fixed it on the face of the driver who dropped his head to avoid the beam.

"Can I see your paperwork please"

The driver turned to his right and removed a clipboard off the passenger seat which he then handed to the torch wielding guard.

The guard took the clipboard into the portable office and shuffled with papers on his desk, after three minutes he unveiled documents validating the delivery of aircraft engine parts for a Bombardier Global S to be fitted by subcontract operatives at InterJet Hanger

He returned to the van and requested that the driver alight and open the doors of the vehicle.

The driver opened the double rear doors and the beam of the guard's torch irradiated a sole wooden crate positioned in the load space of the van. Examining the paperwork in one hand and the torch fixed on stencilled numbers on the crate the guard validated the cargo.

He nodded for the driver to lock the rear doors to the van and return to the cab.

"Ok my friend everything looks in order, but I am afraid you will have to wait as the building is currently unoccupied, I suppose that the engineers will be here soon, I have paperwork informing me that they will be arriving at 0030 hours"

"That is fine I can wait just show me where I need to park my van"

"I suggest that you pull up in front of the hanger doors as you will need to unload using a fork lift truck"

The guard lifted the barrier and the van moved off and took up position in front of the cream sliding hanger doors.

The driver turned off the engine, leaned his head against the door window and nodded off to sleep.

At exactly 0030 hrs. a dark grey Ford crew bus followed by black Ford box van pulled up at the gates to the InterJet compound.

For the second time in 30 minutes the guard's peace had been disturbed and he left the comfort of his warm office and TV to attend to matters at the barrier. Pablo had been given advanced notice of the contingent who were now present at the barrier, and to save time he picked up the appropriate documentation as he went to address the visitors.

The driver of the crew bus opened the vehicle window and presented Pablo with some documentation and the photo ID passes of Five European technicians, all employees of Euro Jet Maintenance Gmbh, Germany. In addition, he handed over passes confirming that these men were all EASA approved engineers licenced to work on a list of specific executive jets.

With all of the paperwork in order Pablo ambled over to the black van. The sole occupant disembarked, handed over documentation and led the tired guard to the rear of the van.

The doors were opened and Pablo's torch light, illuminate four blue roller tool cabinets, and a selection of aircraft lubricants, placed in a small plastic stillage.

Pablo eager to get back to watching the broadcast European league football, gave the driver the thumbs up and returned to the barrier which he swiftly opened. As the driver of the first vehicle restarted the diesel engine, Pablo shouted

"Park in front of the hanger next to that blue van"

The driver shouted acceptance and the mini convoy proceeded to the hanger doors.

Pablo returned to comfort of his cabin and placed his keys next to a black plastic tape cassette used for the camera surveillance system.

As requested he would substitute this tape cassette with the one in the recorder once the technicians had left and before the end of his shift.

He would destroy the tape and deposit in a dumpster on his way home to his little family, in the knowledge that his youngest son would now receive lifelong medical care for his heart condition. This treatment would be paid in full by the mystery man with who had given him the tape to replace. He had no regrets or conscience for his actions, after all he lived in a very corrupt country.

The driver jumped out of the Ford crew bus and his dark blue overall clad shape was silhouetted against the building as he activated the security approach light. He reached a green painted side entrance to the hangers and tapped six numbers into a keypad which unlocked the door and powered up the main lights. Three minutes later an electric motor opened one of the main hanger doors opened to reveal two gleaming white and blue executive jets staged by a powerful array of powerful ceiling lights. On the visual command of the driver, four men in blue overalls disembarked from the Ford and walked over to the open hanger, they were followed by the black box van as that disappeared out of view into the illuminated void.

The black box van reversed guided into position by one of the men was halted between the two multimillion-dollar aircraft. The rear door was opened and two men entered the van and unstrapped the tool cabinets, while two men set up a temporary ramp to the rear of the vehicle. Under the glare of the hanger lights the four men rolled out the four gleaming blue mobile work stations and placed them in pairs by each aircraft. The men then unloaded a selection of aluminium steps and plastic tote bins.

The driver who answered to Martin instructed the driver of the GM delivery van to open the rear doors and the 2.5m by 1m wooden crate was manoeuvred out onto the forks of the attending fork lift truck. With the crate secured, a green diesel powered lift truck revved into life, reversed away from the van and moved at creep speed into the hanger and stopped just by one of the aircraft nose wheels. The driver of the delivery van climbed back into his cab, engaged the key into the ignition slot, and was halted from starting the engine by a gesticulating Martin.

Unaware of his fate the driver lowered the window and turned towards a silenced 9mm round despatched form a Walther pistol in the expert hands of Martin. The direct headshot propelled the driver into a permanent sate of oblivion and he collapsed sideways onto the passenger seat. The passenger door opened and two of the men hauled out the warm but limp body into the rear of the van and closed the doors with a definitive clunk.

One of the men drove the van into the building and his accomplice closed the main hanger door.

Martin stood of top of the crate shouted.

"Please stand around and listen to what I have to say'

The European looking men in overalls obeyed their leader's instruction and gathered around the box and listened intently.

Speaking fluent German Martin spoke.

"Now listen carefully we have only four hours to fix six of the canisters into the fuselage of each aircraft. It is imperative that they will not be found."

"I have studied the plans of both aircraft types and have decided that the best place to hide the vessels would be to place them in the floor void between the passenger cabin and the main fuselage. The other alternative is that we place them in the centre fuel tank however the range would be reduced from 11,300 Km for what is an 11000km flight."

"Any questions "probed Martin

In response to the silence Martin said.

"OK let's get on with the task and I suggest that we split into two teams of three."

Martin jumped off the crate and walked over to one of the unlocked tool chests and removed a hammer and a crowbar. He returned to the crate and hammered the crowbar into the gap between the lid and main body. A large cracking noise proclaimed that the crate was open and Martin aided by one of his colleagues paired back the lid to reveal the menacing contents.

Positioned on wooden saddles within the crate were 8 dark red machined metal canisters 230mmin diameter and 900 mm long. Embedded in one end of the tube was a digital temperature and pressure display below which was positioned a label describing the contents as fire suppression gas. The legitimacy of the red and international standards validated nameplate betrayed the real and deadly contents. There was no lifesaving medium within the innocuous looking vessels, it was in fact a serum of mass murder soon to be unleashed on an innocent population.

In the ghostly stillness and the artificial daylight of the hanger the six men toiled for four and half hours and completed the chilling task.

At precisely 0547 hours, the three vehicles drove out of the hanger into the daylight and parked next to the side door to the building. Martin closed the hanger door ran back to the side door, switched off all the lights and exited to the awaiting transport. He set the alarm and locked the side door to the hanger, and jumped into the Mercedes crew bus.

The convoy stopped at the gatehouse and Martin retrieved the swapped out copy video tape from Pablo.

With a wave from their leader the three vehicles motored off towards down town Buenos Aries leaving no trace of ever having been anywhere the InterJet facility.

Martin placed his foot on the dashboard of the speeding crew bus and turned to his fellow passengers

"Well done team "he said

He returned his gaze forward and to his mobile phone and clicked send to a text.

Back in the Hyatt Lukas Richter's phone pinged.

"*Mission accomplished the bars on both aircraft have been refreshed M'*

Pablo Guzman finished his shift as a security guard at 0730 on that Saturday morning, and drove to his modest home in the run down suburb of Villa da Cava. At 0847 he got out of his ageing Toyota Corolla, he closed the door and proceeded across the road with the front door key to his home held out in his right hand. Sixty seconds later Pablo Guzman was gunned down by a masked machine pistol wielding pillion on the back of a speeding motorcycle, he had just become another statistic of the area's escalating gun crime.

Chapter 29

Grace Wells leaned against the ajar door to the dimly lit office, she peered in to witness her boss scrutinising the three paragraphs printed on an A4 sheet franked CONFIDENTIAL in dark red script.

Tom Leyton hesitated for a minute then beckoned for Grace to enter and with a swift movement of his left hand gestured for her to sit down.

It was 11.00 a.m. on a cold wet Saturday morning in Cheltenham, the unshaven tired eyed Tom Leyton was not aware of the day's weather, he had been in the office all night.

He reached for the red and white coffee mug took a slurp of the contents and the resulting look of disapproval confirmed that the black coffee had turned cold.

Grace quietly scanned the room in anticipation for Leyton to initiate conversation.

Tom Leyton pushed the confidential script towards Grace then banging his hands on the table and shaking his head he punctuated the silence.

"I don't get this; I just don't get this why is Richter getting this veiled text from a mobile positioned at Buenos Airport at 06.30 local time.?"

"Guy informs me that he has taken the jet over to BA for a polo tournament, but why a text so early in the morning and what the hell does '*mission accomplished mean*' for crying out loud.?"

"Well Gov there is clearly something happening in Argentina recall those communications with Richter and the Friedrich"

Tom Leyton brushed back his hair flopping over his furrowed forehead, slid back his chair slowly got up and went over to a white board.

Black marker in hand he scrawled with a squeaking action *Argentina, Tel Aviv, Desal Plant, Viper, JBL, Tornado Ventures,* around the perimeter and *Richter* of the white surface.

"There is a connection and Richter is the common denominator, he is the hub around which all of this activity is linked to"

Grace Wells studied the words, jumped up grabbed a red marker in her left hand and speedily drew a ring around *De sal Plant, Argentina Viper and Richter,* and scribed straight lines between the three. She turned to face a wide eyed Leyton and slamming the marker back on to the table she pronounced.

"They are planning attacks on the desalination plants, somehow Richter's men have infiltrated JBL and the Argentinean connection is the source of Viper which could be a nuclear weapon or something more sinister and deadlier"

Leyton removed his right form his trouser pocket and slapped his forehead,

"Yes yes that is it we all know that that those Nazi bastards all jumped ship to South America after the War"

"Do you know Tommy it is all too convenient, Nazi sympathisers in Argentina building the components of some large bomb off radar"

"Yes Grace my lass, but there are no known scientists with the knowledge to produce a nuclear weapon in that part of the world"

Leyton threw his hands up in frustration.

"What the fuck are they up to and why are desalination plants the target"

Deep in non-communicative thought the two GCHQ agents returned to their seats and endeavoured to figure out the substance of the plot.

"Gov I have something for you to consider"

Leyton raised a flat palm hand to indicate that he wanted silence to think.

All of a sudden and to the surprise the silence, the veteran intelligence man clapped his hands and pointed his right finger at the white board and stared directly at Grace Wells.

"My god it is clear as day Viper Snake ....and come on Wells what is the link???'

Grace Wells rolled her eyes slammed her palms on the edge of the desk and semi raised from her seat shouted.

"Poison Tommy its bloody poison they are going to poison the water supplies"

"Get on there my girl" rejoiced Leyton punching his fist into the air.

"And my guess it is being manufactured in Argentina"

"We need to keep this to ourselves Grace, the fat controller cannot get a whiff of this"

"I need to get Walker on the case and find out what the eff is going on in Argentina and I will speak with the PM"

Wells leaned across the table and to take advantage of the euphoria of the moment put her proposal to her boss.

"Tom, I spoke with Yitzhak and he in turn spoke with his Uncle and well he has fixed it for me to work undercover in Israel as a water authority senior manager, working on one of the sites and in a role facing the JBL projects team. I will be at the coal face"

Leyton stood up and with his back to Grace Wells he scanned the scribbles on the whiteboard, and biting his bottom lip he pondered his next move.

After what seemed an eternity Leyton broke the silence.

"Ok Grace I will speak with the PM's people and get you the posting with Mossad, you will need to brush up on your engineering knowledge, but I suppose you could slide into a more contractual facing role"

"Good call Gov," exclaimed Wells.

With his open palms pushed in front of his shabby attired torso Leyton turned towards his excited colleague, in an attempt facilitate a composed understanding of the proposal.

"Do you really know what you are doing Grace, what you are letting yourself into, this is a dangerous mission and in the event of danger you will be on your own"

"The UK government will have to be non-committal and will deny all knowledge of your involvement, and as for the Israelis they will not protect you."

There was a momentary silence. Then Tom Leyton spoke in a subdued and serious tone.

"This will be more than likely be a one-way mission"

Tom's chilling words rebounded in her head, but she had already decided and in an act of defiance she bolted up from her seat and walked over to her weary boss.

"I can do this Gov, I want to do this, why I am not sure, but it sure beats the hell out of working in this underground drudgery, I need this one Tom, I get the potential dangers, but please do not stop me"

Tom Leyton gave a deep sigh stepped forward to his would be female lead and held her in a tight embrace.

"I care for you Grace, you are a brilliant operative but I know that the world is a savage place, I have first hand experience of the misery and hurt that the likes of Richter' people can impose on the innocent"

"I and well aware of what I am facing Tom" replied Grace.

An emotional Leyton looked into Grace Wells, brown eyes and said.

"I will not stop you, and we have to work towards the higher cause in eliminating this evil, I will not hold you back Grace, and I will do all with in my power to watch your back"

A visibly touched and teary Grace Wells held her boss tight in the embrace and under her breath she gave an emotional response.

"Thank you, Tommy thank, you so much I will not let you down"

They released their mutual encirclement and Grace headed for the door.

"I will set things in motion Grace, I will also arrange some immediate basic firearms training, I suggest that you now focus on getting your affairs in order"

"Understood Gov"

"What I now need to do is to figure out how we can get Walker closer to the action, and I think that I may just have come up with a cunning plan"

The door closed and she was gone and with her out of earshot Tom Leyton collected an encrypted mobile form the desk top drawer and called Guy Walker

"Tom what can I do for you"

Leyton sat back in his seat and through the scrambled and unscrambled ether and explained to Walker what his plan was.

"My goodness Tom this is serious shit you are proposing how will you get approval"

"Guy that is not your concern I have access to the highest office in the Land"

"It is still major league anti-terror tactics you are proposing"

"Well I will have it all in hand by the end of play today you just act normal and I will energise the machine at my end"

The call ended and Leyton dialled a secure line to a receiver stationed in a side office at 10 Downing Street London.

"Good morning Sir, its Tom Leyton I need to speak with the PM please."

Chapter 30

Sunday Morning

John Mawgan shouted goodbye to his wife and closed the front door on his large rented house in the quiet village of Sarrett located on the border of South West Hertfordshire and Buckinghamshire. It had been a hard but very fruitful week for the new head of JBL, he had bagged six large value contracts during his fleeting visit to Tel Aviv. The forthcoming weeks would be hectic as he needed to mobilise a strong team and complex materiel to kick start the initial four large projects in Israel and he had elected to take advantage of the Sunday off to clear his head.

The open garage door revealed a slightly grubby blue and silver road cycle leaning against a dark grey metal work bench. The lycra clad Texan removed his trusty steed, closed the garage door and headed off down the winding high hedge lined country road toward the village of Chipperfield. It was just after the on the cold February morning and it would take some time before John Mawgan was up and performing at his optimum pace.

As he sped through Chipperfield and onwards to the small town of Kings Langley, he noticed but thought nothing of the dark green and mud emblazoned ageing Land Rover Discover innocuously parked on the forecourt of the local dealership.

As Mawgan passed the vehicle it's driver activated a hand held radio which was positioned to his left ear. Four miles to the East a dark blue Ford Mondeo was parked in a getaway to an arable field. The unshaven driver a man of athletic build, acknowledged the call on the radio held in his right hand.

He threw the radio on to the back seat and turned to his shaven head and dangerous looking accomplice.

"it's a go hold on"

With first gear engaged followed by large foot full of throttle the Mondeo's front wheels were set spinning on the soft ground as it accelerated from park and headed west down the narrow single track B road.

Mawgan changed up two gears as he hurtled down one of the plentiful dips in the undulating and winding four -mile stretch of road. There was no traffic as far as he could and he felt a sense of real freedom as the fresh cold fresh air gently attacked his red cheeks. The exhilaration was short lived as from out of nowhere appeared a speeding and erratically driven green Land Rover Discovery. It was so close to his tail he could hear every beat and grumble of the ageing diesel engine as the driver shifted up and down the gears. He looked over his shoulder and was alarmed to see that the dirty green 4 x 4 was less than one metre from his rear wheel. Mawgan removed his right hand from the slightly unsteady handlebars and he furiously gesticulated to the driver to overtake. Despite the clear road ahead the driver of the Land Rover kept hard on the tail of the shakily ridden bicycle, persistent in the act of violently changing up and down the gears. Mawgan considered pulling over however the pursuit vehicle had the whole rear of the bike blocked out rendering it impossible to slow down never mind stop'

"For God's sake you moron get past" he screamed in an angry tone.

Anger very soon became disquiet and then fear as the Land Rover moved closer to the rear wheel of Mawgan's bike

The Texan could hear his heart pounding louder and more rapidly in his ears, and feel his blood cold from fear run through his veins. He attempted to shake off his suitor and preserve life so he peddled faster but it was futile as the two and half tonnes of hurtling steel hung on to him like a crazed limpet. Mawgan was in a state of blind panic and gut wrenching bottomless fear, and he knew that this was not a normal Sunday morning driver or some drunk, he concluded that that this was a determined attempt to scare hell out of him or even end his life.

He frantically peddled harder but to no avail and the bike wobbled and snaked across the lane as a consequence of his fear driven erratic action.

'My God' he thought *'this madman is out to kill me'*

The desperate cyclist was suffering trauma, pounding head, blood pumping in his ears, a dry mouth and hammering pain in his thighs.

As the bicycle and Land Rover reached a dip in an unpopulated stretch of the road the Mondeo peered over the top of the brow of the horizon and headed towards them at increasing speed.

The approaching Mondeo was at approximately seventy metres ahead when the driver flashed the headlights to the oncoming Land Rover which was clearly in attack mode.

The very last thing John Mawgan saw was the Land Rover appear at his side as the Mondeo swerved across the road. The Mondeo hit the cyclist almost head on at 60mph and sped off Westward towards Chipperfield. Mawgan hit his unprotected head on the windscreen pillar of the car at a contact force which killed him instantly his lifeless body and mangled cycle were thrown into the air and landed five meters down the road.

The Land Rover braked hard to a stop, and in a frantic manoeuvre accompanied by revving the engine hard the driver turned the opposite way. The driver then delivered a "coupe de gras" as he drove the two and half of steel and aluminium over the head of the stationary body of John Mawgan lying on the tarmac.

Three miles away a workman completed repairs to the temporary traffic lights on the western exit road from Kings Langley. He collected his tools and jumped into a white and red transit van and drove off in the direction of Bovingdon. To the relief of the frustrated drivers held in the long queue he had released the blockage which had prevented any traffic from departing towards Chipperfield for a frustrating interlude of twenty-two minutes.

Mawgan's body was found five minutes later by a middle-aged woman riding a horse, who immediately called the police.

Ten minutes later Police Sergeant Rob Stansfield of Hemel Hempstead Traffic Division attended the scene on what to all intents and purposes was a hit and run.

Fifteen minutes later the Mondeo and Land Rover were driven into a small industrial unit on the former Bovingdon airfield. The roller shutter door closed behind them and almost straight away a team of men in army black fatigues starting dismantling the two vehicles. As the carnage inside the lockup continued the two drivers and a third man walked over to a rotors running dark grey helicopter, the type and colour not unlike the aircraft used by Special Forces.

After a long flight back from Buenos Aires Lukas Richter was enjoying the comforts of the soft leather reclining seats in the rear of a chauffeur driven Mercedes.

Twenty minutes into the journey from Northolt Airfield to his Holland Park home Richter received a call from the distraught sister of Christina Mawgan, the wife of John. Richter's face turned ashen as he digested the news about John's sudden death, his grip on the phone receiver almost shattering the thermoplastic case.

"How on earth did this happen, have they caught the driver of the vehicle that hit him, what have the police said were there any witnesses"

"None" replied a clearly grief-stricken Caroline Mawgan.

"I am shocked and so sorry this is tragic please tell me of anything you need"

Richter removed a black mobile phone from his inside pocket and dialled a 11digit number.

"Lukas" announced a man's voice.

"Now listen Brian I need you to find out what you can about an alleged hit and run in South West Hertfordshire, the victim is an American John Davis Mawgan, he is a close friend a key employee and one of us"

Richter spoke to Superintendent Brian Fenton of Bedfordshire Police for another three minutes and gave him all the details he had on the accident.

Unbeknown to both participants the full details of the conversation were on Tom Leyton's desk in a blink after the call ended.

Tom Leyton made a long call to a source in Watford Police station and within the hour Brian Fenton would be given fabricated information regarding the incident involving John Mawgan.

Just as the black Mercedes arrived at the Holland Park townhouse, Richter received a text form Fenton informing that the driver in the hit and run had been found and had been arrested for driving over the limit for alcohol. Richter had no reason to believe that the reports from a senior police officer would be untrue. The curve ball thrown by Tom Leyton had led Richter to believe that Mawgan's death was the result of a tragic accident and not at the hand of some opposing faction.

Richter closed the front door of his house and rushed up stair and into his bedroom threw his light blue linen jacket over a chair and laid on the bed.

He awoke thirty minutes later got up from the comfort of his king-sized bed showered and dressed in chinos and a black polo neck pullover. Back in his kitchen Richter fired up his bean to cup coffee maker which produced a cup of smooth piping hot beverage.

The aroma of the coffee alone had lifted his spirits and after two mouthfuls he was ready to get to work on the big problem that needed solving. Who would replace Mawgan at this critical time.

Another mouthful of coffee and he made the call he feared making. He had to tell Alfred the news of the loss of a key lieutenant.

Guy walker was taking advantage of a Sunday off, he had experienced a very hectic few weeks and had little time to catch up on his sleep. He had risen late, taken brisk walk around Mayfair and lunched with friends at his club before returning for a well deserved asleep on his large four seat settee in front of the TV.

At 4.30 in the afternoon Guy's afternoon siesta was disturbed by the ringtone of his encrypted mobile, it was Lukas Richter.

Guy stretched his arms above his head, breathed in and out deeply, rubbed his eyes and with an extended right had grabbed the mobile off the floor.

"Yes Lukas" he yawned as he sat up straight form his semi deep sleep.

"Sorry to intrude on your private time Guy but we need to talk very urgently, I have a deeply serious problem and you are the only am I can trust to solve it."

"What is it Lukas? why is it so urgent"

"We cannot talk on the phone can we meet this evening; I suggest that you come to my house"

"Ok Lukas I will be with you at 18.00 hrs. "replied a rather perplexed Guy.

"See you then Guy, thank you" and the phone went dead.

'Thank you that is a phrase Richter used economically, this must be serious, is he on the back foot or is it a curve ball' Guy pondered.

Guy felt a sense of de ja vu as he approached the high gloss black front door of the Holland Park residence. Richter answered the door and he joined his guest in the kitchen and they both sat down on the dark purple easy chairs positioned near the floor to ceiling sash windows overlooking the road.

Guy observed Richter's uneasy manner, for the first time since they had met his mentor was not his usual confident self and he lacked his trademark assertiveness.

The Austrian leaned forwards and placed his elbows on his knees, a move which Guy mimicked in readiness for what Richter was about to say.

"Guy, I have a problem"

Richter hesitated and appeared restless as he shuffled his body in the chair.

"I am all ears Lukas" replied Guy with a delicate tone of advantage.

"well it is like this .....well I will get to it .... John Mawgan is dead "

"Phew' exhaled an astonished Guy as he fell back into his seat,

"Killed on his cycle by a hit and run driver, and as far as I am led to believe there are no suspicious circumstances."

"How can I help?"

"Guy this leaves me with a big hole in the management at JBL at a very critical time, and as you know we have just won the contracts to build two new de salination water treatment plants in Israel and of a more urgent matter four contracts for the update of four existing plants."

Guy listened intently.

"The immediate emphasis is to complete works on the retrofit works by 21 March on 4 sites",

"I have a first class project team headed up by Steve Hopkins however I am missing over all leadership for the mission."

Richter continued

"Guy I want you head up the JBL operation for me, in particular, I want you to oversee the mobilisation and commencement of the four desalination plant up grades at Sorek, Ashkelon, Palchaman and Hadera."

"Why me Lukas, what is in your thinking"

"Well Guy it goes like this, firstly you have an engineering and contacting background, with a fair amount of overseas experience albeit many years ago. Then you have a solid contractual mind and a good eye for detail, coupled with your air of authority, in my mind you are more than qualified. The fact that you are one of my trusted right and men will also give robust assurances to the client."

Guy continued to listen and remained almost motionless.

"From my perspective Guy you are the right man to carry this, I need a figurehead to lead a very competent and handpicked team, and let us not forget that we have an exacting programme to achieve."

Guy leaned forward and waived his hands in approval.

"That is all fine by me Lukas you have my full support, so what is the next step."

"It is 1855 now, at 1900 my driver will take us to your office where we will be met by Dan Hunt Projects Director, Kevin Harrison Operations Manager Retrofit and Steve Hopkins Project Manager Retrofit"

"Michael is at the office so he will let them in.

The black limo was waiting at the kerbside as Lukas Richter locked the front door of his house, the two passengers got into the car and it glided off at speed into the backdrop of a London winters evening.

For most of the journey there was and uncomfortable silence, Guy observed that Richter appeared troubled, uncharacteristically he sat awkwardly in the lush leather seats, and fumbled with his mobile phone in a vaguely irritable fashion.

Guy in the main looked out of the window, he never got bored of travelling through Central London at night. He sensed that this may be his opportunity to get closer to Richter, and more importantly gain intelligence on the projects being undertaken in Israel.

The car pulled up in St James Street and Richter and Guy proceeded to the seventh floor dimly lit office and made a direct move to the beacon of the illuminated board room.

Sat around the table were four man and Guy recognised one of them as Michael Stuch.

Richter gestured for them to remain seated as he made the formal introductions.

"Good evening gentlemen thank you for coming here this evening at such short notice on a Sunday evening"

Dan Hunt muttered "No problem Lukas 'and the others nodded in agreement.

"I wish we were meeting in less tragic circumstances, the sudden death of our great friend and colleague was an immense shock, I still cannot believe the speed at which all of this has happened"

Steve Hopkins shifted from his casual pose, inclined forward and stared directly at Richter and piped in.

"Was it pure accident Lukas are we sure that there are no dubious motives at play?"

"No Steve he died as a result of an incident involving a hit a run drunken driver, and my high-ranking contacts in the police have informed me that they have a suspect under arrest."

"We have very little time so let us commence Steve can you give us the heads ups on the key events over the next six weeks"

For the next three hours the JBL project team brought Guy up to date with key programme parameters and procurement of critical components and items of plant.

The session ended a little after midnight and it was agreed that Guy would hold a progress meeting on the afternoon of the forthcoming Tuesday.

Last to leave, an exhausted Guy turned off the office lights, locked up and then took the lift to the ground floor and the cold but revitalising London air.

He elected to walk home, this would allow him to clear his head and report into Tom Leyton.

Just after crossing Piccadilly whilst walking North Guy phoned Leyton, who was still at his desk in Cheltenham GCHQ.

"Evening Guy what is the latest" opened a surprisingly lucid Leyton

Guy informed Leyton on the death of Mawgan, his appointment as head of JBL Contracts, the meeting at his office and the main events of the project.

"We are on site on March 3rd to be complete 21 March, it is an accelerated programme which involves the doubling of resources boy on and off site.'

Guy continued.

"All of the key software development has been completed and tested so it is only a matter of programming the computers at the faculties, this will be done remotely"

"There are two main pieces of hardware per installation consisting of equipment and control systems mounted on skid units currently under final assembly and test at JBL's subcontractor at Dorcan Swindon."

"Due to programme restrictions when completed the skid units will be airfreighted from RAF Brize Norton, courtesy of HM Government"

"When are they being transported Guy" questioned Leyton

"As I understand and according to Hopkins these units cannot be completed because of they are awaiting some critical component from an overseas subsidiary of JBL Engineering"

"What and where are these components"

"That I do not know, Richter and Hopkins were vey coy and not forthcoming, my guess that there is something fishy about this gear"

“Well Guy do what you have to but find out what the bloody hell is going on, you need access to Richter’s PC “

“That is easier said than done Tom he never has it out of his site or it is locked in his safe at home, furthermore I would never be able to guess his password or break the encryption”

“Leave that to us Guy just get me access to the hard drive and leave the rest to us”

Chapter 31

It was a little after 0530 on Tuesday morning and the darkness outside proffered no indication to the frenzied activity inside the dark grey hanger on the North side of Biggin Hill Airfield.

Indoor the floodlit unit two aircraft engineers were in the process of signing off the works completed by the two teams of three aircraft mechanics. Over the last twelve hours the skilled artisans had undertaken mandatory 'one hundred hours' checks on two foreign registered executive jets.

Parked between the wing tips of the two luxury aircraft was a red 2 tonne refrigerated Peugeot Van, the open doors revealing the dimly lit interior where 8 containers fixed on a wooden pallet.

A tall blonde haired man wearing black overalls and boots signalled to the driver to close the van doors and set off on the 140-mile journey to Swindon in Wiltshire.

At 0615 all of the mechanics had completed their job sheets and packed away tools into controlled mobile cabinets.

Five minutes later and as the mechanics and engineers were leaving, the man in black handed the completed job packs and aircraft tech logs to the dayshift maintenance manager.

The silver rings on their fingers momentarily touched as they shook hands and the man in black made his way to an awaiting Audi saloon sat in the car park.

Just after the Audi left the compound the driver of the red Peugeot van locked the rear doors moved to the front of the vehicle and jumped into the cab. The dark haired man behind the wheel started the van and drove off to join the swarm of rush hour traffic.

The route around the M25 and onwards on the M4 was torturous as the usual packed commuter trickle was enflamed by an accident at Junction 13 Westbound. Eventually the van arrived at an Industrial Estate at Dorcan on the East side of Swindon in Wiltshire.

The driver halted at the main gates and produced documentation which was examined by an apathetic security guard. The uniformed man handed back the documents and pointed towards a roller shutter door.

"Park by that door mate I will call the stores and let them know you are here"

The driver nodded, put the van into gear and drove towards the door as indicated.

As the van pulled up the grey door opened vertically exposing a red fork lift truck and array of orange and blue pallet racking and a small white office.

The fork lift unloaded the two pallets of the red tubes, placed them on the grey painted floor inside a white lined boundary demarcated as 'Goods in"

The store man was studying the documents when a man in his late thirties and wearing blue suit and tie appeared.

He handed a pile of neatly prepared papers to the store man.

"Morning boss "he responded.

"Good morning Wayne thanks for unloading the pallets, just to let you know these components do not need to be booked in as they will be picked up later this evening, as they are off to another site. They are for use on the project but not for us"

"Do you want me to stay back and load them up Frank?"

"No need to as I am working back and have a couple of subcontract technicians coming in on a late shift to test some panels"

"Ok Frank I will not book them and just leave them here, you know where the keys for the fork lift are don't you"

Frank nodded and walked off into the factory.

At 5.00 pm the shop floor employees finished work for the day leaving only a few members of technical staff and the Manager Frank Williamson in the building.

One hour later there was only Frank remaining at his desk and he was texting on a black mobile device.

Approaching Junction 15 of the M4 was an Audi A6 driven by the short blond haired man dressed in black accompanied by three men in the passenger seat. As the driver indicated to turn off the motorway his phone pinged receipt of a message.

'all clear F'

Frank Williamson was waiting at the unlit gatehouse when the Audi arrived, he spoke briefly to the driver and in the darkness the car repositioned to the welcoming illumination of the open factory door.

The men in the car quickly disembarked and headed in to the brightly lit factory.

They walked past a dark and dusty steel fabrication bay littered with steel sections and blue and red welding sets, they then progressed through an unlit machine shop containing an assortment of up to date CNC machines.

There final destination was a long 900 meter square brightly lit assembly shop served by two 10 Tonne yellow overhead cranes.

Sat on the unsoiled painted floor were eight units comprising an arrangement of small vessels, pipework, valves and control panels assembled on a yellow painted fabricated frame or "skid".

Alongside the skids were the two wooden pallets holding the canisters.

On one face of each skid adjacent to an operational control panel made up of lights, readouts and switches was a laminated sign declaring that the units had past inspection and test and were ready for despatch.

The team of men immediately got to work and disassembled a 2.5meter long spool of pipework reaching from the base to the top of the skid.

One of the yellow canisters was carefully inserted into each piece of pipe before it was reassembled onto the skid.

The work to all of the eight units was completed in three hours and the four men packed themselves into the Audi and they were gone.

Frank Williamson disposed of the used wooden pallet into the waste skip, he set the alarms, locked the factory and he was gone.

Guy Walker arrived at the Wembley offices of JBL Contracts at 09.30, he made his presence known at the reception desk and headed to the lift for third floor.

The lift doors opened to the third floor and awaiting to greet Guy was Steve Hopkins. And Dan Hunt.

Dan Hunt proffered his hand.

"Good morning Guy welcome to the third floor, it is good to have you with us at this very difficult time"

"Thank you, Dan, I really hope that I can contribute and lead us through the very demanding forthcoming months"

Hopkins lead the trio into a large open plan space bordered with a number of private rooms and executive offices.

Totally in character Guy was dressed for action in a well tailored back suit, crisp white shirt and a dark green patterned tie.

The more casually dressed Hunt followed by his colleagues halted in the centre of the work space.

"Good morning ladies and gentlemen' Hunt said in a raised voice in attempt to grab the attention

He cleared his throat and shouted.

"Can I have your attention please everyone…now would be ideal"

The thirty-seven employees put down their pens, ceased rattling keyboards, ended phone calls and all faced the trio standing in the centre of the office.

Dan Hunt reiterated the details surrounding the sad loss of John Mawgan and provided an update on what the police had told Lukas Richter. He then introduced Guy and the new head of the Company, and after summarising Guy's background and pedigree he announced that the new boss would be closely involved with the projects in Israel.

There was a brief question and answer session and everyone returned to their work, and Dan Hunt took Guy over to his office in the corner. The office was of reasonable and size modestly decorated with a pale mauve wallpaper with a smattering of darkened areas evidence where past picture frames had been removed. Positioned against the rear wall was a large dark cherry wood desk and high backed grey chair, against the opposite wall stood a large floor to ceiling bookcase constructed form the same variety of timber as the desk. The room was clinically business-like devoid of any personal touches no mortal would have ever believed that up until four days ago this was the office of John Mawgan.

Guy placed his briefcase on the desk sat down and shuffled around whilst making height and lumbar adjustments to the expensive chair.

Dan Hunt was leaning against the doorframe as he turned to leave he eyeballed Guy.

"I will leave you be for a while I know Lukas is on his way to see you, and I think that he is bringing the laptop which John Mawgan used to use."

"Thanks Dan, I will get settled and I suggest that I sit in on the project progress meeting at two todays, is that ok with you"

"It will be good to have you also, I will get Karen my secretary to send you the past minutes, that should get you up to speed."

At precisely 10.30 Lukas Richter entered Guy's office, he was carrying a black leather lap top case and a lever arch file.

Richter dumped the case on the desk and took out a very up to date lap top, charger and three memory sticks.

"Well Guy I must say that you look ready for business"

"I have a lot to catch up with Lukas but you know me I am a quick learner"

"This is the lap top John used I have had IT take off his personal files and e-mails, on it you will find directories for all of the contracts, finances and HR data."

Guy nodded

"Also on top of your emails is a highly encrypted e-mail account which links you and I only, it is extremely secure the best minds I have met cannot crack it."

"So will I have access to John Mawgan's encrypted e-mails"

"I'm afraid that is no longer possible as you need this to access your own account"

Richter tossed a small black device across the desk.

"What is it enquired" Guy

"It scans your retina and plugs into the PC so no way can you access Johns emails. It will programme the machine the first time you use it"

"Anyway all that you need to know is in the files on his machine."

Richter said as he tapped the black laptop.

"OK Guy let's get down to business"

Guy fell back into the comfort of the soft leather, and with arms folded behind his head he fixed his gaze straight at Richter

"Guy you will need to fly to Tel Aviv this week and meet the senior team at the Israeli Water Company and in particular you need to meet Yoshi Edri, and Abigael Darhan, you see the thing is Mawgan struck up a good rapport with these people it is essential that we build immediate trust after John's death. The meeting will be hand holding. A 'dog and Pony show' the Americans call it I understand"

"I see where you are coming from Lukas, you can count on me, I will get Karen onto flights and hotel bookings"

Richter looked out onto the main office space.

"Also keep on top of Hopkins and his team the start date on site of March is non-negotiable, all the IT work is complete and the equipment is tested and ready for shipment, even that asshole Medway has got your RAF involved. The will be airfreighting eight modules from Brize Norton,"

Richter got up from where he was sat and stood with both hands on the back of the chair and virtually cut Guy two with a laser like stare from his steely blue eyes.

"You must not fail Guy and let me know if any one slacks or does not perform ……they will be dealt with……goodbye Guy call me when you are in Tel Aviv."

And with that he turned and strode out of the office.

Guy sat silent for a number of seconds dwelling on Richter's chilling address, he shook his head vigorously in attempt to rid his mind of what he had just heard.

Guy Walker slept lightly on the flight, dropped his luggage at the Tel Aviv Carlton and took a cab to the offices of The Israeli Water Provision Authority.

He was met in reception by Yoshi Edri who hugged Guy in an endeavour to progress 'bon ami' between the two parties.

"Guy it is so wonderful to meet you Lukas has told me so much about you, he holds you in such high regard. Also please accept my sincere condolences on the loss of your colleague and our great friend John, it was such a shock to us all" boomed the exuberant Yoshi.

"It is great to meet you too Yoshi, I only wish it was in different circumstances, John's death is very hard for us to take"

Yoshi wrapped his arm around Guy in act of genuine affection and guided him to the lift.

They left the lift at the fourth floor and walked down to the end of a corridor of windows and individual office doors. Yoshi opened a light oak door into an executive office suite and Guy followed him past a vacant secretaries' desk and into a large corner office bordered by large windows on two sides.

Sat at a large light oak meeting table were four figures a man a woman and the outline of another man a woman positioned with their rears to the door.

As Guy worked his way into the tightly packed space the two visible characters stood up and offered their hand.

"Good morning Guy, Nadiv Levy head of construction, nice to meet you"

The young woman reached across and shook Guy's hand.

"Hello Guy welcome I am Abigael Darhan Director of Projects."

Guy returned the handshakes "Good morning It is very nice to meet you"

He then turned to the pair behind him and was taken aback at what he saw.

'My goodness its Grace Wells and that Yitzhak fella 'hell Guy lose the surprise' he thought.

Grace had noticed Guy's astonished reaction and took the initiative to ensure that her cover was not blown.

"Guy good to meet you, Esther Gold, I work for the Israeli Government as Liaison Officer for the projects. I am purely in a support role to ensure that progress is not held up by undue or unnecessary red tape in the UK and my Country." "Also as my Government is providing a substantial tranche of the funding it is my job to report back on the progress of the projects."

Guy ceased biting his lip, he felt awkward, *he knew the real reason Esther/Grace was present, he deduced that the potential terror attack was in Israel. His presence at the meeting was confirmation that Richter's evil brotherhood were planning a terrorist event under the cover of legitimate contracting' work. But where when and how were still a mystery.*

"Very nice to meet you Esther I look forward to a good working relationship, as you can imagine I am just getting up to speed with the projects however I have a very strong and competent team with on my side"

Yoshi turned to Yitzhak and made the introduction.

"Guy I would like you to meet Colonel Yitzhak Avraham, ... Yitzhak is our head of security and is on consignment from the military"

Guy exchange a firm hand shake with the tall well-presented athletic man who was dressed a black polo neck pullover and black slacks.

"Nice to meet you '

"Likewise "returned a standoffish Yitzhak.

The introductions over Yoshi clapped his hands, sat down and announced.

"OK Ladies and Gentlemen let's get down to business, today is not so much a programme review more of an overview and an opportunity for Guy to meet the senior team"

He looked around at the assembled meeting and continued.

"Also with today being March the first we have only two days before start on site"

"As you all know we have operatives on all sites making off line preparations to receive the control systems modules and upload the new operating software." Reported Guy.

Abigael raise her pencil in the air.

"What is the status of the modules are they in transit."

"Yes, they are all process tested and have passed all simulations, to my understanding they will be airfreighted from Brize Norton to Sde Dov airport tomorrow. Courtesy of our RAF I believe"

"And next?" questioned a poker faced Abigeal Darhan.

"Well they will be moved by road transport to each plant the first two will arrive on site at Hadera and Sorek on March 5th."

The meeting took and unplanned course and for the next two hours Abigael asked highly detailed questions on the four projects. The meeting came to an end in the late afternoon, Guy had held his own, dug deep into his reserves and thanks to a photographic memory and intensive preparation he had fielded most of the questions.

In the reception he bade farewell to Yoshi and jumped into a hotel bound taxi.

Guy Walker was exhausted a long sleepless flight followed by a pounding meeting, he could only contemplate sleep as he unlocked the door to the hotel suite. To his complete surprise the room was fully lit and sat on the blue settee in the sitting area was Tom Leyton and an almost adolescent looking male who was scruffily dressed in ripped jeans, tee shirt baseball boots and a dark hoody.

"Tom what the fuck !!!!!!!!" exclaimed an irritated Guy

"Guy now stop and listen to me there is something big going off what I don't know but I am here to find out"

"Tommy I'm whacked" moaned Guy as he tossed his light grey suit jacket over a chair by the regulation executive hotel integrated black desk.

"And who is the boy are we playing video games" he added caustically and he threw his tired shell into a lounge chair and kicked off a pair off dark brown suede 'slip on' shoes.

"Guy my friend, I and the boy as you call him have work to do…… meet Hugo or our code breaker."

March 2

In the distance the sun was setting on a beautifully clear day over the hills on the Berkshire Oxfordshire border. It provided a contrasting backdrop to the frenetic activity on the large flood lit concrete apron at RAF Brize Norton where two grey RAF C130 "Hercules" aircraft were being refuelled for a 7 hour 55-minute flight to Sde Dov Airport Tel Aviv Israel.

Close to the rear of the aircraft four dark blue low loader trailers were parked, each one stacked with a skid mounted process unit which had been assembled in a facticity twenty-four miles away in Swindon.

Under the experienced eye of Loadmaster Warrant Officer Robert "Penny" Lane one of the units was being transferred by fork lift to loading rollers extended from the rear of a Hercules.

Penny gingerly rotated his right hand in a downward fashion as the fork lift operator slowly and steadily lowered the skid.

"What are you reading Marshy" Penny shouted to Sergeant Dave Marsh in charge of the fork lift.

"3976 kilos boss"

WO Lane looked puzzled as he checked the manifest as each unit was recorded and labelled as 3912 kilos.

He made a note on the loading manifest and accepted the load as it was in limits and continued with the operation of preparing the two aircraft for the mission.

Two hours later the blinking red strobes disappeared into the darkness as the Hercules made a climbing turn after departing Brize Norton.

The three men sat facing each other in the Tel Aviv hotel suite on the smoked dark glass coffee table in front of them was a powered up dark grey laptop.

Guy attached the retina reading device and logged in and handed the computer to an eager looking Hugo'

The silence was disturbed only by Hugo's frantic tapping of the black plastic keys and an occasional grunt from the twenty-three-year-old.

"Good yes I have it" Hugo gasped "I'm in"

"Is it too early to ask a question?" a cynical Guy asked

Tom Leyton shook his head signalling that it was not an appropriate time.

"I am in and just need one more thing and I should be able to recover the files you want" Hugo rejoiced as he peered up at Guy.

Prompt acknowledged Tom Leyton placed his briefcase on the table, open it and removed a small black plastic box.

Hugo took the box and Guy was flabbergasted when he saw the contents, inside a cast resin replica of John Mawgan's right eye.

"My God Tommy what next, are you boys for real for fs sake"

Hugo touched the lens of the reader with facsimile eye, and beamed as he gained access to the deepest depths of the digital ossuary.

A few dozen key strokes expended and Hugo turned the screen to allow Leyton and Guy full vision.

Tom Leyton scrolled down a series of e-mails to and from Mawgan and Richter.

Most of the words related to the project in Israel and the takeover of JBL contracts and an uncomfortable number of references to Philip Medway.

'I will deal, with Medway later' thought a solemn Leyton.

Leyton slammed his fist down on the chair arm in an act of pure frustration.

"There has to be something in this lot"

Guy took up command of the laptop and trawled the e mails one more time.

"Tom here look at this and turned the screen towards the GCHQ man"

"What I can see nothing"

"Look again Tom"

Leyton grumpily reviewed the screen.

"Tom there is reference to a ship and a delivery of 'Viper' "

"The MV Lawson ETA Rotterdam Feb 28.......that is it 2 containers from Argentina .... whatever Viper it is deadly and heading for Israel."

Tom Leyton grabbed his mobile and made two calls, the first one was to a desk in the Vauxhall Bridge headquarters of MI 5 and MI 6., the second call was to the office of Eileen Moss, the Prime Minister.

Chapter 32

March 3rd Evening

Inspector Gus de Vought of Rotterdam Special Branch produced his pass at the gatehouse to entrance B at the Port of Rotterdam. The day guard had received advanced notification and was expecting the Inspector, seven armed colleagues and an Englishman who all arrived in the two black people carriers.

The security man checked the documents and gave De Vought coordinates which detailed the precise location of two containers which had recently arrived from Argentina on the vessel MV Lawson.

The barrier was lifted and the two vehicles aided by a satellite navigation reference were directed automatically to the containers, such was the sophisticated storage and retrieval system at the port. The vehicles slowly negotiated the route through a dark maze of stacked blue, red, green and white sea going containers.

Sergeant Davide Meijer driving the lead van swivelled his eyes between the navigation aid and the long dark corridor of steel.

"We are here; there we are the two containers on the right hand side' announced Meijer.

The vehicles came to a halt and of the black boiler suited armed officers got out ran over to the units and checked the identification details.

He raised his hand in the air and shouted.

"These are the units the identifications match'

Acknowledging the signal, Inspector de Vought instructed the seven armed officers and Tom Leyton to disembark.

"OK now be careful we need to ensure that this is not a trap" shouted de Vought and signalled to one of the officers who was holding a Spaniel dog on a lead.

"Let the dog loose let him check the containers or explosives" instructed the Inspector.

The handler released the brown and white dog and led the excited animal to the two steel vessels.

After several minutes of furious activity, Max the Spaniel ran over and greeted his master with the news that there was no evidence of explosive residue.

Inspector de Vought rechecked the reference on the container looked over his shoulder and gave instructions to one of the officers,

"Ok these are the units, Willy bring the bolt cutters."

"OK chief" confirmed the large Policeman and he broke the seal on the first container.

Tom Leyton stepped in and grabbed de Vought by the left arm and said.

"Gus no you have to wait for your colleagues we don't know what is in there we could be looking at a nuclear or bio chemical threat."

"Yes Tom I get it I have just received the radio message informing me that my people are at the gate, we will wait here"

There was a hiss of air brakes being applied as the two 8-meter-long dark blue rigid bodied trucks pulled up. On the back of one of the units was an extended cab with small porthole windows, mounted on the second vehicle was a dark blue steel container.

The doors open on the rear of the first unit and four men in light grey overalls jumped out on to the tarmac standing. The leader of the men walked rapidly towards Inspector de Vought.

"Good evening Gus what have we here" asked the leader who clearly knew de Vought.

"Well Den two containers arrived from Argentina original destination unknown but the Brits suspect a cargo destined for use in a large terrorist act, we cannot rule out bio, chems or nuclear, and that is why you and your team are here."

"OK Gus now get your men well back I will take it from here"

The Inspector acknowledged the order and ordered his men and Leyton to behind the pseudo safety of the two large trucks, and for the next fifteen minutes they witnessed frantic activity as Captain Den Jankers and his team prepared.

From the seemingly endless supply of equipment stored in the second truck the men erected a bright blue tent, a temporary shower and an unfolded an array of protective clothing.

Fifteen minutes passed and an impatient Tom Leyton barked.

"When are these men going to be ready we have very little time you know"

Gus de Vought sent a disapproving scowl in the direction of Tom Leyton and said

"Mr Leyton you have to patient this cargo could be deadly we need the experts on this and cannot be hurried."

Leyton's frustration was short lived when he heard the message crackle on the radio.

"Gus we are ready to move in please stay back"

Captain Jankers clothed in a yellow bio hazard suit and an independent air supply lead three similarly attired men towards the first container.

He swivelled the handle on the locking mechanism and opened the door, the headlights of one of the vehicles shone into a container.

"Stand down all clear" Jankers announced through his radio.

"What do you mean" replied Leyton

"Come and take a look Tom, see for yourself"

The unit was empty apart from three concrete blocks secured to the floor. Examination of the second container yielded the same result. Tom Leyton scratched his head in despair, he had been clearly led up a blind alley.

Two hours later the empty handed Tom Leyton and the Dutch Police team packed themselves into their vehicles and left the port.

Fifty kilometres North of Tel Aviv a security guard at the gatehouse to the main plant building at Hadera De salination plant, was talking to the lead driver of two low loader lorries.

"Thank you, all of your paper work is in order, my colleague will direct you to the final delivery area" said the guard.

A guard left the gatehouse walked over to the lorry cab and shouted up to the driver.

"Please follow me sir I will be in the blue pickup with the orange flashing lights."

The convoy under the lead of the pick-up proceed to building 12 right at the heart of the noisy processing plant.

The lead vehicle stopped and the two low loaders were reverse lead through an open entrance and into a large dark grey steel-clad building.

Awaiting were a contingent of engineers, fitters and riggers employed by JBL Contracts, they were under the supervision of a tall blonde haired Swede Gunta Erickson.

To the outside world the snake ring sporting Erickson held a Swedish passport, in actuality he was raised in Germany by one of the disciples of the covenant, this man had a direct link to Lukas Richter.

The two skids were carefully unloaded by an overhead gantry crane and onto custom made bogey trolleys which would allow ease of movement around the well lit high bay portal framed building.

It took only twelve hours of cleverly orchestrated activity to couple the two skid units into the water sampling apparatus which comprised the outlet from the desalination plant.

The fitters seemed unfazed as Erickson and his assistant, an Englishman who answered only to Smith, dismantled and then made good the main pipe after they had removed two complex looking canisters.

Erickson and Smith carefully handled the two red metal tubes and positioned them adjacent to the outlet on each of the two process skids. They opened a large steel box which contained an array of 50mm diameter stainless steel pipe work, valves flanges and fittings.

Under the skilled and watchful eye of Erickson, Smith and another fitter using the assorted fittings and pipe 'hard' connected the outlet valve of each cylinder to the outlet valve of each process unit. Throughout the operation the outlet to the canister remained closed by way of a locked valve. Erickson retained the key to valve set.

At Sorek ninety kilometres to the South a similar operation was in progress under the supervision of 'the man in black' who had worked on the skid units in the UK.

Over the next twenty-four hours, Two RAF C 130's would commence the operation to airfreight to Tel Aviv two more pairs of skid units, destined to be installed at desalination plants at Ashkelon and Palchaman

It was 9.30pm and Richter was sat in the back of his chauffeur driven Mercedes when he received the text from Ericson.

'*H and S locked and loaded, P and A will be ready tomorrow, E"*

Richter enjoyed a small grin, before his more serious call to Friedrich, he did not have the best of news.

A frustrated Tom Leyton had returned from Rotterdam and was working late at a hot desk in the Vauxhall Bridge office od MI6. The floor was at the nerve centre of the British Intelligence section which monitored intelligence and controlled agents placed across the globe. He was pawing through the documents trying to piece together what Richter and his men were planning.

It was 1.30 in the morning and Grace Wells' sleep was disturbed by the ringing of her secure mobile. It was Tom Leyton

"Goodness Tom do you never sleep"

The call had woken Yitzhak who rolled over in bed to look at Grace.

Grace responded by mimicking "*Tom Leyton'* unexcited Yitzhak re visited his sleeping pose and returned to his dreams.

"Just hold on a second Tom"

Grace got out of bed, threw on her towelling robe and headed off to the bathroom, switched on the light and closed the door.

"Ok I can talk"

"Grace I just cannot get my head around what the hell they are up to, Viper, JB Contracts, work in Israel."

"Interestingly enough boss I was talking to some RAF lads who had brought the kit for the works to the desalination plants" "boy can those boys knock it back"

"and "

"Well I told them of my involvement and we started talking about the project and how they had flown over some large units, this fella Lane said he had no idea what they were for but the daft so and so's had got the weight wrong"

There was silence as the wheels of Tom Leyton's brain spun into alignment.

"That's it Grace. that's bloody it! someone somewhere has added something to these units, smuggled it in"

"Viper" screamed Grace "they have hidden Viper'

"Where is this kit destined for Grace"

"The water treatment plants at Sorek, Hadera, Palchaman and Ashkelon"

Tom almost leapt from his seat, he sensed victory was in his sights.

"That's it Grace S and H, P and A that's is it"

"What is it? Tommy I'm not with you"

Tom explained the context of the text Richter had received.

"My God Tommy they are planning to attack the water plants, my guess is Viper is a poison or a bio agent, they are going to dose the water supply to almost ninety percent of Israel."

"Grace you are on the money, we need to stop the final two shipments and seize control of the water plants at Sorek and Hadera."

There was a ping on Tom Leyton's phone announcing that he was to receive a secure e-mail.

"Hold on a minute Grace I have incoming"

Tom refreshed his laptop

'Tom, we have intercepted a call between Richter and F in Argentina it looks as though Walker has been exposed, he fell for the curve ball of the MV Lawson, he has been compromised.'

They concluded by agreeing to accelerate the plan and deal with Walker"

"oh no" Leyton muttered

"Grace You need to get to those two plants you will need backup, I will speak with the PM and she will talk to the Israelis, I will also stop the other two shipments but I now need to get in touch with Guy, he is danger"

"Danger?"

"Yes danger Richter is on to him"

"OK boss I will get mobilised at this end"

"Oh and Grace I will get GCHQ to copy all messages to me and.....take care"

"You too Tommy"

Tom Leyton ended the call and immediately spoke to the office of Eileen Moss and updated her on the situation.

"Thank you Tom I will be onto the Prime Minister of Israel the minute we are off the phone." said the PM.

The call ended and Leyton's thoughts returned to Guy Walker who was in peril.

"Come on Guy pick up the phone" a clearly frustrated Leyton muttered.

Leyton tried several times to get hold of Guy but to no avail.

Leyton banked on Guy being in his office, he slammed his lap top shut grabbed his jacket and phone and requested a driver to take him to St James Street.

Five minutes later Leyton and agent Paul Judd were on their way with the blue light flashing on the speeding grey Jaguar saloon parting the London traffic.

Guy Walker sat in silence, he was facing Richter and Michael Stuch who was holding a Glock 13 9mm pistol.

Richter spoke in a sinister monotone.

"Guy you disappoint me, I trusted you, one of the brotherhood yet you betray our great pedigree. You have put our great project at grave risk"

"Now we must end our association"

"I am not one of your filthy brotherhood the ring was a gift to my Uncle in the war,"

"No Guy we have checked your records we know who brought you up, you are one of us"

There was a voice from behind Richter and Stuch.

"I am afraid not Herr Richter, we fabricated Guy's history and background and presented him on a plate to you."

Guy was wide eyed as he stood trembling behind his desk.

It was Tom Leyton; he was standing in the open doorway to Guy's office.

"The game is up Richter, we are on to you and as we speak we are sending special forces to the water plants and diverting the remaining two flights.......it's over"

Richter turned toward Tom Leyton.

"Michael SHOOT" he ordered

Tom Leyton lunged at Stuch and they both fell to the floor kicking over an office chair.

Leyton pinned Stuch to the floor but his adversary was of younger years and clearly of superior fitness. Stuch summoned up all his strength and pushed his opponent back and then rotated the protesting, kicking and partially winded Leyton against the wall.

The ensuing scuffle lasted another thirty seconds and was brought to an abrupt conclusion with the crack of a gunshot, followed by an eerie silence and eventually Stuch got up and raised the gun towards Guy.

Tom Leyton lay on the floor in a pool of he had been killed instantly with a single shot the head.

From the dimly lit main office appeared a flash and a crack as Sergeant Judd emptied a round into Stuch.

As Stuch fell to the floor he discharged his handgun in a frantic attempt to regain control and the bullet struck Guy in the right shoulder. Judd walked over to towards Stuch aimed his weapon and delivered a deadly round straight at his head.

Guy screamed in pain and swiped out with his good arm missing Richter, who had picked up the live weapon from his dead colleague.

In a final act of defiance Richter aimed the fully charge automatic pistol straight at Guy, but it was too late for the Austrian. Judd stepped forward into the office, he raised his weapon, and in a clinical move which demonstrated a military pedigree he aimed directly at Richter, and fired.

The Austrian banker had been hit hard with a terminal wound to the chest, it would only be a matter of twenty seconds before his life would expire.

With blood covered hands he reached for his phone and texted his two lieutenants in Israel

'I order release now Repeat Release Viper now LR'

The phone rolled out of his hand and Lukas Richter was dead.

Three thousand six hundred miles away a black military helicopter was on final approach into a compound at the Hadera Water Treatment Plant. Sat in the back was Grace Wells accompanied by six Israeli Special Forces operatives all regaled in black combat fatigues, helmets and stab vests. The high pitched scream of the turbines and booming rotors overpowered the silence in the cabin of the helicopter. All seven occupants were deep in thought, a momentary pause to reflect before the heat of action when men and women would likely die. Colonel Liv Greenburg glanced across the dark grey cabin, three men were carrying out vital final checks to their equipment, one was praying and one just gazing into the ether.

Ninety kilometres to the South Yitzhak Avraham supported by an assault force of seven Special Forces operatives was leading a similar operation in the main plant building at the Sorek Facility.

The helicopter touched down on the tarmac apron at Hadera and Sergeant Moshi Abelman waived a raised black leather gloved hand and the four soldiers followed by Grace and Colonel Greenburg jumped out.

Abelman disembarked and lead the group away from the beating machine towards a perimeter fence one hundred meters to the North of the landing site.

Colonel Greenburg held his hand in the air and spoke into the microphone which was integrated into his black light weight combat helmet.

"OK stop here a second and let us get our bearings" "gather round please"

From the top left-hand pocket of his stab vest he produced a rolled up laminated A5 sized plan of the plant.

Under a yellow torch light, the group studied the layout of the plant and their eventual destination.

"OK It is straight ahead for two hundred metres then left for eighty meters." Confirmed Greenburg.

"It will be a large grey building on the right hand of the roadway and we will enter in single file via the door at the side"

"Sergeant Abelman you lead and Grace you follow at the rear, do you all understand"

They all nodded in acceptance.

"OK check your weapons and on the count of five we move"

The seven black clad figures moved at pace through the water treatment complex and arrived at the grey building.

Under the instruction of Greenburg, the troop halted at the main door to the building and awaited the order to enter.

Grace looked at her phone and read the message Richter had sent to Erickson, she was distressed with the content and realised that they had little time if any left to stop the horrific and unimaginable act of terror.

Abelman turned to the group and spoke.

"That is the door and it should be unlocked; the plant room layout would indicate that our target is at the far right hand end of the building"

"As rehearsed we stay together until we are visual with the target then we split up and move either side" added Greenburg

"OK Sergeant you take the lead, night vision goggles on and let's go

Heads low the dark clad figures crept into the well lit building and took full advantage of the abundant runs of pipe work and machinery to provide cover.

Greenburg became visual with the "man in black" who was attempting an operation with a valve on a yellow skid mounted piece of equipment. He was accompanied by three men all armed with machine pistols.

Greenburg removed a small electronic device from his pocket and with one click he switched off all of the lights in the building.

These actions alerted Erickson who cocked his machine gun and shouted

"Take cover I will stay with Viper you need to hold them off long enough for me to complete the task"

Relying on night vision alone Greenburg and his men closed in on Erickson and his three armed henchmen who were stood guarding the Viper canisters.

When in range the Special Forces opened fire and a gun battle ensued as the defenders took advantage of the muzzle flashes in the dark to guide their fire. Two of Erickson's men fell and as he turned to the third they were both hit by incoming munitions. The third man folded over and as he hit the ground he rolled sideways, he was dead, Erickson felt pain and looked at the blood from the rip in his black combat trousers, he had sustained a flesh wound to his leg.

Erickson randomly fired the gun gripped in his right hand as he crawled across the floor leaving a trail of blood. He stopped when he came to the brass valve which connected the deadly Viper to the water supply which fed millions of innocents. Erickson reached for the valve set and stood up which allowed him to place the key in lock and arm the valve. His action was halted when he received three shots to his torso, weakened he curled up and tumbled to the floor. He slid behind a large vessel to protect him from the follow up hail of bullets, however, he knew that was still within hand reach to open the valve and release the liquor of death into the water supply.

He knew he was dying but aware that he could still achieve his objective and with a large intake of breath he outstretched a shaking blood covered hand and grabbed the handle of the valve.

Mustering his dying strength, he attempted to open the valve, but it was too late. Erickson looked up and saw Grace Wells pointing an Uzi machine pistol.

"No you don't" she screamed and gun flipped up as she emptied several rounds into his torso and head.

Erickson's hand slipped off the handle as he gave his last breath.

Grace gasped and placed her weapon by her side, and at that moment she received a message that Yitzhak had secured the plant at Sorek.

An exhausted Grace Wells almost collapsed onto the floor and with her back resting against a large section of pipe she placed her head in her hands. With an unsteady hand Grace sluggishly tapped in Yitzhak's number into her mobile phone, there was a thirty second delay, it seemed like an eternity.

Yitzhak eventually picked up, his dwindling adrenaline was making him tired.

"Grace are you OK. Please tell me it's over "

"It's over my love it's over and for you"

"Yes we made it in time, and the plant is secure"

"And the terrorists" enquired a now nauseous Grace

"All dead"

A pause ensued as they both reflected on the events of the last hour.

Grace still with phone to her ear witnessed a more subdued tone in Yitzhak's voice.

"Grace, I have some not too good news for you……"

"Yes what is its' she replied is an almost petrified tone.

"Tommy is dead, Richter killed him but Richter was killed by M16"

"Oh no oh my God poor Tommy, poor Tommy…." She started to sob.

"It is tragic I know but we achieved our goal, Tom Leyton is a hero"

Forty kilometres to the South of Tel Aviv 3 Israeli Air Force F 16 Fighter Jets escorted the Two RAF Hercules to a Military Airfield at Ein Shermar. The aircraft landed safely and the deadly cargo was safely quarantined.

The attack on Israel and the Jewish people by an evil covenant had been thwarted.

THE END

Epilogue

Guy Walker was dressed in his best attire with the added addition of a sling for his right arm. He walked down the aisle at Gloucester Cathedral and sat down next to Grace Wells.

Adjacent to the alter lay the coffin of Tom Leyton draped with the Union Flag.

The funeral initially was to be a private affair but Tommy Leyton had too many friends, furthermore there would be one very important attendee.

The Prime Minister herself would be giving a eulogy, she had a lot to thank Tom Leyton for he had exposed the fraudulent finance house who had framed her husband. The exposure of the fraud was the cause of the alleged suicide of the international financier Lukas Richter and his deputy Michael Stuch.

She had recently gained popularity and no longer was facing the latent threat from Phillip Medway. Sadly, and to some commentators mysteriously, Medway had died in a car crash in Hampshire.

One person was missing from the huge contingent from GCHQ, Sidney Laing was in prison serving 14 years for treason. In another prison in North West England was incarcerated an IT manager from the Metropolitan Police, he had allowed Hugo access to penetrate their records and informed the Covenant.

There was however a new recruit to join the 6000 plus 'schoolteachers" in Cheltenham, Hugo was now working at GCHQ as the head of cryptology, a very unhappy Holly Jackson was his deputy.

Tornado Ventures LLP was liquidated and the proceeds were given to many charities.

JBL Ltd was bought in a Management Buy Out lead by Guy Walker, funding was provided at attractive rates by the British Government who retained a golden share to appease their Israeli customers.

Later in the year undercover Israeli special forces would destroy a laboratory deep in the jungle in Argentina.

Friedrich and Albert were never traced

Fifteen miles away in Cheltenham a thirty-year old IT consultant who worked at GCHQ was being discharged after a long period in hospital resulting from a hit and run incident two months earlier. He collected his possessions which included a silver snake ring and a key to an industrial unit in Southampton.

In the unit was a brown rust peppered twenty-foot sea container, locked inside were 8 sealed yellow canisters.

The Traitors List by Sidney Tomas

In the bleak days of the late 1930's and with WW2 imminent, an English Industrialist plays host to an alliance of influential businessmen, politicians, senior military figures and one mystery guest. An enigmatic Austrian aristocrat outlines a sinister and a far reaching plan that will see a defeated Germany and financially ruined British Empire rise from the ashes to once again rule the World. Financed by the spoils of war, disciples of this new world order will infiltrate industry, government , commerce and the military.

Seven decades later and a simmering division is building within the population of the United Kingdom . The populist and divisive leader of the GBLP Clive Bousefield supported by senior business leaders and members of the Government, , is whipping up hatred towards the European Union . A proliferation in terrorist attacks on the UK mainland gifts an opportunity for the anti-European camp to condemn the UK Prime Minister David Milner, and further divide the electorate over EU immigration policies.

In what will be a conclusive and bold move to seize power the clandestine brotherhood plan a world shattering event, the assassination of the UK Premier and the President of the United States. They commission the services of covert journeyman, a killer to not only carry out the heinous act but to also detonate a dirty bomb in London.

A man of many aliases, tortured and weary of life in the shadows, he finds love for the first time, however, he struggles to vision a route to a peaceful and legitimate future.

At GCHQ Cheltenham England, rising star graduate Grace Wells teams up with the 'old guard' ex field agent Jack Parker. With help from their team they unravel a series of encrypted messages, naming the traitors and detailing their sinister plans.

What follows is a life and death hunt across 4 continents to find the assassin, Jack encounters an old nemesis , the IRA, whilst Grace is inducted into the dark and deadly business of operating in the shadows. Grace cannot fight her instincts, tipped over the edge by the death of her friends at the hands of ruthless killers, she exercises her right of passage with an automatic pistol.

With only minutes to spare Grace locates the hired killer, however, the outcome, is not as she predicted. The elusive assassin driven by a personal vendetta delivers a twist to the proceedings. The two World leaders are unharmed whilst two of traitors lie dead.

The Author

Sidney Tomas

After a successful career the author embarked on fulfilling a lifelong ambition to become a writer of fiction.

Inspired by extensive World travel and the works of top fiction writers coupled with a vivid and wide imagination Sidney put pen to paper.

In May of 2019 Sidney set off on a solo motorcycle tour of India and South East Asia.

During the exciting and sometimes gruelling schedule Sidney penned 70,000 words of his first novel "the Covenant of the Ring'.

Sidney has already commenced work on his second novel "The Traitors List' an International thriller based on a conspiracy by a clandestine organisation to destabilise modern day Europe.

Today keen cook (Masterchef 1996 Television Finalist) Sidney lives in Cambridgeshire.

Printed in Great Britain
by Amazon

66901157R00180